After ten years as a tel
Ella Hayes started her
so that she could work
her young family. As a̶n̶ ̶a̶w̶a̶r̶d̶-̶w̶i̶n̶n̶i̶n̶g̶
photographer she's documented hundreds of
love stories in beautiful locations, both at home
and abroad. She lives in central Scotland with
her husband and two grown-up sons. She loves
reading, travelling with her camera, running and
great coffee.

Scarlett Clarke's interest in romance can be
traced back to her love of Nancy Drew books,
when she tried to solve the mysteries of her
favourite detective while rereading the romantic
chapters featuring Ned Nickerson. She's thrilled
now to be writing romances of her own. Scarlett
lives in, and loves, her hometown of Kansas City.
By day she works in public relations and wrangles
two toddlers, two cats and a dog. By night she
writes romance and tries to steal a few moments
with her firefighter hubby.

Also by Ella Hayes

The Single Dad's Christmas Proposal
Their Surprise Safari Reunion
Barcelona Fling with a Secret Prince
One Night on the French Riviera

The Prince She Kissed in Paris
is **Scarlett Clarke**'s debut book
for Mills & Boon True Love.

Look out for more titles from Scarlett Clarke,
coming soon!

Discover more at millsandboon.co.uk.

BOUND BY THEIR LISBON LEGACY

ELLA HAYES

THE PRINCE SHE KISSED IN PARIS

SCARLETT CLARKE

MILLS & BOON

First published in Great Britain 2024
by Mills & Boon, an imprint of HarperCollins*Publishers* Ltd,
1 London Bridge Street, London, SE1 9GF

www.harpercollins.co.uk

HarperCollins*Publishers*, Macken House, 39/40 Mayor Street Upper,
Dublin 1, D01 C9W8, Ireland

Bound by Their Lisbon Legacy © 2024 Ella Hayes

The Prince She Kissed in Paris © 2024 Scarlett Clarke

ISBN: 978-0-263-32133-3

06/24

BOUND BY THEIR LISBON LEGACY

ELLA HAYES

MILLS & BOON

This one goes out to my sons James and Matthew,
who will probably never read it but will hopefully
get to Lisbon one day and enjoy it as much as I did!

CHAPTER ONE

WHAT THE HELL was Edward saying to Will? Because Will was exploding off his chair, gesticulating at the solicitor so hard Quinn could practically feel the waves of his fury pulsing through the soundproof glass. And then his head whipped round, his eyes seeking hers, locking on.

She felt her blood draining. Why was he looking...no, glaring at her like this? She was only in line for some small token of Anthony's affection: a keepsake or maybe a donation for the homeless shelter where she volunteered. That was why she'd been asked to come, to be 'on hand' at the reading of Anthony's will. That was why she was waiting out here while he was in there for the important business.

Outside the family. Outside the boardroom. Waiting for a small bequest. Made sense. Nothing else did. Could! Because Anthony had more than done his legal duty by her already. Giving her a home when Dad died. Caring for her, supporting and guiding her, even granting her the interiors contract for the Thacker Hub hotel in Kensington when she was just starting up her business, still wet behind the ears. She owed Anthony Thacker big time, and he owed her precisely nothing. But now Will was bruising her with his eyes, and he wouldn't be doing that without a reason, would he? Not when, for years, he'd barely looked at her at all.

She cut free, forcing her gaze to the floor. What was going

on? She didn't know Will, had never quite got the chance to get to know him, but it didn't take a microscope to see he was bleeding hard, wounded by whatever Anthony had put in that will.

But why would Anthony do that—hurt his son—when he'd loved him so fiercely, respected him for the great job he was doing as Thacker's Head of Business Development? Anthony had admired Will's drive, his sharp intellect. Not so much his gambling and his casual sexual encounters, admittedly. They'd used to fight about that apparently, but the fight was because of the love, because Anthony wanted better for Will.

That was how she'd read it anyway, from the distance of her own life, and it tallied with all the things Anthony had said during those long chemo afternoons: that he loved Will more than life itself, wished he'd handled things better, drawn him in closer, especially after his mother left, drawn him in and held him there instead of losing his grip, messing up…

Confessional talk. Out of character for Anthony. She'd said to him that it was Will he should be talking to, that it wasn't too late, but he'd said it was, that Will would see it as a selfish act, just a father trying to salve his own conscience before the inevitable happened. She hadn't known what to say then because what did she know about the way Will saw anything?

That was the thing about Will. Everything about him was a guess. Like guessing he'd gone from being shyly kind to her when she'd first moved in, to being distant, because she'd been grieving too hard for Dad at the time, feeling too displaced in the strange house to respond to him properly. And like guessing that the reason he didn't hang around for long during his uni holidays was because he really did have better places to be than the Cotswolds house, better things to do than joining her and Anthony for pub lunches and mad rural hikes.

And of course, Christmas at home couldn't possibly compete with skiing in Chamonix, staying at his friend Jordan's family ski lodge, could it? Easter? Guess he did the right thing there, never coming home at all, staying 'up' so he could revise, because it paid off. He got a First, not that she went to the graduation. There were only tickets for family. Nothing she didn't know, but when Will said it to her, it had felt like a stone sinking in her chest.

That was the stone she could feel again now, sinking lower. And it was so stupid, so wrong for them to be distant like this when they had Anthony in common, this terrible grief to share. And no, Anthony wasn't *her* father, and no, he hadn't been the easiest person, but was it any wonder after losing his eldest son to a speeding white van like that, then losing his wife eighteen months later to some hedge fund manager with a place in Jersey, all while steering Thacker Hotels to ever greater success? He wasn't perfect. He'd made mistakes, especially with Will, but he'd been good to her, and she loved him, missed him, wanted to talk about him. But Liam the Scumbag had gone, found some other girl to love, so she couldn't talk to him, and Sadie was a diamond, always a good listener, but she hadn't known Anthony, whereas Will…

Her heart twisted. Talking to him made sense. And she'd thought he'd see that, want to talk to her too, but when she'd touched his arm at the funeral, trying to build a bridge, all she'd got back was the same curt nod he used to give her when he arrived at the hospice—dismissive. *Hurtful!* And then he'd stepped back, turned a cold shoulder.

And she didn't deserve that, didn't get it, because Will wasn't heartless. If he was, he would never have hovered in her bedroom doorway all those years ago with his kind blue eyes and his hands pushing into the pockets of his jeans, saying he was sorry about her dad dying, that he knew how she was feeling, that if she wanted to talk—

'Quinn?'

Edward... Standing in the open doorway, holding the door she hadn't heard opening. Could he see her mouth going dry, her blood trying to march backwards? If so, it wasn't showing on his face, and it certainly wasn't changing anything because he was opening the door wider, stepping aside for her.

'Could you come in now, please?'

Quinn was shaking her head, frowning. 'I don't know if I can—'

He cut in, relieved. 'See, Edward. She can't do it anyway—'

'No, Will!' Cutting right back in, pinning him hard with her clear gold-brown gaze. '*She* isn't saying she can't do it. *She* was going to say that doing it inside six months is going to be a stretch.'

He felt a flame thrower blasting his ears. Putting him in his place, and rightly so. He'd been rude, letting the old wounds bleed too freely. He inclined his head by way of apology, which she accepted with her eyes.

Her eyebrows drew in again. 'The problem is I have other work scheduled, other commitments...'

'Which *I* understand...' He forced out a smile, opening his hands to seem reasonable and calm, which he wasn't. But he'd thrown his toys out of the pram with Edward once already and that hadn't got him anywhere, so calm and reasonable was the only option. In any case, whatever he thought about Quinn Radley, this one wasn't on her; this was on Dad, one hundred fricking percent. He gave a little shrug. 'I'm just saying that if you were to turn the project down on the basis of being too busy then—'

'It won't make a blind bit of difference.' Edward's voice was sharp as glass. 'For the third time, William, the terms of the will are this: you inherit Anthony's estate *only* when the Lisbon hotel has been up and running for three months; you must take personal charge of the project from here on in and Quinn is to be your interior designer. It is not negotiable since Quinn's personal bequest is contingent on her doing the work…' His gaze shifted to Quinn 'Work which you were already discussing with Anthony, I believe?'

She gave a strange sideways nod. 'We talked about it…' And then she was closing her eyes, evidently reining in some emotion. 'When Anthony first bought it, I mean, before he was diagnosed…'

In other words, before the project rolled into the long grass. Why couldn't it have died there instead of coming back to bite him? Blasted hotel! He'd *told* Dad it was going to be a massive waste of time and money.

Granted, Bairro Alto was a prime location, but the building was sprouting grass for goodness' sake! Roof, walls—every nook and cranny. As for the interior, that was a whole other can of festering worms. And all for what? A paltry eighteen en suite bedrooms and one master suite! Payback period— for ever! Dad's insane passion project, a little *amuse bouche* because he loved Lisbon and 'fancied a challenge'. Maybe it didn't say much for his sense of filial duty, but he'd intended to slap it back on the market the second it fell into his hands. So much for that plan!

'I understand, Quinn…' Edward was shuffling his papers together. 'You weren't expecting a rush job. If you're tied to other clients for the time being, then we must wait.'

Except it wasn't *we*, was it? It was *he*, Will, who must wait for Quinn, work with her. *Her* of all people, at Dad's behest!

He felt his blood rising, a vice tightening somewhere. Had Dad not had eyes to see with? Had he *not* noticed him opting out of family life circa six months after Quinn arrived? Had he never asked himself why?

He ground his jaw. Of course not, because he wasn't Pete. Pete, he'd have noticed. Every blink, every breath! But he'd never been captain of the rugby team, had he? Holding up the trophy, muddy and triumphant. He'd never had swimming medals to line up on a bedroom shelf. No bear hugs and back slaps for Will. Just the searing devastation of losing his brother, best friend. The light in the room; the light in the dark. All the dazzling light.

God, how he had missed him. The thump of his schoolbag going down on the hall floor; the rhythm his feet made walking; the different, leaping rhythm they made when he was bounding up the stairs. The sound of his voice, that rich chuckling sound of his laughter, that bright flash of his smile. He'd been everything. To him. To Dad. To Mum…

How he'd had to fight to fill a single toe of Pete's shoes. To be seen. Noticed. Taking Mum cups of tea that she'd let go cold. Pulling the blanket up around her shoulders when it slipped. Rubbing her feet to win a pale smile. Pushing himself at school to make them both sit up. Top grades across the board—better than Pete ever got.

Not enough to stop Mum taking up with Gabe the hedge fund jerk though, was it? Not enough to stop her from leaving, making the hole he was trying to fill even bigger, but he'd banked the hurt and pushed on harder, faster, focusing on Dad. Duke of Edinburgh Gold! Maths prize! Science prize! Inching his way into Dad's field of view. Working admin jobs at Thacker HQ in the school holidays to impress him, riding shotgun in the BMW like Pete used to. Weekends, he'd pitch in, working on the old convertible with Dad to please him, because that car was Dad's pride and joy.

Jeez! He'd been smashing it six ways to Sunday, feeling pretty good about himself, so close to worthy that when Quinn first came, hollow-eyed and beautiful, aching with grief over her dad, he'd thought nothing of reaching out to her, wanting to be kind, because why wouldn't he want to soothe her when he *knew* her pain, could feel it living inside him every single day that Pete wasn't around. But she'd curled like a leaf, shutting him out, which he got too, because pain could be like that, wanting to keep you all to itself. He'd thought time would do its healing work. And he was going to uni, anyway, spreading his wings...

Oh, but he hadn't bargained on coming home to find that Quinn was the new apple of Dad's eye. Quinn this. Quinn that. Cooking together, laughing at their little in-jokes. He'd told himself it would be petulant to react, that Dad and Quinn were bound to fall into a rhythm since they were living in the same house. He'd reined in the negativity, tried not to mind, but then came that Christmas pub quiz, Dad's friend coming in, wanting to join their team, Dad saying he could if Will didn't mind moving to another team because of the numbers—*Will*, not Quinn by the way—saying it in such a way that he would have looked like an utter stick-in-the-mud if he hadn't smiled and got up. Enough to turn a stomach, hollow it out. Heart too. That night he'd decided. No more fighting for his place. Easier to back off, leave them to it.

But now he couldn't back off, make himself scarce. Heaping insult onto injury, not only had Dad saddled him with this hare-brained, budget-busting renovation project from hell, but he'd saddled him with the cuckoo in the nest as well—the cuckoo he'd spent the last decade trying to avoid! And all he wanted—*all* he wanted—was to move quickly, get the infernal thing done so he could get his life back, not to mention his inheritance. But now Quinn wasn't even sure she could fit him in!

He inhaled to cool his blood, slid his gaze through the window to the sea of high-rise buildings bleeding shadows in the low February sun. There had to be a workaround. Some way of speeding things up. Roof, façade, walls, windows. Three floors, eighteen beds, bar, dining, reception. His stomach pulsed. *Maybe...*

He turned to look at her. 'Could you work piecemeal?'

'Piecemeal?'

She was looking at him as if the concept was alien. Well, he could relate! Everything about this was alien, the opposite of comfortable.

He licked his lips. 'Look, I'm no expert on old buildings but I imagine renovation isn't a linear process. Some areas are going to be ready for your input ahead of others. I'm just wondering if you could dovetail into the workflow so we can keep everything moving.'

She see-sawed her head, weighing it up. 'It's a possibility. The challenge would be keeping the finished areas clean.'

'Would that be especially hard? I mean, have you seen the building?'

'No. Only photos. And some preliminary sketches from the architect.'

'Same here...'

Which suddenly seemed ludicrous, given what lay ahead. He felt a tingle, resistance trying to bite, but he tamped it down. No way round it. This was a needs-must situation.

He drew in a breath. 'Quinn, do you think you could make time for a quick site visit?'

She blinked. 'Go to Lisbon, you mean?'

Too tempting not to deadpan.

'Ideally, yes, given that that's where the building is.'

Her eyes held him, busy replaying the last three seconds, and then suddenly her face split and she was chuckling, giving herself up to laughter, a sound he could feel somehow in his own body, feel tugging a smile up through him, and he didn't want to give in to it because Quinn was the one making it happen, pitching him back to the Cotswolds house—her and Dad, shoulder to shoulder at the kitchen table, laughing over some stupid video on her phone—but he couldn't hold back the rumble in his chest, couldn't keep his traitorous cheeks from creasing. At least he wasn't alone. Edward's lips were twitching too.

And then she was coming back down to land, rolling her eyes at herself, touching two fingers to her sweet, curving lips, catching one short, clean fingernail with her teeth. 'In case you're worried, I'm not usually this dumb.'

'I'm not worried.' Not about her anyway. He pulled himself straight. 'So, about Lisbon; if I can fix up a visit with the architect, could you spare a day?'

She lowered her hand. 'I could, depending on the day, obviously.'

'Would a weekend be easier?' Anything to speed things up. 'Assuming the architect could make it…' And assuming she didn't mind leaving her boyfriend behind. If she had one. He let his eyes run loose. Eyes, lips, dark corkscrew curls grazing the smooth curve of her cheek. Of course she had one! She'd been lovely at seventeen, and she was even lovelier now. Excluding himself, what man on earth could walk past her?

Her mouth twisted to the side. 'A weekend *could* work…'
Do the decent thing, Will.

'If it helps, you could bring your other half, on the company, obviously, make a weekend of it.'

Her gaze flickered for an intriguing beat, then sharpened. 'Thanks for your consideration, and for the generous offer, but that's not the issue…'

And none of his business either, if her tone was anything to go by. But then, suddenly, she was sighing, frowning, shaking her head a little.

'I'm sorry. That didn't come out quite right.' She inhaled and then her gaze cleared. 'I don't have another half, but even if I did, I wouldn't let him get in the way of work.'

Why was he getting an *ever again* vibe? Was it her mouth? That little bit of tightness there. Or her eyes? That touch of bruised steel.

She gave a little shrug. 'The reason I'm havering is because I volunteer at a homeless shelter. I have my regular nights, but sometimes things can change, so I'd need to check the schedule before committing to a date.' Her lips set. 'I don't want to let them down.'

Surprising about the boyfriend, but this wasn't. He didn't know her ins and outs, which was the way he liked it—why he'd always changed the subject quickly if Dad struck up about her—but no denying she was the warm, caring type. Hands-on.

Sitting with Dad through all his chemo sessions. And when Dad moved to the hospice she was invariably there when he arrived—running late because of work—taking up the slack—*his* slack—which felt like a slap. Doing so easily, smilingly, all the things he had to grit his teeth to do. Raising Dad up, the skin and bones of him, to help him drink. Blotting his mouth afterwards. Taking his hand. All the touchy-feely stuff that should have come naturally but didn't. But it did to Quinn. Warmth was her superpower. And at the funeral she'd aimed it right at him, put her hand on his arm…

He pushed the thought away. 'Kudos on the shelter work.'

She blushed. 'It's nothing.'

He felt his brow pleating, a weight shifting inside. It was categorically not nothing. How he spent his downtime was nothing. No doubt Dad had moaned her ears off about it, painting him black. Gambler! Womaniser! So what if it wasn't quite like that. So what if he'd let Dad think it was for the craic. It still amounted to nothing. Was that what she was thinking now: that he could do better with his time? It wasn't in her gaze, but who knew?

He looked at Edward. 'Do you happen to know anything about Dad's architect?'

'Yes.' Edward consulted a note. 'She's called Julia Levette. She's English, living in Lisbon, has a lot of experience with old buildings and the pertinent regulations. I've got a number here.'

'Great.' He switched his attention back to Quinn. 'I'll give Julia a call; see if she can offer us some possible dates.'

'Good.' She nodded a smile then turned to Edward, making to move. 'Are we done now?'

'No...' Edward's lips pursed. 'Not quite.'

She sank back, and he felt his heart sinking too, beating fast irregular beats as it went. The solicitor was drawing two envelopes out from underneath his papers. And then his eyes flicked up, moving between them as he talked.

'As I explained to you both earlier, Anthony adjusted his will to incorporate the stipulation about the Lisbon property just a month before he passed. At the same time, he gave me these envelopes: one for you, Quinn, and one for you, Will.' He slid them over. 'I don't know what's in them, just that Anthony wanted you to have them today.'

High white laid, Dad's stationery of choice. His name writ large, that resolute line scored underneath. *Blue-black ink.*

He felt his throat tightening, a vague burning sensation building behind his lids. Dad had used the fountain pen, the one he'd gone halves on with Pete to buy him a million Christmases ago, the one they'd taken ages over choosing so it would be exactly right.

He closed his eyes. Of all the stupid things to stir him up.

CHAPTER TWO

Dearest Quinn,

I write this wondering if I'm doing the right thing, so be assured, if you conclude with your smart head and warm heart that I'm not, then don't think any more about it. Live free and be happy, because I don't mean for you to carry the burden of my mistakes.

But, selfishly perhaps, and especially now that you know the contents of my will, I need to air them, put them into context, tell you things I haven't spoken about before. If I fall short, forgive me. When it comes to matters of a personal nature, I don't communicate well.

You'll recall me telling you about my boarding school days, where survival depended on not showing what was going on inside. Sadly, it's been a hard habit to break! But I must try now so you understand my anguish over Will, my desperate need to make amends for not being the father he deserved.

How to begin? With Pete, I suppose, the son I could never talk about. You must have found it frustrating, but there are things, guilts I cannot reveal, even in a letter—even to you, who always listens so well. For now, suffice it to say that Pete was a lively boy. Charismatic. Sporty. Pete made it easy for me to seem like a good affectionate father, because he won trophies, medals, tangibles I could applaud openly.

Will was—is—so very different. Thoughtful, reserved, sensitive. As a boy he looked up to Pete, adored him, lived a little in his slipstream, like younger brothers do. But Pete adored Will equally, looked after him. I see so clearly now that Pete got me and Judy off the parental hook by assuming the role of Will's caretaker, freeing us to pursue our own lives and careers.

Truth to tell, Quinn, Pete was the glue in our family, the paper that covered our cracks. When he died, those cracks all gradually reappeared—in mine and Judy's marriage, in the entire fabric of our lives.

But here's the thing: after the initial devastation of Pete's death and those first few terrible weeks, Will mustered a strength I never knew he had. I won't go into everything here because to think of it breaks my heart. Let's just say that I think, in his own way, he was trying to fill the void his brother left, trying to make good.

Sadly, as you know, Judy went on to meet someone, too sick of me and my faults to try any longer. She thought that since Will was doing so well at school he should stay there, keep living with me—thought that the combination of Jersey and getting to know her new partner would be too much upheaval for him after everything he'd been through already.

Another painful time, but Will rallied again, asked if he could work for Thacker in his school holidays. And he started helping me with the Morgan, which wasn't fully restored back then, getting to grips with the engine far better than I ever did.

Don't get me wrong, we were still feeling Pete's loss, Judy's absence, but Will seemed to settle. Sometimes he even seemed happy. You probably don't remember seeing him like that because you'd just come to us, full of sadness.

But then he went off to university and he changed. I wondered if he was simply adjusting to the big wide world, or if some girl had broken his heart. But he wouldn't talk, or engage beyond the minimum. You'll no doubt remember how taciturn he was whenever he came back.

It bothers me, Quinn, that I don't know what was going on in his head, or in his life back then, bothers me that we never got back the ease we had so briefly. And I don't understand his gambling and the rest.

Apologies! That's my cancer brain rambling. You know this already. What you don't know, and what I've only just realised myself, is that it also bothers me that he works for the company. He does a sterling job, but I don't know, deep down, if it's what he really wants, or if on some level he's trying to be some imagined version of Pete. I'm ashamed that I don't know the man he is inside, grieved that he's drifted so far away from me that I can't touch him any more, help him.

Which is where you come in, darling girl. If you no longer wish to take on the Lisbon hotel then I understand, but for Will's sake, I urge you to see it through. As you know, he thinks it's a terrible idea and, financially speaking, were it to be run on the lines of the current Thacker model then he would be absolutely right. Too smart by half, my youngest son! But you are also smart, and your idea for the hotel has my hearty blessing.

As you know, I wasn't thinking about profit when I bought it. I just wanted to rescue it, challenge myself with something different. What different looks like will now be down to you and Will.

Why involve Will at all? I hear you wondering. Well, the one thing to be said for imminent death is that it makes you reflect. And, reflecting on everything, I got to thinking that tying Will to the renovation, with you by his side, might open his eyes up, stretch him in new ways, make him think about what he truly wants from life. He might even absorb some of your wondrous creativity! At the very least, he will hopefully make a dear friend in you, which is my greatest wish. And for you too, to find a true friend in him.

Your father didn't want you to be alone, Quinn, which is why he asked me to take care of you should anything ever happen to him. I have tried to do my best by you, but I must leave you now, which means that Will is all you have left of me and my family.

I know he will be angry about what I've done, but he's a good man with a good heart full of sadness. All I want for him is to rise, find peace and happiness in whatever form it comes. If I can go towards the light knowing that you've got his back, that you will help him find his own true light, then I will rest easy in my heart.

Go well, Quinn.
Your ever-loving guardian,
Anthony

CHAPTER THREE

ROSSIO SQUARE, gently warm in the pale morning sunshine. And the plash-plash of the fountain was soothing, but the sweeping waves of black mosaic tile running side to side seemed to be alive, pulsing around her feet as she walked, messing with her head, which was all she needed when her poor head was already messed to the max!

That letter…

Those words…

Circling for days, tugging her every which way. Anthony had said she could forget it, live free and be happy if she thought he was wrong to have written it. He said he didn't want to burden her with his mistakes, but that was exactly what he had done! And now what was she supposed to do?

She owed him so much but—*seriously?*—helping Will find his light! Helping him when, aside from that one time, he'd never shown the slightest interest in her, made the slightest effort to get to know her, when, on the few occasions he'd actually been around her, he'd sailed wide or been curt. As for the funeral, he'd been downright rude, stepping back like that, turning away so she'd been left with her stupid hand grasping at air.

Was that what Anthony wanted for her? To be jumping through Will's hoops only to land flat on her face?

Her heart pinched. *No.* He wanted her to land on her feet

smiling, with Will smiling alongside. He wanted her not to be alone, to find a friend in Will, and he wanted Will to be happy.

She dropped down onto a bench, losing herself in the sparkling froth of the fountain. All very laudable, but was it achievable? She felt a knot tightening somewhere. She wasn't up for putting herself on the line just to be dissed. Hurt. Not again, not after Liam.

She'd bent over backwards to design the right look for his café, sidelining her real clients in the process—not exactly at their pleasure—giving him her time, her skill, her advice, all so he'd feel her love. Oh, and he'd been so grateful, hadn't he? All over her like a rash, pulling her into bed, eyes aglow, saying 'I love you' over and over again. Saying it with texts. Flowers. Roses by the dozen, little cards with cupid arrows…

Her heart clenched. Some love! Because when it came to the crunch, when she had needed him, when she was tied up juggling work, and the hospice, and the shelter, too tired to see him—*sleep* with him—his love had died a sudden death. And no, maybe it wasn't great for him that she was stretched so thin, but it was worse for her, being the one who was stretched. And he knew—*knew*—that Anthony was dying, that the long hospice hours would come to an end. He could have stuck it out, supported her, for God's sake, but no. Too busy tomcatting around, finding someone else to buy roses for!

Liam was a selfish, cheating, grade-A jerk! She was well shot of him. But knowing it didn't stop the thoughts coming, the same thoughts that always came. *Why?* Why could she attract attention but never hold it? What was wrong with her? Sadie would say 'Nothing', give her the stern eye, tell her she was being too down on herself, that she rocked. But she was twenty-nine now, still rocking it single.

Oh, she'd masked up with a little feminist zeal for Will's benefit, hadn't she? Because he'd irked her, assuming she was havering about coming out here because of some guy. She'd rattled a bit of steel because she didn't want him seeing in her eyes that that was exactly her pattern: putting the boy-friend first, falling over herself to be available, not wanting whoever she was with to be deprived of her love, but also— *crucially*—not wanting to deprive herself of theirs. Living for every sweet act of intimacy, that sublime headrush feel-ing of being wanted, cherished…

She bit her cheek.

Needy Quinn!

Always chasing unicorns. Was it because Mum had died just as she, Quinn, was drawing her first breath? Had she somehow sensed she was losing something irreplaceable even as she was coming into the world, so that ever since she'd been snatching at love, twisting herself to make it fit, even when it didn't?

She sighed. Who knew? And anyway, what did any of this have to do with Will? Other than that, if she couldn't convince the ones who'd at least started off liking her that she was worth sticking around for, then what chance did she have of convincing him, indifferent to her at best, that she was his friend in need?

Her heart tugged. But she owed it to Anthony to try, didn't she? Because he'd been beset with this stuff for weeks be-fore he even wrote that letter. Guilt over Will. Going to his grave with all that heartache. How could she not feel for him now when she'd been feeling for him every day for weeks? That letter was just the grim icing on the cake, churning her up even more, so she couldn't stop thinking about it, about Pete, and Will.

Pete, the son she'd never met, the one Anthony would

never talk about, but that photo on his desk spoke volumes. Pete, frozen at sixteen, tanned, tow-haired, smiling, his legs crossed, elbows on his knees, meeting the camera's eye all comfortable in his skin; Will beside him, mirroring the pose, except that his brown head was turned, tilted, looking at his brother, the adoration clearly visible on his face, his expression so sweet and open that it was impossible not to feel warmth burling, impossible not to fix on that face over and over again.

The last ever photo of the brothers together. That was what Marion, the housekeeper, had told her the day she'd found her holding the frame in her hands. Taken on holiday in France, she'd said, just weeks before Pete was knocked off his bicycle and killed.

She felt her eyes prickling, welling. Unimaginable, losing a beloved brother like that. Will had been fourteen. Fourteen, yet only weeks later, drawing strength from some hidden place Anthony didn't even know about, devastated by loss but launching himself at cracks, trying to fill the void. She swallowed hard. Rudeness aside, curt nods and miles of distance aside, she couldn't not feel for the boy Will had been. And Anthony must have known that about her, known that if he trickled in just a bit more information he could turn her to his side, hitch her to his cause.

She pressed her fingers to her eyes. *Fine!* She'd try her best. Except, what did she have to build a friendship with Will out of? Only that one sweet moment of kindness long ago, which he was bound to have forgotten about, and that other moment in the boardroom when she'd said that stupid thing about the site visit which had made him smile.

Crinkling eyes, twinkling blue, the planes of his face turning handsome…

She felt the knot inside loosening a little. That moment had felt nice, as if they were getting along, as if they could. And he had seemed genuinely impressed about her work with the homeless. Impressed and a little bit introspective, a little bit softer. Her stomach swooped. But, of course, that was before Edward had given them their letters…

What had Anthony put in Will's letter? That he loved him, respected him, was sorry for tying him to a project he had no love for, with a partner he had no love for, but that it was for his own good? Or was it straight-up business, laying out their vision for the hotel, laying it on thick about her 'wondrous creativity', about how different this hotel was going to be from all the other Thacker hotels? Whatever it was, it was unlikely to have gone down well.

It was why she'd bailed on flying out with him, so she didn't have to sit with him on the plane, trying to make conversation, worrying about which gears were grinding away inside him. Flying out last night, staying over, had seemed like a better plan, and maybe he thought so too because when she'd called to tell him he'd sounded fine about it. Maybe he'd been faking civility, or maybe he was just relieved that he didn't have to sit with her either.

She glanced at her watch, felt her stomach swooping again. No bailing now, though. She rose, forcing her feet to walk. At least it would be easier seeing him for the first time since the will reading with Julia Levette there to act as a buffer. And who knew? Maybe when Will saw the building with his own eyes he would feel switched on, inspired. That would make everything easier.

Lisbon was such a great city after all, faded but elegant. How could Will fail to be caught up in the sight of these Pombaline buildings with their Juliet balconies? And if those didn't grab him, then maybe he'd fall for the scrum of candy-coloured buildings jostling for space on the surrounding hillsides, orange roofs fencing with the crisp blue of the March sky. Crazy pavements. Rumbling yellow trams. Warmth. Light. Life! Oh, and what about those custard tarts? To. Die. For.

She felt her step lightening, a sudden smile straining at her cheeks. Surely Will could find something to love here.

CHAPTER FOUR

'YOUR FATHER WAS lucky to get his hands on this...' Julia was running her eyes over the façade with a sort of beatific smile on her face. 'So many of these old buildings sit unclaimed for ever, all because the laws of inheritance here are so complicated.' And then she was turning, looking at him again, her smile tapering somewhat. 'I won't get on my soapbox about it, though, bore you to death.'

What to say?

He forced his lips to smile then lifted his gaze to the building, trying to seem thrilled with what he was seeing: pale gold stucco, mottled and crumbling; weathered boards where windows should have been; tufts of grass sprouting from every unfortunate crack. Right now, the word 'lucky' was not even a bottom feeder in his personal lexicon for this project. 'Ignorant', on the other hand, was headlining. Because ignorant was how he was feeling right now in front of Julia, who seemed to know so much more about Dad's love for Lisbon and its architecture than he did, and was clearly wondering, behind her eyes, why that was.

If only Quinn was here. Oh, and the irony of that particular thought wasn't lost on him either. To think he'd been relieved when she'd said she would make her own way out. Relieved that he wouldn't have to sit beside her on the plane, making polite conversation, pretending she wasn't the spanner in his works, pretending he wasn't noticing her honey skin and the warm, floral smell of her.

Now, all he could think was that he could have used the time to grill her about the building, about what Dad was thinking, and that if he'd been able to do that then at least he would have been able to talk to Julia like a competent adult instead of standing here floundering like some prize idiot.

'Is this Quinn, coming now?'

He turned, following Julia's gaze, felt his heart catching. *There!* At the street end, coming towards them. Green coat, orange scarf, chunky black boots, not that different from his own brown ones, and those glorious dark curls, bobbing to the rhythm of her walk. He felt a smile coming, a swell of relief. Smiling because of the relief, obviously.

He looked at Julia. 'Yes, that's her.'

'Hmm.' Her eyebrows flickered. 'Anthony said she was lovely.'

His chest went tight. He didn't need Julia Levette reminding him how enamoured Dad was—*had been*—with Quinn. But he couldn't very well say nothing, could he? He was getting a vibe that Julia already thought he was a bit strange, so if he didn't declare himself a member of the Quinn Radley fan club, especially as Quinn was on his team, then the architect would likely give him another of those cryptic, assessing looks.

He geared up with a smile. 'Yeah, Quinn's great.'

Not 'lovely', because he didn't want Julia getting any fanciful notions. Of course, 'great' needed fleshing out, substantiating.

He cranked up his smile a touch. 'She has a good eye...'

Illustrate with examples, Will, to show you at least know something...

'Dad gave her one of our hub hotels to do when she was

more or less straight out of college. Budget rooms—compact, you know—but she came up with some ingenious designs to make the most of the space, then styled the hell out of it so the rooms looked top class…' Sage-green walls, splashes of orange in the soft furnishings and en suite bathrooms, setting off the white bedding, adding a bit of on-point zing to the ubiquitous white bathroom suite. Green and orange! He felt a beat of recognition. She clearly had a thing for green and orange.

Julia's eyebrows lifted. 'Well, space won't be an issue here. There's nothing compact about this building.' And then she was shifting her stance, altering her demeanour, smiling a broad, welcoming smile. 'Quinn! How lovely to meet you! Are your ears burning?'

Quinn took Julia's outstretched hand in both of hers. 'Lovely to meet you too, Julia.' And then she was turning to meet his gaze, her own suddenly tentative. 'Hi, Will.'

Eyes… Lips… One corkscrew curl lighter than the rest, tumbling from a place somewhere north of her left eyebrow. But where were the words? The simple reply he'd felt rising but couldn't find now because somehow, he was flying backwards in his mind to Dad's sixtieth, seeing her in silver again, seeing her smile, her *glow*, feeling that same traitorous tug inside, that same intolerable craving.

And then it was too late. She was turning back to Julia, smiling full beam, a little chuckle in her voice. 'Why would my ears be burning?'

Julia laughed. 'Because Will's been singing your praises to the high heavens, that's why.'

Outrageous exaggeration!

'Is that right?' Her gaze came back, holding him, turning a quizzical second into an agonising hour, and then she was smiling at Julia again, blushing a little, the way she had in the boardroom when he'd complimented her for volunteering at the homeless shelter. 'That's very nice to hear…'

He felt resistance scrambling up his walls, an urge to say that she shouldn't read anything into it, but then, just as quickly as it came, the urge was gone. So what if Quinn was surprised, flattered? She *was* a good designer, *did* have a good eye. Whatever else he felt about her, he wasn't above acknowledging that.

And hey, wasn't this what being calm and reasonable looked like, felt like? Hadn't he spent the last few days telling himself that, no matter how much it went against the grain, this was the way he had to be with Quinn now, because getting the best out of her, getting her full cooperation—aka speedy cooperation—was going to be a whole lot easier if he squashed his animosity flat and jumped through the wretched hoops Dad had set out for him.

His gut clenched. Dad had probably written as much in his letter, not that he'd read it. His desk drawer had swallowed it readily enough. Why torture himself reading Dad's justifications for hanging this crumbling albatross around his neck when reading them wasn't going to sweeten the medicine, change anything? He was encumbered. And that was all he needed to know, thank you very much.

'Right…' Julia was bending to a bag by her feet, pulling out hard hats, handing them over. 'Not very fashionable, I'm afraid, but we need to comply.'

'Because these are obviously going to save us if the roof caves in!' Quinn's eyes came to his briefly, full of mischievous light.

He felt an answering smile twitching, a little glow of camaraderie. The hard hat thing always mystified him too.

'Now, now, Quinn.' Julia was giving Quinn the stern eye, pulling a fat door key out of her pocket. 'There's no chance of the roof caving in. We got as far as supporting it, making it safe, before...' Her eyes came to his, softening with an apology for skimming so close to the bone, he supposed. 'Before we put everything on hold.' She drew a clearing breath. 'But the hat will save you from any loose debris dislodged by birds and so on, so it's wise to wear it, as well as being mandatory. Oh, and while we're on the subject of safety, please don't wander off when we're inside. The building is hazardous in places.'

'I was only joking about the hat...' Quinn was placating now, plonking her hat on, reaching round to tighten it. And then her gaze caught his, catching alight, emptying his lungs. 'Come on, Will. Get with the programme!'

The programme. The renovation.

The push and pull of Quinn. Eyes... Lips... Smile...

He lifted his hat, ramming it on hard, feeling the awkward grip of it, the stiff spring of its straps. How to breathe? How to think straight? He ground his jaw. Losing time every time she looked at him wasn't what he'd expected, bargained for. He didn't want this. Didn't like it.

Oh, God!

How was he going to get through this day?

Wrought-iron balusters. Mahogany rail, splitting in places but, in the right hands, not beyond redemption. She snapped a few pictures then lowered her phone, fighting a shiver as she ran her eyes around the damp-mottled walls of the stairwell. These abandoned buildings were always dank, uniquely bone-chilling, but once the roof was fixed and the building was watertight again, there was nothing here that couldn't be made good...

'Quinn?'

Will!

Concern in his voice. *Irritation.* Her heart seized. Irritation because she was doing her usual, wasn't she? Getting so caught up in light, and texture, and potential, that she'd inadvertently left him alone with Julia.

Poor Will!

Out of his depth with the architect, with this entire project. Ever since they'd come inside he'd been deferring to her, relying on her to broker the discussion, but she needed to take pictures because he was in a hurry, talking about doing things piecemeal. Maybe that wouldn't be possible in the end, but if she didn't have the reference material to work with then it definitely wouldn't be.

She clapped a hand to her hat and leaned over the balustrade. There he was, looking up from the ground floor, his face pale in the light spilling from the skylight window above. His throat was pale too, the portion of it she could see above the collar of his dark shirt. Dark shirt, grey herringbone coat. He looked good. But then Will always did, whatever he was wearing.

Jeans and tee shirts on those rare summer days he'd been home from uni, before he'd taken himself off to some other, better place…that chunky blue sweater he'd worn the Christmas they'd all gone to the pub for the quiz. His thick brown hair had been longer then, damply tousled from the falling snow they'd ploughed through to get there. *Strange…* Talking to Anthony on the way there, but on the way home silent… She blinked. Why was she even thinking about that?

'Hey!' She switched on a smile, beaming it at him. 'What is it?'

His brows crimped. 'Are you coming, or what?'

Imperious tone.

She laced her own tone with deliberate sweetness. 'Yes, when I've finished what I'm doing.'

He made a little impatient noise. 'What *are* you doing?'

She held her phone out. 'Taking pictures, videos. Making notes. I can't keep everything in my head.'

'Oh.' His expression relaxed a little. 'Sorry. I didn't know.' And then his face disappeared, and the stairwell filled with the sound of his leaping boots. Elongated intervals—two treads at a time. And then he was arriving, thrusting his hands into his coat pockets as if he needed something to do, as if now that he was here he didn't quite know what to say.

She felt her heart giving. Impossible not to feel for him. Out of his depth with Julia. Out of his depth with her too, but standing here all the same, looking awkward, endearingly vulnerable. She could feel softness stirring, as it had outside when Julia said he'd been singing her praises. Same look in his eyes now as then. Resistant, but porous somehow.

But she couldn't say anything, couldn't make an overture without a definite 'in'. Besides, the last time she'd tried he'd dissed her. Once bitten and all that. So, it was a case of pretending to be oblivious to the whole running up two flights of stairs thing, pretending that the only thought in her head, the only possible topic of conversation, was the building.

She smiled. 'I'm sorry it's taking a while. It's just a long way to come back if I find I've missed something.'

He shook his head. 'Don't apologise.' And then his mouth stiffened. 'I'm just...'

Floundering. Grieving. Did he even know he was? Was he able to admit it to himself? She felt a beat of indecision, but only a beat.

'I know.'

His eyes flared briefly, then softened a little.

Relief swept through. Any kind of softness was good and infinitely better than the cold shoulder she'd got at the funeral.

And then, as if he wanted to shake the moment off, he was moving across the landing, lifting his gaze to the skylight. 'If you do need to come back though, just come. As often as you need. On the company, obviously.'

'Anything to speed things up, huh?'

'Yes.' His eyes came back. 'As long as your own schedule permits, of course.'

'Oh, of course.' She raised her eyebrows at him, so he'd know that she'd caught the all too obvious afterthought.

And then suddenly, unexpectedly, he smiled. A warm smile that creased his cheeks, lifting his face into the realm of drop-dead gorgeous. 'I like that I don't have to pretend with you, Quinn.'

Mediterranean blue eyes. Eyes that could easily stop a heart, catch a breath out, make a voice struggle to form a word.

She swallowed. 'Pretend?'

He shrugged. 'You know how I feel about this project, know that I want to hatch and dispatch it ASAP.' His voice dipped low. 'Julia isn't in the picture, and I don't want to let on. I sense she'd be affronted if she knew how much I *don't* love this building.'

Her heart fell. It was good that he was confiding in her, definitely a step in the right direction, but what he was confiding wasn't. He wasn't seeing the good as she'd hoped, feeling inspired. And his expression was only soft right now because she wasn't Julia, someone he had to pretend with. Her heart paused.

Then again, that he was up here talking to her like this was something, wasn't it? She felt a tingle. Okay, so maybe the waves weren't parting for him on the building front, but there were other fronts, the main one being that, after years of more or less ignoring her, he had just vaulted up two flights to talk to her. That was progress. The kind of progress she could put to good use...

She shot him a smile, going with a conspiratorial tone. 'Where is Julia, by the way?'

'On a phone call.'

'Ah...' So she had a bit of time to dip a toe in the water, see how cold it was.

She lifted her phone to seem semi-preoccupied, framed a shot. 'Well, I suppose the building *is* quite hard to love at the moment...' She tapped the screen, then looked up and around, sighing for effect. 'Of course, damp's a killer, makes everything seem so hopeless. It can be hard to see past it...'

'Oh, here we go. You're about to tell me you can, aren't you?'

Challenging gaze. Wry smile.

She felt a smile of her own stirring. He might have rumbled her, but she could roll with it.

'Well, of course! I mean, I wouldn't be much good at my job if I couldn't see my way through this stuff.'

'And you think, what? That if you sprinkle your fairy dust I'm suddenly going to fall in love with this crumbling pile, leap about with enthusiasm?' His eyebrows went up. 'Sorry to disappoint you, but that's not going to happen.'

She felt a 'Why?' rising but bit it back. They weren't close enough for whys yet. Better to go with humour.

She slid her own eyebrows up. 'I wasn't expecting instant results, to be honest.'

Something ruffled the surface of his gaze momentarily and then a sheepish smile softened his features. 'Just as well, since I have nothing in the creative vision department.' His eyes made a quick, hopeless sweep of the landing. 'I look around and all I can see is a massive headache.' And then he was moving over to the wall, running his fingers over a bad section, setting off a small avalanche of loose plaster. 'Case in point.' His eyes came back, half triumphant, half despairing. 'I see a crumbling wall and after that it's all panic and white noise in my head. What do you see?'

She felt tenderness blooming in her chest. His honesty was disarming. As for fairy dust—pointless. What Will needed to banish his white noise was information.

She rooted a pen out of her pocket then went over to join him by the wall, digging the nib into the plaster, raddling it backwards and forwards to loosen it, scraping off a small section until the underlying masonry was visible.

'What I see are solid walls with areas of loose plaster—plaster that can be knocked off and redone. It's not a problem.'

Bemusement in his eyes, and interest, which could only be a good sign. Whatever she did, she mustn't stop talking.

'Now, if the supporting walls were crumbling then that would be a headache, but the bones of this building seem good to me. It just needs a little TLC.'

'TLC? Is that right?' He put his hands to his mouth, mimicking a loudhailer. 'Understatement alert!'

She couldn't hold in a chuckle. 'Okay, a lot of TLC. But there's plenty of good stuff.' She felt her heart rising, a ball of enthusiasm starting to roll. She set off along the corridor, touching a door frame. 'These frames are still good, and most of the doors are too.' She turned, walking backwards so she could see his face, judge his reaction to what she was saying. 'The stair balusters are wrought iron so they only need a clean, and the rail might look ropey right now, but it's mahogany so it'll refurbish a treat.'

'I'll buy that.' He was following now, his mouth twisting into a reluctant but twinkly smile. 'I'll go so far as to say I'm pleased because it sounds quick.'

She felt mischief sparking. 'Well, at least you're pleased about something!'

His eyes flashed. 'I have my moments.'

Smiling moments. Twinkly moments. *All good!*

She looked up at the broken, elegant ceiling. This was going to be a harder sell, but she had to try. She licked her lips, steeling herself. 'On the downside, restoring this ornate plasterwork won't be speedy. It's going to need a specialist, but it'll be worth it because—'

'Quinn, stop!'

Loud eyes. Contorting face. Some kind of horror…

Her heart lurched. 'What?'

His hand shot out, stretching into the void between them. 'Don't move—'

But she couldn't not move because her back foot was already descending, going down, down into…

Oh, God!

Nothing. Air instead of floor. And then everything was tilting, rushing in, out, spinning past, ceiling, plaster, her own hands clawing at frantic air and then somehow, *somehow*, Will was there, seizing her elbows, yanking her hard against him as he launched himself backwards, dragging her clear.

Cripes! He was breathing hard, panting warm gusts into her hair. 'Are you okay?'

Was she? She was shaking all over. *Vibrating.* She could feel her heart banging against her ribs, banging against his chest, but banging was beating, and beating was good. Beating meant she was alive. Alive, and in his arms—his, of all people's—being held tight, so tight and close that she could smell the warm, lingering trace of soap or shower gel, or maybe it was cologne. *Whatever!*

Why was she even noticing that? The scent of him, the way he was just the right height. *For what?* Why, when her head was still reeling, was it running off on stupid tangents, coming up with insane ideas, such as how good it would feel to snuggle in closer and stay there, just breathing, feeling close and warm, feeling safe, feeling—

'Quinn…?' He straightened suddenly, leaning back to look at her. 'Are you okay?'

Concern in his eyes, kindness, turning the air soft, filling it with some sweet, tugging charge.

She nodded. 'Yes. Thanks to you.'

He shook his head minutely, as if he didn't want to hear it, but why wouldn't he want to? He'd saved her from an almighty tumble. Her stomach dived. Or something worse.

She checked in, taking inventory. No hat, no phone. Fallen, dropped—lost. Without her even noticing. A blind second… a broken link. A gap in her memory. And then the world was trying to tilt, or maybe it was her head reeling again. She forced herself to breathe, reconnect with his gaze.

'Will, what happened?'

His eyes held hers for a beat, then his features set hard. 'Oh, nothing much. Just a minor, complete absence of floor.'

She blinked. 'What?'

But before he could answer she was moving, twisting out of his arms, turning to look back along the corridor. For a long second, she was silent, taking in the sight he almost hadn't seen himself, wouldn't have seen at all if he'd been remotely interested in the dilapidated ceiling. A hole. Four floorboards wide, its edges rotted and crumbling.

'Oh, my God.' Her body seemed to deflate and then she was turning round again, her voice close to a whisper. 'You're right.' Her eyes flickered, taking a moment to settle on his. 'Complete absence…'

The state of her… Ashen-faced. Shock beating behind

her lovely eyes. His heart kicked. Why the hell hadn't this wretched building been checked for safety before their visit? All very well dishing out safety helmets—which, by the way, seemed to come off far too easily—but what about the fricking floorboards, actual holes that people—*Quinn*—could fall through? If he hadn't been here...

His heart kicked again, nailing him in the stomach this time. If he hadn't been here, spreading his gloom about, she would never have been walking backwards in the first place, trying to enthuse him, get him to see the good. He felt his insides shrivelling, his mouth drying to dust. This was all his fault.

'Thank you, Will...' Her hand was on his arm, squeezing gently, warmth in her gaze, pouring out gratitude he didn't deserve. 'If you hadn't been here...'

'Don't.' He swallowed hard, removing her hand as gently as he could manage. 'If I hadn't been here, you wouldn't have been anywhere near that hole.'

She let out an incredulous breath. 'Hang on a minute.' Her eyes were striking up, pinning him. 'You're not blaming yourself for this, are you?'

'Who else? If you hadn't been trying to get me onside—'

'I'd have still walked along here, eyes on the ceiling, taking photos...' She was shaking her head at him, frustration brimming. 'It's what I *do*, Will. All the time. I get distracted, caught up in what I'm doing.' Her lips pressed together, tight with impatience. 'If you knew me at all then you would know that about me, know that I'm not just saying it. This time it was the staircase, the stairwell. I was walking up, taking pictures—thinking about the space, what I could do—and, before I knew it, I was on this floor and then you came...' She shrugged, sighed. 'But if you hadn't I'd have carried on, blazing my own ill-advised trail.'

He felt his heart cramping. Why was she doing this, trying to make him feel better? She owed him nothing. Especially after the unforgivable way he'd behaved towards her at Dad's funeral. And feeling guilty about it straight afterwards, *still* feeling guilty, didn't make him a good person.

But she was good through and through. Oh, he didn't know her, no, but he could feel her, the sweetness in her, the warmth. He'd always been able to feel it. It was why he'd tried to reach out to her when she'd first arrived at the house, because he could see what she was, couldn't bear that she was hurting and alone. Even Dad had succumbed, hadn't he? Let Quinn run through him like a hot knife through butter, bringing out his hidden sides. Dad, who hadn't been given to warmth, letting his hair down, smiling. Dad who'd made hard work of everything except, ironically, work itself.

Making hard work of things. As he did. *Was* doing right now. Whoa! Was he turning into Dad? Resistant. Armoured. Or was he there already, stiffly cast in the old man's mould? No more the open-hearted eighteen-year-old he'd once been but thirty-one and calcified.

He touched his face. Hadn't he felt these muscles rebelling just minutes ago when she'd made him smile? Jaw cracking, pain blooming. The price of a smile. The price of being Will Thacker. Oh, he might have been sticking to the script he'd written for himself, to make nice with Quinn for the sake of the project so she would roll things along quickly, but fact was, deep down, he was still fighting it tooth and nail, wasn't he? Setting his face against it so hard that she was having to sing for her supper, work to drag a shred of interest out of him, and that wasn't fair, wasn't right. His heart pulsed. See how it had nearly ended.

He lowered his hand, drew her back into focus. He had to do better, apply himself properly. Not for Dad's sake, but for hers. He inhaled deep into his lungs. It wasn't as if he didn't have the skills. No, he couldn't see through crumbling plaster, but he knew how to bring a project in, and yes, renovating a building was different to developing a new site, but it all boiled down to planning, budgeting, managing, which were definitely his bag. So, no more making things hard, for himself or for her. Especially her. He set his lips. And he wasn't letting her take the blame for what had happened either.

'I'm not buying it, Quinn.' Her chin lifted in a gesture of defiance, but that was all right. He was feeling sure-footed now, lighter somehow. 'I think you'd have stopped at the head of the stairs, looked around, then gone back down because, whatever you say about getting caught up, I think you'd have been mindful that we'd be wondering where you were.' He opened his palms to push the point. 'So you see, my fault.'

Her brow pleated. 'Are we still arguing about this?'

'Absolutely.'

Her gaze tightened on his, as if she thought she could make him fold with her eyes, and then she was puffing her cheeks out, giving up.

'Well, you're right about one thing. I do try to be mindful.' Her eyes flashed. 'But I'm also right because I do get distracted...' She frowned, considering for a moment, and then her eyes brightened. 'Why don't we go halves?'

Sharing the blame. Not as convivial as sharing a pizza—which he could totally murder right now—but it was something. Better than stringing this out anyway, which was the likely alternative since she seemed to be as stubborn as he was. Besides, wasn't working together all about compromise?

'Okay.' He sighed, labouring it to make it seem like he wasn't a pushover. 'If you insist. We can split it.'

'Cool.' She beamed a triumphant smile but then suddenly

her gaze stilled. 'We're going to have to zip it too because I just remembered what Julia said outside...'

'About what?'

'About *not* wandering off.'

'Ahh!' How could he have forgotten? And Julia was bound to be off the phone any second, wondering where they were. He felt a flick of schoolboy panic. 'We should go down.'

She nodded. 'Yeah...' But then, incredibly, she was turning in the opposite direction. 'I'll just get my hat and my phone...'

What?

He grabbed her arm. 'No, you don't!'

Her eyes filled with bemusement. 'I was *obviously* going to be careful.'

'You're not going to *be* anything, Quinn! And you're not going anywhere near that hole either.' He squeezed her arm to make her stay. 'I'll get them.'

Something flickered through her gaze—surprise perhaps, gratitude, maybe a combo of the two, and then she broke into a smile that split his atom. 'Thanks, Will.'

'No problem...' Unlike breathing. Functioning. He cut free and scanned the floor ahead, glad of the distraction.

There, against the wall beside the lethal chasm, one white hat. One phone in its—*surprise, surprise*—orange case.

He went to the wall, flattening himself against it, testing the floor with his foot between each sideways step.

Wasn't today just the gift that kept on giving? Confusion at every turn. Warm, golden feelings he had no idea what to do with. And now here he was, risking life and limb for a hat and a phone because they were hers. Of all people, hers!

'Be careful, Will...'

He paused. Her concern was touching though. He bent his knees, scooping up the hat. 'What do you think I'm being?'

'I just...' And then she made a noise that sounded suspiciously like a giggle being smothered.

Was he amusing now? He planted his foot, ducking a second time for her phone. To be fair, he probably did look like a bit of a berk, inching along like this in his smart overcoat and safety helmet!

When he got back, she was smiling at him hard. 'You were amazing!'

Definitely laughing at him, but that was fine. He could deal with that.

He pressed his lips together, nodding. 'I know. I was actually thinking the same thing.'

Her face stretched. 'Oh, and so modest!'

He nodded again. 'That too.'

She stared at him for a blink, and then suddenly she was laughing into his eyes, making the warm golden stuff flow again. What was she doing to him? Making him want to be funny, making him feel...

Focus!

He held out her things. 'Here you go.'

'Thanks.' She took them, holding his gaze for a sweet, tangled beat, and then she was jamming on the hat, brushing her phone off, tapping the screen to life. 'Oh, thank goodness.' And then she was looking up again, her eyes twinkling like magic. 'After all your heroics, I'd have been gutted if it was broken!'

CHAPTER FIVE

WILL DIPPED HIS CHIN. 'So, you've got trades primed, ready to go?'

Julia nodded. 'More or less.'

Impossible not to look at him—to *stare!* He was so different. Ever since they had rejoined Julia—ambling back through as if they had only been in the adjoining room waiting for her to finish on the phone—Will had been shouldering the load, taking notes, displaying the smarts Anthony used to so admire.

'What about specialist plasterers?' His eyes came to hers briefly, stirring a warm little ripple inside. 'I'm informed that restoring plasterwork can take a while.'

'It can, but I have a team lined up. They could start in a couple of months.'

'No earlier?'

Focus, Quinn!

She cut in. 'Will…' His gaze came back. Warm. Disconcertingly attentive. 'A month isn't going to affect the time schedule on a project like this. If the other trades are starting soon, it would be better to hold off on the restoration plasterers because they're going to need scaffold towers erecting and those will only hinder access for the other trades, slowing them down.' She smiled to soften the blow. 'No point robbing Peter to pay Paul.'

His eyes signalled resignation. 'Okay.' And then he was turning back to Julia. 'I suppose we need to prioritise the roof anyway.' His lips moved as if to smile, then flattened into a line. 'And the floors too, for safety.'

Her heart quivered. Upstairs... Pulling her from the brink... Holding her tight, breathing into her hair. That close, safe feeling. Then arguing with her about whose fault it was that she'd almost taken the express route to the floor below. Blaming himself for making her work at getting him onside when it wasn't he who'd asked her to do that at all, but his father.

And yes, she might well have stumbled down a hole anyway, because she *did* get distracted, but she'd been walking backwards upstairs expressly because of Anthony, because she'd been thinking about what *he* wanted her to do for Will—stretching Will's horizons—and of course Anthony meant well, wanting her to open Will up, but many a slip and all that. Like at that pub quiz...

Her heart pulsed. Oh, it was all coming back now: Anthony asking Will if he'd mind joining that other table because some friend of his had pitched up and wanted to join them... Will smiling, getting up. But it had felt a bit off to her, made her heart hurt for Will, and maybe it had made Will hurt as well because he'd been silent all the way home.

Typical Anthony! Blinkered once he'd got a notion in his head. Maybe it was a strength in business, but it didn't work for family, for Will. And he'd come to see it too late, hadn't he? Regretted it too late.

She drew Will back into focus. But she couldn't get into all that with him. Not yet. For now, she was just glad they had 'upstairs'—the saving part, and the funny part when he'd gone back for her stuff—because it was their secret now, a warm little strip of connection between them that was making everything feel better, more hopeful.

'So, you're saying all new pantiles?' Will was frowning now, tapping calculations into his phone.

Julia shrugged. 'If you want to turn this around quickly then new is the best option. Reclaimed materials take time to source.'

'And what's the lead time on new?'

She held in a smile. He was relentless. Even the über-serene and consummately professional Julia was beginning to look a fraction jaded.

'I'll have to check with Filipe.' And then Julia's gaze was moving, flitting between them. 'That's Filipe Alexandre. He'll be your project manager. He's very good, speaks excellent English.' She riffled in her bag, producing two white business cards which she handed over. 'Filipe's details. If you have any questions about trades, materials or scheduling, he's your guy.' She smiled. 'I'll call him later, give him the green light, then I'll touch base with you again next week, let you know when the trades are starting.' And then suddenly she shuddered. 'God, it's cold in here. We should have taken this to a café or something.'

'We can still do that.' Will looked over, checking in, then shot Julia an eager smile. 'What about lunch? We could all go grab a bite…'

Julia pulled a disappointed face. 'Oh, I'd have loved that, but I've got another meeting, so we'll have to call it a day.' She frisked her hands together. 'Unless you've got more to do, in which case I'll give you the key and you can drop it off at my office later.'

Will looked over. 'Have you got everything you need?'

'Absolutely…' She felt an icy shiver tangling with her spine. 'I'm actually freezing as well.'

He smiled then looked at Julia. 'Decision made. We're leaving.'

* * *

Quinn opened her coat then tipped her head back, closing her eyes. 'Oh, this is heavenly…'

He felt a smile tugging at his lips. 'You're easily pleased.'

Because they were nowhere yet. Just outside on the cobbled pavement, minus Julia, who'd whizzed off in her little car moments ago.

'What's not to be pleased about?' She fanned her coat out wider, smiling blindly at the sky. 'It's gorgeous out here.'

Bang on, but not for the reason she was thinking! He shut his eyes to stop them staring at her. Staring was a new problem, along with breathing. And his pizza pangs were getting to be a problem. But what were a few more starving minutes if Quinn wanted to make like a lizard on a rock?

He inhaled, letting the warm dry air cycle through his lungs. Definitely nicer out here than inside. Of course, as Julia said, once the boards came off the windows and the roof was sorted, the whole place would feel different—lighter, airier. Even he could almost imagine it…

'You've got hat hair!'

He opened his eyes.

Quinn was looking at him, holding in a smile rather badly.

Was he really so comical? He felt the air softening. He used to be, didn't he? Around Pete anyway. Pete had brought it out in him. And he'd brought it out in Pete. Mum used to say they were like a pair of flints sparking. His heart caught. A pair reduced to one. As much use as one hand clapping. But now Quinn was looking at him the way Pete used to, hanging on the edge of a smile, and he could feel that vital spark jumping again, an irresistible light rising. So, he had hat hair? Well, he could work with that!

He bent over, raking at his hair until he could feel it standing on end, then straightened, meeting her gaze. 'Better?'

She made a satisfying little snorting noise. 'Erm...'

He felt his cheeks creasing, an enjoyable chuckle rumbling. 'Too much?'

Her eyes narrowed by a playful margin. 'Just a touch.' And then she was smiling full beam, twisting her hands together as if she was itching to sort him out.

He would only have to drop his arms, offer up a hopeless little shrug, and those hands would involve themselves in his hair, he could tell. Smoothing him out, fingers softly teasing, but that would be...he felt his head trying to swim...also too much. Off the scale. Especially after what had happened earlier. Hard enough even before that, staying level around her, but afterwards—*ever since*—he'd been going full tilt trying not to remember her warm skin smell and how it had felt to hold her close, to feel the spiralling softness of her hair against his face. If she hadn't twisted free...

He smiled to reset, dealing with his hair himself, talking on as if he hadn't just been thinking what he'd been thinking. 'By the way, in case you're wondering, you don't have hat hair...'

She laughed, winding a finger into her curls. 'Oh, the hat hasn't been invented yet that could stand a chance with mine!' And then her eyes were sweeping over him, approving, softening into his. 'You've got it now...'

And there his breath went again, catching.

Her head tilted. 'You look very smart.'

Which sounded like a cue, a way to move things along so that he wasn't dangling here at the mercy of her amber gaze, losing his breath and most of his wits.

He smiled. 'Smart enough for an outdoor table somewhere?'

Her face split. 'Definitely! It's been a million years since breakfast.'

And, just like that, he was thinking of a tease, wanting to

be funny for her, wanting to make her eyes glow and twinkle, which was stupid—*self-defeating*—because her eyes were the problem, and her smile, and the way her cheeks lifted, dimpling. Making that happen was only going to tangle him up again. But he couldn't help it, couldn't switch off the desire to see himself reflected in her smiling eyes.

He slid his eyebrows up. 'Would that be a million years on this planet, or in some other universe?'

Her gaze solidified. 'Very funny!' And then she was starting along the street, laughing, drawing him along in her slipstream, blinding him with her light. 'When you know me better, you'll know that as well as getting caught up in things, I'm rather prone to hyperbole.'

'That's some view!' Will was sipping his beer, gazing out over the sweep of the city.

She wanted to agree but speaking would draw his gaze back to her and then she would blush, because the view she was busy appreciating was him. His lovely profile: that fine, straight nose, that sweet, full mouth, that lovely thick brown hair lifting off his forehead in the faint breeze. He was just in his shirtsleeves now, rolled back, because slogging up to this terrace restaurant had proved too much in a coat. All through lunch, she'd had to stop her eyes from sliding to his shoulders, his chest, his arms. But now that his gaze was otherwise occupied, her eyes were running amok, taking in his contours, the sprinkle of dark hair on his thick forearms—arms that had pulled her from the brink, held her tight.

'What did you say the square down there was called?' He turned, putting his glass down, and then his eyes were lifting, locking onto hers.

She swallowed. 'Rossio. Although it's really King Pedro the Fourth Square. He's the poor soul stuck on top of the column.' Which maybe she shouldn't have mentioned, because Pedro was Portuguese for Peter, wasn't it? She felt her chest tightening. She'd never said Pete's name to Will before, had never heard him say it either. Was he making the connection? Maybe if she just kept talking…

She picked up her glass, sipping quickly. '*Rossio* is roughly equivalent to our English word "common", as in common land. Back in the day, it was where the executions happened.'

'Nice.' His eyes flickered, without a trace of Pete, thank God, and then his gaze narrowed a little. 'How do you know all this?'

What to say?

She didn't want to upend him now—upset him—not when they were getting on so well, having actual fun, when he seemed to be stepping up on the project front, albeit still in a tearing hurry. Pace was going to be a hurdle, not one she wanted to face yet, not when he was proving such a sweet surprise, messing his hair up like that to look like a scarecrow! She felt warmth unfurling. In a million years she'd never have guessed he could be so slapstick, so completely adorable.

But she couldn't let the sunshine, and the wine, and his ocean eyes lull her into La-La Land. Anthony had wanted her to help him find his light, and she couldn't do that without touching the dark, without ever mentioning his father.

She set her glass down, bracing a little. 'Your dad told me.'

Something moved behind his eyes, but he wasn't turning his face away, which was good.

'As you know, he liked talking about Lisbon. I guess some of it stuck…'

His lips tightened. 'Right.'

Was that resistance starting? She dug in. No way was she losing him now. 'There's nothing like seeing it for real, though.' She aimed a smile into his eyes. 'I was out first thing this morning, walking…'

Empty streets. Pale sun. Sky turning blue.

His features softened. 'Sounds like a nice thing to do.'

She felt a flick of relief and, in the same beat, a spark igniting. 'It was so quiet, Will. Mellow. Or maybe it just felt like that because it's warmer here than it is in London right now and the pavements really *are* golden.'

He smiled, then turned to the view. 'Incredibly, it's my first time here.'

Because of Anthony's love for the place, he meant. She felt her heart lifting. Maybe it was only an oblique nod to his father, but it felt like a milestone, a tiptoe step towards a possible future conversation with him about Anthony, and everything that went with that. For now, she was glad of this new thing they had in common.

'It's my first time here too.'

His gaze swung back. 'Really? I assumed…' His lips pressed together. 'I mean, the way you led us up to this place…'

'No, I saw it earlier from down there, that's all. Thought it might be worth a try.'

'Hmm.' And then he broke a smile. 'You've clearly got a good radar for pizza.'

'Honed over many years!'

He chuckled and then his gaze settled. 'So, what else did you see?'

Interest in his eyes, irresistible warmth.

She felt a fresh smile surging. 'I saw—walked down—Rua Augusta. It's one of the main drags, pedestrianised, very pleasant. There's a massive arch at the end, the Arco da Rua Augusta, which leads into a vast square, and beyond that, literally across the road, is the river.'

'The Tagus?'

Raised, earnest eyebrows.

She felt her lips curving, her heart dancing. 'Apparently so.'

His eyes smiled back, crinkling. Crinkling her breath, her focus.

She picked up her glass to reset. 'I stayed there for a while, then came back up another street and stumbled upon the Santa Justa lift—which I still can't get over!'

He shook his head. 'Me neither.' And then he was turning to look over the rail. 'It's a weird-looking thing, isn't it?'

She followed his gaze, feeling the little heart dip that happened every time she looked at the grey iron tower with its great boxy top that didn't fit at all with the terracotta roofs around it.

His eyebrows drew in. 'Incongruous, but oddly compelling.' And then his eyes found hers. 'Did you go up it?'

'Heavens, no! It gives me the heebie-jeebies.'

He pulled a sheepish face. 'Not just me then?'

She felt a warm rush of fellow feeling, then yet another smile coming. 'No, not just you. I had a quick look then walked up to Rossio Square, which has these insane waves of mosaic running side to side. You can't really see them from here but, trust me, they make you feel tipsy when you're walking across, even when you've only had coffee!'

'Sounds awful.'

But his eyes were smiling, twinkling into hers, making her heart soar. How was this turning out to be so easy? All those years of distance, and now they were flowing together, mingling like tides.

She smiled. 'Not *awful*. Just weird—but in a fun way.'

'I'm sold!' He grinned, then he was turning, looking down at the square again, his voice shading towards wistfulness. 'I wish I could have...'

She held her breath. Was he about to say something about Anthony, that he wished he could have come here with him? That would be a breakthrough, would open things right up...

But then suddenly his features were darkening, hardening, his whole demeanour changing. When he turned back to look at her, his gaze was cool, bordering on disdainful.

'Is that why you came over by yourself last night, Quinn?' His eyebrows arched in a blatant challenge. 'So you could hit the streets first thing, get some *exploring* under your belt?'

Her lungs emptied. What was he doing? Saying? Why was he looking at her like this? She felt maddening tears prickling, her shoulders starting to blaze. And why was he even asking when his tone said it all, that he knew it wasn't the reason? He was poking her deliberately.

Why? When they'd been getting on so well, having fun, for goodness' sake! Was it a trust thing, some kind of bizarre honesty test? Did he want to hear her say: No, I came last night so I didn't have to sit with you on the plane, wondering what the hell to say to you, wondering what Anthony put in your letter? Was that it?

She swallowed, paddling hard. Well, if he wanted to know, then she could say that, minus the letter part. Getting into that... She baulked. Too many unknowns! Besides, she couldn't risk him asking her about her own letter, all that *leading him to the light* business...

She inhaled carefully. But the rest was fine, maybe even desirable, because what was the point of trying to be friends with him if she couldn't be honest with him about herself? Fears. Feelings. Steering clear of Anthony, and Anthony's letter, was one thing, but his question—however barbed, however oblique, concerned the two of them, and it was true there was now, somehow, such a thing as the 'two of them', however new, however fragile, and this new, fragile thing would never grow, never flourish if she sidestepped this, let it wither her. So...

She set her glass down, then fastened her eyes on his. 'No, that wasn't the reason, Will...' *breathe* '... I just thought it would be easier on both of us if we met at the building, given that the last time we saw each other was at the reading of the will.'

His lips parted, and then something seemed to shift behind his gaze, absorbing his attention. Was he going back, replaying it in his mind? Ranting at Edward. Glaring at her through the glass. Trying to unhook her from the project, getting slapped down for it by Edward. Talking about piecemeal and dovetailing for speed. Then softening. Chuckling over her dumb site visit question. Praising her for her voluntary work. Her heart caught. And then it had been the letters, the soft rasp of those envelopes sliding over the table, the colour draining from Will's face...

She shook herself. 'I thought if we had the building to focus on, and Julia with us, then it would give us a chance to acclimatise, to start afresh.'

'Right.' His gaze held her distant for a long, unsmiling second, and then he was draining his glass, putting it down again with an air of finality. 'We should go. We don't want to miss our flight.'

Just like that! Without comment, without feeling! Cutting her off—effectively.! She felt a knife twisting somewhere. It was the funeral all over again, the same hot prickle playing with her spine, bothering her eyes, same stupid hand left grasping at air. Was this how it was going to be with him? Hot. Cold. Up. Down.

She reached for her things, swallowing a sob. To think she'd been enjoying his company. Relishing the sweet surprise of him, the way his eyes could twinkle all warm, the stupid things they had in common: a passion for thin crust pizza and a vague unease about the grey, neo-gothic structure that was the Elevador de Santa Justa! Relishing him, tingling inside because of him when, all this time, he'd been saving his biggest surprise for last, this cruel trick up his sleeve, this talent for turning light to dark in a heartbeat, fire to ice.

She bit into her lip hard. Well, she'd learned her lesson. No more opening up so he could shut her down. No more flying her hopes high for him to just cut loose. She stared into the depths of her tote, breathing through.

For Anthony's sake, she couldn't give up on him, but she wasn't setting herself up for another fall either. She'd done it with Liam, helping him, getting nothing of worth back. And no, Will wasn't her boyfriend and she definitely didn't love him, but for some reason he had the power to hurt her, and she hadn't signed up for being trampled on, dissed, put through the mill. She wasn't standing for it, and he was going to know all about it!

'Quinn…'

She looked up. He was on his feet now, gesturing for her to come, a slight, polite smile fixed on his face.

She felt a knot yanking tight in her chest, a furious surge of rippling energy. She pushed up from her chair, switching on the brightest, widest smile she could muster just for the sheer pleasure of knocking his paltry effort clean off the wicket.

'Chillax, Will. I'm coming.'

CHAPTER SIX

'HEY, WILL THACKER…' Catherine's voice slid into his ear from behind and then she appeared beside him, her long blonde hair swinging. 'What are you doing after?'

Code for: do you want to invite me back to your place and take my clothes off? A month ago, he might have called a cab, taken her home, but now he could feel his stomach turning at the thought. Not that she wasn't attractive. He just wasn't interested, couldn't imagine being so ever again.

He shucked the ice in his glass. 'I'm going home.'

'Aww, darling.' She flicked a glance at the tables. 'Did you have a bad night with Mr Blackjack?' Her fingers connected with his nape, stroking. 'I could take your mind off it.'

He reached up, removing her hand, smiling to soften whatever level of blow it might be to her. 'No thanks, I'm good.'

'Aww, Will…'

She was leaning away now, pouting, contriving to look hurt, but she was way off the mark because hurt didn't look like that. Real hurt, jugular deep hurt, was what he had seen welling in Quinn's eyes, what he had inflicted on her, all because he'd lost the plot. And now he couldn't stop seeing her eyes, feeling her pain, feeling it twisting inside him with all the crushing guilt and remorse. And he couldn't stop replaying the way she had left him at the airport—that scant good-bye then striding off through the barriers without a backward glance—because replaying it hurt and he deserved to hurt, deserved to feel that knife twisting over and over again.

'Why don't you have a drink with me, Will?'

Catherine! Still looking at him, still flirting. *Why?* Couldn't she read him at all?

He shrugged. 'Because I don't want to.' He downed the last of his drink and got up, battling a sudden hot swell of emotion. 'I'm sorry, but can't you see? I'm done here.'

He drew in a steadying breath. So that didn't work, didn't take his mind off anything. He couldn't focus on the cards long enough to count them, and Catherine wasn't Quinn.

Not even close...

He flicked up his collar, aimed a nod at the doorman and set off walking. *Quinn...* Hanging on the edge of a smile, waiting for him to be funny. Looking at him the way Pete used to, drawing the clown out of him like Pete used to, putting little pieces of his old self back. The happy pieces. The light-as-air pieces. Making him feel how he used to feel before the mirror cracked. And more besides. Feeling her warmth flowing, that sweet, tingling connection. Losing himself in her smile, in her gaze, in the way her lips sipped wine from a glass...

And then he'd caught himself, hadn't he? Caught himself on the way to saying that he wished he'd been with her walking through the city that morning, and in the blink of an eye, it had all come rushing back, that *she* was the one who had pushed him out of the nest, the one who'd filled Dad's bandwidth—Dad, who was all he had left because Mum had chosen Gabe over him, deserted him when he'd been trying so hard to fill the hole in her heart Pete had left! Crashing over him like a wave that *Quinn* knew stuff about Lisbon because she was firmly, eternally, in Dad's fricking camp! God help him, in that split second it had exploded to the surface, all the animosity he'd pushed down, all the hurt and anger.

Oh, the chagrin! To have caught himself flowing towards her—*the enemy!*—flowing towards that place with her that he had sworn off going to with any woman ever again. When she would only hurt him too, reject him as Mum had. As Louise had, at uni, after he had risked his heart with her, trusted her with his story, poured out all his pain, all his venom over Dad and Quinn's precious little party for two. She'd wrapped him up, loved him, only to cut him loose six months later. Too intense, she'd said. Too messed up!

Too much for Louise. Not enough, not important enough for Mum. He'd made up his mind then: no strings, no pain. Hook-ups only. Easy enough to come by at uni and at the casino. Added bonus—Dad disapproved. Oh, the pure joy of payback, of shoving Dad's nose right in it, watching it wrinkle every time he brought a woman home and led her upstairs. Not as often as Dad made out when he was bending his ear about it. Not a *'constant stream'*. Just more than Dad himself who, as far as he could tell, wasn't getting any action at all!

All of it exploding, hitting the fan in that nanosecond in Lisbon, making him want to lash out at Quinn, sting her. So he'd grabbed a spanner to throw in the works, the question he was ninety-nine percent sure he already knew the answer to, just to watch her squirm. Oh, but she had come back at him with such honesty, talking such sense, that it was he who was left squirming, teetering on the edge. And he couldn't find a foothold, a way out of the mess he'd made, so he'd shut down, closed himself off, hurting her more. Evidence of it in her eyes, all over her beautiful face. But she'd remodelled it into a shield to hold against him all the way home, then split without a backwards glance the second her feet hit the ground.

And now he was wretched to the marrow. Aching. He couldn't hold focus at work, at the blackjack table, anywhere. All he could think about was Quinn: the way she'd made him feel before the ugly stuff had twisted him up. Lighter of heart. Freer of spirit. Like his old self. As if anything was possible. Tenderness. Intimacy. Love...

He flagged a cab and got in, turning his gaze through the window. All the things he'd put at the bottom of his list. At the top was making it in Dad's world, making Dad proud of him, but he had smashed through that barrier years ago, ceased to think about it, because he had found his niche in the business, was happy in it. His heart caught. It was the rest of his life that didn't make sense now. And maybe that was because Dad wasn't here any more to provoke, or maybe it was because of Quinn.

He drilled his fingertips into his temples. If he could turn back time he would, undo the hurt, because maybe she was the enemy in his messed-up head, but in his messed-up heart she was golden, the thrill he couldn't stop feeling, and he wanted to see her, say sorry, fix things. But every time he went to call her, he lost his nerve because fixing things would mean untangling threads that might ignite another bitter fuse inside him, cause another conflagration.

He dropped his hands to his lap. But he had to do something. Three and a half weeks since he'd broken their wheel. The longer he left it, the harder it would be to fix. Like Dad's blasted hotel.

Three and a half weeks...

He felt a tingle. A reasonable enough period, surely, to make another site visit feel appropriate. Sensible, even.

Filipe Alexandre was doing a good job of keeping them well appraised but, even so, this was *his* project. Wanting to cast his own eye over things was completely reasonable, and wanting his interior designer present was also completely reasonable. And he was in Paris next week, anyway, which was even better. He could fly to Lisbon from there, meet Quinn at the building like last time, assuming she could make it, would agree to come…

His stomach dipped. If she did, would she suss that he was taking a leaf out of her book, meeting her there to avoid the awkwardness of flying over together, meeting her for the first time since their last visit, with Filipe between them to temper the air? And if she sussed that, would she see that what he was trying to do was make amends and, if she did see that, would she let him?

CHAPTER SEVEN

'HE EMAILED YOU?' Sadie looked up from putting on her jacket, her expression halfway between cross and curious. 'And what did he have to say for himself? *Sorry*, by any chance?'

Her heart crimped. Maybe she shouldn't have mentioned the email, just that she might need to swap a couple of shifts, but since the older woman was her friend as well as the shelter manager, and since she had mercilessly bent her ear about Will, she could hardly blow her off now just because she was in turmoil and didn't want to talk about it.

'That would have been a nice touch, but no...' She pulled her own jacket on, using the moment to push down the hurt. 'He wants us to go see how things are going with the building.'

'Will there be anything to see yet?'

Her own first thought exactly! Filipe was keeping them up to speed with progress, but it was still early days. Her second thought, which she'd instantly discounted as too needy and pathetic to entertain, was the one that was busy surfacing in Sadie's light green eyes.

'Do you think he could be using the trip as an excuse? As a way to see you?'

She offered up a shrug, not trusting herself to speak.

'Perhaps he's feeling bad...' Sadie was running up her zip

now, her expression brightening. 'Maybe he wants to see you face to face so he can apologise.'

Something snapped inside.

'He could apologise face to face here, Sadie! Where we both *happen* to live. He's only had, let me see, three weeks, three and a half days to pick his moment.'

'Not that you're counting...'

She felt her bristles stiffening then collapsing. Sadie was only trying to lighten her up, but she couldn't make herself feel lighter, not even for Sadie.

She swallowed. 'I'm sorry but that isn't helping.'

Sadie nodded slowly. 'I can see that—' little shrug '—sorry.' And then she was letting out one of her deep wise sighs. 'You know, Quinn, maybe things aren't quite what they seem with him. I mean, we see it with our service users all the time, don't we? Behaviours that can make you think one thing about a person, then you find out there's more to it, more to them.'

Her heart caught. 'But the *more* part is what I *thought* I'd found! We were getting on, having fun. I thought we were connecting.' And then he'd flicked the switch, pitched her into blinding darkness. She felt an edge hardening somewhere. 'But clearly, I was wrong. I don't know what's real with him and what isn't—what makes him tick, who he is!'

Sadie's eyebrows slid up. 'You'd like to find out though, wouldn't you?'

Her stomach locked. Would she? Still? In spite of everything?

That light in his eyes... That mad thing he'd done with his hair to make her laugh... The way the corners of his mouth curved up just before he smiled. They way he'd saved her, held her without awkwardness, looking at her as he had that other time, when she was seventeen, concern etched on his face, kindness. All the good in him. Her heart twisted. But he'd stung her too, more than once. How many times before she was a mug? How much, even for Anthony's sake, could she take?

She reconnected with Sadie's gaze. 'I don't know. I keep thinking about Liam, all the effort I put in, the big fat nothing I got out of it.'

Sadie rolled her eyes. 'Liam O'Connor was a waster, transparent from the start.' She turned to her locker, pulling out her street-duty rucksack. 'I told you to watch yourself with him right after I met him that first time. Look past the roses, I said.'

She felt her neck prickling. Sadie had said that. But what made her think Will wasn't a waster too? It wasn't as if she'd met him, taken his measure.

'So now you're saying, what? That I should look past the thorns...'

'I'm just saying don't be too quick to judge him, that's all.' Sadie sighed. 'From what you've said, it seems he's had a lot to contend with in his life.'

Her heart gave a little. Nothing she didn't feel to her bones for him, even now. But still...

'So have I, but I don't ride roughshod over other people!'

Sadie shook her head. 'I'm not saying what he did was right, Quinn, but I think you should give him time.' And then her gaze was softening, reaching in, full of kindness. 'Yourself too.'

Time. In Lisbon. Getting tied up in Will Thacker's capricious knots!

'Well, I don't have much choice as far as that goes, do I?' She yanked her rucksack out of her locker, fighting a sudden urge to slam the door shut. 'This isn't a quick makeover job we're trying to pull off, so Will and I are going to have lots more *lovely* time together!'

'Come on, Quinn.' Sadie's tone was cajoling now. 'He saved you from that hole in the floor, tried to take the blame for the whole thing, then went back for your stuff. There's a good guy in there somewhere.' Her gaze lit. 'Plus you like him. Tingles were mentioned. Goosebumps...'

Should have kept her mouth shut!

She shouldered her pack. 'I did like him, yes. Now I just feel like an idiot!'

'Maybe he feels like one too...'

'Oh, I doubt that!'

Nothing remotely sheepish about the way Will had sat on his phone talking business all the way to the airport! In the lounge as well: call after call. Oh, and on the plane he'd put his seat back and closed his eyes, taking a moment out of his busy schedule to excuse himself, blaming the lunchtime beer. By the time they'd landed she couldn't even bring herself to look at him. She'd forced herself to say goodbye at the barriers because she couldn't allow herself to be as rude as he was, and then she'd taken off. Maybe he had felt like an idiot then, but since she hadn't looked back to see, it was open to speculation.

'Come on, let's do the rounds.' Sadie was pulling the door open, ushering her through. 'A couple of hours in the London cold will soon have you longing for Lisbon, even if Will Thacker is part of the package!'

Sadie was right. Checking in with the rough sleepers had definitely given her a bit of perspective on everything. Next to theirs, her problems were beyond trivial.

She sprung the microwave door and took out her cup, going over to the window. Quiet street. Lamplit. Neighbour's cat doing its own nocturnal rounds. She was lucky. Nice roof over her head, not even a mortgage because of Dad's life insurance. A career she loved. Friends. And Sadie, who'd been her tutor at college and was now a cherished friend-cum-auntie figure. Older. *Wiser!*

She sipped her cocoa. She could line up her blessings no trouble, but there was still the enigma of Will. What was *with* him? Why had he suddenly turned on her like that? If only she could see inside his head. Reaching out to her all those years ago, then changing, as Anthony said, after he went to university, growing more and more taciturn. Coming home less and less, keeping himself to the edges of things when he did.

For years now, he had been like a ghost passing through her orbit, only ever appearing in snatches. Car shows when Anthony was putting the Morgan in for the concours, bending over the engine, his deft hands busy with some fiddly thing that Anthony couldn't manage, fixing it but then always leaving straight after. And what about that time at Anthony's lavish Gatsby-themed sixtieth birthday party when she'd gone all out in a glorious silver-fringed flapper dress that had made her feel every inch like Jay Gatsby's Daisy Buchanan? Will had been there at the start, impeccably handsome in his tux. She had caught him looking at her from across the room at one point, thought maybe he would like to dance, but when she had gone to look for him just half an hour later, Marion said that he had left.

For some stupid reason it had stung. Stupid, because it was completely in keeping. Will was a past master at leaving, beating a retreat when he'd had enough, presumably, or got bored. Or when something else appealed more: skiing instead of Christmas; dinner out instead of at home with her and Anthony. Always coming through a door only to stop and turn round again, as if he'd changed his mind. Always changing his mind, throwing himself into fricking reverse!

Reverse, reverse, reverse!

Her heart paused. But what if he couldn't simply reverse, physically remove himself, then what? She felt a tingle, her heart picking up again. What would Will Thacker do if he found himself trapped in a situation he didn't like? For instance, if he found himself forced to travel with someone he had knowingly hurt…infuriated? She bit her lip. Would he perhaps choose to hide in plain sight by making back-to-back business calls? Oh, and when that option ran dry, when it was flight mode time for the phone, would he put his seat back, perhaps, close his eyes, blame it on a single lunchtime beer?

On point, Will!

In character, just different tactics. Curling up. Bowing out. No remorse!

Wait a minute…

She parked her cup on the sill and pulled out her phone, calling up his email.

Hey Quinn. I'm in the Paris office on Wednesday and thought it might be worth coming back via Lisbon to see how things are going. Any chance you could make it for a site visit at eleven o'clock on Thursday morning? I'm jammed otherwise, so it's Thursday or bust for me, at least for a while. I'm keen to meet Filipe—as you are, I'm sure—and to see how the roof's coming on. Totally understand if you're already committed but if you could possibly find a way to make it that would be really, really great! Hope to hear from you soon. Best, Will.

No remorse, but there were lines aplenty to read between, weren't there? Words and phrases jumping out.

Paris office…jammed otherwise…this Thursday or bust…if you could possibly find a way…really, really great!…

She felt her breath stilling. How hadn't she seen it straight away? He was either desperate to check progress on the building or desperate to see her. Her pulse moved up. Desperate to see her but *not* to fly with her. Hence Paris. Hence stealing her own trick, stealing it because he was...

Oh, for goodness' sake!

Was Sadie right after all? Was he feeling bad, feeling like an idiot? Could it be that this trip wasn't about the building at all, but solely about seeing her? She squeezed her eyes shut. Or was she just chasing unicorns again, tilting the mirror to see what she wanted to see like she always did? Everything was a guess with Will. It might really be all about the roof, and meeting Filipe.

Except... He didn't need her there to look at a roof, did he? And if this was only about business then his email wouldn't have been quite so...so...breathless. She slipped her phone back. No. Will wanted her there, no question, and, bruised as she was, it was a stretch to imagine that all he wanted to do was sting her again, in which case was he, in fact, planning to apologise?

Her heart bumped. And if he did, then what? Did she cave, or stick, let herself like him again so that she could move forward with Anthony's agenda? Or would it be better to keep him at arm's length no matter what, let time tell? She bit her lips together. *Great!* So it was back to Sadie, and giving herself time to look past the thorns, giving Will time to do whatever it was he had in mind.

She folded her arms. *Fine!* She would give him time, go to Lisbon, but she was keeping her wits about her this time. No letting his smile blind her if she found herself in its bright beam. No letting his gaze soften her stupid. And she definitely wasn't flying back with him. *No, no, no!* She would stay the weekend, fly back on Sunday. Hadn't she been playing around with an idea that the hotel rooms should reflect the city itself? She could use the weekend to explore, start gathering inspiration, soak up some lovely Lisbon sunshine while she was at it.

She felt a smile coming. Yes. That would do very nicely. It was the perfect plan.

CHAPTER EIGHT

FILIPE'S GAZE SHIFTED past him. 'Is this Quinn, coming now?'

His stomach lurched, or maybe it was his heart. Hard to separate the two when his insides were bunched together like this, twisting as one. Maybe he shouldn't have positioned himself with his back to the street end, but having sight of the corner would have been too distracting. It had seemed better to face Filipe, to at least give the man the impression he was fully attentive, which he wasn't. Not by a long mile. Because of Quinn. Because, forty minutes after take-off, his brilliant plan to come straight from Paris to avoid awkwardness had started to seem a lot less brilliant and a lot more like the act of a coward, and the thought of seeing that in her eyes, along with all the other damage he'd caused, was churning him up inside. But he'd made his bed now so…

He took a breath and turned, felt his heart rising against a cold plunging tide. Quinn indeed, coming up the street as before, except this time she was in plimsolls, loose pants and a soft-looking shirt, all cream. Her tote was orange, of course.

He swallowed his heart back down. 'Yes, that's her.'

'She's going to need a jacket on inside.' Filipe glanced over, gesturing to his own clothes but meaning Quinn's—that they would get dirty.

'Yes, probably a good idea.' He smiled, trying to seem casual, to seem as if he wasn't frantically trying to read her mood. Impossible, given that she was focusing on the pavement ten paces in front of her. Was that deliberate, so she didn't have to look at him, or was she simply watching for loose cobbles, of which there were many. Was she going to give him the cold shoulder? Fair enough if she did, but still, the thought of it…

Breathe, Will.

She was here, wasn't she? She'd come. Although what did that really count for since she was bound to the project, the same as he was? Her email had been efficient but not unfriendly. In fact, borderline cheery. He had felt a wave of euphoria reading it, anyway. That was the thing to hold onto and the fact that she was looking up now, smiling on approach. At Filipe.

'Filipe…' She stretched out her hand for the project manager to shake. 'Lovely to meet you.'

'Nice to meet you too, Quinn.' Filipe was twinkling, obviously smitten. 'I was just saying to Will that you'll need a jacket on in there to protect your clothes from the dust.'

Her gaze stayed on Filipe, along with her smile. 'One of those fetching hi-vis ones, I hope!'

Filipe chuckled. 'They're all the rage inside, along with the hats. Very "in".'

She laughed back. 'Well, I'm nothing if not an ardent follower of fashion, so please, do your worst.'

His chest went tight. She wasn't looking at him, smiling at *him*. Was she punishing him? If so, it was working. He could feel cracks opening inside, pain poking its fingers in. He scanned her face, looking for signs of cruel intent. A suggestion of tension along her jaw. Her smile a touch too wide, not quite reaching her eyes…

His heart pulsed. *Idiot!* She probably would like to punish him, but that wasn't what she was doing at this moment.

Likely she was struggling to meet his eye because of the pain he'd caused her. Easy to be casually cheery in an email. Hadn't he pitched his own that way? But face to face was a different story. Doubtless, she was waiting for him to make the first move, which was entirely right since he was the one who'd broken them in the first place.

Come on, Will.

He collected himself and smiled over. 'How was your flight, Quinn?'

She stiffened for a beat, and then she was turning, regarding him with a level gaze. 'It was okay, thanks…'

He felt his ribs tightening as something shifted behind her eyes. For a piece of a second it stilled and then there was movement, a smile ghosting over her lips.

'Somewhat better than the last one.'

His stomach clenched. Talking above Filipe's head. He searched her gaze. Did she expect him to respond? Did he have a choice? Because not responding might seem like a rebuff and he couldn't do that to her again, not when the whole point of this trip was to make things right.

He drew a breath. 'Yeah, that wasn't such a great flight.'

Her gaze narrowed with interest. Or maybe it was surprise. Either way, it seemed as if she was expecting more.

He licked his lips to buy a second. 'It was a bit…bumpy.'

'Bumpy?' Filipe handed them hard hats. 'Did you hit some turbulence?'

Quinn flashed Filipe a smile. 'Yes, we did.' And then her gaze was on his again, bolder now, challenging. 'One moment we were cruising along just fine, then the next: wham!' She put her hat on, reaching round to adjust the band, eyes still trained on his. 'I'd be interested to know the science behind that.'

Filipe shifted stance. 'Fast-moving air currents.'

He ground his jaw. Could Filipe not read the situation, see that this would be a good time for him to go and measure something?

'Pretty scary, huh?' The man was grimacing now, looking at each of them in turn.

He mirrored the grimace to be polite, then rammed his own hat on. He had felt scared, sitting at that table with Quinn, before the mayhem took him over, and he would have to try to explain himself to her, but there weren't enough meteorological metaphors in the world to cover the necessary bases, none that Filipe wouldn't pick up and run with anyway. If only he could bail out of the conversation somehow, but if he did Quinn might feel as if he was shutting her down so, not an option. All he could do was keep going...

He secured his own hat, fastening his eyes on hers to block Filipe out. 'Re the science, it could have just been a...a rogue current. Or a...a spontaneous electrical storm close by that caused that sudden fatal drop. Chaos in the cockpit, instruments spinning, complete loss of control—'

'Don't listen to him, Quinn.'

For the love of God!

Filipe was shaking his head, grinning. 'Will's teasing you. Pilots never lose control. And the planes are built to withstand electrical storms. It can be frightening sometimes but you're always safe.'

Quinn's gaze slid to Filipe. 'Well, that's reassuring.' And then she was turning back, the hint of a twitch playing at the corner of her lovely mouth. 'As for you, teasing me like that...'

He felt his heart pause and then suddenly it was off again, beating hard happy beats, because her eyes were filling with light that looked like laughter, laughing at Filipe and the snafu they'd got themselves into. And it didn't mean he was off the hook, but the ice was broken, lying in pieces all around, and it was such a weight off that he could barely believe he was standing on the pavement not floating above it.

Her gaze held his for one more heartening second and then she was turning to Filipe. 'Shall we go inside now? I'm dying to see what's going on in there. Also, I'm feeling quite excited about this lovely jacket you promised me...'

'I know I've said it already, but I'm amazed at what you've achieved in three weeks, Filipe.' Will was stopping yet again, casting his eyes around, and then he looked over. 'Don't you think?'

She felt her heart squeezing. Ever since they'd come inside he'd been conferring at every opportunity, catching her eye, holding onto her gaze as if he was trying to keep the plates spinning, as if he was scared that if he didn't she would go cold on him.

As if! Not after he'd replied, *in metaphor*, to her gibe about the flight, the gibe she couldn't keep in because the bad Quinn inside her wanted a little payback. And then Filipe had chimed in, turning the whole thing into a comedy, and she had tried not to show Will that she was laughing inside because the root cause of it—the hurt he'd caused her last time—wasn't remotely funny, but he'd been looking at her so earnestly, his face such a picture—and so damn handsome—that she couldn't keep it from him, not for the world. And maybe that wasn't keeping her wits about her, but that didn't seem important now. What was important was that Will hadn't tried to dodge her bullet, which meant Sadie was right. He was feeling bad about last time, wanted to make amends, and that changed everything...

'Absolutely.' She shot him a smile. 'It's like a different building.' And then, because his steady gaze was stirring warmth in her cheeks, she turned to let her eyes make one last sweep.

So very different, as she'd known it would be, as she'd told him it would be. Gone was the stale damp smell. Gone were the cold and the gloom. Now sunlight was streaming in through the opened-up windows, illuminating a haze of dust—because the place was teeming with builders: banging and scraping; hammering and drilling; shouting and laughing; clomping up and down the stairs and across the floors in their heavy boots.

'Well, we put a big team on it as you asked, Will.' Filipe was standing with his hand on the newel post, waiting for them, and then he was leading the way back downstairs, raising his voice above the din as he went. 'The floors are all sound now, so we can really crack on. And in a couple of weeks the roof will be fully watertight, not that we're likely to get much rain.'

Will's eyes glanced into hers as he stood back for her to go first, his voice dipping low. 'Good news about the floors.'

She felt the warm tug of before, the bond that was still there somehow, in spite of everything. She couldn't hold in a smile.

'Indeed.'

And then they were descending and she was tuning in to the scuff of his following feet, imagining his lovely face and the smooth curve of his shoulders in his green-and-white-striped shirt. And she could feel her stomach tensing because very soon they were going to be alone and she was dreading it, but at the same time she couldn't wait. And then it was the last step and she was following Filipe along the wide hall-way, through the open door, and out into the bright hot glare of the midday sun.

'Any final questions?' Filipe gestured to their hats, indicating that they could remove them.

Will peeled his off, handing it over. 'I guess my only question concerns timeframe.' He raked at his hair, then glanced over. 'Specifically, how long before Quinn can get involved?'

Still in a tearing hurry, which meant Anthony couldn't have revealed all her creative, time-consuming ideas to Will in his letter after all. It was a relief, knowing for sure, except that now, on top of everything else they needed to talk about, she was going to have to raise it, and that could be tricky.

'At least a month…' Filipe's eyes found hers. 'Although if you could take a look at the plans for the proposed bar and lounge area soon that would be useful. I'll need your final decisions on layout so we can get the plumbing and wiring in the right place.'

'No problem.' She slipped off the hi-vis, handing it back with her hat. 'I've got some ideas sketched out already.' No need to say that they were only half baked because her mind had been elsewhere for the past month. 'I'll work on them some more when I get back and send you something as soon as I can.'

'Great!' He put out his hand. 'Nice to meet you, Quinn.'

'Likewise. Thanks for your time today.'

Then it was Will's turn to do the hand shaking and the pleasantries.

And then it was all done, and Filipe was going back inside and, finally, they were alone.

CHAPTER NINE

HE PULLED IN a breath. He was all scudding pulse and wrenching gut, but he wasn't holding this in for another second, not when she had let him back inside her gaze before they'd even set foot in the building, carried on engaging with him as they went around, talking and smiling, not just for show, for Filipe's benefit, but for real. No frost. No daggers. He owed her this from the depths of his heart.

'I'm sorry about last time, Quinn. So, so sorry...'

Her eyes welled slightly. 'I know.' And then she was blinking, smiling a bit. 'You wouldn't have tried to explain yourself in meteorological terms if you weren't.'

'I couldn't not try.' He felt his heart catching. 'I wanted to show you I was ready to talk about it, explain...'

She gave a soft nod. 'So, what happened, Will?'

And now here it was, all the hurt surfacing in her eyes, all the pain and confusion he'd caused. His heart clenched. She deserved a five-star explanation, toffee sauce, sprinkles and a flake, but now that the moment was here, what could he say?

That he'd caught himself liking her, *more* than liking her, and it had thrown him for a loop—triggered some hateful gremlin inside, whispering to him, reminding him that she was the enemy, the one who'd come between him and Dad, stirring him up so much that he'd derailed them on purpose;

that once he'd done that he couldn't find a way back, so he'd shut down, even though it hurt to do it—and hurt her as well?

He ran his eyes over her face. Even if she took it on the chin that she'd been the secret object of his animosity for over a decade she would want to know why, and then what would he say? Because the answer was a twisted vine with deep tangled roots, roots that reached into the darkness, and if he couldn't even make himself go there, how could he go there with her? But he had to say something, something true that also tied in with the meteorological metaphors.

He drew in a breath. 'I had a bit of a meltdown.'

Her lips pursed. 'Yes.'

Good going, Will!

Telling her something she knew already. He felt his pores prickling. Maybe moving would help.

He motioned to the street end. 'Can we walk and talk, find some shade?'

She hesitated then nodded. 'Okay.' And then she was diving into her bag, coming up with sunglasses. 'Do you mind if I wear these?'

'Why would I mind?'

She made a sombre shuttering motion with her hand. 'Hides the eyes. Windows to the soul and all that.'

He turned to walk, feeling an unexpected smile rising. 'Listen, I don't need to see your eyes to know your soul is good. It's mine we should worry about.'

'We'll see.' He felt her shoulder nudging his arm, a little playful, but then her tone was downshifting, serious again. 'So, about this meltdown?'

His stomach roiled. No way round it. The only option was to come clean, put his heart on the block, at least partially, because how could he explain it otherwise? Just a layer or two, peeled back carefully, and then maybe, somehow, the rest would come to him…

He glanced over. 'I think it happened because I didn't expect to like Lisbon so much.' He swallowed hard. 'Or you, Quinn.'

'What?' She stopped dead, pushing up her sunglasses, the windows of her soul displaying an array of indecipherable comings and goings. 'What did you say?'

Was she really making him repeat it? Hard enough saying it the first time. But he was in the thick of it now. No choice.

He inhaled. 'I said that I didn't expect to like it so much here or...'

'Yes...?'

His heart pulsed. *This* was the part she most wanted to hear—that he liked her! He felt his eyes staring into hers, his breath trying to leave. How could it mean anything when, aside from that one time, he had never given her the time of day, never done anything worthy of her attention or favour? Yet here she was, waiting for him to say it, anticipation burning in her gaze as if it mattered, as if *he* mattered, counted somehow, to her.

Beyond feeling!

He felt the air softening, a smile coming. 'Or...to like *you*, Quinn. But I do like you. Very much.'

Her gaze stilled, then it was filling with a glow, lighting up with a smile that caught him in the throat. 'I like you too.' But then in the next moment the glow was fading, and she was frowning, puzzling. 'But you didn't expect to like me?' She looked down for second, blinking, then her eyes came back, wide, wounded. 'Why? Can you unpack that, and the whole meltdown thing as well, because I don't understand...'

His heart seized. Of course she didn't because, aside from that slip at Dad's funeral, he'd always tried to keep his feelings hidden. Must have done a better job of it than he'd thought too, because she seemed not to have the slightest inkling. A good thing for her sake, but a problem for him, because being honest, which he wanted to be, without potentially hurting her all over again, which he definitely didn't want to do, didn't leave him much rope. And yes, thinking about all of this beforehand would have been a good plan, but he hadn't wanted to sound rehearsed, like he was trying to save his own skin, instead of whatever this was sounding like.

Think, Will!

And then suddenly it was opening up. A path through the tangle. Somewhat treacherous, but a path at least.

He drew in a breath, nodded into her gaze. 'Yes, I can. I mean, I'll try to.' Anything to fix this, to bring her smile back. He swallowed to buy a moment, then looked into her eyes. 'You know how Dad and I didn't see eye to eye on this project?'

Small nod. 'Yes.'

'Well, maybe you also know...' Because who knew what Dad had told her? 'Or maybe you don't, but that's a ball with a very long chain.'

Curiosity flared in her eyes, but he wasn't going to elaborate, dig down into that particular crypt. This was only about context.

'Where I'm going with this is that I might have let the project become a bit of a totem for all that stuff with Dad, used it as a legit way to harangue him—I say *legit* because the hotel is, without a shadow of a doubt, a terrible investment.' He felt his chest tightening, his voice tightening with it. 'You probably got that I couldn't fricking well believe the will! Red mist central! Forcing me to take it on, *knowing* I was dead against it. Way to rub—no—*grind* my nose right in it!'

Breathe, Will.

'My total bad, of course, for going in there expecting a smooth ride: something for Mum, a chunk to charity, the rest to me. I was going to put the place straight back on the market, but instead—'

'You were lumbered.'

'Understatement alert!'

Her eyes flickered, registering the reference, and then her gaze cleared. 'So you set your face against it.'

'It was already set. The will just set it harder.'

'And, by association, I was included?'

His gut tensed. He could see the hurt in her eyes, but he couldn't bail now. He'd led her here after all. If he didn't admit to some resentment, then this explanation wasn't going to fly, but he needed to tread softly.

He nodded. 'Honestly—yes, but I knew it was wrong to feel that way. You didn't write the will. None of this is your fault. You're tied, like me.'

She let out a sigh. 'Okay.'

'When we came out last month, I was resigned to just getting on with it since I couldn't change it, but I wasn't feeling it...' An image flew in, making a smile tug: Quinn, raking at the wall with her pen, scattering debris. 'Not until you took me in hand, tried to open my eyes up—'

She puffed her cheeks out. 'Your eyes were more open than mine! You were the one who saw the hole in the floor.'

'It's not the only thing I saw...' He felt the guilt shifting again. 'After what happened, I knew I had to take my share, show you I was stepping up.'

A smile touched her lips. 'It wasn't lost on me. You were on fire with Julia after.'

'And I felt better for it, for involving myself. And then we went for lunch, and it was so warm, and pleasant. And I was looking at the view...' *and you* '...thinking how wonderful everything looked...' *especially you* '...and you were telling me bits of history, telling me about your walk, and

I found myself thinking how nice it would have been to be with you…'

'But then…?'

His insides coiled. The trickiest part—building a bridge between the warm fuzzy stuff and what happened next. The truth with a small change of emphasis…

He swallowed hard. 'Okay, just bear with me here. You know how sometimes when you're falling asleep you can suddenly jolt awake because you've fallen off a kerb or something?'

Her eyebrows went up. 'You fell off a kerb?'

'Yes, sort of…' This had sounded so much more plausible in his head. Would she get it, understand at all? He inhaled, tightening his gaze on hers. 'In that moment, it's as if I suddenly caught myself in the act, liking Lisbon, getting sucked in. I remembered it was Dad's dream, not mine—something he thrust upon me, something I was angry about, tied to because of him, and because of that I shouldn't be letting myself enjoy anything about it.'

Her mouth tightened. 'So then you thought, what…?' Hurt was surfacing in her eyes, glistening. 'That since you couldn't enjoy it, you might as well dump on me, stop me enjoying it too?'

'No!' His heart seized. 'It wasn't like that! It was nothing against you! It was all me—my mess…total internal combustion. Meltdown! And I couldn't level myself out afterwards, so I shut down. And I know that hurt you, and I'm sorry because you didn't deserve it.'

She looked away. 'No, I didn't.'

His heart sank. After all that, turning her head away, not forgiving him. What could he do, say, to turn this around?

You could play your last card…

He paused to breathe, pushed his hands through his hair. 'I

wanted to call you, Quinn. To say sorry. I got my phone out a million times to do it, but after the way you strode off at the airport, I couldn't get up the nerve.' He swallowed hard. 'So, I thought if I engineered a trip…'

Her gaze swung back, interested now. 'Engineered?'

'Yes.' He could feel the tips of his ears starting to blaze but if this was what it took… 'I wanted to see you. Fix things. I thought I'd stand a better chance if I made it seem like it was business.'

She inclined her head. 'I did wonder.'

His pulse quickened. Her gaze was brightening, opening by a few heartening degrees.

He ventured a half-smile. 'But you said yes, anyway.'

Her eyes flashed. 'I was curious, okay? I didn't like the way we left things and I figured, since you seemed desperate to tack this trip onto the end of your Paris trip, that it was possible you were feeling the same.' She dipped her chin at him. 'Unless not flying—*avec moi*—from London was pure coincidence?'

Rumbled! But what better feeling than when it was coupled with seeing amusement growing in those gorgeous gold-brown eyes?

'Not a coincidence, no.' He couldn't hold in a smile. 'I did wonder if you'd spot it.'

Her eyes flared. 'What—the pupil becoming the master?' And then, joy of joys, she was laughing, that same infectious chuckle she'd let loose on him in the boardroom that day. 'Only completely totally!' And then she was shaking her head. 'Seriously, though, initial awkwardness aside, it would have been so much easier talking in the airport lounge using plain speech, instead of outside the hotel in code with Filipe chiming in every two seconds. He must have thought we were both mad as hatters!'

Warm eyes. Warm smile. Was he forgiven? He couldn't push her to say it. The main thing was they were through it, *somehow*, sweltering on this pavement but smiling at each other, twinkling.

He offered up a shrug. 'I'm not saying every idea I have is a good one.'

'Can I quote you on that, as I see fit?'

Adorable mischief in her eyes. How could he possibly say no?

He opened his palms. 'Any time.'

She grinned. 'Good!' And then she was turning to look along the street, still smiling. 'So, now that we've sorted all that out, how about we find ourselves some shade and a couple of cold ones?'

CHAPTER TEN

'THIS IS PERFECT!' Will was smiling round at the pretty square and then his eyes met hers, seeming to light on the small doubt she could feel nagging. 'Don't worry, I'm not going to decide suddenly that I shouldn't be letting myself think that. No more kerbs, Quinn.' He shook his head. 'Been there, done that, not going back.'

Conviction in his eyes. In his voice.

She felt something giving inside, a hot ache filling her throat. Yes, he had hurt her the last time they were here, but now he seemed so aware, so tuned in to her, just as he had all those years ago, standing in her doorway, the same warmth and kindness shining through his gaze now as then. She had let him pass her by back then, but not this time—*no way!*— because just twenty minutes ago he'd looked into her eyes and told her he liked her and, in spite of all the messy explaining that followed, that was a huge step forward, not only because it had touched her stupid, needy heart but because it was going to make carrying out Anthony's mission easier...

She let her eyes loose on his face. Smooth arching brows, straight nose. That adorable upturn at the corners of his mouth. And those eyes, royal blue in this light, windows to a tortured soul. She could feel her heart flowing out, wanting to soothe that soul, because he was under her skin now— *somehow*—must have slipped under when she wasn't looking.

Maybe when he'd been pulling her back from the brink that day, or when he'd been messing up his hair to make her laugh. Or maybe it was the subtle but completely obvious desperation in his email that had broken her open, or his gallant stab at explaining himself in front of Filipe.

Whatever!

He was inside her now, running through her veins, beating inside her heart.

Sadie was right! She wanted to know Will—likes, dislikes…all about him. This wasn't only Anthony's mission now, but hers too. She wanted to draw Will close, dig into his shadows, help him find his light—which he might discern any second if she didn't stop staring at him like this and reply to what he had said like a normal, non-misty-eyed person!

She smiled. 'I'm glad because it doesn't get much better than this: hot sun, cold beer…' she glanced up at the riot of violet blossoms above them '…incredible jacarandas!'

He tipped his glass towards her, his gaze soft, his smile fond. 'Incredible company.'

Oh, no! No, no, no! One thing to be feeling him inside her, noticing *him*: the perfect fit of his shirt, the way the breeze was lifting his hair, wafting the light fresh smell of his cologne about, quite another for him to be noticing her. *Flirting!*

Not that she didn't like the idea of it because, heaven knew, she did—Will was super gorgeous! But this wasn't just some cute guy making eyes at her, shooting tingles up her spine. This was Anthony's son! She had to work with him, launch a hotel with him. And all that feeling-him-under-her-skin business aside, he was patently a bit of a mess—with regard to Anthony especially—signs and tells the whole time he was talking, things she couldn't ask him about because she didn't know him well enough yet. And maybe he was right, maybe he wouldn't melt down again over liking Lisbon, or her—

hopefully not her—but that didn't mean he wouldn't combust over something else, and that something might very well be her ideas for the hotel, their impact on his precious timeframe.

So, however lovely it was to be feeling this sweet electricity shuttling back and forth between them, however tempting it was to flirt back, she mustn't. There were bumps ahead, a million possible hurts waiting for her if she wasn't careful. She needed to nip it in the bud right now. Tactfully, of course.

She raised her eyebrows at him. 'Oh, stop it! You're just sucking up now, trying to get on my good side.'

'Of course I am.' He smiled a lopsided smile. 'I've been on your other side, and I didn't like it much.'

Her heart squeezed. Damn him and his silver tongue! On the other hand, hadn't he just handed her an opportunity to show him where she stood?

She smiled. 'Well, you're on the right side now: we're friends again! In fact, I think we should drink to it.' She raised her glass towards him, trying to keep her voice casual. 'Friends?'

Something moved behind his gaze, and then he was leaning forwards, touching his glass to hers. 'Friends.' For an eternal, heart-thudding, tingle-inducing second his eyes held hers and then he was setting his glass back down, scanning the square. 'So where are we, exactly?'

On safer ground, thank goodness! She gulped down a mouthful of beer to chase the Will-induced dryness from her mouth then parked her glass. 'I don't know exactly, but the old building behind you seems to be called Carmo Convent, and the kiosk where we got the beers is called Carmo Kiosk, so I'm guessing... Carmo Square?'

He broke a smile. 'Detective Quinn!' And then his smile was fading. 'Dad would have known, wouldn't he?'

Her heart missed. Was Will actually starting a conversation about his father? To what end? His gaze was almost wistful, definitely tentative. One thing for sure, if she didn't seize the moment, it might slip away.

She nodded. 'Yes, undoubtedly…'

Anthony, who had loved Lisbon openly but had struggled to show real love to this smart, kind, messed-up guy sitting opposite. She felt hot tears welling and looked away to hide it, running her eyes over the graceful arched structure in the middle of the square. Maybe it had been a fountain. No sign of water now, though. Just a group of lively teenagers sitting chatting on the shallow steps around its base. Did they have fathers who loved them, who showed it openly, like Dad had with her?

Don't!

She inhaled to reset, then turned back to Will, drawing up the good stuff with a smile. 'Your dad would have known what that structure over there was, and he'd have known the history of the convent too.'

'You loved him, didn't you?'

Soft blue gaze. Intent.

She felt tears prickling again. 'Yes, I did…' She wanted to add *in spite of everything*, but maybe there were enough eggshells under her feet already. 'I mean, he took me in, gave me a home.'

He nodded slightly, and then he was picking up his drink, settling back in his chair. 'Our dads were at uni together, right?'

She felt a little jolt of surprise. But of course he would know this, must know about her mum too, her whole history. All the things they'd never talked about, and now here they were, getting into it, which was weird but also nice.

She let a smile rise. 'Yeah. They shared a flat for a couple of years. Different degrees though. My dad did History and Politics.'

'And then he went into the Civil Service?' Will's eyes took quick measure then lit with a smile. 'Don't look so surprised. Dad filled me in before you—' And then his expression was changing, clouding. He leaned in again, setting his beer down. 'I'm sorry about your dad, Quinn. It must have been so hard for you, not having anyone...'

Stirring her pain, making it flow. No relatives on Mum's side because Mum had been orphaned as a child, had come to Britain from Nigeria to study architecture. No relatives on Dad's side either because he was an only child born to older parents—Grandad and Grandma—who had both died before she was twelve. All those years, just the two of them, because Dad wouldn't date anyone, no matter how much she'd nagged him. He'd used to say he had his hands full enough with her and that, in any case, Mum was the only one for him. Then, at fifty-one, he'd discovered the lump at the side of his neck...

'Hey...' She felt Will's hand sliding over hers, squeezing gently. 'I'm sorry. I was just... I didn't mean to upset you.'

She blinked, found her eyes were wet. 'You didn't.' She wiped her face with her free hand, smiling to reassure him because he looked so concerned. 'Kindness just stirs up the sediment, that's all. Brings things back.'

He nodded. Deep light in his gaze. Understanding.

But of course he understood. He'd lost his brother, hadn't he? Judy by default. And Anthony... It was what she had thought he was lining up to talk about—Anthony, and the grief they shared—but he seemed to have put them on a different path. Not that it mattered. Any path with Will was a good one.

Incredible that they were sitting here talking like this, after years of only existing on each other's periphery, when only a single piece of the past could be said to properly belong to them. A moment in time. Her stomach clenched. A moment she had let die, possibly to their cost. And now they were skating close to it with this talk of Dad's passing, weren't they? She bit the edge of her lip. If she took him back to that precious moment in her doorway, opened up about it, thanked him for his kindness, then maybe he would open up in return, keep this sweet momentum going.

She blinked herself back into his gaze. 'To be honest, I don't mind at all that you brought it up because I don't have anyone to talk to about that time.' She let a beat pass. 'Not anyone who was actually there, I mean...'

Movement in his eyes. Recognition. He knew what she was talking about.

She turned her hand over inside his, squeezing so he'd feel how much it had meant. 'You were very kind to me, Will. Sweet.' He was blinking, making a burn start in her throat, behind her eyes, but she wasn't stopping. He needed to know this. 'I've never forgotten the way you reached out to me that day, and I'm sorry I couldn't find it in me to respond, but that's because it *was* hard for me. I was so grateful to Anthony, and to you, but Dad was my everything. Losing him, having to leave my home for yours, feeling everything strange around me was unreal. Even though I knew it was coming down the track, I still couldn't believe how quickly my life changed, that I was truly alone in the world.'

'Quinn—' he was frowning, shaking his head now '—you don't have to be sorry. I didn't take offence, lose sleep over it. I got it.' His hand squeezed hers and then he was taking it back, picking up his glass. 'You forget. At eighteen I was well-acquainted with grief.'

And at thirty-one he was getting edgy, his eyes darting, going past her, as if now that he'd brought up the subject of his teenage grief, he wished he hadn't. Was he worried she was going to press him, push him to talk? She wanted to, because getting to know him was suddenly all she could think about, but not if he wasn't ready, if it was going to cause him pain.

She touched a finger to her own glass, keeping her voice gentle. 'I wasn't forgetting anything, especially that. I just wanted you to know that what you said that day meant the world even though I couldn't show it.'

He put his glass back down, seeming to settle. 'I'm glad then.' He gave a small smile, but in the next moment it was gone. 'I have an apology of my own to make, actually.'

Her pulse picked up. 'Oh?'

'It's why I mentioned Dad—you loving him like you did.' He sucked his cheeks in then blew out a sigh. 'At the funeral I behaved very badly towards you and I'm deeply sorry for that.'

What to say?

But then he was continuing, saving her the trouble.

'I don't know what got into me.' Something checked in his gaze. 'Actually, that's not true. I do know.' He rubbed a hand over his face. 'Dad was there for you, Quinn, so you loved him, and because you loved him you could show your sadness easily. I couldn't do that because...'

She held her breath. Was he about to give her the inside track on what was behind his tricky relationship with Anthony, something she could maybe offset with some small hint from Anthony's letter?

But then he was shrugging, spreading his fingers on the table as if in defeat, sending her hopes plummeting. 'Let's just say that my feelings for Dad were—*are*—less clear cut.' Another shrug and then his eyes came to hers, a little bit hopeless. 'Truth is, I envied you at the funeral because you were feeling all the things we're supposed to feel, and I wasn't. When you put your hand on my arm it felt like, I don't know, you were expecting me to cave, or cry or something, because that's what you were doing, and it just made me feel worse. Lacking...'

So he'd shrugged her off for the guilt and shame of not being able to muster the appropriate feelings. Her heart twisted. If only she could tell him that Anthony had gone to his grave feeling guilty for not being the father he had deserved—that if he had felt 'lacking' at his father's funeral then Anthony was as much to blame for that as he was, if not more.

But how could she tell him that now? Trickling in warm hints from Anthony's letter was one thing, but revealing wholesale that Anthony had shared his guilt and anguish about him with *her* might spark his envy again—that, and everything that went with it—and that could set them back by a mile. Bad enough that her plans for the hotel might do that anyway without adding fuel to the fire.

'I'm not trying to make excuses, Quinn.' His hand touched hers briefly, sending a tingle through her. 'I just wanted to explain, say sorry.'

Always saying sorry when so much of what he was apologising for wasn't his fault.

Enough!

She aimed a smile into his eyes, loading it with all the light she had inside. 'And now you have, and I appreciate it, and I'm okay about it. And now I think we should move on.'

His gaze softened then brightened. 'Literally or figuratively?'

'Both!'

His eyes crinkled. 'What do you have in mind?'

'Seafood! I've heard there's an excellent little place down the hill there. Want to check it out?'

He grinned. 'I think it'd be a crime not to.'

CHAPTER ELEVEN

'So this is Rua Augusta. And down there…' Quinn was sweeping her arm out like a circus ringmaster, turning her head to follow its line '…is the famous arch!'

He followed her gaze to the end of the street, felt his breath stilling. Pale…towering…magnificent. As if someone had just plonked down a version of the Arc de Triomphe. It drew the eye, then led it all the way through itself to the blue sky and the wispy clouds beyond. Stirring, but utterly present, utterly accessible. Quite something!

He pulled in a breath to dispel an unexpected quiver. Had Dad stood here on these same ornate cobblestones feeling this same surge of emotion? Must have. Because he'd come back to Lisbon time and time again, hadn't he—bought a fricking ruin!

He pushed the thought away and looked at Quinn. 'Impressive!'

Smiling eyes. Warm light. Sunglasses perched on her head, or rather buried in those gorgeous dark curls, curls that were lifting a little in the faint breeze.

He felt the tingle he couldn't stop feeling tingling harder. What was she doing to him? He didn't do relationships, didn't go deeper than a night or two with anyone, but he wanted more of this, of *her*. How could simply being with her, talking to her, feel so liberating, like balm for the soul, when it was also so hard, taking him perilously close to difficult edges, stirring old resentments?

Seeing her eyes welling over Dad in that Carmo place had been tough, twisted the knife inside, but in the next moment she had been welling up looking at him, thanking him for that one time in his miserable life that he'd been decent to her, actually apologising to him for not springing up out of her grief to welcome his effort at comforting her. He had felt surprised she remembered—touched. Although, for some reason, he'd never forgotten it either, so maybe it was just one of those memories that stuck...

'Shall we walk on so you can see it up close?'

She was dropping her shades now, raking the curls back into place—curls he'd felt against his face the day she'd nearly fallen...soft, fragrant, abundant...

He smiled to break the spell. 'Sounds good.'

She smiled back. 'Okay.' And then she was turning, setting off, stepping out like she did.

He fell into step beside her, adjusting his stride to hers, trying not to smile like a total goof. It felt ridiculously good to be walking with her, breathing in little bursts of her perfume. Such a lovely street too—wide, airy, pedestrianised. No high-rises here, no modern city skyline. The pale buildings running either side of them were four storeys high at most. He let his eyes skip along the narrow first floor balconies, then over the tables and parasols of the street cafés they were passing. Glinting glasses. Happy holiday faces. But then his eyes were skipping back to Quinn, because not looking at her every few seconds seemed to be impossible.

Quinn...

Spinning the very air into gold, bringing light to the dark—realisation! To think he'd only ventured into 'Dad territory' with her as a prelude to apologising for his behaviour at the funeral. But by the time he'd finally got back to it after all the detours, it had all become clear in his mind, that what had pushed him over the edge that day was envy. Because he didn't feel as she did, didn't feel as he had at Pete's funeral—insides wringing, heart breaking with every struggling breath—and not feeling like that had put the guilt hex on him, inflamed the rest—anger...respect...love...hate—strands he couldn't twist together into manifest grief, strands that were still tugging him a million different ways.

No wonder he was all over the place. With himself. With Quinn. Flirting with her one moment, holding her hand the next, wanting to soothe her heart. And then it had been *her* hand, *her* palm turning over so that it was scorching his, making his blood rush and his heart pound. Turning over her scorching palm like that after quite pointedly declaring them to be friends. Subtext: *and only friends, so stop flirting with me, Will.* Which was exactly right and probably a very good idea. Except it didn't tally with the warm twinkly vibes she was giving out all the time, vibes he couldn't get enough of. And so here he was again, glancing over, and here she was again, catching him out, flooring him with another of those smiles.

How much easier this would be if he could see her purely as a friend, but something was happening here, something he couldn't control. And he was tied now, couldn't simply bolt as he used to, as he had a million times before. Car shows, when he had gone along expecting it to be just Dad then found she was there too, stealing the show in her trim jeans and smart wellies. Family gatherings when the sight of her with Dad was too much to stomach.

Dad's sixtieth! Looking like some silver angel so he couldn't take his eyes off her. How he'd wanted to go over and spread her wings, touch her, taste her. And then she'd looked up, right into his gaze, catching him *in flagrante* with his tongue hanging out. He couldn't stay after that. The kicker was, he'd felt bad about Dad, worried that he would feel hurt that he'd cut out, but he'd never said a thing. His stomach clenched. He probably didn't even notice.

Oh, and now here he was again, seething about Dad, grating himself raw over what Dad did or didn't notice. If Dad had spent less time noticing what he chose to do with his leisure time and more time noticing that his actual sphere of interest at Thacker was commercial development, not commercial suicide, then he might have thought twice about lumbering him with a crumbling folly, one he couldn't wait to—

'Hey, you!' Quinn was eyeing him through her shades, frowning a little. 'I'll give you a penny for them.'

He felt his muscles loosening, a smile coming. 'Believe me, they're not worth that much.' He aimed a finger at her forehead. 'And definitely not worth wrinkling your brow over.'

'Hmm.' Her lips curved up. 'I'm not convinced but I'll let it lie.'

Just as well. When it came to the millstone, she was firmly in Dad's camp. He was on board, true—*committed*—but being on board didn't make the whole thing a good idea.

And then suddenly she was pushing up her sunglasses, filling his gaze with hers. 'Will, I need to talk to you about something.'

His stomach dipped. Anxiety in her eyes. Disquiet. Was it something about Dad, something that was going to grind his gears? Or was he just grabbing at that because he was self-absorbed? He searched her face. It could be something else—something personal to her. Maybe she needed help with something—advice…support. He felt the flurry inside subsiding. He could do that: be sensitive, supportive.

'Okay.' He smiled, loading his gaze with understanding vibes. 'Hit me.'

'It's about the hotel…'

'Oh.' He felt a sudden, ridiculous urge to laugh. The hotel was safe territory. There was nothing she could say about the hotel that could touch him. Dad had seen to that. He opened his palms. 'What about it?'

Her eyes held his for a long beat and then she drew in a breath of the fortifying variety. 'I know you're keen to get the renovation done quickly so you can get rid of it—'

'Too right!'

Something flinched in her gaze, catching him in the chest. *Too forceful, Will!*

He drew in a quick breath, smiling to smooth things over. 'Look, I'm not immune to the charms of Lisbon.' He flicked a glance at the great arch to make the point. 'As I said earlier, I'm fast coming round to it as a place, but the hotel is a non-starter!'

Her brow furrowed. 'Did you and Anthony never talk about it…?'

He felt his heart pause. 'What do you mean?'

'I mean, you do know it wasn't about the money, right?'

He felt his bristles stiffening, a fuse trying to blow somewhere. 'It patently wasn't about the money, Quinn, otherwise he wouldn't have bought the blasted thing, so yes, I did get that! And because I got it, at that point I—not very cordially, I admit—declined to show any further interest. So, to answer your question—no, Dad and I didn't talk about it—which I'm sure you know already, so I don't even know why you're asking me.'

She gave a noncommittal shrug, seemingly unfazed. 'I was just checking, that's all.' And then she was stopping, tipping her head back to look at the huge arch that was now right there, towering above them. 'Do you think when this was built the King, or whoever commissioned it, was thinking about cost?'

He followed her gaze, running his eyes over the expanse of pale stone, the mighty pillars, the intricately carved details around its central clock face. There was a statue on top, a figure with arms outstretched, but it was facing away from them, looking out over the square he could see through the arch now, the one she had told him about last time that was right beside the Tagus.

He drew in a steadying breath. 'Probably not, but this is a monument. Its sole purpose is existing. It isn't an eighteen-bedroom hotel that's never going to earn its keep.'

'What if the hotel *could* be made to earn its keep, though?'

The air pulsed. 'I'm sorry...what?'

Her eyes descended the arch and came back to his. 'It's what I want to talk to you about, but please...' She stepped in close, putting her hand on his forearm. 'Would you let me say everything I have to say before you say anything?'

Not a problem since he was close to speechless anyway. 'Okay.'

She took her hand back, beckoning him to follow her to a shaded area by the plinth, and then she was turning, fastening her eyes on his. 'As you've just so eloquently confirmed, when Anthony bought the building he wasn't thinking about profit. He just loved this city, hated to see so many elegant buildings going to ruin. He thought if he could buy one it would be a fun little project to work on, something different.'

Like a money pit!

'As you also know, he asked me if I'd like to be involved, which I did, obviously. He wasn't all that clear about what the hotel should be other than that he wanted it to be different to the standard Thacker offering.'

Fair enough. Dad had built the business on the back of a model that had barely changed in thirty years after all, but still, maybe because she was suddenly speaking more quickly, he could feel his pulse quickening, a vague unease ebbing up his spine.

'Even though Anthony wasn't bothered about the money, my first thought was the same as yours, that with the cost of the reno and with only eighteen bedrooms the hotel would be a long time coming into profit. My second thought was that if we positioned ourselves at the top end, not only would the numbers look better, but Anthony would get something that wasn't just different but properly exciting too.' She swallowed. 'I'm talking an exclusive Lisbon hotel, Will! Every room unique, luxurious. Bespoke boutique!' And then she was exhaling as if she had been holding her breath the whole time. 'What I'm getting to, trying to tell you, is that your dad really liked that idea, that bespoke boutique is basically *the* plan for the hotel.'

His lungs locked. And she'd been sitting on this all this time! When he'd been upfront, honest from the off, crystal-clear about wanting to get this thing done and dusted! Letting him say as much, smiling at him as he'd said it, staying silent, not even a ripple, a hint.

For crying out loud! Didn't this just take the biscuit? Dad's will—lumbering *him*, hanging the project around *his* neck, but this wasn't actually his gig at all, was it? It was the fricking 'Anthony and Quinn Show' all over again. Country walks, car shows, dinners out. Laughing together, cooking together! Well, they'd cooked up a storm this time, hadn't they? Left him high and dry. Out. Of. The. Loop.

Of all the places to tell him, too. On the street…people going by. He ground his jaw hard, willing the burn behind his eyes to stop, his lungs to draw in air. He couldn't lose it. Not here, not while the hurt was biting this hard. The thing to do was stop. Divide. Conquer. Separate out the threads—the Quinn stuff from the Dad stuff; the Dad stuff from the

Mum and Pete stuff. Anger...pain. Loneliness...pain. Resentment...pain. He could feel the sparks jumping, scorching, but he couldn't let them fly. He'd blown it with Quinn before and he couldn't—*wouldn't*—do it again. Not without counting to ten. Not without giving reason a say in the matter.

He forced himself to look at her. Wide eyes. Primed. Anticipating a reaction. Dreading it. He slowed his breathing, pushing everything down. It couldn't have been easy telling him all that. Tiptoeing into it, double checking how much he knew before starting. That long exhale at the end, as if it had been pressing down on her chest for a while, which it must have been, because—*face it*—if he had been standing in her shoes, would he have wanted to tell *him* that the agreed plan for the hotel was not the quick hatch and despatch job he'd thought it was but something else entirely, something protracted and eye-wateringly expensive? He swallowed. No, he wouldn't. Not before he had to, and especially not after their other ups and downs.

He drew in a deeper breath, felt it clearing his head. Fact was, it wasn't Quinn's fault that she was interested in the hotel, wasn't her fault that she had hatched a plan of her own, and it definitely wasn't her fault that from the second Dad showed him the details he had refused to be interested at all. Truth was, if he was out the loop it was as much his fault as hers.

'Will...?' She was worrying at a fingernail with her teeth, something she seemed to do when she was nervous. 'Are you going to say something?'

Because having seized the moment, forced herself to tell him everything, she wanted a reaction. Something—anything but this nerve-jangling silence. And then—*finally!*—his gaze was reanimating, reconnecting.

'Yes, I am…' He sighed. 'I will… I'm just trying to get my thoughts in order.'

What thoughts, though? He didn't look as if he was about to explode, but he didn't look delighted either. He was being annoyingly cryptic—and cryptic wasn't doing her nerves any good. She could feel her arms folding across her front, anxious prompts rising on her tongue.

'Are you upset? Cross?'

'No!'

Straight back at her. Frowning as if she was mad for thinking it but then, in the next moment, he was rubbing his head, offering up a weary-looking smile.

'Don't get me wrong. I was for a moment but I'm past it now. Now, I'm just trying to assimilate…'

Trying to assimilate something he should have known already, would have, if he and Anthony had ever talked properly, if Anthony had connected with him like a father should, forced himself past his emotional hangups for his son's sake.

She felt her heart softening. 'I'm sorry I didn't tell you before. I wanted to, but I didn't know how you'd take it, if you'd blow a fuse, or feel hurt, or…'

'All of the above?'

'Exactly!'

Her chest went tight. And it wasn't fair, was it? Never knowing which way the wind was blowing. Always having to walk this tightrope between him and his father. And maybe it would clear the air if she just let it all out, told him.

'Will, you've got to understand: this thing between you and your dad makes it hard for me—hard for me to say certain things, to know how to *be* with you about him, or about anything concerning him, like the hotel. We're coming from such different places, you and I…'

Acknowledgement in his eyes. No need to elaborate. He knew what she was saying.

'I wanted to tell you from the get-go, not only because it was the right thing to do, but also to honour your dad, because it was *our* plan, *his* dream...'

A dream he would never see realised now because the cancer had rubbed him out, the way it had rubbed Dad out. She felt her sinuses tingling. Precious lives cut short. Precious time lost—time that Anthony could have used to make things right with Will, that Will could have used...

She swallowed hard. 'But for that exact same reason I couldn't raise it with you! You're all about getting the hotel done quickly, getting rid of it because Anthony forced it on you, and I can understand that...' She could feel grief and anger thickening in her chest now, hot tears clogging her lashes. 'But you also want to throw it off for the simple fact that it was his dream, because you can't stand it, can you?' Something pulsed behind his eyes that made her own well hotter, wetter. 'I don't know what all your issues were with him, and I'm not asking you to tell me, not if you don't want to, but you need to know how it feels for me, Will! I'm stuck in the middle! I want to do right by him, and I want to do right by you, and I care about both of you, but I can't...' She forced a sob back down. 'I can't even *move* in this straitjacket!'

For a second, his eyes stared into hers and then his face was crumpling and he was moving in, taking hold of her face, wiping her tears with his thumbs. 'Oh, Quinn, please don't cry.' Shaking his head, his gaze blue and full. 'I do get it— all of it.' And then his focus was shifting, turning inwards. 'I'm sorry it's such a mess.'

Her heart pulsed. But would he try to untangle it? For her—for himself. That would be a leap towards the light. She could prompt him, perhaps. A tiny nudge. *Except* that would mean speaking, moving, and she didn't want to do either of those things because his gentle touch was giving her tingles, and his body was so close, and her face was tilted upwards in his hands so she was looking at his lovely mouth, and it wasn't much of a stretch to imagine how things could…

'Sorry…' His focus was back, arrowing in, stealing her breath. 'Are you okay?'

'Yes.' Except for her mouth, which was going dry, and her ears, which were pulsing with fast thick heartbeats because now he seemed to be stuck again, locked in the moment, or maybe it was she who was trapped, or maybe it was time stretching, slowing everything down, which was why it was easy to see his eyes lowering to her mouth, easy to see the slow parting of his lips, the tip of his tongue pausing there, then the slow deep swallow, the up down movement of his Adam's apple.

And then suddenly he was jerking his hands away as if she were white-hot metal, pushing them through his hair.

'Sorry…' He stepped back, his hands making a second, slower, pass and then he was sighing at the ground, talking to the ground. 'You must be sick of hearing that from me by now.' He shook his head. 'I'm certainly sick of saying it.'

Sorry for what, though? For looking at her mouth? For thinking about kissing her? Or maybe she had misread, was just projecting her own heat-of-the-moment confusion onto him.

'It's all right.' She inhaled to steady herself. 'We've both got things to be sorry for.'

'Me more than you.' Another sigh, and then his gaze was lifting by tentative degrees, filling hers again. 'I can see I haven't made it easy for you, and I want to wipe the slate clean, but you're going to have to help me.'

Her heart gave. Asking for help, trying so hard.

'Okay, but how?'

He gave a little shrug. 'Just...talk about Dad...if you want to, I mean. Whenever you want to. Don't skirt round him. Or me, for that matter.' He stepped closer, his gaze deep, and full. 'Promise me, Quinn.'

She felt tears aching again, in her throat, behind her lids. This was all for her, not for himself. Because it was still there, moving behind his eyes, that secret pain he kept over Anthony—pain he was forcing himself over, like a hurdle, for her sake. That he was doing this for her maybe wasn't a startling leap towards the light, but it might unlock a few doors. At the very least, it would make talking about the project easier.

She swallowed the ache back down and smiled. 'Okay. I promise.'

'Great!' His eyes crinkled and then he passed a hand across his forehead as if he was, indeed, wiping the slate clean. 'So, now we need to talk about your plan for the hotel.'

Her heart bounced. 'Talk about, as in...'

Did she dare to even hope that he would run with it?

He raised his eyebrows. 'As in: I've got a few things to say about it, but I'm ready to listen and discuss it.'

She felt her lips curving, a mad urge to fling her arms around his neck, but that was out of the question. Besides, he was talking on.

'The only thing is, we should really be making tracks...' He threw a glance at the clock on the arch. 'I've got to get my bag out of left luggage before we go through. We can talk in the cab.'

Her heart stalled. No, they couldn't!

Oh, God!

How had they managed to spend three hours together without once touching on the return journey—a journey she wasn't actually making?

'Quinn?' He was looking at her, his brow furrowing a little. 'What's up?'

Where to even begin?

She bit her lip. 'I'm sorry, Will...'

'What about?'

She swallowed hard. 'I'm not leaving today. I'm staying the weekend, flying back midday Sunday.'

'But...' His gaze narrowed in confusion and then it was clearing, meeting hers. 'Please tell me you didn't do that because of me, because you didn't want to risk a repeat of last time?'

Her heart pinched. No point denying it. He could surely see it written on her face anyway.

She nodded. 'Sort of...'

Pain in his eyes. Regret.

Nothing she wasn't feeling too in huge, desperate spades.

She licked her lips quickly. 'It wasn't the only reason, though...' Which might soften the blow for him, if not for herself. 'I thought it'd be good to spend some time here exploring the city. I've got this idea, see, to draw inspiration for the individual bedrooms from the city itself. Colours. Textures. That kind of thing. I'm going to look around, see if it could be a viable approach.'

He received this with a slow nod. 'So, where are you staying?'

'The Metropole.'

'Right.' His lips pursed and then he was drawing himself up. 'Well, maybe we could get together in London then, next week, or whenever suits...'

She felt an ache tugging, wretchedness winding through, but if she didn't force herself to seem bright about the prospect then he was only going to feel worse.

'Sure.' She smiled to warm him. 'I'll hopefully have some firm ideas by then—only for discussion, obviously.'

'Obviously...' He smiled a pale confounded smile and then, as if he wasn't sure if it was the right thing to do or not, he stepped in quickly and kissed her on the cheek. 'Have a good one, Quinn!' And then he was turning on his heel, striding away up Rua Augusta, disappearing from sight.

She touched the place he'd kissed, swallowing down tears along with the scream she could feel rising inside.

How could they not catch a fricking break? Why did everything have to keep going wrong?

CHAPTER TWELVE

'UNBELIEVABLE!'

'Sorry, *senhor*?'

Curses! He must have said it out loud. And now the taxi driver was staring at him through the rear-view mirror, obviously thinking he'd missed some fresh instruction.

'It was nothing.' He shook his head at the man, waving his hand to dismiss it. 'I was talking to myself.'

'Ah!'

The driver's expression said it all: *Like a madman!*

Like a mad man who was trying very hard right now *not* to put his mad fist through the window.

He clamped his mouth shut to make sure nothing else slipped out. *Unbelievable!* Why was everything with Quinn one step forward, two steps back? Just when he'd turned himself round, allowed himself to see some merit in her bespoke boutique idea—just when he'd started seeing things from her side, feeling things from her side, fate had drawn a line, dumping him on the wrong side.

He looked out of the window, taking in nothing. Or maybe it was the right side. For him. For her. Because he had just come pretty close to blowing it back there, hadn't he?

His stomach roiled. He had only set out to comfort her. A pure impulse from a pure place because she was crying—because of him, and Dad, and the position they'd put her in—

and he couldn't bear it. And she had let him touch her, let him wipe her tears away. No recoiling. No stiffening. Just looking up at him, reaching in with that warm liquid gaze of hers, and then he had got stuck, couldn't shake himself loose, couldn't stop his eyes going to her mouth, imagining how her lips would feel under his, wanting so badly to taste them that he'd almost succumbed...

He shut his eyes. Thank God he hadn't because this was Quinn Radley. In itself a complication too far, never mind that they were working together, hence colleagues, hence off-limits to each other. And even if, for a tantalising second, it had seemed that she was looking at him with longing in her eyes, seemed that maybe she wanted him to kiss her, it was probably just his febrile imagination tripping because she was lovely, because being with her, spending time with her, was reminding his body that it had wanted her ever since the night of Dad's sixtieth.

He rubbed his hands over his face, reconnecting with the view. Just an old thread getting tangled up with the new ones, almost landing him on the wrong side of the line. His heart clenched. But if this was the right side, then why didn't it feel right? Why was his pulse going hard, his fist itching to break something? Why was he feeling devastated that she wasn't here with him, filling his head with her ideas for the hotel? Dad's dream—calling him out for being against it simply because it was that! He swallowed hard. She was right, of course.

He drummed his fingers on his thigh. At least Dad had had a dream, though. What was his? A pang caught him in the gut.

And what the hell was he going to do with himself in London all weekend? Rattle around in the big old house feeling the irksome absence of Dad? Call Mum for a few minutes of awkward catch-up conversation? Hang out with his partnered-up friends, pretending he was cool with being thirty-one and single? Or he could fritter his time away at Aspinalls. Tempting, *not!* And meanwhile Quinn would be here, in the warmth and sunshine, searching for creative inspiration—*alone*. Drinking alone, dining alone, possibly being approached by some random guy. His heart lurched. Not possibly, *probably*, because she was stunning, and far too friendly for her own good...

An airport welcome sign flashed past.

He felt a hot wave rising, pulsing up his spine and then suddenly it stopped.

What the hell was he doing?

Just because he was booked to fly didn't mean he had to! He could cancel, go back, book into the Metropole, spend the weekend with Quinn, searching for colours or whatever, listening to her ideas, thrashing things out. This was business after all. *His* business! Why wouldn't he want to be involved? And it wasn't as if he didn't want to see more of the city...

And if he stayed he could keep an eye on her, because she was bound to go off the main drag, intentionally or otherwise, not thinking of danger. From her own lips—that was what she did all the time! He could keep her safe, protect her from random strangers. And as long as she didn't mind him tagging along then wouldn't it be the perfect opportunity for them to get to know each other better? After everything they'd been through, that couldn't hurt, could only help on the project front, especially now it was sprouting arms and legs.

He felt a smile coming. He wasn't sold yet, but it was quite the curve ball she'd thrown. A smart take on things. It was giving him a buzz anyway, or maybe the buzz was in collaborating, working with someone who had creative vision. He didn't have much to offer in that department, but he was curious, wanted to learn, and at this very moment his favourite teacher was walking through Lisbon without him. Not a situation he could allow to continue, at least not without giving her an alternative option!

The driver was pulling in now, cutting the engine, turning round. 'Twenty euros, *senhor.*'

He flicked a glance through the window. The taxi queue was heaving, snaking back for miles. If he let this cab go, it would take him ages to get another once he'd retrieved his bag and he didn't have time to waste. He had to get back, find Quinn, see if she was open to the idea of a partner in crime.

He pulled out a hundred, offering it up but keeping hold. 'Could you wait, please? I'm going in, then coming back out.'

The man looked confused. 'You come back, *senhor*?'

'Yes.' He felt his hands moving, trying to illustrate. 'I'm going in to collect a bag, then I want to go back to the city.' He circled his finger so the guy would get it, trying and failing to stop a smile breaking his face apart. 'I'm not leaving Lisbon today.'

CHAPTER THIRTEEN

IT WAS STUPID to be feeling this deflated. A solo weekend in Lisbon was exactly what she had planned, after all. Time to explore and gather ideas—ideas which, from the sound of it, Will might actually consider. Lots to feel positive about.

She looked down at her plate, at the untouched tart with its sprinkling of cinnamon on top. It was just difficult to feel positive right now while this big Will-shaped hole was busy expanding inside, a hole that even a custard tart couldn't fill.

Ridiculous!

It wasn't as if they were close…as if she knew him beyond bits and pieces. And heaven knew things hadn't been easy with him, or between them. But she was missing him all the same, aching with missing him. The sight of him. His smile. All his blue depths and warm lights. He was under her skin, she knew that, but seemingly he was much deeper under than she'd thought, so deep that it had been all she could do not to tear up Rua Augusta after him, beg him to stay. If she had, would he be sitting here now or would he have stepped back in surprise, looked at her as if she were mad?

Impossible to say, which was why she had let him go. Because even though it had seemed he was dismayed she wasn't going back to London, she could well have been reading too much into it, projecting her own disappointment into his eyes, seeing what she wanted to see because for a moment back there it had felt as if he was going to kiss her, and the tingling idea of it was taking a long time to clear from her blood, her brain. It was why she was still sitting here in the Praço do Comércio, not a hundred metres from where he had left her an hour ago, trying to fortify herself with coffee and a *pastel de nata*, trying to pull herself back level. But it wasn't working.

And now her phone was pinging. Sadie, no doubt, checking in to see if she had been right about Will, about him engineering this whole trip so he could see her!

She picked it up and her heart slipped sideways. Not Sadie but Will...

Hey, you. How's the exploring going?

She felt a smile rising, breaking, her heart lifting. They didn't do chatty texts, but it was perfect timing. Just the sweet, tingling boost she needed.

She bit down on her lip, texting back.

Not very well. Got waylaid exploring the merits of pastéis de nata at a very nice café in the Praço do Comércio and I'm still here.

Which café?

She felt a frown coming. How could that matter? Still...

Martinho da Arcada.

Ah! Opened 1778. The oldest café in Lisbon!

She laughed out loud, attracting a curious glance from a woman at the next table, but she didn't care. He was filling her well, making her day.

She tapped out a reply, giggling inside.

What??? Since WHEN are you the font of all Lisbon knowledge?

Since I bought a guidebook!

She laughed again, feeling a tease coming.

That'll come in handy in London!

Not remotely! But it's proving useful here...

Her heart bounced. *Here?* But he was at the airport, surely! *Unless...*

She lifted her head slowly, scanning the square to her left, then the arches up ahead, feeling faintly sick, faintly idiotic. And then her heart stopped dead. *There!* Under the great arch. Guidebook in hand. Looking this way and that. And then his eyes found hers, flashing sweet recognition, knocking the air clean out of her lungs. And then he was on his way, coming towards her through the crowd with his nice long stride, walking until he was right there in front of her, smiling, twinkling.

'Hello.'

She felt her eyes staring into his. How to breathe? How to speak when her heart was this full, but then suddenly that brimming heart was jumping her to her feet, and before she knew what she was doing she was flinging her arms around his neck, hugging him for all she was worth.

'For God's sake, Will! What are you doing here?'

He laughed. 'Apart from being strangled, you mean?' And then his arms were wrapping around her in turn, hugging her back. 'Let's just say I couldn't leave. Not when we were on the point of having a very important discussion about the hotel from hell.'

No bile in his voice, though, only lightness. And his arms holding her. No stiffness, no reserve. Just warmth, affection. She breathed him in. Was he really only here because of business, because this hug was feeling more like heaven than business and, wishful imaginings aside, thinking about it again, it had sort of felt that earlier he did want to kiss her...

Oh, hell!

And she had started this hugging. Spontaneously for sure, because it was so good to see him, but if he had been thinking of kissing her before, what must he be thinking now? What signal was she sending out? Aside from the wrong one! Which was the right one, secretly, but that was her business. *Whatever!* In one more second this could turn sticky, and with everything else they had going on—Anthony, and the project, and Will's issues with those things—sticky was the last thing they needed.

She released him quickly, smiling past the annoying blush that was suddenly tingling in her cheeks. 'It was a good call!'

'You think so?' He looked pleased—*relieved*—but then his eyes were clouding. 'You really don't mind me crashing your party? I mean, just say if you do and I'll go.'

After only just getting here! Was he for real?

She fired him a look to set him straight. 'There's no party to crash. And there especially won't be if you leave.' She motioned to the table. 'Shall we sit?'

He split a grin. 'Okay.'

She took her own seat, watching him settle. Guidebook,

but no bag. No jacket. Had he left them at the airport, or had he booked himself into a hotel? She felt a tingle starting, a vague skittering sensation in her veins. Gorgeous as it was to see him, what was the plan here?

She smiled over, tucking a curl back to seem casual. 'So, now that you're here, how long are you staying?'

His gaze faltered then stilled, clearing into hers. 'That's up to you.'

The tingle skittered into her stomach.

'I don't own Lisbon, Will.'

'No, but you weren't planning to spend your weekend with me either. Just because I took it upon myself to come back doesn't mean you have to fall in.' His lips set. 'I'm not trying to force a situation on you, Quinn, impose myself...'

She felt her heart melting. That he would come back to find her, fully prepared to disappear again if she wanted him to, was beyond adorable.

'You're not, and you wouldn't be.'

'You're sure?'

Still the doubt!

'Of course! Which part of the whole mobbing-you-with-an-unsolicited-hug thing didn't you get?'

He smiled a lopsided smile. 'Now that you put it like that...'

Which maybe she shouldn't have, because now she was thinking about how lovely he'd felt to hug, all smooth cotton and muscular shoulders, and thinking about it was turning her bones to rubber.

She inhaled to reset. 'So, have you booked a place to stay?'

'Yes...' His smile turned sheepish. 'I got a room at the Metropole, actually. I thought staying in the same place made sense, but if you think it's too much...'

What? He was worried that staying at the same hotel,

along with the other two hundred or so random people staying there, would bother her! His insecurity was startling but
so utterly endearing that she couldn't not smile, couldn't resist teasing him a little bit.

'Well, it is quite stalkery of you, but it's also very convenient! I'll be able to knock you up first thing so we can hit
the streets before the crowds get going.'

He smiled, and then his gaze was softening, filling hers.
'You're very nice, do you know that?'

She felt her heart squeezing, heat prickling behind her lids.
How was he able to stir her emotions like this, tug her heart
out with a word that her English teacher used to strike out
for being insipid? There was nothing insipid about it! Nothing insipid about the light in his eyes or the warmth pouring
into her chest.

She swallowed to find her voice. 'So are you.'

He baulked. 'Thanks, but I'm not so sure.'

Her heart bumped. Did he not see the good in himself?
She so wanted to dig into that, but maybe this wasn't the moment. This moment called for a light touch.

She slid her eyebrows up. 'You're not sure if you're nice
or not?'

He inclined his head, faintly wary, faintly bemused. 'I
guess.'

'So, why don't you let me decide? Show me your best, nicest side all weekend, and I'll do the same, then at the end we
can judge how nice we both are.'

A wry smile lifted his mouth. 'In other words, you want
me to suck up to you all weekend?'

She felt a giggle rising. 'If that's what it takes, yes. But
remember, it cuts both ways.'

'Hmm...' His eyes darted to her plate, came back twinkling.
'So if I sign up to this pact, do I get to share your custard tart?'

Oh, he was good! Going straight for the jugular.

She looked at the tart, trying to quash another giggle, then met his gaze. 'Asking isn't nice, you know.'

'Oh, I'm sorry.' He pressed a hand to his chest. 'My bad.' And then he was resting his forearms on the table, leaning in, his eyes glinting with mischief. 'You're right, of course. I should totally have waited for you to offer.'

And again! Running his smart rings around her, tickling all of her funny bones at once so that it was getting harder and harder to keep a straight face.

She pursed her lips to stop them from twitching, going for a derisive look. 'You can go off people, you know.'

His eyebrows flashed. 'But not off me, surely, because I'm nice.'

She stared at him hard, trying not to succumb, but then her traitorous lips were curving and his were too, and it was the best feeling in the world to be sitting here laughing together, a custard tart between them and a whole weekend ahead of them, the fun already starting.

CHAPTER FOURTEEN

'SO THIS VIEWPOINT is called...' He licked his lips, concentrating. 'Mira-dour-o de Sã-o Pe-dro de Al-cân-ta-ra!'

Quinn pulled a wincing face. 'Or something along those lines anyway...'

He felt his lips twitching. Always teasing him, just like Pete, making him feel light as air. Carefree.

He feigned chagrin. 'Are you trying to say my Portuguese pronunciation sucks?'

She laughed. 'Not *trying* to...' And then she was smiling into his eyes, doing the placating thing. 'To be fair, I don't know what it should sound like, but I'm fairly sure that *that* isn't it.' And then she was turning, making for the fountain, calling back over her shoulder, 'Ten points for trying though.'

He felt warmth bursting inside. Such a good decision to come back yesterday! Sweet delight on her face when she'd caught sight of him. That unexpected hug! Then it had been the two of them doing battle over the custard tart, until it had struck them that they could simply order more.

Afterwards, they had wandered around the Praço do Comércio, Quinn mulling over the bright yellow walls of the surrounding Pombaline-style buildings as a potential accent colour—*Pombaline-style* and *accent colour* being new phrases in his developing creative lexicon—but then, for some reason, she'd switched to teasing him about his guidebook.

He felt a chuckle rising. Not his fault that random facts were his thing. How could she not have found it fascinating that the square was one hundred and seventy-five metres by one hundred and seventy-five metres, and that before the earthquake of 1775 the site had been home to the royal palace? How could she not have wanted to know that the red suspension bridge they could see to the west was the 25 de Abril Bridge, named for the Portuguese Carnation Revolution of that same date in 1974?

So much fun plying her with facts, seeing her eyes twinkle, feeling it feeding some starved thing inside him, feeding it like a drug. All through dinner too—a candlelit blur on some restaurant terrace overlooking the Tagus—wine and teasing, a few stabs at business chat. Trying—*failing!*—not to lose himself in her eyes, in all her lovely animation.

And now she was playing with a small dog by the fountain, rubbing its head, laughing at its antics. So lovely—too lovely in that sundress, her smooth golden shoulders catching splashes of dappled sunlight, her collarbones dusky with shadow, making his lips want to…

Oh God! Telling himself that this was all about business and keeping her safe was all very well, but there was more going on here, wasn't there? A scary kind of more. The kind of more he hadn't courted—*wanted!*—let himself think about for years. And he didn't want to be thinking about it now, even entertaining it, because this was Quinn—Dad's little pet—the last person in the world he should be thinking about more with.

His stomach seized. But how to switch off these feelings, draw back, when he didn't *want* to dampen anything, when he wanted more? More of her time, her laughter, her loveliness, more of this tingling, glad-to-be-alive feeling. His heart pulsed. And what of her feelings? What would drawing back do except hurt her, make her think he was shutting down on her again? His heart caught. He couldn't do that to her. Not again.

He inhaled, letting his gaze widen. Trees... Paths... People...

Resolution! Nothing for it but to keep the inner crazy well-stoppered and carry on. After all, it wasn't as if anything could happen between them—rules of the workplace and all that. He felt his pulse settling. No... As long as he stayed on the right side of the off-limits line, he was safe, fine to let himself enjoy this for what it was, which, right now, was Quinn coming up, a little breathless, full of smiles.

'Did you see the cute dog?'

He felt his own smile spreading. 'I did.'

'And you weren't tempted to come over, give him a cuddle?'

They seemed to be walking again, heading for the parapet.

'I didn't want to butt in.'

Her eyes narrowed. 'You're not scared of dogs, are you?' And then, quickly, 'Not that there's anything wrong with that... I mean, lots of people are.'

Always that kindness with her, that irresistible warmth of spirit. No wonder he was a barrel of confusion.

He shook his head. 'No, I'm not scared of dogs, although—caveat—if a dog is scary, I reserve the right to be scared.'

She chuckled. 'Well, that little one was soppy. That's my favourite kind: pure-bred soppy!'

'Figures.'

'Are you saying I'm soppy?'

'No, but you're warm.'

She seemed momentarily stunned, and then she was putting her hands to her cheeks, laughing. 'Especially now, thank you very much. You're making me blush.'

No more than himself, at least on the inside, but twisting it up into a bit of fun would soon cure them.

He put his hands up. 'Sorry, but you know, there *is* this ongoing pressure to be nice!'

She laughed, and then she was drawing in a large breath. 'And on that *nice* convenient note, I'm going to change the subject.'

'To—?'

'The hotel.'

Business—the perfect antidote to whatever this was.

He smiled over. 'What about it?'

'I was just thinking about what you said last night, about the commercial perils of offering choice...'

He felt his business brain waking up. 'Only because consistency is what I know.'

'I get that, but you raised a valid point.' And then she was stopping, turning to face him, her eyes serious. 'If you're a guest looking to pay top whack for a unique room then it *absolutely* follows that you're going to want the room you want, not some disappointing second choice option if that one isn't available.

'And I know I said I've seen it working in London, and that all the rooms should be equally desirable, and that with so few rooms, filling them shouldn't be difficult but see, now I'm wondering if we shouldn't rein back on the bespoke angle a bit.' She gave a little shrug. 'I mean, we could easily go top end with something less avant-garde, less polarising...'

He felt himself staring into her eyes, his heart sinking in his chest. Was she doing this for him? All because he'd raised a point based on his über-narrow experience with the Thacker business model. Talking about compromise for his sake! It was even-handed of her, beyond touching, but he didn't want this. He hadn't come back here to pour cold water

on her ideas. Yes, he had questions, but mostly he was en-
thralled, excited. If she couldn't see that, wasn't getting it,
then clearly, he needed to spell it out.

'Quinn, come…'

She blinked. 'Where?'

He felt a flash of impatience and grabbed her arm. 'Just
come, okay?' Because there was a gap opening up by the
parapet railing which would heal over with other tourists if
they didn't claim it quickly, a place where they could talk
without getting in anyone's way.

When she was safely installed and looking at him again,
he drew a breath. 'Whatever you're thinking, you need to
stop, okay? I don't want us to go less avant-garde and I can
see from your face that you don't either.'

'But what you said—'

'Is irrelevant.'

'No.' She was shaking her head at him, using a slow, emphatic tone. 'You *have* got a point.'

Were they really here again, arguing the toss, like on the
day she'd nearly fallen through the floor? If he didn't nip this
in the bud right now, it would run and run.

He pressed his gaze into hers. 'But you've got more points,
good ones too. As you just said, we don't have many rooms
to fill so there'll always be someone ready to…' He felt a
tingle. 'In fact, now I think about it, there's an easy way to
circumvent the whole disappointment angle with a booking
system that only shows details of the available rooms for the
date being searched…'

Her eyes flickered. 'That could work…' And then her gaze
was reanimating. 'So you really believe my idea's a goer?'

'I do…'

And even if he didn't, he would still be saying it, because
she believed in it, wanted it—not even for herself but to hon-

our Dad's memory, to bring his Lisbon dream to life—and if she wanted it, then so did he—not for Dad but for her—to make her happy, to honour her.

The balance sheet didn't matter. He'd only chafed at the cost with Dad to provoke him, to cause him grief, because that was the way things were with them. But Dad wasn't here now. Now it was just the two of them and a broken building that needed all the TLC they could give it. Bottom line, whatever it cost, Thacker Hotels could afford it.

For pity's sake, Thacker Hotels could take a hit like this a thousand times over and not feel a thing! And if that meant he was somehow chanting Dad's mantra—fix the building just because—then it was all down to Quinn, because she was filling his well with that glow in her eyes, igniting something bright and kinetic inside him. And he wanted her to see it in him, feel it flowing through him, because she was the one who had put it there.

He took gentle hold of her shoulders. 'I believe in you, Quinn, believe you can create a hotel like no other.'

Her eyes flared. 'Steady on.' But she was smiling with obvious pleasure, blushing, blinding him.

He felt his own face breaking apart, a ripple of pure happiness taking him over. 'I think clients will be banging the door down by the time you've finished. Bespoke boutique! Quinn Radley exclusive design! All in the heart of Lisbon!'

'Whatever you're on, can I have some, please?'

Biting her lip again, drawing his eyes there, making his blood rise, his pulse hammer.

He turned her to face the view, leaning his arms on the rail to stop himself from wrapping them around her. 'It's just this place...' *And you.* 'I mean, look at it...'

Orange roofs...pastel buildings... Castelo São Jorge on

the opposite hill, knee-deep in green trees and, to the south, like a blue hem, the mighty Tagus.

'My, but you've got it bad, haven't you?' She was eyeing him softly. 'Like your dad.' And then she was turning to face him, her expression serious. 'So, you're absolutely sure about avant-garde?'

That doubt again. There was only one way to chase it away.

He contrived a solemn nod. 'Absolutely. I'm completely, one hundred percent *for* avant-garde. I just have one question...'

'Okay.' Her eyes narrowed. 'Hit me.'

He paused for effect, clamping down hard on the chuckle he could feel vibrating, then contorted his features into the same look of puzzlement that used to crack Pete up. 'What exactly is it again?'

'Whoa...' Will was holding his arms out, clowning a tight-rope walk across the undulating mosaic waves. 'Trippy or what?'

She felt a fresh smile tugging, warmth filling her chest. 'I did warn you!'

He flashed a boyish smile, making her heart skip and tumble, then he was off again, teetering on his way, drawing amused looks from everyone around him.

So funny! So gorgeous!

And so onboard with the exclusivity angle for the hotel. Onboard with jacaranda purple and tram-yellow and Tagus-blue. Giving her licence to do her creative thing, licence to talk about Anthony—not that she had much as yet since, for some reason, it still felt a bit sticky—and being the best company imaginable. Oh, and what about the way he'd taken her arm up there at the viewpoint? That warm, firm grip of his hand then standing so close that she could smell the soapy clean scent of his tee shirt…

'You were right…' He was coming up now, cargos hanging low on his hips, hair blowing in the slight breeze. 'Rossio Square is insane!' He grinned. 'Literally the most fun you can have with your clothes on!'

Her stomach dipped. Way to send her thoughts barrelling in precisely the opposite direction, to a 'clothes-off' scenario! Imagining what those shoulders would look like naked, that chest, that torso. Abs, navel, snail trail…

Oh, God!

And now she could feel a flush spreading upwards from her chest, warming her gills. Could he see it? Was he feeling it too? This crackle on the line, this tingling static.

Maybe.

Maybe that was why he was turning, casting his eyes over the square again—to give them a breathing space, to let the air clear.

'I guess you're already considering mosaics for the bathrooms?'

Safe ground.

She felt her pulse steadying. 'Yes. It's an obvious way to reflect the city.'

He turned back, his eyes twinkling. 'Get me—grasping the obvious! Maybe I'm catching on to this creative vision thing at last.'

'Could be!'

He smiled, then smiled again, hesitantly. 'So, I actually have an idea…'

And again, way to melt her heart. Trying so hard, being so sweet with it.

'Go on…'

'Okay...' Another smile. 'You know that funicular we went on?'

The rattle and clang. Warm air rippling through the carriage. Warm little jolts of his biceps against her shoulder, scorching jolts of his thigh against hers, jolts that sometimes lasted for more than a whole second. But there was something else too, tickling her behind her ribs, sparking mischief. She simply couldn't resist.

'Ahh... You mean Ascensor da Glória... Opened 1885. Electrified in 1912. Two-hundred and sixty-five metres long, ascending forty-four metres, which is, *interestingly*, an eighteen percent gradient.'

His lips set, though his eyes were smiling. 'Are you mocking my guidebook again?'

'No, I'm being nice.' She touched her chest, fighting a jag of laughter. 'Showing my appreciation. Without your guidebook, where would I be, not knowing all that?'

'Hmm.' His eyebrows lifted. 'You can go off people, you know.'

Borrowing her line, making her arms ache with wanting to fling themselves around his neck. But she couldn't do that again. *Too confusing!* She could use one of his own lines back at him though, seeing as he'd started it...

'But not off me, surely...' She hugged herself, preening for effect. 'Because I'm nice.'

He laughed. 'You're a menace, that's what!'

'But cute with it, right?'

Something moved behind his gaze and her heart tripped. *Oh, no!*

She hadn't meant to flirt. It had just happened. Because of this sweet charge in the air between them, stealing her focus, his too, from the look of it, which was not good—not good at all! If she didn't sweep this moment clean, and quickly, it was going to get messy.

She licked her lips. 'So, getting back to your idea...' She smiled into his eyes, pushing hard. 'I want to hear it.'

His gaze held her for a loaded beat then it cleared. 'Right. Well, the carriage was covered in graffiti, if you remember, and the walls up the slope too. I don't see much in the tagging, but I think some of the graffiti is cool, and it's everywhere so, you know, it's part of the Lisbon experience.'

Of course it was. There was street art everywhere here.

She felt a smile coming. 'You're right...'

He gave a little smiling shrug. 'Just a thought.'

'A really good one. And quite avant-garde!' Making ideas tingle and rise. 'Maybe floating panels of graffiti because we wouldn't want to overwhelm the space, and with a nod to the carriage itself we could incorporate some curved slat detailing to echo the wooden seats—around the bed headboard possibly, or to divide the room—reclaimed wood if we could get it, for its patina... Oh, and some soft metallic touches to invoke the mechanical—grilles or fretwork—and maybe a feature naked bulb...you know the ones with the fancy orange filaments...?'

'Sounds great!'

'Take a bow then because it's your idea.'

'Er...*no*...' shaking his head at her as if she were mad '... I said "graffiti"! You've just outlined a whole room concept in the space of five seconds. You're the one who should be taking a bow!' And then his gaze was softening. 'You're amazing.'

Admiration in his eyes and something else too. Something soft... Magnetic... Blue layers shifting, swirling, as if he was imagining...*thinking*...that she...he...they... Her stomach pulsed. Such a tantalising thought, but she couldn't let it be more than that. She was supposed to be helping him, *working* with him, for pity's sake!

Besides, she wasn't a prospect, a safe bet. She was a false flame, a dead end, someone men liked for a while then discarded because she didn't have what it took. And Sadie could tell her she was better than those men till she was blue in the face, but they couldn't all be wrong, could they? Fact was, she was twenty-nine and still single, not by choice.

Not. Like. Will.

Her heart thumped. Because he was a player, wasn't he? Anthony had said so, used to complain about it… She felt her insides tightening. Was that what this was all about—this warm intensity in his eyes a prelude to some well-practised move? Was he measuring his chances, wondering if she would be up for a little weekend fling? Her heart thumped again, harder. But no! That didn't add up, didn't tally. Will was warm, attentive, kind. He was funny. Sweet. She wasn't getting 'player' vibes. Then again, what did she know about vibes? Reading people was Sadie's strength. Sadie, who'd got the measure of Liam right away, while she'd still been tripping the light fantastic, high as a kite on the scent of his roses—

'Hey, are you okay?' Raking his hair back, half smiling, half frowning. 'Don't tell me you get so few compliments that you're actually stunned to silence when you get one.'

'No, I mean…' *Come on, Quinn!* 'Sorry. Thank you. It was nice of you.'

'I wasn't being *nice*.' And then a smile touched his lips, a smile that didn't look remotely like a player kind of smile. 'I was being truthful.'

She felt the air softening, her limbs loosening. Of course he was. Truth in his eyes…warmth, kindness. How could she have let herself think he had casual designs on her? Maybe in some other orbit he was that guy, but not in hers.

'Listen…' He was stepping back a little, pushing his hands into his pockets. 'I don't know what you had in mind for now, but I could actually do with making a few calls before close of business, so maybe I'll shoot back to the hotel for a bit.'

Because he wanted some space? Or was he trying to give her some because he'd detected her minor freakout and thought she needed it? Or maybe he really did have calls to make. *Whatever!* A timeout probably couldn't hurt, although, ironically, suddenly the last thing she wanted was to be apart from him.

'I didn't have anything lined up, but I could do with a bit of sketching time, so if you don't mind me shooting back with you…'

His eyes crinkled. 'Not at all, although, fair warning, when I said "shoot" I really meant "limp".'

She felt a smile rising, all the good feelings rising with it. 'Are you trying to tell me I've driven you too hard today?'

He see-sawed his head and then he split a grin. 'Yep!'

Impossible, irresistible Will…

She felt a smile breaking loose, filling her cheeks. 'I'll bear that in mind for tomorrow then, when I'm planning the itinerary.'

CHAPTER FIFTEEN

HE LEANED BACK in his chair. Praça do Comércio was pretty impressive by night. Buildings all lit up, and that statue too—José I and his trusty horse, Gentil. He felt a smile prodding. Quinn had liked the horse's name but had only just managed not to roll her eyes when he'd told her that the sculptor's name was Machado de Castro.

Fun times! Good food! And still half a bottle of wine to go…

He picked up his glass. Calling that timeout earlier had been the right move. An hour for business, then an hour in the hotel gym followed by a long cold shower had given him time to reset his dial, remind himself that Quinn was a work colleague. Because somehow he kept forgetting. Too high on whatever magic she was sprinkling.

Back there in Rossio Square he'd felt the joy inside cresting, pulsing out of him in waves bigger than those trippy mosaic ones: the joy of feeling good like he used to; the joy of watching her jump on his graffiti idea and spin it into gold; the joy of simply being with her, feeling every single one of his wires connecting. And maybe he had let it show too much, been too intense, like with Louise all those years ago. Maybe that was why Quinn's gaze had gone from warm to wary…

He sipped, swallowed. But things were better now. Even keel. Oh, he couldn't stop himself feeling light as air around her, couldn't stop himself wanting her, but he could keep it inside better—he *must*—because she was who she was, and they had serious work to do.

'Hey...' She was back, sitting down. 'Sorry I was so long. Why are there never enough facilities for we girls?'

Now here was an open goal...

He set his glass down, contriving a pained expression. 'I don't know. We girls do suffer, don't we?'

Her gaze solidified. 'Oh, ha-ha-ha.'

He felt a chuckle coming loose. 'Sorry! Couldn't resist.' He reached for the bottle. 'How about a top-up?'

'Oh, go on then—just the full glass, mind.' And then she was laughing quietly, tucking a stray curl behind her ear. 'I don't know where I heard that, but I can never resist saying it.'

So funny—so lovely!

A thought which was probably dancing a jig all over his stupid face.

Sensible conversation, Will...

'It's a good one.' He refilled her glass then his own, then parked the bottle. 'So, all in all, a good day, inspiration-wise?'

'Definitely!' She scrunched her face up. 'My head's buzzing.'

'I get that feeling too, when I'm about to secure a new hotel site, when it all starts coming together.'

'So, you like the hotel business?'

Surprise in her eyes, in her voice. Perhaps his big, bad attitude to Dad's project had skewed her perception.

'I do but, to be fair, probably not in the way you're thinking. Dad built the business so I signed up, but hotels per se don't excite me. It's the mechanics of business I love, the push and pull, expansion, strategizing and so on...'

'So it could be widgets and you'd be just as happy?'

'Maybe...who knows?'

She grimaced, making him laugh.

'I take it liking business for itself is an alien concept for you.'

'I suppose.'

'So, that begs the question: did you always want to be an interior designer?'

'No...' She picked up her glass, exuding mischief. 'I was aiming for astronaut, but I'm scared of heights so, you know...'

He felt his cheeks creasing. 'Ah, now I get your reluctance to ride the Santa Justa Lift.'

Her eyes flashed. 'You got me!'

'Seriously, though, was it a calling? I mean, I know you studied design, but was it always interiors you liked?'

'Yeah. I like homey stuff, making things nice.' She took a little drink from her glass then set it down. 'My mum was an architect so maybe I inherited something from her—not her patience though! Seven years is a long time to study...' She let out a little sigh. 'Doesn't seem fair that after all that effort she only got to practice for a few years.'

His heart dipped. Because her mum had died in child-birth, hadn't she? Not remotely where he'd meant this conversation to go.

'I'm sorry, Quinn.'

'It's okay.' She gave a little shrug. 'I've had twenty-nine years to get used to it. I don't miss her or anything because you can't miss something you've never had...' Her gaze drifted for a moment then came back, softening. 'Harder for you, I think...'

He felt his blood draining. What was she doing, blindsid-ing him with Mum like this?! He didn't want to talk about his mother—didn't, ever, with anyone—but if he clammed up it would rock their boat, put a dent in things, and he wanted that even less.

He swallowed to buy a moment. 'It was hard, yes.'

'And now?'

His heart clenched. 'Now it's just awkward, stilted and excruciating.'

'So, you haven't been able to…'

'What? Get over her waltzing off into the sunset with Gabe the hedge fund jerk when I was fifteen?' Because that was what her eyes were asking. 'Strangely enough, no!'

She pressed her lips together slowly. Signalling that the floor was his?

Well, she could take it back because he didn't want it! His heart pulsed. Then again, if he didn't take it, where would that leave them, except on opposite sides of an awkward silence?

He drew in a breath. 'Look, don't get me wrong. I get that she and Dad weren't in a good place before Pete died. I get that Gabe seemed like a better bet than Dad, but after that the only song I can seem to hear playing is the one about how she abandoned me.'

'Which is completely understandable.' She was leaning forward, her eyes welling with kindness, making his own prickle. 'You were fifteen. You'd been through so much already…'

Blue lights flashing… Uniforms at the door… His legs failing… Dad's grey face… Mum curling like a leaf, disappearing inside herself…

He swallowed. 'It didn't seem fair.' He could feel the familiar ache spreading, the familiar hot, thick spot swelling in his throat. 'Not when I tried so hard to take care of her after Pete died. I did everything I could to make her happy, to bring her back to herself, but I failed. And then she left, and I *know* I need to put it behind me, but I can't. She wrecked everything and now I can't look at her the same, can't feel any love…'

Quinn's hand slid over his. 'And that hurts you all over

again, doesn't it? Because it's not who you are inside, not the person you *want* to be with her.'

He felt a warm wet swell starting behind his lids. How could she know, articulate so easily what he had never been able to?

He drew in a breath to push it all back, to steady himself. 'Something like that.'

Her hand squeezed his, and then she was taking it back, picking up her glass. 'If you want to move on, you know the only way is to forgive her, don't you?'

Soft gaze. Hopeful light. She made it sound so simple, so doable.

He lifted his own glass, knocking back a mouthful. 'Is that your recommendation?'

Her lips quirked slightly. 'Well, speaking as a motherless child, with obviously zero experience of mothers, I'd say it's worth a shot, worth thinking about at least.'

Telling him she didn't miss what she'd never had, but there was a chink in her gaze saying precisely the opposite—telling him that if she'd been lucky enough to have a mum she would never have let things go stale without a fight.

He felt his heart pinching. Was he an ingrate, too trapped inside his own grudge to see the wider view? Who knew?

He reconnected with her gaze. 'Maybe I'll do that then. Think about it, I mean.'

She smiled. 'You've got nothing to lose, everything to gain.' And then she was setting her glass down, flattening her hands on the table. 'Right... Didn't your esteemed guide-book say that taking in a Fado show was a must?'

CHAPTER SIXTEEN

'OH, LOOK—! VINYL!' Will was stopping, taking in the array
of tightly packed boxes. 'Do you mind if I have a gander? I
love looking at this stuff.'

She felt warmth burling. Every moment something new—
something delightful. Gorgeous Lisbon—gorgeous sunshine!
And Will, beyond gorgeous in his faded jeans and light orange shirt—seemingly a vinyl addict. Best weekend ever!

She smiled. 'Knock yourself out. I'll go on though. There's
a stall up there with some interesting bric-a-brac. Catch me
up?'

'Okay.' But then his hand was coming out, staying her.
'No wandering off, mind.'

Her heart dipped. Referencing last night's little misunderstanding in Alfama. To be fair, the protective gleam in his
eyes was adorable, a little bit dizzying, but still…

'For the umpteenth time, I did *not* wander off last night.'

'You disappeared.'

'Only into the tile place we were standing right next to!'

'You didn't say you were going in.'

'I thought you saw me. Besides, where else would I have
gone?'

His hands went up. 'Who knows? It was dark. There were
crowds. My senses were dulled by the Fado singing and you
do have a talent for vanishing into thin air.'

Setting his lips but his eyes were crinkling, twinkling blue. Impossible not to smile, not to capitulate.

She pressed her hands to her chest. 'Okay, Scout's Honour! I promise not to leave the market.'

He grinned. 'Okay, see you in a bit.' And then he was turning, getting stuck in, hunting for jazz, no doubt, which he apparently loved, Miles Davis especially.

She let her gaze linger on his back for a few tantalising seconds then set off.

Feira da Ladra Market—flea market, or perhaps 'thieves' market, Will's guidebook had tendered both. *Whatever!* Strolling round was the perfect lazy Saturday morning activity, a bit of a rest after yesterday and, concerns about her wandering off aside, Will seemed happy—*relaxed*—which was such a weight off after the Judy conversation last night.

She stopped by a rail of vintage dresses, half looking. She wouldn't have gone anywhere near Topic Judy if she hadn't had two glasses of wine and a golden opportunity. Still, even with licence to talk about Anthony, for some reason actually doing it still felt tricky. Too tricky to risk touching on anything Anthony had put in his letter anyway. But in his letter, Anthony had described Judy's leaving as a 'painful time' and, given that he had never talked much about Judy, and given that she wanted to know Will to his bones, know how he felt about things, she couldn't stop herself from giving him a nudge...

She felt her lungs tightening. And then it had all come out—pain that was more like devastation, trotting out the facts in his man's bitter voice, but the facts didn't make sense to the boy who was still so obviously bleeding inside. And not to her either. After everything they'd been through as a family, couldn't Judy have at least stayed in London until Will finished school? To be around for him, to be a fricking mother! If he couldn't find any love inside for Judy now, then no wonder.

She swiped at the dresses and walked on. But two sides to every story and all that. Forgiveness would be a start if Will could manage it. Not easy. But if he didn't, he would be dragging this stuff around for ever, miserable on some level, just as his father had been, and that was no way to live and, especially, it was no way to die!

She came to the bric-a-brac stall and stopped. There were piles of everything, including a somewhat cool porthole mirror. She leaned over to inspect it. Maybe things wouldn't work out for Will with Judy, but at least he had said he would think about trying to reach out…

'You like, *senhora*?'

It took a second to locate the small, beady-eyed old woman who was smiling at her from across the mountain of lamps and pictures and vases.

'Yes, I do.' She smiled back. 'Can I pick it up?'

'*Sim, senhora…*' The woman's hands lifted. 'Yes, of course.'

Antique gold…deep frame…filling suddenly with Will's smiling face.

'I'm impressed, Quinn—you're right where you said you be!'

She looked into his eyes in the mirror. 'Of course I am! I did promise. Also, you weren't very long so, you know, not enough time to escape your clutches.'

'Clutches!' His face in the mirror chuckled then disappeared as he came round to stand beside her. 'You make me sound like the Dark Lord.'

'I didn't say evil clutches.'

'Good…' His gaze pinned her for a cloudy beat. 'Because I'm only trying to look after you.'

Way to melt her heart and all of her bones.

'I know. And I appreciate it.' She offered up a smile. 'You're very noble…' Not that she could let herself linger on that confusing thought. 'So, did you buy anything?'

He flashed empty palms. 'No. I flirted with buying something from the Fado section but then I remembered that I don't like super cheery music.'

She felt her insides vibrating. Last night's Fado show was lovely, but after four consecutive slow, impassioned ballads, which to their untrained ears had sounded more or less the same, they'd slipped out to explore the Alfama streets.

'It was all quite heartfelt, wasn't it?'

He grinned. 'Just a bit.' And then his eyes flicked to the mirror. 'So, are we buying that, or what?'

'Not today.' She set it down, smiled an apology at the woman, then propelled him on before the woman could start a sales pitch. 'It's given me an idea or two though, so all good. I'll come back when I know what I'm looking for.'

'Fair play.' And then he was looking over. 'So, what's on the agenda now?'

Aside from crushing on him every single second?

She shook herself. 'If your feet are willing and able, I wouldn't mind seeing the pink street…'

His gaze narrowed. 'I remember seeing that…' And then the guidebook was coming out, absorbing his attention. 'Oh, yes… Rua Nova do Carvalho, former red-light district and crime centre, now über-trendy nightspot. Bars, cafés… Located Cais da Sodré.' His eyes snapped up, full of teasing light. 'Super, a mere ten thousand steps away!'

She felt warmth bursting inside, happiness. He was so good-natured. Such perfect company.

She aimed a smile into his eyes. 'Yes, but then after that,

I was thinking we could jump in a tuk-tuk, spend the rest of the day cruising.'

'Yes!' His fist shot up, punching the air. 'I've been waiting for *ever* for you to suggest that!'

Quinn was eyeing him over her glass, patently trying to hold in a smile. 'Are you *dancing*?'

He checked in with his body, felt a chuckle coming. 'I might be...' Because how could he not when the music was this catchy, and the sun was this warm, and the Tagus was yards away, glinting blue? When he was with the kindest, loveliest girl he had ever known. He grooved his shoulders at her for fun. 'What's wrong with a little chair dancing?'

'Nothing...' A smile broke across her face. 'I suppose I just...'

'What?'

She looked shy suddenly. 'I guess I just don't see you as the dancing type.'

'Thanks. No offence taken.'

'Will—' admonishing him with her eyes '—I didn't mean it as a—'

'Black mark on my character?' He took a sip of his beer, letting his smile out slowly. 'Chill. I'm just teasing.'

She gave him the side-eye. 'Not nice!' But then her expression was warming again, brightening with interest. 'So you *do* dance?'

He felt a little sagging sensation inside. 'Well, no, not routinely, so I see your point, but I've had my moments on the dance floor—admittedly, mostly drunken ones when I was a student—but I've been told that I don't totally suck in the rhythm department. What about you? Are you the dancing type?'

'Am I...?' She leaned forward, fixing him with a merry

deadpan stare. 'Will, I like dancing so much I dance with my vacuum cleaner.'

In which case...

His heart pulsed. Did he dare? Would the people around them laugh? He felt a smile coming. Maybe he was crazy, finally losing it, but right now he couldn't care less.

He set his glass down and got to his feet. 'Come on then. Show me.'

Her face stretched. 'You're joking, right?'

'Do I look like I'm joking?'

She let out a giggle. 'Sadly, no.'

'So, let's dance.' He held his hand out. 'Unless I'm to be bested by a Hoover.'

'Oh, God!' Rolling her eyes at him, but in the next breath she was parking her glass and getting up, letting him lead her onto the promenade that separated the tables from the river, and then she was standing, staring at him, laughing. 'You're mad, you know that?'

'Yep...'

And if this was madness, then happy days, because it felt great—great to be moving his hips to the beat, letting himself go, seeing amusement shining in her eyes. And now she was moving too, extending her arms with graceful hands, swaying her sublime body this way and that, laughing into his eyes.

So lovely!

Hair up today, loose tendrils grazing her neck. Green vest with a white one underneath, showing those kissable collarbones and that delicious dusky hollow between her breasts. Turning now, rotating her hips, hips he wanted to feel moving under his hands, hands that wanted to slide over that neat gyrating rear, that rear smoothly encased in blue jeans, jeans cropped mid-calf above her white trainers—simple... elegant. Beautiful.

And off-limits!

He spun away. What was he doing, letting his eyes off the leash? Thoughts, desires. So much for cold showers and keeping it in! Why wasn't his body getting the memo? This was Quinn! They had a job to do together, one they both had to get through to get their respective dues.

Gah! But that was the whole problem right there, wasn't it? That this *was* Quinn! Not the cuckoo, not Dad's pet, but something else now, something wonderful. Every blink, every breath of her a blast. Just being with her...talking to her... God, she'd even got him talking about Mum last night, which he never did, with anyone. Listening so well, giving him something to think about, lifting some weight off his chest just by listening, releasing him, so that now he was walking—*dancing*—on air. Oh, and maybe letting his eyes roam wasn't right, but it was only looking, not touching. Only dancing, a bit of fun...

He danced himself back around and started in surprise. There were other people up and dancing with them, going for it! And then Quinn was coming in close, swaying, beaming.

'See what you started.'

He felt his head shaking, words rising. 'Not me. You!'

She pulled a confused face then moved back, laughing, reaching up into the air with her hands.

All very well looking confused but it was true. He hadn't started this. She had. Because he would never have got up with anyone else. It wouldn't even have crossed his mind to, because he wasn't the dancing type, especially not in broad daylight with only a small beer inside him! Only with Quinn, because—spinning again, weaving her hands through the air, circling her shoulders—he felt weightless around her, on fire, light and bright as a flame. And now she was turning, flashing a smile into his eyes, and he could feel his heart soaring, leaping and flying, flowing right out...

Right... Out...

Oh, hell!

It couldn't be, could it? This feeling... Was he somehow falling in love with Quinn Radley?

'Hey...' She was moving in again. 'Where's your groove gone, mister?'

If only she knew!

And then, mercifully, the catchy track was ending, giving him an out.

'Song's finished.' He shrugged, finding a smile. 'I'm afraid one dance is all I've got.'

Her cheeks dimpled. 'Well, I'm glad I got to see it, then.' And then she was giving his shoulder a little nudge, propelling him back to their table through a ripple of applause from the other tables.

He smiled round to acknowledge the crowd. Did he seem normal to them? Or could they see that he was a man reeling? His heart pulsed. Could Quinn?

'By the way, you're definitely not an embarrassment on the dance floor.' Twinkling up at him as he seated her, making his heart flip but also soothing it somehow, settling it back down.

He took his own seat. 'I hope that's not compared to your Hoover.'

'Oh, no! You're way better than that.' Her eyes flashed a tease. 'You're at least as good as my floor mop.'

'Nice!'

'That's the objective!'

Back to banter. Back to easy flow. Maybe he could just tick along like this. His heart clenched. No choice really. It was way too soon to declare himself, or to even know if these feelings were love feelings or crush feelings. His heart clenched again, tighter. And what about the elephant in the room? He didn't feel any animosity for Quinn now, couldn't imagine feeling it ever again, but that gremlin had swooped in once before, hadn't it, ruining everything. Old sores. Like the one with Mum, hurting on and on. Quinn had said if he didn't forgive his mum he would never heal, so it followed that if he didn't somehow come clean to Quinn about her role in his misery, then it could only come back to bite him…

'We should get back…' Quinn was spearing the last olive, popping it into her mouth. 'Miguel will be wondering where we are.'

Miguel. Their smiley tuk-tuk driver, full of mischief and fascinating factoids.

'You're right. We've been a while…' He signalled for the bill then remembered something. 'Hey, Quinn…'

'What?' Twinkling gold-brown eyes.

He felt a warm spot pulsing in his heart, a smile unfurling. 'Thanks for the dance.'

'Here we are! Miradouro de Santa Luzia!' Miguel pulled the little vehicle in sharply then shuffled round in his seat to face them. 'The best place in Lisbon to see the sunset.' His gaze darted to Will then came back, glinting with mischief. 'Very romantic!'

For heaven's sake! He was at it again. Loaded looks, twinkling eyes. Why? Because she and Will had been leaning into each other a lot? Only so they could hear themselves over the road noise! Or was it because Will had handed her out of the vehicle at Belém Tower with an exaggerated gentlemanly flourish? That was just clowning, Will trying to make her laugh. As for the dancing, Miguel couldn't have seen that unless he'd left the tuk-tuk and walked along the promenade and, in any case, it wasn't close dancing, nothing he could read into. She felt a flush stirring. Unless he was reading its lingering effects, the tingles she couldn't stop feeling because of the way Will had been gazing at her, moving his body in sync with hers. A crazy, hazy, über sexy moment! But it was gone now. A bit of fun, that was all.

She aimed a smile into Miguel's eyes. 'You are a very bad man! We've told you already, we're just friends, colleagues…'

'Yes, yes, yes…' He waved a dismissive hand. 'But still, it's romantic. You must go. Enjoy a *ginja* shot, watch the sunset. I can wait…'

Will leaned forward. 'But you already waited an hour in Belém.'

'It's okay.' Miguel shrugged, oozing charm like honey. 'You can give me a very big tip!' He flashed white teeth. 'A very big tip always helps.'

Will laughed. 'Okay, done! A very big tip it is!' And then he was looking over, his expression slightly baleful but twinkling. 'Shall we go check out this sunset, then?'

'Why not…?' Since Miguel wasn't giving them a choice anyway.

A few respectful yards from the vehicle Will started chuckling. 'Miguel's something else, isn't he?' He smiled over. 'Worth every single euro, though!'

She felt her heart softening. 'Yes…'

Not just Miguel, though. Will was something else too. Every kind of wonderful. Liam would have been walking through this little park chuntering, not chuckling, feeling manipulated by the Brazilian, not seeing what Will had clearly seen: that Miguel was poor, needed all the tips he could get.

If only Miguel knew that he needn't have given Will that wily little push because Will was generous, would have tipped him handsomely anyway. All the time, rewarding good service, being subtle about it. Like at that tapas place. Slipping two blue notes under his glass as they got up to leave—more than the bill itself had come to. And yes, he could afford to be generous, but not everyone with money was, unless they were angling for something for themselves. Liam. Roses. Case in point!

She pushed the thought away, focusing ahead. They were stepping onto a wide pillared terrace now, lush with clambering vines, teeming with tourists. A woman was selling *ginja* sour cherry liqueur shots from a stall at the side and a busker was perched on the parapet playing soulful guitar, but it was the view opening up through the crowds that stopped her breath. Lisbon and the Tagus, the sun behind painting everything gold.

'Wow!' She looked up at Will. 'Miguel was right. This is incredible!'

'It is.' He smiled, making her breath stop again, but then suddenly his gaze was going past her, lengthening. 'Hang on. There's a better spot…' His eyes snapped back, full of mischief. 'Ready to run?'

Her heart pulsed. 'What?'

But his hand was already grabbing hers, tugging her through the crowds, until they were at the very end of the terrace where the parapet butted up to a high sheltering wall. A quiet spot, almost secluded.

He released her, panting a bit. 'Sorry for the mad dash, but it's a prime spot.' He motioned to the parapet. 'You can sit and chill with the view while I go back for some *ginja*.'

She felt her heart squeezing. All this for her!

She smiled. 'It's perfect, but please don't worry about the *ginja*…'

'What? And disappoint Miguel. No way! You know he's probably got a commission thing going on with the *ginja* woman, right?' And then his eyes were crinkling. 'Besides, don't you want to taste it? It's like a thing here. We should give it a go...'

So adorable. And so very sexy with his hair blowing in the breeze, sun gold turning his blue eyes green. Her stomach pulsed. All the things she shouldn't be noticing!

She shook herself, smiled. 'Okay, you've convinced me. We can be Ginja Ninjas.'

His chin dipped. 'Seriously?' And then he was chuckling, shaking his head. 'So lame!'

'This is lovely.' Quinn was sipping, tasting her own lips. 'Sweet!' And then she was looking up, a little glow in her gaze. 'Almost as sweet as you with Miguel.'

'Sweet?' He forced his eyes not to revisit the lips she'd just tasted. 'I've never been called sweet before.'

'Well, you are.' She wrinkled her nose. 'My ex would have whinged about being leveraged into giving a big tip.'

He felt his stomach tightening. The thought of Quinn with anyone else, especially a tightwad, was a total gear-grind.

'Sounds like a right jerk.'

'Oh, he was.'

At least she wasn't holding onto any candles!

He took a sip from his cup. 'Miguel's shirt is patched in three places, and his trainers are coming apart. He isn't well-off. Also, he's been great—pleasant, knowledgeable. He deserves a good tip.'

'Which you'd have given him anyway, without him having to ask.' Her gaze softened. 'You're so tuned in, Will. Sensitive, just like your dad said...'

His heart caught. 'What...?'

Because Dad had never said anything like that to him, given him any indication he had ever noticed anything on the fricking inside of him at all! Just the bad stuff. Faults and failings. Blackjack, whisky, women. He would never shut up about those.

She gave a little shrug. 'He just said it…'

But then she was blinking, her cheeks colouring as though she was wishing she hadn't mentioned it.

His fault. Because he was suddenly tight as a drum. Spine, shoulders, jaw. Reacting in spite of what he felt for her, in spite of himself, in spite of asking her not to skirt around the subject of Dad.

What he had meant was that she shouldn't skirt around her affection for Dad, around the hotel and the plans they'd made. But *this*…this was a curveball, a real stinger. Why had Dad never dipped below the waterline with him, taken *him* aside to say stuff like this? Why tell Quinn? And now, what? Was she waiting for him to pick up the baton, chat on merrily as if his gut wasn't wringing itself tight? Was she expecting him to light up with interest, ask her what else his own father had divulged?

His heart pulsed. *Not fair, Will!* Strain, showing on her face, in her eyes, because she was caught in the middle again—caught there because he had asked her to be open, asked her not to tiptoe around him and Dad, caught there because she was doing exactly that!

He needed to level out, say something.

He set his cup down to buy a moment then met her gaze. 'I'm sorry for freezing like that. I…' He could feel his heart pinching, his throat drying. 'I'm just surprised. I didn't know Dad thought that about me…'

The planes of her face softened. 'Oh, Will, he did…' And then her eyes were welling, glistening into his. 'He just wasn't very good at expressing it.'

'Except to you, apparently!'

Her eyes closed and regret crashed in. Why had he said it like that, in a whiplash tone? He felt his insides twisting. How to walk this impossible line? Half of his heart lost to her, the other half bitter. And now the two halves were tearing him apart because he'd been cruel when none of this was her fault.

'I'm sorry, Quinn...' He seized her shoulders so that she would feel his regret, all the desperation inside. 'Please... Please look at me... I didn't mean it...'

'You did...' She screwed her face up tightly, swallowing, and then her eyes opened, blinking into his. 'But I don't blame you, Will...'

He felt his throat constricting. Why not? Did she get him, understand somehow, in spite of everything? And if so, could she see how much it meant, see how the warmth she was giving out was turning him inside out, making him want to...?

'Oh, Quinn...'

And then somehow her face was in his hands and he was moving in, brushing her lips with his, taking her mouth. Soft... Warm... Cherry sweet... His pulse spiked...*responsive!* Rising towards him now, sliding her arms around his neck, kissing him back, tasting him back. He could feel his blood heating, beating hard, pent-up desire dragging at him, taking him over. He wanted more...to give more, so she would feel his love, feel it from the very heart of him— deeper. Warmer. He teased her lips apart with his tongue, felt the brief incendiary touch of hers, but then, all of a sudden, she was pulling away, pushing at his chest.

'Stop, Will. Please.'

He jerked his hands away, heart pounding. 'What?'

'We mustn't.' Closing her eyes, swallowing, shaking her head as if it was a battle to get the words out. 'I want to, so much. But I can't...'

He felt a protest rising, collapsing. Telling him what he

already knew, what he'd told himself over and over again. They had a job to do, one that would go easier if they kept their relationship on the straight and narrow.

'You're right. I'm sorry.' He inhaled to steady himself. 'We're working together. Mixing it up is probably a bad idea.'

'Yes...'

He felt a spike of adrenaline. That 'yes' lacked conviction, as if it was only half an answer. And there was something flickering through her gaze that felt like a hammer blow coming. He could feel himself tensing, bracing in anticipation.

'It isn't only that, though...' She pressed her lips together tightly. 'It's that I don't want to lose you.'

He felt his heart pausing, the tightness inside relenting. 'But you wouldn't...' Because wasn't getting together the exact opposite of losing each other?

'No, I *would*...' And then her gaze was turning inwards, full of anguish and latent fury. 'I'm single for a reason, Will! I'm no good at relationships. No one ever stays with me.' Her hand caught his, squeezing hard. 'And I couldn't bear it if that happened with you.' And then, maybe because the confusion he was feeling was showing on his face, her voice tipped over into impatience. 'Don't you see? I've got too much to lose... You're the last and only link to a huge part of my life!'

The words seemed to hang in the air, echoing, reverberating inside his skull. So this was the punchline? The lethal blow. That he was nothing but a link to Dad?

He felt his blood draining, a hot swell rising behind his eyes. Falling for her, getting tangled up in the thought of her... All this time thinking about not crossing over work lines, but somehow stowing a secret hope in some secret recess of his heart that once the work was done...

Idiot, Will!

Hung up on 'some day' when what she was offering was

never—because of Dad! Because of this precious link—to what, exactly? Because Dad was gone, and he was…

His stomach turned. What was he? Other than sick. Heart. Belly. Soul. He couldn't think, speak, vent, couldn't even let it show; because Quinn had a right to her feelings, same as he did, even if they were incomprehensible. And he couldn't freeze on her because of the hotel. Nothing to do then but suck it up, stay behind the line she was drawing.

He swallowed hard. 'Fair enough.' He squeezed her hand gently to seem onside, then put it away from him, forcing out a smile. 'No hard feelings, right?'

For a long second her eyes searched his, as if she wanted more, expected more, but what more could he say—*give*—when simply holding himself upright was taking every ounce of strength he had? And then, finally, she blinked.

'Of course not.' She smiled a smile that looked like his own felt, and then she turned back to the view. 'Look, the sun's gone down.'

His heart flinched.

And didn't that just sum it up!

CHAPTER SEVENTEEN

SADIE INHALED AUDIBLY. 'What happened after that?'

She felt her heart crimping. What had happened was trudging back to the tuk-tuk feeling depleted, faking jollity all the way back to the hotel for Miguel's sake, then bursting into tears in her room because all she'd been trying to do was share a fragment of Anthony with Will, to make him happy. But it had backfired, made him hostile instead—which she totally got because Anthony should have told Will all that stuff himself. Then somehow her understanding had backfired as well, making Will's gaze go all soft and intense...

And then the kiss had happened, and it had felt so right, like heaven, until confusion took hold, shook her up. And even though she was the one who'd pulled away, and even though Will had smiled and said 'No hard feelings', and even though he'd brought her all the way home from the airport, joking about being nice to the last because of their pact—which surely demonstrated that everything was all right between them—she wasn't feeling all right at all, which was why she was on the phone to Sadie at midnight, keeping the older woman from her shelter duties.

She swallowed down a sip of tea. 'We went back to the hotel, muddled through dinner. And this morning we had to be at the airport for ten so... Probably a good thing.' Her heart pinched. 'He insisted on bringing me home from the airport though, which was nice.'

'*Very*, given that he lives on the opposite side of London.' Little pause. 'So, now you're in turmoil...'

Her heart pinched again. 'What do you think? I just don't know if I did the right thing, putting the brakes on. My head says yes, but I don't know...' Because for a moment, after she'd explained herself to him, Will had looked broken, and it was messing her up, messing with her heart. Seven hours back—seven hours churning away over it, seven hours reliving that kiss: the tenderness of it, the warm, perfect fit of his mouth, the hot, dragging ache of desire that was still dragging. She swallowed hard. 'I just can't seem to think straight.'

'Well, let's start with those brakes.' There was a small pause while Sadie sipped her own tea. 'Why *did* you put them on?'

'Because it would only end in disaster.'

'Why?'

Her chest went tight. 'You know why!'

Sadie sighed. 'I'm taking you through a process, Quinn. Please answer...'

She closed her eyes. 'It would end in disaster because all my relationships do.' She felt a flick of weariness. 'You know that, Sadie. I'm not a safe bet. And this is Will! I'm supposed to be helping him find himself. If things went bad between us then, for a start, that plan's a bust. I'd be failing Anthony, denying him his dying wish. And I'd be losing everything that's been dear to me for the past decade. I'd be emotionally homeless.'

'So, the head has spoken. What's the heart saying?'

'I don't know, hence the phone call.'

'Okay, well, perhaps we need to slide some doors.'

She felt a smile coming. Sadie was invoking her favourite movie.

'Door one: you keep the brakes locked on and you and Will stay friends. Maybe you become best friends! Hanging out. Brunch on Sundays! Sometimes you go double dating. The Thacker connection is strong with you...'

Invoking Yoda now!

'But then the day comes, which it will, because I've seen his picture in Tatler and he's gorgeous, not to mention seriously loaded, which shouldn't factor but, you know...' little breath '...the day comes when Will gets married. He asks you to be his best woman. Nine months later, he asks you to be godmother to his firstborn. Your Thacker connection is sealed, eternally assured.' Sadie's voice filled with a knowing twinkle. 'How does that sound?'

'Unappealing.' She parked her mug on the bedside table. 'Can we do the other door?'

'We don't have to. You're already rattling the handle.'

True.

She plucked at the duvet. 'Maybe I am, but should I be? I need advice, Sadie. I don't know what to do, or how to feel. Please, tell me what you think.'

'Oh, Lordy...' Sadie drew in a weighty breath. 'Are you sure you want to hear?'

'Yes.' Because Sadie was older, wiser, the closest thing she had to a mother. Plus, Sadie was generally right about everything.

'Okay, well, for a start, I think you're head over heels in love with him.'

Her heart paused. *Impossible!* Because Will was practically a stranger. Yes, she liked him. A lot. Cared about him a lot. And yes, he was under her skin, but only because he was a bit damaged, and that kind of thing always tugged at her heartstrings.

As for those other tugs and tingles she was always feeling around him—the ones that happened when his eyes crinkled or his nice shoulders shifted—par for the course, surely, because, as Sadie said, Will was gorgeous. And yes, his kiss had put the hex on her, got her craving and pining, which symptoms maybe did bear some resemblance to a love type of yearning, but equally, it could just be a physical thing— infatuation! Just a stupid crush playing her for a fool, trying to turn her against the door one scenario, which was clearly the most sensible and enduring one.

She adjusted her grip on the phone. 'I think you're wrong.'

'Well, let's pretend I'm not. Let's pretend that you and Will love each other, so we can deal with your biggest fear: that if it doesn't work out, you lose your connection to the Thacker family.'

'All right…'

'Question: what would you actually be losing? I mean, to be blunt, Anthony's gone. You'll always have your memories, *that* connection, but you never met Judy, and you never had much to do with Will in the past, so if things were to end, then, aside from losing a straggle of random outliers, what is there, really, to cling to, except an idea? And I know how important the idea of family is to you, I know you were devoted to Anthony, and I get why you've taken his dying wishes to heart, but what I think—straight up—is that you're letting your loyalties get in the way, and pointlessly.

'Anthony did a good thing by you, Quinn, but by his own admission he made plenty of mistakes in his life. It seems crazy to me that you'd deny yourself a chance at love with Will for his sake, especially when Will clearly has feelings for you too.'

'Oh, God, Sadie...'

Way to mess her up even more, dangling possibilities from Will's side—possibilities that, thinking about it... She felt her heart giving.

The way he'd turned round at the airport and come back, guidebook in hand. The way he'd pulled her over to the railing at Miradouro de São Pedro to reassure her he was all for avant-garde—not just for it but coming up with ideas of his own! Clowning all the time to make her laugh. Confiding in her about Judy. Oh, and dancing by the Tagus! Looking out for her all the time, taking care of her. Keeping tabs. Always capitulating...apologising...trying. Bringing her home from the airport for the sake of their stupid pact, bent on showing her his nicest side. She felt her throat constricting, tears welling. As if he even had any other side!

'And as for this business of helping him find his so-called light, you seem to think it must be something he plucks out of himself, that it shouldn't have anything to do with you, but what if it does?'

Her heart stumbled. 'What?'

'I'm saying, what if Anthony meant *you* to be Will's light?'

Her heart stopped dead. 'Don't be daft—Anthony wasn't matchmaking! He didn't think like that. He was categorically the most unromantic man I've ever known.'

'Well, tying you both into a prolonged hotel renovation sounds like a pretty foxy move to me.'

'But he...'

Sadie wasn't right. Couldn't be. Could she? What did it matter anyway? Anthony was gone, so there was no asking him. No making sense of anything.

'I can hear your cogs whirring, Quinn.' Sadie sighed. 'Maybe the best advice I can actually give you is to stop thinking so hard.'

'After just giving me a whole lot more to think about!'

'It's only conjecture. What isn't is that Will saw you to your door, which shows he's trying to right the ship.' She paused. 'You can come back from this. The project's a long one. You've got time to work things out, get to know each other better. Who knows, maybe you did the right thing, calling a halt this time.'

'What do you mean, *this time*?'

'Just that I think there'll be a next time...' And then there was an extended pause, a sense of distraction. 'Listen, love, I've got to go. Fred's signalling through the door. Looks like trouble in the dorm.'

'Okay, go!'

But Sadie was already gone.

She parked her phone and sank back into the pillows. How not to think about Will and everything that went with him? How not to miss him...want him? Still, as Sadie said, they had time, and maybe that was exactly what she needed. Time to straighten out her head, and find out what was really going on in her heart.

CHAPTER EIGHTEEN

MARION'S HEAD BOBBED round the door. 'I'm off now.' Her eyes made a quick assessing sweep of his face. 'There's a plate in the fridge for you.'

As if he could eat anything while his brain was burning like this. But if he didn't show her some enthusiasm she would only worry. Bizarre that the housekeeper seemed to care more about him than his own mother did.

He smiled into her eyes. 'Thanks, I'll get it later.'

'Make sure you do.' Her lips flattened. 'You look tired.'

'I am…' Tired, wrung out, confused, sad. Could she see it? No matter. He wasn't up for talking about it. He smiled again. 'Have a good evening, Marion.'

'You too, Will.'

Footsteps echoing, fading. Door banging. Silence.

He got up to refill his glass then slumped back down on the sofa. Could it really be that all he was to Quinn was a link in a chain she didn't want to break? If so, wouldn't he have felt it, seen it for what it was? Or was his lens so twisted by love that he'd put a rosy spin on that light in her eyes, seeing it as warmer, fonder, deeper than it really was?

He drank, felt the whisky burning. No. Yesterday, it had definitely felt like it, but now he wasn't so sure. Maybe his lens was rose-tinted, but the way she'd leapt up to hug him when he found her in that café was real. Pure joy. All weekend long, that same feeling: connection, affection. Back and forth. He wasn't imagining it. And he wasn't imagining the way she'd kissed him back either, all warm, sliding her arms around his neck. Pulling away but in the same breath saying she wanted to—'so much'—but couldn't because all her relationships went bad, that she couldn't bear it if it happened with him, couldn't bear to lose him. Then the sucker punch. That stupid, precious, incomprehensible link!

His heart paused. Then again, was it really so incomprehensible?

He sat forward, swirling his drink. She was an orphan. All out of links, all out of family—except for his. And maybe his family didn't amount to much now, but still, if it was all she had… He felt his heartbeat picking up. Would she not cling to it like a raft, even at a subconscious level, perhaps find the fear of losing it surfacing involuntarily at the wrong moment, say, in the middle of a kiss, find it asserting itself as suddenly as his own scars were prone to doing, rupturing in an instant, putting whiplash words into his mouth at precisely the wrong fricking time! It was absolutely possible. So slow on the uptake, Will! The writing was blazoned on the wall. Quinn volunteered at a homeless shelter, for pity's sake, giving her time and attention to those enduring the thing she most feared—dreaded—being without: loved ones. Ties. Roots. Place!

He felt his heart twisting. All things he could give her, wanted to give her from the depths of his soul. He set his glass down. But he'd jumped the gun because of his own messed-up history, because of his own messed-up head, because she seemed to get him, understand him, and he was so desperate to be understood by her. Accepted. Loved. But desperation was a poor hand, one he wasn't playing again.

He got up and went to the window. Twilight now…bats

flitting. He felt his pulse settling, the mist clearing. Lucky for him he'd taken her home, leaning on the pact they'd made, because it had seemed like a good way to bounce them back from that kiss, show her that from his point of view they were good. And yes, maybe there was a part of him that had been hoping she might open up the conversation, which she hadn't, but they'd parted on smiling terms, which meant he had a head start now. He would call her tomorrow, fix up a lunch, show her she wasn't lost to him, that he wasn't about to break any links.

And maybe he was crazy for letting that hopeful voice inside start whispering *some day* again, but he didn't want to switch it off, didn't want to kill off his hope yet. Not when time was on his side, when he could use it to show her that he was steadfast, dependable. That he could be a sound business partner and, most of all, a good friend. Maybe then she'd come to see him as a win-win prospect!

CHAPTER NINETEEN

THE CAB PULLED up and Will smiled, mischief glinting in his eyes. 'Here we are!'

She looked out and started. 'Lisbon!' She felt her jaw trying to fall against a rising smile. 'I had no idea there was a restaurant called Lisbon in London!'

'There isn't.' Will handed the driver a twenty with instructions to keep the change and then his eyes came back, twinkling. 'I paid a guy to repaint the sign. It's really called The Lucky Star Takeaway.'

Her smile won out. How she'd missed this—*him!*—even though it had only been four days since she'd last seen him.

He sprang the door. 'Come on. Sadly, I'm on the clock.'

On the clock but making time for her all the same, calling her the day after they'd got back. Business lunch, Thursday! What it felt like though, was that he was trying to smooth things out, get them past that kiss. But smooth was good, exactly what she needed. Or maybe it was just the sweet, sweet sight of him she needed.

Whatever! Right now, she was floating on air.

Inside, the host led them through a sea of white damask and glittering crystal to a table by the window. A prime spot—of course. *For her.* Her heart pulsed. It was all for her. This beautiful restaurant, this table overlooking the Thames...

She swallowed hard and turned to meet his gaze. 'This is amazing, Will. Thank you. Such a view!'

His eyes crinkled. 'I'm glad you approve. I figure if we're talking business, we might as well do it in style, right?'

In style, in a blur. It felt like the same thing. A fantastic dream. And then somehow their plates were being cleared and their glasses were being replenished, and the rest was falling away so it was only Will again, smiling over, drop-dead gorgeous in his business suit.

'I'm curious...' He inclined his head. 'What got you volunteering at the homeless shelter?'

Drop-dead gorgeous and working so hard. All through lunch talking earnestly about the project, and now he was switching tracks to keep them running along smoothly. The problem was that his efforts seemed to be having the opposite effect, drawing deep, velvety warmth up through her, fresh longings. She couldn't seem to stop her eyes from drifting to his mouth, and to that patch of golden skin at the base of his throat where his collar was open. And she couldn't stop remembering the way his lips had felt, what that brief, sweet scorch of his tongue had done to her body, her core—

'Quinn...?'

Eyes. Face. So dear. So beautiful. So utterly—OMG! Her heart pulsed. It was true! Everything Sadie said. She could feel it surging inside, rampaging through her veins. How could Sadie have seen it and she not? She was absolutely mad for him, past saving. Head over heels in love.

Her heart thumped. But she couldn't say it, go anywhere near it. Not after shutting him down like that in Lisbon, not when loving him didn't guarantee a happy ending—not when she needed to process and couldn't, because he was taking up all of her bandwidth. Nothing for it but to dig deep and push through, as if climbing over the table to kiss his face off was the last thing on her mind.

She forced herself to swallow. 'Sorry. I was just thinking about my friend Sadie...' Not a lie, and a neat segue! 'I got involved through her...' She felt a ripple of calming warmth at the thought of the older woman. 'She's my friend now, but back in the day she was one of my design tutors. She set us a brief to design an interior space for a homeless shelter which was compliant, functional, nurturing. I liked that she speci-fied "nurturing". It felt generous of spirit.'

He smiled a tingle-inducing smile. 'I like it too.'

'Anyway...' She blinked to reset. 'Turned out Sadie was a volunteer. I don't know why but the idea spoke to me so I asked if I could go along.' She felt a flick of incredulity. 'That was ten years ago. Sadie's full-time now, and I'm still there...'

He let out a short, astonished breath. 'Wow! And what do you actually do?'

'Street patrol, mostly. Checking in with the rough sleep-ers, seeing that they're okay.'

'Okay being a relative term?'

'Sadly, yes. We try to get them to come in, especially the women and girls, but a lot of them don't like the shelter. Some of our service users have mental health problems, addictions. They can be disruptive, aggressive sometimes.'

His eyes flared. 'So, it's dangerous?'

'Potentially, but the permanent staff are trained to deal with it. Volunteers are trained too but generally we don't encounter problems—verbal abuse sometimes, but most of the rough sleepers don't mind us. Some of them like to talk.' She felt an ache in her chest. 'They get lonely, feel invisible.'

'You are officially blowing my mind.'

Admiration in his gaze, tugging at her strings, making her blush.

She reached for her glass to deflect. 'Do you do anything outside work?'

His expression fell. 'Nothing useful or remotely noble.' He touched a finger to the base of his glass as if he was toying with a thought, and then his eyes flicked up. 'Until quite recently, I was a regular at Aspinalls.'

Her heart pulsed. And now, what? He wasn't a regular any more? *What to say?* She sipped to buy a second. Maybe he just wanted to talk about it.

She set her glass down. 'Anthony did mention the casino.'

His lips flattened. 'Oh, I'm sure he did! The old goat didn't exactly approve.'

She felt a stir of recognition, took care to make her tone gentle. 'Was that the attraction?'

His ocean-blue gaze stilled. 'Very perceptive!' And then he was picking up his glass, tilting it this way and that. 'Lest you think I'm bitter and twisted, it wasn't all spite.'

She felt her heart twisting. So hard to see him hurting like this, ridiculing himself, because that was what was going on behind the bravado—pain, hurt, bitterness. If only she could tell him how much Anthony had loved him, how deeply he regretted his mistakes, but last time it had backfired, and she couldn't risk it again. Not here. Not now. Better going with the tide.

'So you *like* gambling?'

'Not exactly…' He took a hefty sip and then, unexpectedly, he broke into a smile. 'I liked counting cards.'

Her ribs went tight. 'But isn't that—'

'No, it isn't illegal.' He shrugged. 'It's just arithmetic. Exercise for the brain.'

'There are other ways.'

'So I've discovered.' His gaze fell for a beat then lifted, attached to a wry smile. 'I mean, what's bigger and more exciting than gambling on a bespoke boutique hotel in the heart of Lisbon, right?'

'You're getting a gambling thrill out of it?'

'No!' His features drew in. 'I was joking, Quinn.' And then he was shaking his head, his gaze softening. 'But if the thought of me gambling bothers you then I won't do it ever again.' His chin dipped a little. 'Is that what you'd like: for me to promise?'

Depths in his eyes...depths within depths.

She felt her stomach tingling. So Sadie was right about this too. He did have feelings for her, strong enough to change his ways, do for her what he wouldn't do for his father.

Her heart pulsed. So, there were feelings running both ways then, but she couldn't act on hers, not after Lisbon, and, for the same reason, he was unlikely to either—aside from giving her lunch at the best table in the house and a heartfelt promise to quit gambling, neither of which she could think about right now when he was looking at her like this, waiting for her to reply.

She nodded, pressing her gaze into his, loading it with all the love inside. 'I would, Will. Very much.'

'Okay, I promise—Scout's Honour—no more gambling.' He smiled. 'From now on, I'll apply my brain only to work and to our hotel!'

And then he was talking about dessert, something about a 'deconstructed' Portuguese custard tart, but it was fading in and out because all she could hear playing over and over were the two words that she'd never heard him say in the same breath before.

Our. Hotel.

CHAPTER TWENTY

HE DROPPED HIS holdall and pulled out his phone. It had
pinged as he was riding up in the lift and it could only be
Quinn, replying to the text he'd sent from the taxi.

He tapped the screen, felt a smile breaking loose. Quinn
indeed!

Sorry Budapest negotiations are dragging. *sad face emoji*
To cheer you up, master suite WILL be finished tonight if it
kills me and it is going to be FAB-U-LOUS! So sad...aka furious...that you're in meetings all evening and can't video
call. Even sadder that you're not here to share the moment
because it feels like a milestone and Filipe is no fun at all.
I'm in his bad books because the bathroom fittings I ordered from Paris have been delayed again which means
the plumbers can't get on and now this is 'holding up the
whole project'!!! Anyway, hope your meetings go well tonight and that Team Thacker prevails. I'll send pictures of
the finished suite! See you in London next week. Q x

He slipped his phone back and went to the window, staring out over Rossio Square. If only she knew he wasn't in
Budapest! He felt his smile fading, his stomach tightening.
Coming here to surprise her like this was tantamount to pinning his heart on his sleeve, wasn't it? Putting himself on

the podium, finally. Then again, hadn't he been on this trajectory ever since that 'Lisbon' lunch three months ago? A supposed business lunch that had ended up with him promising to give up gambling for her.

Transparent, much!

As was going out on street patrol with her and Sadie that night in London, love, and admiration, leaking out of him the whole time. As for taking her along the coast to Cascais last month for her birthday, obvious surely, unless her other friends also took her for champagne lunches on yachts!

He felt warmth unfurling. Her face that day—all smiles on deck. Hair bound up with a colourful scarf, blowing in the breeze, her long brown legs killing him in white shorts, her eyes aglow with fifty shades of mischief.

'You're spoiling me, Will! Not that I don't totally deserve it because I'm the one who's here, putting up with Filipe!'

Later, they'd found a park to walk through, trees and cacti cohabiting in a magical dappled woodland, and after that, back in the charming little town, they'd happened upon a gallery, and that abstract in oils of the 25 de Abril Bridge that she just 'had to have' for the master suite because it was 'perfect'!

His heart pulsed. Perfect, like every moment was with her. Catch-ups and debriefs in London, but also Sunday brunch as friends. Portobello Market, galleries and jazz clubs—because education cut both ways! Always fun, always easy. And maybe that was because they didn't feed the demon by talking about Dad, or maybe it was because Quinn had a warm, wonderful way with her but, whatever it was, he was feeling good on it. Drinking less, taking care of himself. He was even looking into the issues around homelessness—not that he'd mentioned it to Quinn yet—talking to the board about Thacker Hotels doing something significant in that regard.

And here, the hotel was coming on apace, which was down

to Quinn and the team, but he was keeping his finger on the pulse too, extending himself, even discovering a bit of chutzpah he never knew he had! He felt a smile coming. That was what Quinn had called it anyway, when he'd persuaded Michelin-starred chef Xavier Rankine to leave the Aurelia in Paris to take control of their restaurant. Opening was six months away still, but Rankine was going to put them on the map. As was Quinn's luxurious avant-garde décor...

He felt his heart softening. Giving her all, spending days at a time here to get things done. Did she really think he wouldn't have crawled through broken glass to be here to celebrate her completing their flagship master suite? Wild horses couldn't have kept him away. Because she was everything now, and he wanted her to know it, feel it, and maybe he was misjudging, misreading her signs, but at the same time it didn't seem possible because every time they were together he could feel the air crackling two ways.

He crossed the room to the mini-fridge. The bottle of fizz was there, just as he'd asked. And two flutes. Damask napkins to wrap them in.

Champagne, then dinner at her favourite place. After that, who knew? He flicked a glance at his watch. But first, a run to calm his nerves. Then it would be time to give his favourite interior designer the surprise of her life!

The plastic sheeting round the door rustled frenetically then disgorged Filipe.

'Hey, Quinn!' His eyes darted to the painting she was unwrapping—the striking abstract that she and Will had found in Cascais. 'It's seven. Everyone else has left. Are you coming?'

In other words skedaddle, which was *not* happening!

She smiled to placate him. 'No, not yet.' She scanned the

rich blue wall—blue for the Tagus—fixing on the blank space where the painting was to go. 'I'm on a roll, Filipe, so close to finishing…' And it wasn't as if she had anything better to do since the one person—*the only person*—she would have walked off the job for wasn't here. She turned back to him. 'You don't have to wait. I've got my keys. I know the alarm codes.'

He peeled off his safety helmet. 'You shouldn't be here alone.'

She forced her eyes not to roll. He meant well but he was such a stickler!

'I know, but I'll be fine, honestly. I mean, the hallways are clear. I'm not going to trip over any ladders, fall through any—'

Her heart clutched then fluttered, spraying tingles. Oh, the way Will had caught her that day, crushing her against him— so quick, so strong. Nothing to how he was now though! Honed from every sublime angle, skewing her senses every time they were together. It was getting harder and harder not to say something, not to throw herself at him, especially when he was close, when she could feel sparks crackling between them, hear the rhythm of his breathing actually changing around her. When he was so damn attentive and indulgent! Champagne lunch on that yacht for her birthday, then dis-covering Cascais: that beautiful, lush little park, that amaz-ing gallery. And coming on street patrol with her in London, winning Sadie right over, and herself even more. Signs all the time. Tingles all the time.

But nothing was moving forward. He didn't talk about Anthony, or Pete, so she didn't feel that she could either, even though she wanted to. Stuck for weeks, revolving in the same old doors, and it wasn't enough, God help her. She wanted more: to know more, give more, feel more, emotionally...physically. She wanted to love him, drown in his heat, feel his body on her, inside her, everywhere. God, just the thought of it was misting her up, stealing her...

Brakes! Now!

She blinked, reconnecting with Filipe's frowning gaze. 'Look, if I finish tonight then I can get back to London a day sooner. I've got clients backing up that I really need to deal with...' Was he caving? Maybe a tease would clinch it. She angled her head, smiling into his eyes. 'Plus side: you get to *not* have me around tomorrow, messing up your schedules.'

His frown softened. 'Fine! But please text me when you leave so I don't spend the night worrying about you.'

She felt her heart softening. He could be such a grump, but he was kind to the marrow.

'I promise.'

'Okay.' He nodded a smile then turned, fighting his way back through the plastic. 'Goodnight, Quinn.'

''Night, Filipe.'

She listened to his boots crunching down the hall then pulled out her phone. Nothing more from Will. Her heart pinched. Stuck in Budapest when he should have been here, sharing this!

She tapped, setting her Miles Davis playlist going—Will's favourite, growing on her too. She parked her phone, surveying the room to 'Moon Dreams', felt her mood lifting. This was nice work at least!

Finishing touches!

She felt a tingle, a smile coming. Maybe she could send Will a little video of the finished rooms, do her grandiose TV presenter impression to make him laugh. He'd like that.

She picked up her scissors, bending to the package again, but then her heart lurched. Footsteps—coming along the hallway. A heavy, purposeful stride. Filipe? *Of course.* She felt her breath flowing out on a wave of relief. He must have forgotten something.

She straightened. 'Filipe? Is that you?'

'No, it's me!'

Her heart stopped, then vaulted. 'Will!'

And then the plastic was rustling, parting, and he was appearing. He set a bag down on the floor, casual as anything, and then he was looking up, smiling. 'Hello!'

She couldn't move, couldn't breathe. He looked so gorgeous—tanned, scrubbed...better than heaven. And she was in her oldest paint-spattered jeans and vest, wearing *eau de fresh paint* if she was lucky!

His eyes flicked to the scissors in her hand. 'Are you going to put those down or are we reenacting *The Shining*?'

She felt the dam breaking, joy bursting. 'What the hell, Will?' And then, before she could think a single thought, the scissors were falling and she was launching herself at him, flinging her arms around his neck. 'You came!'

'Did you really think I wouldn't?' He was laughing into her ear, hugging her back, all warm and tight. 'Like you said, milestone moment...'

She closed her eyes, breathing him in. It was so good to see him. But what was she supposed to do with all this leaping joy, all this love inside? How did she get from here to where she wanted to be?

She swallowed hard. 'So it was all a ruse—late-night meetings?'

'Yep! That was last. We got it all signed off this morning.'

'So you thought you'd have a little fun?' She felt her lips curving. 'I hate you!'

He chuckled softly, his breath warming her ear. 'Yeah, I'm kind of getting that.'

But he wasn't pulling away, wasn't disengaging, not even

slightly. If anything, he was enfolding her more, pulling her closer. She could feel his muscled torso through his shirt, her body responding, her nipples hardening. Could he feel her—feel her heart beating, the bubble of happiness bursting, spreading inside her? Because something was changing, altering the air, the mood, the temperature. Definitely the temperature!

She felt a sudden, crushing desire to cry. Because the point was past now, wasn't it, for stepping back as if there was nothing between them? It was long gone. Without a word. No more pretending. No more holding back. Too late now to step back into the spin of those doors. This was a sliding door moment, and she was sliding, for better or for worse. She could feel her hand moving to the back of his neck, her fingertips touching the hair they'd been itching to touch for months.

'Oh, Quinn...'

His voice was low, urgent, wringing tears out of her, putting a crack in her own.

'Don't ask me to stop, Will, please...' Because touching him was all she wanted to do. Skin. Hair—glorious hair... soft, thick, slipping between her fingers just so.

'I'm not asking you to stop...' He was breathing into her hair, nuzzling, his lips grazing her temple. 'But I need to know...' And then he was pulling back, taking her face into his hands, stroking her cheekbones with his thumbs. 'Are you sure?' His eyes were reaching in, drinking her in, as if he couldn't get enough. 'Because I can't go down this road with you if you're not sure...' His expression tightened. 'It would kill me, Quinn.'

She felt her heart giving, her whole body tightening and tingling to his touch as if she were an instrument he was playing. 'I'm sure, Will. Please...' She closed her hand around a fistful of hair, pulling him towards her a little. He resisted for a beat, the ghost of a smile on his face, and then he was coming for her, his lips taking hers, bold, confident. Such a perfect mouth! Such a perfect fit...so warm. She felt the scorching tease of his tongue and parted her lips, letting him in. She could feel her heart exploding, or maybe it was her pulse. She was liquid, melting, wet between her legs already. Could he feel it through her jeans because his hand was there now, as if he knew she needed just that.

'Oh, Will...' It was involuntary, from the depths of her. She felt her hands going for his shirt buttons, tearing at them until she was touching smooth, hot skin.

'Quinn...' His lips were on her neck now, his hands roaming, torturing her nipples, sliding down, cupping her butt, drawing her in hard against him. 'Have you any idea how much I want you?'

She felt her breath coming in short bursts, a smile breaking. 'I can feel it.' Rigid along his considerable length, a length she couldn't wait to unwrap. She went for his zip, just as he gripped the hem of her vest.

'You first.' His eyes were hazy, hooded. She did the honours, button, zip, then raised her arms so he could peel off her vest.

For a long moment his eyes gazed at her and then he leaned in, kissing her mouth again. 'You blind me, Quinn.' And then she was being lifted, swung up into his arms. 'Do we have such a thing as a bed?'

She was trembling inside, weak with longing, lost in the warmth of him, the strength of him.

'Yes, we have a bed. Super king-size, dressed to the nines!'

Quinn put her glass to her lips, eyes twinkling. 'I didn't anticipate christening the master suite quite like this...'

He felt his heart swelling. Quinn, naked. Almost too lovely

to look at. Was this real or was he dreaming? Had he really just been inside her, losing himself in her sighs, feeling her body rising, exploding with him, blowing all his fuses at once? Not how he'd expected that hug to turn out, but he was so glad about it, so freaking happy!

He bent to kiss her shoulder. 'Me neither.'

'Are you sure…?' She raised her eyebrows. 'I mean, you did come prepared!'

He felt a flash of warmth around the gills. 'Keeping a condom in my wallet is an old habit…'

Wait! Was she laughing at him? He felt a beat of ease, a smile loosening.

'I've had a few shameless moments in the past, all right—I admit it.' He slid his eyebrows up to tease her back. 'I didn't hear you complaining anyway!'

She laughed. 'Nothing to complain about!' She took a sip from her glass then set it down, smiling. 'You're not just a pretty face is all I'm saying, lover boy.' And then she was snuggling in close, nuzzling his neck. 'God, you must think I'm fickle as hell, tearing your clothes off after saying no last time, but those things I said before stopped making sense to me weeks ago. I've been going crazy since then.'

So he had been right then, about the air crackling both ways. He felt warmth spreading, stowed his glass so he could lie down and draw her into his arms. 'I'll bet I've been going crazy for longer.'

She moved her head back a little, eyes locking on his. 'So now you've got my attention, William Thacker.' A smile touched her lips. 'How long?'

Silver angel…

'Since the night of Dad's sixtieth.'

Her gaze stilled. 'But you didn't even talk to me! You left early.'

His stomach pulsed. Questions in her eyes—questions he should have seen coming if he'd been thinking straight, thinking at all, instead of oversharing.

And then she was shifting, sitting up, her gaze curious. 'Why *did* you leave that night?'

What to say? That he'd hated himself for finding her attractive when she was the one who'd supplanted him in Dad's scant affections?

He raised himself up, angling himself to face her. 'It's complicated.'

'I'm good with complicated.' Kindness in her eyes. 'Please, Will…'

His heart gave. If he didn't try, didn't risk the vortex, what was the point of all this? Making love—*love*—not having sex. Wanting her, weaving dreams around her. If he didn't brave this then it was all for nothing, and he couldn't bear the thought of that. But he couldn't bear the thought of hurting her either, so it was thinking of a way in, a gentle way, a way that would give her a shot at understanding.

He shut his eyes, inhaling to find some clarity, then met her gaze. 'I guess it's all to do with Pete really…' And here it was arriving, right on cue, the burn, the ache. Throat. Eyes. Always the same. He swallowed, blinking back hard. 'He was everything to me, Quinn. Brother. Friend. Protector, in a way.' He felt a smile trying to rise past the pain. 'He was so funny. Brought it out in me too. Man, the way we carried on, laughing till our sides were aching. Over the stupidest things. He had this infectious laugh, you know, that sort of kept yours going…

'He was popular. Good at sport, good at everything. He could have let it go to his head, but he didn't. He was kind. Thoroughly decent.'

'Like you…'

Her gaze softened, but he couldn't let himself get lost in her warmth. He had to get through this, finish somehow.

'It wasn't just me that worshipped Pete.' He felt his ribs tightening. 'Mum did, lit up when he came in the room. As for Dad, God you should have seen him, smiling like a normal fricking parent, slinging his arm around Pete's shoulders...'

Her hand touched his forearm. 'Breathe...'

He inhaled, steadying himself. 'When Pete died, Mum tuned out. Dad got even more hooked on work. I felt—*was*—invisible. I tried telling myself we were all grieving, tried to help Mum, and I told myself to cut Dad some slack. But we were a sinking ship. And then Mum left, so all I had was Dad, except he didn't make himself all that available.

'I figured it was up to me to push, because I needed a parent, Quinn, needed to feel that *I* mattered. I interested myself in Dad's stuff: the Morgan he was rebuilding; the business. As soon as I was sixteen, I asked him if I could work at Thacker in the holidays. I wanted to ride into work with him, show him I could be useful, that he could be proud of me.

'It took a bit of time, but things got better. We were getting on, doing all right, but then...' He looked into her eyes. Was she seeing it, getting it yet? He didn't want to actually say it—*couldn't*.

And then suddenly it was there in her gaze—recognition. Then tears welling.

'Then I came...' She blinked, throat working. 'I came between you, didn't I?'

He felt his heart seizing. 'You didn't mean to, I know that.'

'That's why...' Her gaze turned inwards. 'Oh, how could I have been so blind? So much is making sense now. You were always backing out of rooms at home. You never spent holidays at the cottage.' Her eyes came back to his, glistening. 'You couldn't bear the sight of me, could you?'

His heart wilted. 'For a long time, no...' This had better prove cathartic in the end because it was causing a lot of pain. He swallowed. 'At Dad's sixtieth, you were dazzling. I wanted to come over. I wanted to dance with you, hold you, and I couldn't bear myself for wanting it, because you had Dad's ear, his time, all the things I didn't, so I left. But it wasn't your fault. Any of it. It was Dad's. I made an effort for him, but he never did the same for me. He never got me, Quinn, never even tried...' He could feel the burn again, the tearing ache, the boy inside howling. 'He never loved me because I wasn't Pete. I wasn't golden, good enough, ever! No matter what I did, no matter how many hours I put in at Thacker.'

'No, Will! No!' She was shaking her head now, throat working. 'You're wrong, so wrong, about your father.'

His heart pulsed. Was she actually defending the old man?

'What do you mean?'

'Anthony *loved* you, Will... So much.'

Wet eyes, reaching in, making it worse somehow, making his blood pound.

'Well, excuse me if that went right past me.'

'He did! He was sorry for everything that went wrong between you.'

His body tightened like a zip. 'Which you would know, of course, because he talked to *you*, didn't he?' He could feel his gorge rising, dredging all the old animosity back, and for some reason, maybe because she seemed to be siding with Dad, he couldn't make himself stow it. 'Dear old Dad, bending your ear, confessing to his favourite saint, instead of—here's an idea—taking the direct route—taking the time and trouble to talk to me. You never thought to tell him that!'

'Stop it, Will!' Her eyes flashed. 'I *get* that you're hurting, I do, but please listen. He made mistakes but he cared about you. It's all in the letter he wrote me—it's why he wanted me on this project with you. He asked me to help you, be your friend…'

His lungs emptied.

No… It couldn't be true. Everything they'd shared had felt spontaneous. *Real!* He felt his teeth clenching, grinding. But it wasn't. Yet again, this wasn't about him. It was about Dad. *Pleasing* Dad! Being his friend *for Dad*. Doing it all *for Dad*. All…

He felt his eyes looking at their tumbled sheets, a hot wave rising inside, rising and rising. From the bottom of his trashed heart he did not want to hurt her, but why should he be the only one hurting when there was so much hurt to go round?

He sprang from the bed. 'And did he ask you to sleep with me as well?'

Her face paled. 'How dare you?' And then her mouth was tightening, her eyes blazing white-hot fury into his. 'Get out, Will!' Rising up onto her knees, as if making herself taller would make her louder, more emphatic. 'Get out! Now!'

His heart caught, but only for a beat, and then the bile was back, hurtling through his veins. 'Oh, don't worry yourself, Quinn.' He snatched up his clothes, heading for the door. 'I'm already gone!'

She felt the words ringing in her ears, stinging, reverberating, her throat thickening, hot tears sliding out, tickling her cheeks.

Will…

How could he have said such a thing, even thought that Anthony, that she…?

She felt a shudder taking hold and sank down, pulling the sheets up around herself.

He couldn't think it, believe it.

No! She drilled her fingertips into her temples. *No, no, no.*

He was only venting, striking out like a wounded animal because she'd spoken up for Anthony, trying to defend him, intercede. Lashing out because of all the pain inside, hurt he'd hidden behind a façade—drinking...gambling...casual encounters which didn't require trust. Hurt he'd kept bottled when he should have let it out to those who should have listened, who should have been strong enough, brave enough, to take it, instead of copping out—Judy, Anthony!

Her throat constricted around a sob. And unwittingly she'd made it so much worse. All those years of coming in, only to find her and Anthony together, finding them laughing maybe. She felt her chest heaving, another sob rising. Oh, she could see it all now through Will's eyes. Her hand on Anthony's arm. Her arm linked through Anthony's when they were walking to the pub. Sitting by him on the sofa, getting him to watch the kind of movies she used to watch with Dad. Popcorn! Trying to make Anthony into Dad, trying to coax him into being what he wasn't, what he'd never been, and all because she'd needed a parent, needed it so badly that she couldn't see what she was doing to Will, dislodging him from the spot he'd fought so hard for. Bad enough trying to fill Pete's shoes without having to battle her as well. No wonder he'd left all the time. No wonder he'd resented her.

No wonder! Her heart clenched. *Stupid, Quinn!*

Blind to the last, to the very end. Even while the red flags were going up—that tightness along his jaw, that cool edge sharpening in his gaze—she'd just kept on talking, hadn't she? Banging Anthony's blasted drum in his face, hellbent on trying to help, but all she'd done was push him over the edge and now he was gone.

She felt fresh tears scalding. Love light in his eyes just hours ago, *making love* to her right here, taking his tender time with her, pouring himself into her until she was helpless, out of her mind with pleasure and love... Rare... Precious... *Real!* Her heart reared up. Not something to let slip through her fingers, not when it had taken her this long to find it. She might have given Will his marching orders but she loved him, heart and soul, and she wasn't letting him go. This wasn't the end!

Phone!

She'd call him, apologise, beg him to come back, and then they'd talk, sort all this out.

She scrambled off the bed and ran into the other room, but before she even got to her phone the pressing silence declared everything she didn't want to know. Dead battery. Killed off by Miles Davis. And of course her charger was at her rental apartment. And Filipe had asked her to text. She felt a flick of panic. What time was it? If Filipe was trying to check in and couldn't get through, he might come back, might be coming up the stairs right now!

She looked down at her naked body and dived for her clothes, dragging them on quickly. The room! She ran back in, straightening and plumping, hauling the massive silk bedspread into place. Filipe had remarked on it just that morning, so she couldn't leave it anything less than pristine. Then it was the bottle and the glasses, napkins, wiping and tidying. Ridiculous to be chambermaiding when what she needed to be doing was hightailing it after Will.

The Metropole. He always stayed there. He was bound to be there.

Please, God, let him be there!

CHAPTER TWENTY-ONE

HE PUSHED THE great door shut and dropped his bag.

Silence.

But of course. Because Marion wasn't expecting him back today and Dad was—

He pulled in a breath. Just as well. He was in no fit state for company. What he wanted was a drink.

In the office he poured a Scotch, knocking it back as he went to the desk. He was so tired. Tired of fighting. Tired of reacting, of revolving inside these same old doors. He sank into his chair, forcing his gaze through the leaded panes to the giant beeches at the outer reaches of the garden.

Oh, Quinn...

She was right to have sent him packing. He'd been cruel, out of order. But only because of this festering sore inside that he needed to lance and drain. The boil of Dad. His heart pinched. And yes, the boil of Pete too. How it hurt, turned him inside out to admit it, but he had to face it. He'd loved Pete to his bones, but after he died he'd resented him too, for shining so brightly, for leaving Mum bereft, Dad, all of them, aching and angry. To have that much hold, so that functioning without it was impossible, wasn't healthy. No one should have that much power!

He rubbed his hands over his face. But power only gripped if you let it and he couldn't, not any more. Fighting with

Quinn had shattered more than his heart. It had snapped his strings, floated him free. Oh, he'd been seething, yes, bruised and broken all the way to Rossio Square, but then he'd remembered her stricken face, her eyes wide with shock and disbelief and hurt, and remorse had cracked him open.

He'd turned back, calling her over and over, getting voice-mail over and over because she was blocking him, shutting him out. And then, standing outside, surveying the burnt-out shell of himself, he'd realised he would be no good to her anyway, no good to himself, until he'd dealt with the demons inside, forced himself over one last hurdle.

He put his hand to the drawer and pulled it open, taking out the envelope Edward had slid over the desk to him an eternity ago...

Dearest Will,
Already I imagine you curling your lip at my saluta-
tion, but whatever you think you are dear to me, dearer
than you could ever imagine. My admiration for you
knows no bounds.

You are strong, Will. And sensitive. A powerful com-
bination. You succeeded where I failed, conquered your
natural reticence and shyness to reach out to me, but I
couldn't conquer my demons in turn and be the father
you needed, deserved. I go to my grave knowing that
I have failed you as utterly as I failed your brother.
Yes! Failed him too, beyond redemption. I should have
leaned on you, Will, confided in you, but something
inside me wouldn't allow it. So now I must write out
my guilt, burdening you further, for which I am deeply
sorry.

Pete was killed because of me. Because I refused to
drive him to rugby practice. Mum was out that day, if

you remember. It was raining. Pete came into the office, asking if I could take him. Three miles. Only three miles, but I said no, because I was busy. I told him to take his bike. He was good about it, the way he always was.

   'Okay, Dad. It's fine.'

   The last words he ever said to me.

   Now you have even more reason to hate me, but know that you will never hate me as much as I hate myself.

   My message to you, Will, is to live your life free of me, because I am not worthy of your pain. All very well, you must be thinking, when I have tasked you with finishing my Lisbon hotel, but my reason for doing that is not to irk you, but to appeal to your great good spirit and do one thing for me.

   Please, take Quinn into your fold. Be a friend to her. She is worthy of your time and your affection. I promised her father to take care of her because he didn't want her to be alone in the world, but now I must leave her, and she will take it hard. Quinn is good at hiding her issues behind her smile, behind her warm, generous nature, but she needs an anchor in her life, and I urge you to be that anchor, Will. I hope that in working together you will become friends. It is my dearest wish that you do.

   I love you, Will. Try to remember that.

Dad

Oh, Dad...

He felt his chest heaving with a sob, tears scalding his eyes. Why hadn't he said any of this before, to his face?

Oh, God! And Pete... *Pete!*

That day. Rain slanting down. And Mum was out, yes, visiting a friend in hospital. He'd been in the kitchen, raiding the fridge, when Pete had stepped in, backpack on, hands tightening the straps of his bike helmet.

He'd flashed a grin. *'See you later, squirt!'*

The last words he'd ever heard from Pete's lips.

He drew in a deep breath, wiped his eyes then looked at the photo he kept by the phone. Pete smiling straight towards the lens. His own smile directed at Pete, as it always was.

'See you later...'

And he had expected to see him later, never thought that... And Dad wouldn't have thought it either, that Pete would never come hurtling back through the gates, spraying gravel the way he always did. Dad had been busy. But he was always busy, always working weekends, building the business. And for a seasoned cyclist like Pete, three miles was nothing, even in the rain. How many other dads hadn't driven their kids that day and got lucky, got their kids back safe and sound?

He felt his heart cracking, tearing. Why had Dad kept it to himself? He should have let them in, told them, let them all talk about it. Yes, he would still have felt guilty, of course he would, but maybe a little less so for sharing, a little closer to him and Mum for sharing. Who knew? The only thing for sure was that life was precious—too precious to waste fighting and hiding from the people you loved.

His heart pulsed. And the one he loved most of all, loved with all his heart, was where? In Lisbon? In London? He slipped the letter back and got to his feet. He had to find her somehow. Tell her everything, *share* everything, so he could start living his life—a life he couldn't imagine spending, that he was categorically *not* going to spend, without her.

She swiped her card and slipped through the opening gates. Would he be here? His car was, every sleek black inch of it, but he might well have taken a cab to the airport so that didn't say much. Her heart twisted. If only she'd managed to catch him before he'd checked out of the Metropole but, rushing, she'd dropped the stupid champagne bottle, wetting the bedroom carpet, and she couldn't leave it like that. She'd had to clean it up, crying the whole time because she couldn't call him or the Metropole to leave a message, or even a cab to come pick her up and speed her there to make up for lost time. And then it was too late. But it had seemed that he might come home. So here she was.

She drew in a breath, heart pounding, and set off across the familiar gravel to the familiar blue door—imposing, immaculate. She glanced at the knocker. Ought she to knock, or use her key? She bit her lip, opting for the key, but as she pushed it into the lock the door gave sharply inwards.

'Quinn!'

Will!

Weary-looking. Blotchy, as if he'd been crying.

He let out a short, astonished breath. 'What are you…? How…?' His hands mimed an exit motion. 'I was just coming to look for you.'

'Where?'

As if that was even important, but he was answering anyway.

'Lisbon. London. Wherever you might be…' He shook his head as if he thought that maybe she wasn't real, and then his gaze was clearing, opening into hers. 'But you're here, thank God.' And then his face was crumpling. 'I'm sorry, Quinn, so, so sorry for saying what I said, for being cruel, insulting. Unfair.' His hands lifted in a gesture of hopelessness. 'I didn't mean any of it. Please, tell me you know that.'

She felt her heart constricting. He was taking the blame again. Always taking the blame. Not this time though.

'I do. Of course I do. But it's not your fault, it's mine. All of it. It's why I'm here. To say sorry that I stole Anthony from you.'

'You didn't…' He was shaking his head, frowning. 'Dad was never available to me, not really. He never would have been—'

'Yes, he would…' She could feel her eyes prickling, a lump clogging her throat, but she had to say it, confess all. 'I couldn't see it before, but after our fight I could, so clearly. When I first moved in, I remember that you and your dad did talk, that things were normal, seemed normal between you. But then you went to uni, and I had him to myself…

'I didn't mean to do it, but I latched onto him hard, Will, trying to make him like my dad, because I missed my dad so much, the way we talked, the things we used to do… I missed—still miss—the way Dad was with me, that close-ness we had. And Anthony was so good to me—of course he was—but the truth is, he wasn't like Dad, not at all. And I keep imagining how we must have looked to you, walking arm in arm, sitting together watching movies, but it wasn't what it seemed. *I* was always the one linking my arm through his, not the other way round. And *I* always picked the movies we watched, made the popcorn, trying to do movie night, but he'd often pick up a book halfway through, or fall asleep.'

Will twisted his mouth to one side. 'He always was an old curmudgeon.'

Was he actually trying to make her laugh right in the middle of her heartfelt speech? The one she'd rehearsed all through the flight! *No matter.* She was finishing this if it killed her.

She tightened her gaze on his. 'That's my point. What you saw, backed away from, was as much fake as it was real. Your father was difficult, Will. Troubled. He found it hard to show affection. But underneath I always felt he was a good man, and I miss him. But he wasn't my father, he was yours. And I'm sorry for any pain I've caused you.'

'Oh, Quinn.' His eyes were glistening, smiling at the same time. 'Just come here, will you?' And then he was pulling her inside, pushing the door closed, taking her shoulders in his hands. 'None of it matters. Now I've read Dad's letter I know that for sure.'

Her heart pulsed. 'You've only just read it?'

'Yes.' His lips tightened. 'I stuffed it in a drawer the day I got it because I thought it would be full of rubbish, Dad trying to justify the terms of his will.'

Which, from the look in his eyes, it wasn't.

She felt her heart flowing out to him, her hand going to his cheek. 'Do you want to talk about it?'

His gaze softened and then he broke a smile full of heart-stopping warmth. 'I do. I want to talk about everything, but not right now.'

Oh, that light in his eyes, darkening to a haze, giving her all the feels, all the happy tingles, making her lips curve, her eyes want to cry. 'So, what did you have in mind for right now?'

He chuckled and then he was leaning in, lifting her chin with his thumb. 'I have a notion to kiss the woman I love then take her to bed.' His lips brushed hers, sending a tingle thrilling through her body. 'What do you think?'

She closed her eyes. How could a heart feel so much joy and relief, so much love for one person? And he loved her too, and they were going to work everything out. She felt her lips curving, smiling into his mouth, felt him smiling back. 'I think being kissed and bedded by the man I love with all my heart sounds absolutely perfect.'

EPILOGUE

Six months later...

'WOULD THIS BE the moment to remind you that not every idea you have is a good one?' Quinn was looking at him, half smiling, but also perturbed. 'I mean, seriously, you want us to take a tuk-tuk ride when the Hotel Antonio opens in T minus ten seconds?'

He looked at Miguel. 'She's prone to hyperbole. We open in three hours, and we have staff in place.'

Miguel grinned then looked at Quinn. 'Please get in, *senhora*?'

The perfect accomplice!

'Fine!'

She got in.

He slid in beside her and then Miguel was taking off, hurtling the little vehicle down the narrow street.

He held in a smile. If he'd learned anything about Quinn over the past year, it was that she was a grafter. She couldn't bear to take her hands off the wheel, even for a second, but it was all under control.

He looked over, catching her smile, feeling his heart flip and tumble.

Beautiful Quinn. Saving him. Filling his heart with happiness every second of every day. She was a primary colour. Like Pete. And soon, hopefully, she would be *his* primary co-

lour. It was what this little excursion was about, because what
better day to ask her than this one? The opening of the Hotel
Antonio, named for Dad, of course. Because why wouldn't
they have called it after him? For all his faults he'd brought
them together, and that called for some heartfelt recognition!

Quinn looked over. 'Where are we going then?'

He glanced at Miguel. 'Nowhere really. Just driving around.'

Her eyes narrowed. 'Why?'

'Because otherwise you'd be running around like a head-
less chicken, and you need to stop and breathe.'

'In a moving tuk-tuk?'

'Yes.'

'Hmm.'

They were entering the Praça do Comércio now, approaching their destination. He felt his veins tingling. Time for part
one!

'Miguel, could you please pass me the bundle?'

Miguel obliged.

'What's that?'

He wanted to laugh. She was like a meerkat on fast forward. 'It's something I've been working on that I want to
give you.'

Her eyes lit. 'A gift?'

'Sort of…' He handed it over. 'Open it.'

She lifted the flap, pulling the papers out of the envelope,
scanning the pages, and then she was looking up, her eyes
filling with tears. 'You're building a village for the homeless?'

He nodded. 'That's the plan.'

Her lips wobbled then stretched. 'Why?'

He felt his own eyes tearing up. 'Because there's a need.
And because I can. And because it means a lot to you.'

'Oh, Will.' And then she was launching herself at him,
hugging him tightly. 'I love you so much.'

And there went his heart, bursting again. He wrapped his arms around her, burying his lips in her hair. He lived for this, for pleasing her, because she pleased him all the time, blew his mind, all the time.

He breathed her in. 'It's not settled yet. I can't put it into action until we've been running Antonio for three months and the will comes into effect, but the board is on board, so to speak.'

She took his face in her hands and kissed him. 'It'll happen, I know it, because you're driving it, and you're the best.' And then she was smiling into his eyes. 'Totally worth taking time out for. Thank you.'

And then she suddenly seemed to notice that they'd stopped. 'This isn't driving around. We've stopped.' Her eyes narrowed. 'Why have we stopped, Will?'

Miguel was turning in his seat, smiling fit to burst. 'Because we have reached our destination.'

'Arco da Rua Augusta?'

He felt a smile rising. 'Yes.'

Miguel's eyes flicked to his then to Quinn's. 'So, I'll leave you alone for a few moments then...'

Way to give the whole thing away!

'What's going on?' Quinn was eyeing them both suspiciously, the ghost of a half-smile on her lips.

'Nothing...' He patted his pocket covertly, checking for the ring box, then leaned back against the seat, trying to hold his smile in tight. 'Nothing at all.'

* * * * *

THE PRINCE SHE KISSED IN PARIS

SCARLETT CLARKE

MILLS & BOON

My husband John, my mom Lori Beth,
and my dad Martin. My kids, Jack and Hannah.
Teddy, Joe, Katelyn, Laura, Justin, and Sara.
My brother Nate, my SIL Kelsey, and Papa Jim.
My family and friends around the country (my
St. Louis and Portland in-laws, Aunt Julie, Madi,
Christina, my brother DJ, nieces Kyrstan and
Samantha, Ayme, Ashley and Mama Donna).
My Thursday critiquers: Dyann, Dennis, Cathy,
Dora, Tenaya, Kristy, Nora, Claire, Goldie, Rod,
Jan, and Ed. My teachers: Dr. Anne Farmer,
Mrs. Flory, Ms. Austin, Mrs. Young, Mrs. Schrock,
and Mrs. Long. Melodie, Stephanie, Kimberly, and
Dee Dee, and my Lakeland ladies, Marta, Ashley,
and Rachael. And to Steve, who will never read this
book, and his wife Lisa, who has excellent taste.

CHAPTER ONE

PRINCE NICHOLAI ADAMOVIĆ braced his arm against the balcony doorframe as the wrought iron beams of the Eiffel Tower lit up with hundreds of sparkling white lights. The display no doubt dazzled the hordes of tourists who, despite the late hour, would be thronging the Pont d'Iéna and surrounding streets to snap the perfect picture.

He'd seen it plenty of times, had frequently dismissed it as nothing more than a cheap trick to attract visitors and romantics.

But tonight, he, too, watched the show.

When would he have the freedom to be in his own hotel room alone again? Without security guards or press or his family lurking about?

Or worse, a wife.

The lights performed one last dance before settling into a steady golden glow. A beacon for all of Paris to look to. One of hope, history and love.

He snorted. Love was for books, movies and the occasional lucky sap who stumbled upon their soulmate. For people like him, love was not always an option. Especially when the law of his country required that he have a wedding ring on his finger before accepting the crown.

A cold fist tightened around his heart. It wasn't enough that he would lose his father and take over the ruling of a country growing far faster than anyone had anticipated. No, he also had to tie himself to someone he didn't love. All because of an archaic decree.

He quelled his anger as he turned away from the window and crossed the room of his luxurious penthouse suite to the bar. One of the benefits of this night alone was being able to indulge in a glass of bourbon without raising eyebrows. He wasn't anywhere close to the level of the President of the United States or the King of England. Hell, there were actors and actresses more recognized by the general public than he was.

But that was all about to change with the construction of Kelna's first major port that would welcome ships from across the world. Multibillion dollar companies were courting his country, pouring money into building new roads, bridges and other infrastructure that would benefit Kelna's people for decades. The media had started to take notice, requesting interviews and snapping the occasional picture of Nicholai, his sister, Eviana, and his father.

King Ivan Adamović of Kelna. A benevolent ruler loved by his children, respected by his staff and revered by his people. The kind of king one wished could rule forever.

He stared down into the amber liquid in his glass. What would the tabloids do if they knew the truth? That if the doctors were right, the Prince of Kelna would be king before the year was out?

He took his first sip, savored the slow burn down his throat. He'd accepted his fate to be king from an early age. He just hadn't expected it this soon. He'd bought into the myth all children wanted to believe about their parents: that they would always be there. Ivan hadn't always been around the way other fathers could be. He was a man who firmly believed in duty. But Nicholai had never doubted he had his father's love and, equally important to him, his father's trust.

He would rule. He had to.

Even if the thought of sitting on his father's throne, of wandering the palace halls knowing he would never again hear the booming laugh or smell the musky scent of cigars smuggled past the royal physician, twisted his chest into knots so tight it hurt.

And, he thought grimly as he wandered back to the window, he wouldn't have the outlets he did now to deal with the loss. The limited freedoms he currently enjoyed would vanish. Nights like this, where his security team slept next door instead of standing guard in the halls and concerns about paparazzi were minimal, would disappear.

His fingers tightened around his glass. A picture of him on his private balcony, brows drawn together, lips pressed into a thin line, had made it onto the front of one Italian publication that favored dramatic headlines and excessive punctuation.

"Kelna's Bachelor Prince!" the title had screamed. According to an "inside source," the Prince was currently unattached but "open to finding someone to share his life and the throne with." The resulting furor, and the number of single women suddenly vying for his attention, had become irritating at best.

Eviana had found it amusing. Nicholai had not, especially when he'd discovered how news of the palace's search had reached the media. A trusted palace aide, Franjo, had let a photographer into the palace under the guise of taking photos of one of the royal art collections. Two months later and the slash of betrayal still cut deep. Nicholai was a private person by nature. Letting his guard down was not something he did easily. That he had relaxed around Franjo, even considered the man a friend and had shared with him that he was contemplating marriage, had made him feel like a fool.

Never mind that Franjo had done it for a mere five thousand euros. All to cover a gambling debt. Had he just come to Nicholai, Nicholai would have helped him.

Neither here nor there.

It was done. It had taught him a valuable lesson. The more Kelna grew, the less he could trust outsiders.

Thankfully, the architecture firm he was meeting with to-morrow had been arranged and vouched for by his father, one of the few people he trusted without reservation. It would be his last event before traveling home to Kelna. With money pouring in, work had already begun on essential projects like schools and bridge renovations.

For one of the few projects that benefited the royal family, a new ballroom, Ivan had requested bringing in an out-side organization from the States. Nicholai preferred keeping things within the country. But Ivan had made a good case for it, pointing out that a firm with no ties to Kelna could bring a fresh perspective and help incorporate elements that would ap-peal to the swell of tourists they were anticipating in the next couple of years. That the lead architect of the firm was an old university friend of Ivan's, one he trusted to be discreet, had helped sway both Nicholai and his sister.

That and an ironclad confidentiality contract. No more gos-sipy speculation about his love life. No more lurid headlines and photographs of him with various women dredged up from the past, with reporters venturing guesses as to who his lucky future bride might be.

If only they knew the truth. He wasn't just open to finding someone. He had to.

Shortly after his father's diagnosis, the prime minister had approached him. Dario Horvat had served for years. He was someone both Ivan and Nicholai could count on, even if his views tended to be even more traditional than the King's. So when Dario had told him about the Marriage Law, an anti-quated law that hadn't been enacted in over two hundred years, Nicholai's initial shock had quickly given way to anger. He'd just found out it would be a miracle if his father made it to next summer. Learning he had to marry within a year of as-cending the throne or he'd lose the crown was the last thing he'd needed to hear.

But Dario had persisted. The last five kings had all ascended the throne well into their fifties and sixties, decades into their marriages. Nicholai would be the first king under the age of forty since before the Napoleonic Wars had decimated Europe.

"Your family is respected, Your Highness," Dario had told him. "Imagine the turmoil Kelna would experience if they lost two kings in one year amidst so much change."

Phrased like that, there had been no point in arguing. The law itself was kept quiet. The last thing Nicholai or the palace needed was a bevy of women suddenly vying for the spot of future queen and possibly bringing the wrong kind of attention to Kelna. Marriage would calm some of the concerns and elevate him in the eyes of the traditionalists. It would also give the country something else to focus on besides the loss of their beloved king. A new princess, a royal wedding and above all, signs that despite Ivan's passing, the line would continue. The throne would be secure.

He'd always known he would marry. Had hoped there would be affection, perhaps even love involved. He thought he'd have more time to find someone on his own.

But he didn't. Such was the nature of duty.

Even now, Dario and a select group of trusted advisors were compiling a list of prospective candidates for him to review when he returned to Kelna. A strategic process. One that would identify women compatible with both the Prince and country. In the coming months, they'd find a way for him to discreetly meet the candidates and see if one would do the role of queen justice.

He glanced down at his watch. Ten minutes past eleven. The meeting was scheduled for nine o'clock in the morning. Sleep had eluded him since the doctor had given him Ivan's updated prognosis. On the nights he did manage to fall asleep, he usually woke an hour or two later, his mind racing.

But he at least needed to try. He tossed back a generous

gulp of bourbon and started to turn away when a movement on the roof caught his eye.

There. Beneath the light of the Paris moon, a woman sat on the roof of the east wing of the hotel, her back to him. Dark blond hair tumbled halfway down her back. Intrigued, he watched as she turned her head to look at the Eiffel Tower and smiled slightly as she raised what looked like a bottle of wine in a toast before taking a long drink.

His amusement vanished as she turned and scooted closer to the edge of the roof.

God, no. She was going to jump.

He grabbed the handle of his balcony door, then cursed as he remembered his security team had insisted on installing new locks that remained bolted during his stay. His head jerked up in time to see the woman move again. His heart shot into his throat. He didn't have time to call for help. He grabbed the key out of the desk drawer and unlocked the door, running out onto the balcony just in time to see the woman brace her hands on the roof's edge.

"Stop!"

His command was lost to the sounds of traffic below and a brisk spring wind that flung his words into the night. With a quick glance at the roof a dozen feet below, he pulled himself onto the balcony railing, uttered a quick prayer and leaped. For a breathless moment, there was nothing but the air rushing past him. He landed with a jarring thud that made his teeth rattle in his skull.

Get up. Get to her.

He rolled to his feet and sprinted across the rooftop.

"Stop! *Ne saute pas!*"

The woman's head snapped up. She turned, her eyes growing wide as she saw Nicholai barreling toward her. She pushed to her feet, the city at her back, and raised the wine bottle up over her head.

"Don't come any closer! I'm armed!"

He stopped, holding up his hands as his gaze darted between her and the roof's edge. She was slender, a good foot shorter than he was. If he could just get close enough to pull her away, he could probably subdue her and summon someone on the ground below for help.

"I'm not going to hurt you—"

"I can see you still moving. I'm not that tipsy."

The snarky tone surprised him.

"I just want to help you."

"Help me?" The woman glared at him, fierceness radiating off her small frame in palpable waves that, had the situation not been so dire, would have made him smile. "Help me how? By shoving me off a roof?"

"Stopping you from jumping off a roof."

"Stop me from…" Her voice trailed off as she stared at him like he'd sprouted horns. And then she did the last thing he expected.

She threw her head back and laughed.

Dealing with a crazy hulk of a man had not been in Madeline Delvine's plans when she'd sneaked out onto the roof of the hotel that night.

A very handsome, very irritated-looking hulk of a man she acknowledged as her laughter subsided and he continued to glower at her. With her fingers still wrapped around the neck of the wine bottle, she started to step back and put a little more distance between herself and her unexpected visitor.

His eyes widened.

"Stop!"

Before she could blink, he darted forward with a speed she hadn't anticipated, wrapping his strong arms around her waist and yanking her forward. Their legs tangled and he stumbled, falling backward and pulling her down with him. The bottle slipped from her fingers, hit the roof with a clink and rolled away. She landed hard on his chest.

A broad, muscular chest.

"What are you doing?" she snapped. She braced her hands on his shoulders, intending to push herself away. But her traitorous fingers just curled into the white material of his shirt as a scent that reminded her of wild woodlands wrapped around her.

Her breath hitched. She looked up to see the man watching her intensely.

Wow.

In the chaos of the moment, she hadn't got a good look at him. But now, as her eyes roamed over his face, she realized what a travesty it was that someone who was probably drunk was also incredibly attractive. Dark, wavy hair had been swept back from his forehead, a couple stray wisps curling on his neck. She could only guess at the color of his eyes—green, perhaps?—beneath thick brows currently drawn together in a frown. His strong nose reminded her of a Greek statue, the square jaw softened by the tiniest dimple in the middle of his chin.

The man wasn't just attractive. He was devastatingly handsome.

"You can let go of me now."

Her voice came out husky and breathy. The man's frown deepened as he moved his hands from her waist to her arms, anchoring her against him.

"No. I'm going to call 112 and have the emergency services send someone over—"

"Hey!" she snapped.

The man's eyes widened a fraction, as if he wasn't used to being interrupted, before they narrowed again.

"Listen, ma'am, you—"

"I was enjoying a lovely bottle of cabernet sauvignon, when some rampaging man comes leaping across the rooftops like he thinks he's acting out 'The Murders in the Rue Morgue.'

If you need to call the emergency services for anyone, call it for yourself."

His grasp on her arms slackened. She used the opportunity to push herself up and back away. She glanced around and spotted the wine bottle glinting in the moonlight. Keeping the man in her line of sight, she inched over and picked it up.

The man sat up slowly, holding up his hands.

"There's been a misunderstanding."

"What clued you in?"

His lips twitched. "I saw you sitting on the edge of the roof. When you scooted closer, I thought you were going to jump."

She shot a quick look over her shoulder and grimaced. From this angle, she could see how the riser she'd been sitting on could look like the edge.

"There's another five or six feet of roof on the other side. I was just enjoying the view." She looked around. "Did you climb up the fire escape, too?"

"Not exactly."

Perplexed, her eyes roamed over the roof. Where on earth could he have come from…

Her mouth dropped open as she spied the open door to the balcony of one of the west wing's penthouse suites.

"You didn't…" That had to be more than a ten-foot drop, not to mention the gap between the balcony and the roof of the east wing. "Did you?"

He stood and grimaced. "That's going to hurt tomorrow."

"Of course it's going to hurt," she retorted. "You jumped off a balcony! You were worried about me jumping off a roof, so you jumped off a balcony and nearly got yourself killed!" She rushed forward and circled him.

"What are you doing?"

"Checking for injuries."

"Are you a nurse?"

"No, but I do have four siblings. We've all done our fair share of patching up each other's injuries."

Nothing looked out of place, no obvious scrapes or bleeding. She finished her assessment and stopped in front of him.

"You should see a doctor tomorrow. Just to be safe."

He looked down at her with a strange expression on his face, as if he couldn't quite figure her out.

"I'll do that."

"Good." She huffed out a breath. "Even though I didn't need saving, that was very heroic."

"I'm not a hero."

She arched a brow. "Maybe you're not familiar with Superman? Can leap tall buildings in a single bound? I'd say that makes you a hero."

His soft chuckle rolled over her, a deep sound that made her pulse beat just a little faster.

"Thanks, Miss...?"

"Delvine." She stuck out her hand. "Madeline Delvine."

His hand engulfed hers and she swallowed a gasp as warmth flowed up her arm.

"Well," she said, pulling her hand back and hoping he hadn't noticed her reaction to his touch, "thank you again for the attempted rescue."

"I apologize for scaring you."

"Thank you, and likewise."

He reached down and picked up a couple things off the roof.

"Yours?" he asked.

"Oh, thank you." She held out her hand for the sketchbook, then frowned as he looked at her drawing.

"This is very good."

Her cheeks flushed. "Thanks."

She'd drawn the tower when she'd first come out on the roof, combining her view with how she imagined it looked from the iconic bridge that arched over the Seine. Even though it had been more whimsical than technical, she'd been pleased with it.

Her would-be rescuer pointed to the couple she'd drawn on

the bridge, the man holding the woman tight against his side, their faces turned to the tower.

"Who are they?"

Madeline shrugged. "A couple in love. I imagined them watching the tower light up right before he proposes. Or maybe she tells him they're finally expecting a baby. Happy things."

It was one of the things she loved about her work. Imagining not just the buildings themselves, but the people who would occupy the space, whether they were simply passing through or staying for decades.

"You're a fan of 'and they all lived happily ever after?'"

Something dark flowed beneath his words.

"Yes." She grinned. "I even picked up a copy of *Pride and Prejudice* from a bookstore on the Left Bank this afternoon." When his frown deepened, she asked softly, "You don't believe in happily ever after?"

His expression evened out into a mask as smooth as glass and as sharp as obsidian.

"Life isn't a fairy tale."

An answering frown crossed her face. "No." Her ex-fiancé Alex's smug smirk flashed in her mind. Between his misogynistic expectations regarding her role as his future wife and his obsession with his own appearance, he had been more villain than hero.

She pushed thoughts of Alex away. "Doesn't mean there aren't fairy-tale moments."

"Oh?"

She flung out her arms. "You're on a rooftop in Paris under a blanket of... Well," she amended as she glanced up, "you can't see the stars all that well. But still, stars above, the Eiffel Tower in the background, a bottle of wine." She looked over at the iconic structure. Before her mysterious would-be rescuer had charged onto the scene, she had been staring at it for nearly twenty minutes. Traveling to Paris had been at the top of her wish list ever since she could remember. A list she was just now starting to tackle after working her way through her architecture degree and certifications. Never had she thought her career would bring her here, that she would get paid to bring dreams to life in the most incredible places around the world.

If her stepfather could see her now, working in the field he had introduced her to, succeeding like she'd always talked about it, he would be so proud of her. He'd always encouraged her to go after her dreams, to balance her love of family and home with having adventures.

She'd been temporarily derailed by Alex and the box he'd tried to shove her in. But she'd broken free.

Some of her earlier happiness returned. She wrapped her arms around her waist and smiled.

"It doesn't get much more fairy tale than this."

"Don't fairy tales include romance?"

Her eyes darted from the Eiffel Tower back to the man.

"Most do, I guess." *Unless you attract frogs instead of princes.* "But they don't have to." She held up the bottle. "My fairy tale is pretty simple right now."

His lips quirked. *What*, she wondered, *would a full-on smile look like?*

"I don't like leaving you out here alone."

She sighed. "I told you, Mr.…." She frowned. "I didn't get your name."

He stared at her, that considering expression on his face again.

"Nick," he finally said.

"Just Nick?"

"Just Nick."

"Well, Just Nick, I'm twenty-seven and can fend for myself up here." She smiled to soften the bluntness of her words.

He walked toward her. Her breath hitched in her chest. In a city swirling with scents, most of them pleasant, some of them not, his cedar-like fragrance crept into her senses once more.

"I don't think a mugger would care how old you are."

"Probably not." She made a show of glancing around. "I don't think too many muggers crawl across the roofs of Paris."

He made a noise that almost sounded like a growl. "I'm not leaving you alone."

"Well then, I guess you'll just have to join me."

As soon as the words were out, she inwardly cringed. What was she doing? Inviting a strange man to spend time with her on the roof of a hotel at midnight? She'd promised herself that she would have an adventure in Paris. But flirting with a man who had just tackled her was a little much. Misguided as his actions had been, he'd been trying to help, not score a date. The last thing he probably wanted was to drink wine with a tourist.

And then he smiled at her. A full-on smile that blew past the walls she'd erected against the male sex after her breakup and sparked a warmth that spread through her body and left her breathless.

"I'd be honored to join you, Madeline Delvine."

CHAPTER TWO

NICHOLAI STRETCHED HIS legs out as he perched on the riser Madeline had been sitting on when he'd first spied her from his balcony. He had to admit, from this vantage point the Eiffel Tower looked larger than life. Even in his brooding, jaded mood, the romanticism of the tower was hard to ignore.

As was the woman sitting next to him. They had been sitting in silence now for several minutes. Unlike most of the people he knew, she seemed comfortable with the silence. She sat now with a small smile on her face, taking an occasional sip of wine and watching the Paris nightlife speed by on the street below. He'd declined her offer of a drink, content to sit and enjoy the moment.

He blinked in surprise. He couldn't remember the last time he had felt content. Certainly not content with something as simple as sitting next to an interesting woman.

And Madeline Delvine was one of the most intriguing women he'd met in a very long time.

He glanced at her out of the corner of his eye. Blond hair cascaded around a surprisingly strong face. Unlike the few previous women he'd been involved with, who would have accepted compliments like "dainty" and "fairylike" with pleasure, Madeline would most likely laugh that deep, throaty laugh before pointing out her square jaw and straight line of a nose were anything but dainty.

Yet the longer he looked, the more he liked what he saw.

Dark brows arched above dark blue eyes. She glanced at him and, when she caught him looking, blinked before ducking her head, a tiny smile flirting about her lips. Full lips were a pleasing contrast to the sharp, elegant slash of cheekbones. Her angled chin made her look feminine and strong and mischievous.

But it wasn't just her unique beauty that caught his attention. It was the simple, deep serenity on her face. All the incredible restaurants, the lauded landmarks, the finest museums just a breath away. And she looked like she'd won the jackpot, sitting on a rooftop drinking wine.

"You have questions."

He blinked as she turned to face him, the little smile spreading into an impish grin that revealed the small, charming gap between her front teeth.

"I do?"

"You keep looking at me like you can't figure me out."

He couldn't. He wasn't recognized on the streets by many. But having a conversation like this, with a woman who had no idea who he was, who his family was, was a novelty. One that needed to be treated with caution. He would be hard-pressed to believe this had been an act to entice him out onto the roof for paparazzi photos, an interview or even seduction.

But stranger things had happened. He would not walk blindly into a trap. Not again.

"I am trying to figure you out."

"So ask."

"Just like that?"

"Just like that. For example, where are you from, Nick?"

He debated for a moment, then took a leap of faith. "Kelna."

Her wrinkled brow told him he'd been right to assume she wouldn't know about his home country. A challenge to overcome as he brought Kelna to the world stage, but one that, in this moment, he was grateful for. The opportunity, for one night, to be just Nick.

"I've never heard of it."

"It's a little country on the coast tucked between Croatia and Montenegro."

She leaned back, her eyes alight with interest. She offered him the bottle again and, after a moment, he accepted it. The intimacy of placing his lips where hers had just been stirred something in his chest. The wine, dark and velvety, lingered on his tongue as he handed the bottle back.

"Hvala vam."

"You're welcome, I think?" At his nod, her smile grew until her eyes crinkled. "What language do you speak in Kelna?"

"Croatian and English, although there are others, too. Serbian, Bosnian, a little bit of Italian."

"And how does someone from Kelna find himself in Paris?"

His pulse kicked up as his eyes sharpened. Was she digging? But he saw nothing suspicious in her demeanor. No hint of artifice in the midnight depths of her eyes.

"Business."

"Ah." At his questioning look, she shrugged. "I would press for details, but I'm also in Paris on business. My boss swore me to secrecy."

"Oh?"

She laughed. "I'm going to say as little as possible so I don't slip up. J.T. told me very little, except that we have the potential to land a big contract with someone very important. I've never seen him so excited."

"Then we won't talk about business. Is this your first time in Paris?"

"Yes." She sighed happily and tilted her head back. The moonlight kissed her throat, made her skin shimmer with silver light. "It's more than I ever imagined it could be. There are so many places I want to travel. I've only been out of school for a short while, and I'm just now starting to make money," she added with a laugh. "Getting to kick off my traveling adventures in Paris is pretty incredible."

"You're from America?"

"I am. Just outside Kansas City."

"Tell me about it."

Her brief hesitation piqued his curiosity.

"I spent a lot of my childhood along the banks of the river a few miles east." Her smile widened. "My favorite part was watching the fog roll in from the water over the fields in the spring. Although I liked winter, too."

He chuckled. "Was there anything you didn't like?"

Her dimples deepened. "Not really. In the winter the snow dusted everything with white. I'd wrap myself in a thick blanket and sit on a wraparound porch with Paul and my sister Greta."

It all sounded so quintessentially American he couldn't help but smile.

"Who's Paul?"

"My stepfather." She glanced down at her sketch pad. "The first time Paul and I spent time together, just him and me away from my mom, he took me to the Nelson-Atkins Museum of Art in the city." She scrunched up her nose. "I was a bit of a brat to him at first. But instead of making me feel guilty, he asked for five minutes. Five minutes and if I didn't like it, we'd leave and he'd buy me ice cream on the way home."

"I'm guessing it was more than five minutes."

"Two hours. He had to bribe me with ice cream to get me to leave. It was magical." She smiled. "It was where I fell in love with art. And when I started to see what my mom saw in Paul. He was the best dad I could have ever asked for."

"Where is he now?"

"He died. Two years ago." Grief poured off her in a sudden wave. That he could sense it, almost feel her anguish, shocked him. He'd never experienced such a connection to anyone other than his father and sister. Being a royal meant keeping your emotions in check, maintaining control.

He nearly reached out to her and stopped himself just in

time. Touching her would just create another connection, one that would further tempt him and make it that much harder to leave at the end of the night.

"I'm sorry, Madeline."

"Thank you. He was nearly twenty years older than my mother. They managed to have three more children. And he never made my sister or me feel like we weren't one of his own."

"Sounds like a good man."

"He was the best. Told me there was nothing I couldn't do. Nowhere I couldn't go." Her smile returned as she turned her head to gaze out over the eastern reaches of Paris. "But as much as I'm loving it here, I can't picture living anywhere but Kansas City. I love adventure, but I also love going back home."

"I know the feeling."

"You like living in Kelna?"

"I love it." The honesty of his words surprised him, as did the desire to talk, to share with someone. "We sit on the coast of the Adriatic Sea. The water is impossibly blue. Limestone cliffs, mountains, fields of olive trees. There's a sense of community, from the largest city to the smallest town, that I have yet to find elsewhere in the world." His eyes roamed over the rooftops spread out before him. "I enjoy traveling, seeing new places. But nowhere gives me the same pleasure as when I come home."

"It sounds beautiful."

She reached for the wine bottle. Nicholai picked it up and handed it to her. Her fingers brushed his. The slight graze hit him hard. Judging by the widening of her eyes and her slightly parted lips, she experienced the same spark.

"I'm going to have to add it to my travel list." Her voice was breathless, the tiniest hint of a blush stealing across her cheeks as she looked away and sipped from the bottle.

The desire to tell her who he was, to invite her to visit him in Kelna, was so sudden and fierce he almost said it out loud. This might actually be the first time he had had a conversation with a woman simply because he wanted to talk to her. To spend time with her. Yes, there was an attraction there. Madeline was a beautiful woman.

But there was something else, something deeper pulsing beneath the initial spark. He wanted to explore it, to get to know her more. To continue the fantasy this evening had provided. One where he was a man enjoying his evening in Paris with a fascinating woman who had no designs on his title or his wealth.

For what?

He would sit on the throne in less than a year with a queen by his side. A queen he most likely hadn't even met yet. The last time he'd seen the list compiled by the prime minister's task force, he had recognized names. But he couldn't even summon the faces to go with them. He had no right to explore any type of romantic interest with another woman. He couldn't offer them anything at this point aside from a night or two of intimacy. Some men would thoroughly enjoy such an arrangement. He wasn't one of them.

Unnerved, he stood. This woman interested him more than anyone or anything had in a very long time. He needed distance. Now. Before he did something he regretted.

"It's getting late."

Madeline glanced down at her watch. Her eyes widened.

"Did we really just talk for over an hour?" She shook her head. "I was enjoying our conversation so much I didn't even realize how long it had been."

Me, too.

For one idyllic moment, he entertained the dream of what it would be like to be normal. To ask Madeline to meet him in the morning for coffee, to explore the Louvre and travel to the top of the Eiffel Tower. To enjoy her company without wondering if paparazzi were lurking around the next corner.

The illusion vanished as quickly as it had appeared. He wasn't just a civilian. He would be fortunate if this little impromptu encounter with a random American wasn't splashed all over the tabloids by tomorrow morning.

"I'm sorry." He cooled his tone. "I have an early meeting. Otherwise, I'd stay."

He saw the flash of hurt, the smoothing of her face as she saw right through his excuse. Meeting or not, he was pushing her away, and she knew it.

"Of course." Her tiny, sweet smile nearly killed him.

She leaned over and picked up the sketch pad at her feet. Her fingers grabbed the bottom of her drawing and, before he could say anything, tugged. The penciled illustration of the Eiffel Tower tore free.

"Here."

He stared at the drawing, then back at her.

"For me?"

"Yes." Her eyes crinkled at the corners. "Something to remember Paris by when you go back home."

"I can't—"

"Yes, you can." She pressed the drawing into his hands before flipping through the sketches in the book. Images of Sacré-Coeur's elegant domes, vine-covered shops in Montmartre and the book-filled windows of Shakespeare and Company flew past. "I have plenty. I want you to have this. Please."

The *please* did him in. He nodded, unable to express his gratitude with words for fear he'd say something else, like telling her he wanted to see her again.

Let her go.

She grabbed the empty wine bottle and walked past him, a heady, sweet scent lingering in her wake. Angry with himself and, for the first time in a long time, the role he was bound to, he followed.

She moved toward a door in the wall marked *Escaliers*, tossing the wine bottle into a refuse bin by the door. They both reached for the handle. Their hands brushed. Her sharp intake of breath pierced his armor. He looked down to see her face tilted up, eyes wide and lips parted, her blonde hair glowing in the moonlight. She watched him without guile, without assessment. She simply looked at him as a woman looked at a man she desired.

He couldn't have stopped himself if he'd tried. He leaned down and kissed her.

Madeline's brain slammed to a halt even as her pulse kicked into overdrive. Nick was kissing her. And not just kissing her, but doing a very good job of it. His lips firmed on hers as he slid an arm around her waist and pulled her against him.

She should resist, her rational mind screamed at her.

But where's the adventure in that? her heart whispered back.

She gave in to temptation and twined her arms around his neck, pulling him closer. He groaned, his hands flattening against her back, warmth seeping in through her shirt. When his tongue teased the seam of her lips, she smiled and opened her mouth to him.

Her fingers crept up into the thick silkiness of his hair. Every touch was heightened, every sound amplified as they kissed, exploring each other with excited yet gentle touches, the sweetness of discovery mixing with the illicitness of a rooftop rendezvous. Whether it was the magic of their surroundings or simply the heady masculinity of the man kissing her like he was starving—even as he cradled her like the most precious of jewels—she'd never experienced a kiss like it before.

One hand drifted up into her hair, fingers tangling in her curls as he anchored her head in a firm grip and trailed his lips across her cheek. Warmth bloomed in her chest.

He pulled back, keeping one hand in her hair, the other pressed against her back. He lowered his forehead to hers, a gesture that somehow seemed more intimate than the kiss they had just shared. Their labored breathing mingled in the night air.

She raised her head, something twisting in her chest at the regret in his eyes.

Tension gripped her. "You're not married, are you?"

He let out a quiet chuckle. "No."

"Girlfriend?"

"No girlfriend, no fiancée, no wife."

She relaxed and let out a breath. "Okay."

He pulled her closer for one long, blissful moment, then released her and stepped back, her drawing now wrinkled but still clutched in his hand.

"But I'm not free to pursue this." He looked out toward the darkened spire of the tower. "No matter how much I want to."

Disappointment and the all-too-familiar bite of rejection rose up before she squelched it. She'd just met him. They'd talked for a while and, yes, shared the sweetest kiss she'd ever experienced. But she would not lose sleep over a man who was setting a very clear boundary.

"It's all right," she said with what she hoped was a casual smile. "Thank you for my adventure."

His gaze swung back to her and he frowned. "Your adventure?"

"I promised myself I'd have an adventure in Paris, and this definitely counts as one." She gestured toward the balcony. "But next time, Superman, use the stairs."

With that final pronouncement, she opened the door to the stairwell and descended. She made it back to her room, closing the door and locking it behind her before sinking down onto the bed. Her room, tucked into a corner, offered her a simple street view.

Slowly, she sucked in a shuddering breath, then released it. Her hand drifted up, her fingers settling on her swollen lips, physical evidence that she hadn't just imagined her too-handsome would-be rescuer.

She flopped back on the bed and stared up at the ceiling. She'd dated before, had had a couple boyfriends here and there. And then Alex, of course.

And look at how well that turned out, she thought cynically.

But none of them, including the early days with Alex before he'd revealed his misogynistic malarkey, had come close to inspiring the kind of sensations Nick had with one simple kiss.

With a deep inhale, she sat back up and moved to the shower, turning the water to blistering hot. Yes, it had hurt when he'd stepped back. But, she reminded herself as she stepped under the scalding spray, she wasn't interested in relationships anyway. Not for a while, at least. Not after Alex, less than a month into their engagement, had delivered his ultimatum that she find another job when they got married or he'd call off the wedding. Alex had loved that he was dating an architect, name-dropping her job title anytime they went out to one of the many parties he'd liked to attend as an up-and-coming lawyer with a prestigious firm in Kansas City. What he hadn't loved were the long hours when she was on a demanding project and couldn't go to one of said parties, or how her career soared while his stayed stagnant.

Anger slithered through her. In the early days of their dating, she'd told him how important her career was to her. How the hours she'd spent with her stepfather, watching him draft plans for airports, courthouses and skyscrapers had led to her passion for architecture. How, after his death, it had been a way to keep his memory alive.

At first, she'd thought Alex asking to spend more time together was romantic, that he couldn't bear the thought of them being apart. But it had been control, not love, that had dictated his words. Just like it had been control that had led to their last fight, when he'd once again asked when she was quitting her job.

"I've told you how important my career is to me," she'd said as he'd stood in the living room of her apartment, hands in his pockets, shoulders thrown back in an arrogant stance as he looked down his nose at her.

"Yes, I know, you loved drawing as a kid, you spent time with your stepdad, blah, blah, blah," Alex had said with a scoff. "Stop living in the past, Maddie. What's more important? His memory or a life with me?"

She'd been wringing her hands, wondering if leaving Alex was the best thing, if he hadn't been partially right about her obsession with her career. But once he'd asked that question, the answer had been so clear and so strong it had been an easy matter to slide the diamond ring off her finger as she'd walked over to him, dropped it in his hand and told him to get out of her apartment.

Alex had been a controlling, narcissistic jerk. And she'd ignored the warning signs until it was almost too late.

Don't think about him, she ordered herself as she washed her hair.

She had just spent an hour on a rooftop in Paris with a handsome, mysterious stranger. She'd experienced the most wonderful kiss of her life…so far. And instead of mourning what might have been, on bad days she'd be able to look back at this night and spin dreams about who the enigmatic Nick was. A foreign spy, a technology billionaire, a prince in disguise.

Cheered by her wild imagination, she stepped out of the shower. Tomorrow she would meet with J.T. and the rest of the team from Forge Architecture and find out what the top-secret assignment was. One day she would make time to date, to fall in love, get married and have a family. For now, though, her career, her family and her friends were more than enough. They'd become even more important as she'd carved out a life for herself in the aftermath of her broken engagement. Unlike Alex, her loved ones gave her room to breathe and supported her dreams. Her career offered independence and, now, the chance to travel.

She definitely didn't need another relationship tying her down now.

But as she lay down, Nick's handsome face crossed her mind. She couldn't suppress the question that arose as she drifted off to sleep.

What if...?

CHAPTER THREE

MADELINE WRAPPED HER hands around her mug of tea and relaxed in her chair as the morning sounds of Paris washed over
her. Birds tweeted overheard. Soft music played quietly from
speakers hidden in urns overflowing with vivid pink blooms.
On the other side of the stone wall, car engines purred as the
occasional horn beeped. Her sketch pad lay nearby. After her
cup of tea, she'd draw the courtyard before her team arrived.
Another memory to take home.

She glanced at the glossy black leather binding. Buried toward the back was a sketch she'd done this morning as the
buildings of Paris had turned to rose in the dawn light. A
strong blade of a nose. A long, handsome face marked by a
square jaw with a dimple in the middle and a reluctant smile
tilting up one corner of full lips.

And the eyes…the eyes had been the hardest. She'd drawn,
erased, drawn again, then finally settled for the best she could
do. Nothing would capture the brooding intensity, the hidden
depths that had slowly flickered to life the longer they'd talked.

She sighed. Nick had quickly turned from an unwanted in-
truder to, so far at least, her best memory of Paris.

So far.

It would be hard to make a better memory. But she still had
all of today and the promise of tomorrow. Still had a mystery
that her boss, J.T., would unveil within the hour. Content with
her thoughts, she settled deeper into her chair. A week ago, she

never would have imagined herself sitting at a table laden with breads, jams, fruit and juices spread out on a neat white table-cloth with the spire of the Eiffel Tower visible in the distance.

She loved her job.

"Oh, my God."

Madeline looked up to see Julie, Andrew and Chris walk into the courtyard. Julie's and Andrew's eyes were round as saucers as they took in the tiered fountain splashing off to the side, the cobblestone pavers and the leafy trees arching overheard.

Chris shot her a megawatt smile. She suppressed a groan and gave him a polite smile in return. A few years older than her, Chris, with his sun-streaked blond hair, lanky build and skin tanned to gold thanks to hours spent outside, appealed to a lot of women. He'd hinted more than once at getting to-gether for an after-work drink. But she didn't mix work with relationships. That rule extended to coworkers and clients. Per-haps she was being overly proper, but it wasn't worth the risk.

No relationship was right now. Not after she'd been so spec-tacularly wrong about Alex and got sucked into his self-cen-tered world. She had always considered herself a good judge of character. Had she let the idea of being in a relationship, of moving on to steps like marriage and kids, blind her to the warning signs of who Alex was beneath his handsome charm?

She frowned. She hadn't thought this much about Alex in nearly six months. It had been well over a year since she'd kicked him out. She'd been content to focus on her career, enjoy time with her family and friends. What had brought this on?

Him.

The answer appeared before she'd even fully formed the question in her mind. Nick had been the first man she'd felt something for in a very long time. But her attraction to him had also brought her fears to the surface.

A good sign, she told herself firmly as she greeted her colleagues, *that you're not ready for any kind of dating.*

"Good! You're all here," a voice boomed across the courtyard.

James Theodore Sanderson, affectionately known as J.T., walked out of the double glass doors as if he were making an entrance onto a stage. With an old-fashioned moustache the color of steel gracing his upper lip, the ends curled into extravagant flourishes, and thick jowls that descended into an even thicker neck, J.T. reminded her of a bulldog with a never-ending smile. He'd been like that ever since the year he'd guest lectured in one of her college classes, offering her first an internship and then a job at his firm once she'd passed her exams. While no one could ever replace her stepfather, J.T. had been both a mentor and a paternal figure in her life.

He slapped his hands together and beamed at them. "Are you ready, *mes petits enfants*?"

Julie, a curvy woman in her forties with a quick smile and a brunette bob that framed her round face, arched a brow. "For?"

"The reveal."

Madeline couldn't help but laugh. "You're practically shaking, you're so excited. I've never seen you like this over a contract before."

"It's a big one."

A buzz hummed through Madeline's veins. In the five years she'd been working for Forge, three as an intern and two as a fully licensed architect, she'd fallen in love with each and every project she'd tackled. J.T. loved his work, too. But after forty years in the business, including thirty running his own firm, little got him this excited. It had to be something big.

"Our client is on his way down to meet with us. I have your nondisclosure agreements on file." J.T. sobered, the twinkle disappearing from his eye as he leaned forward and speared them with an intense gaze. "Not a word of this project, nor who we're working for, must be shared with anyone, including your families. Not until we receive approval from his public relations team."

Andrew, a former university classmate of hers with a stocky build and thick beard, rolled his eyes, the gesture magnified by his oversize glasses.

"We signed the paperwork, J.T. Either you trust us or you don't."

J.T. held up his hands. "Fair." His eyes shifted and a smile spread across his face.

"Ah, Your Highness! I was just briefing my team."

Julie's eyes grew round as she mouthed, "Your Highness?"

Excitement skittered through Madeline. They'd worked with business leaders and politicians and even a couple of local celebrities, but never a member of royalty.

"Please, Mr. Sanderson, there's no need for formalities."

Madeline froze. She knew that voice, smooth whiskey roughened by that sexy accent.

This isn't happening.

Slowly, she turned her head.

He dominated the courtyard with his presence. Navy suit, complete with a crisp white shirt and silver tie, screamed custom tailoring and money. His dark hair had been tamed back from his forehead, the chiseled planes and angles of his striking face on display for all to see.

Their eyes connected. Did she imagine the flicker of recognition, followed by something darker? Or did he truly not recognize her?

She wasn't sure which was worse.

"Team, this is His Royal Highness, Prince Nicholai Adamović of Kelna. His father, King Ivan Adamović, is an old friend of mine."

Oh, my God, I kissed a prince.

Everyone stood and introductions were made, J.T. announcing everyone's names and titles like a proud father introducing his children.

"And this is Madeline, one of my best design architects."

"Your Highness." She bobbed in place, keeping one hand wrapped tightly around the back of her chair.

Nick—no, Prince Nicholai—inclined his head, the same as he had to the others. His professional demeanor took the edge off the panic fluttering around in her stomach.

Okay.

She released a breath. She could pretend like last night had never happened, too. Even if it stung that he was able to pass off their conversation and kiss so easily.

"I look forward to working with you."

He nodded to her, then turned back to J.T. She swallowed hard and glanced up at the tip of the Eiffel Tower. Had it been less than ten hours ago that she had admired it with the man standing just feet away? A man who had listened to her, shared pieces of himself, then kissed her like she was the most precious thing in the world.

A man who had just now dismissed her as if they had never met.

Stop it.

As heroic and intriguing as he'd seemed last night, his cool dismissal made it clear that that's all it had been: one night. If she was going to maintain her professional role, the only option she had was to remove herself from her emotions and do her job.

Nicholai sat at the head of the table, and they all sank back into their chairs.

"Have you shared the details of the project yet, Mr. Sanderson?"

Nicholai's voice commanded everyone's attention, low and deep.

"Not yet. Would you care to do the honors, Your Highness?"

"Nicholai, please," the Prince said with a wave of his hand. "Titles and formal addresses are for government functions and black-tie events." He glanced around the table, his eyes landing on each member of the team. Madeline could swear she heard Julie let out a deep sigh, a noise that made her lips twitch, given that Julie had been happily married for nearly twenty years.

And then Nicholai's gaze landed on her. The air disappeared from her lungs, leaving her chest tight and her skin warm. Something flickered in his eyes—something dark—then disappeared as he continued his perusal of the table.

"My father, King Ivan Adamović, rules Kelna. It's a small country slivered between Croatia and Montenegro. Mountains, fields and a small stretch of coastline along the Adriatic Sea. Our country has a population of less than five hundred thousand. But our economy is strong, primarily powered by tourism along our coast. That's about to change with the addition of a new seaport that will allow us to serve close to three thousand ships a year."

His expression didn't change. But his voice deepened, the pride in his country's accomplishments evident despite the professional veneer that kept his handsome features smooth.

"We've experienced an influx of money from those who want to see the port succeed, enough that we've been able to advance projects like the building of new highways, railway repair, new schools and other projects." His smile flashed, cool but no less potent. "With the rise in interest, we'll be hosting more official visits to our palace. A palace that has not been updated in forty years. That's where your team comes in."

Excitement chased away some of Madeline's tension.

"The palace is a conglomeration of Roman and European styles. It started off as a fortress along the coast, similar to Diocletian's Palace in Croatia. Many of the rooms have been updated over the years. But some, like our ballroom, saw little use. Until now, money was not something our country had a great deal of to spend on vanity projects. Other than the necessary maintenance, rooms like the ballroom are like time capsules from various eras. The Napoleonic Wars, the Industrial

Revolution." His lips twisted into a wry smirk. "The result is certainly...interesting."

"Eclectic," Julie offered.

"A kind way to put it," Nicholai said with a smile. "While we don't want to destroy the history of the palace, we do need to bring these rooms into the twenty-first century. Our first project is the grand ballroom." He gestured to J.T. "We've arranged for your team to fly out tomorrow morning for an initial meeting to review the code and zoning analyses already conducted by members of our team and to discuss details. Then we'll tour the original ballroom, the site for the new one, and, if time allows, the highlights of our palace before flying you all home the next day. We'll reconvene four weeks later to view your initial designs."

Madeline's eyebrows raised as she shot a look at J.T. They had never completed a design for a project in a matter of weeks. Had J.T. actually agreed to this?

"Is there a problem, Miss Delvine?"

Madeline's head swung around. Nicholai stared at her, the silkiness of his voice contrasting sharply with the emotion seething in his eyes. An emotion that looked uncomfortably like repugnance.

Was he upset that she had left so abruptly last night? Or was he irritated that the woman he had indiscreetly kissed was going to be in his life for the foreseeable future?

She raised her chin. Prince or no prince, the man was not going to bully her.

"I have concerns about the timeline, that's all. The predesign phase alone can take a month, and developing schematic drawings another month to two. However," she added with a nod to her boss, "I imagine J.T. has something in mind. He wouldn't have accepted the project otherwise."

"Quite right," J.T. said in his booming voice. "It is a tight timeline. The progress check-in isn't for a final delivery, just to present the schematics and a couple artistic renderings to the royal family. From there it will go to a community panel. King Ivan wants the country to be a part of the process and emphasize that the ballroom will be used for a variety of events, including ones for the people of Kelna." J.T. shot a smile at Madeline. "I appreciate you asking, Maddie."

She sat back. Even though she admired the King's including his people in the decision-making process, the accelerated timeline still made her uncomfortable. But she trusted J.T. If he said he thought it was possible, then it was. He wouldn't risk the reputation of Forge in committing to something he couldn't do, not even for an old friend.

J.T. passed out a folder containing pictures of the palace. Despite the plethora of styles, from the pervading Roman grandeur to the touches of ornate Gothic and classic Renaissance influences, the palace was stunning. Limestone walls gleamed like diamonds in the aerial shots, brilliant white made all the more dramatic by the blue sea a stone's throw away. Many of the rooms still proudly boasted their elegant history with soaring ceilings, marble pillars and intricate stained glass windows. Coupled with the modern touches that had been introduced over the past few decades, it was a lovely and unique structure.

The current ballroom, however, made her wince. A long, thin room, it looked like something from a British country manor. The ornate crown molding, while beautifully carved, seemed ostentatious and overwhelming coupled with the low ceilings. Chandeliers dripping in crystals shrank the room even further. It seemed as if someone had ignored the adage "less is more" and stuffed every possible thing they could into this room.

The next photos, however, made her sit up. The site that had been marked for the new ballroom took her breath away. A grassy expanse sat next to the existing ballroom. Beyond the green, pine trees flanked a clifftop that plunged down into the sea. A stunning garden was visible in the distance.

As she flipped through the photos, designs etched themselves in her mind.

Her earlier excitement returned. This, she felt in her bones, was going to be an incredible project.

"Given how busy tomorrow is going to be," J.T. said, "you have the rest of the day to yourselves. We'll meet in the lobby tomorrow morning at 7:00 a.m. for our flight."

Madeline quickly stood. Perhaps she was imagining the tension between her and Nicholai. But real or not, she wanted to get as far away from it as possible.

"It was nice to meet you, Your Highness," she said with a quick bob. She scooped up her folder and headed toward the door.

Run up to the room. Jot down some of these ideas. Then stroll down the Champs-élysées and pretend like I can afford—

"Where are you headed to?"

She inwardly groaned as Chris fell into step beside her.

"I'm not sure. I had a couple ideas I wanted to write down. Then maybe go out for a walk. What about you?"

"I'm headed to the Musée d'Art Moderne. You should join me."

He flashed her a smile and she knew a moment of frustration. Why couldn't she be attracted to someone like Chris? Someone who was interested in her, who shared her passion for architecture?

But no matter how hard she tried, she couldn't summon anything more than feelings of friendship.

"You could bring your sketch pad," he added with a nod to the book in her hands. "Show Matisse and Picasso a thing or two."

The comment teased a genuine smile from her. "How about I text you after lunch, see where you're at?"

His face fell, but he nodded. "Sure."

They entered the cool interior of the hotel. Chris headed toward the front door while Madeline walked to the elevator, her mind almost immediately returning to the man just a few dozen feet behind her.

A prince. She had kissed a prince. One day she would tell her mom and her siblings, maybe even Julie. One day, it would be one of those moments she looked back on with fondness and a dash of excitement.

But right now, it was just frustrating. How was she supposed to work for someone who had gone from talking with her on a rooftop and kissing her senseless to acting like she was worse than the dirt on his shoes?

They'd have to talk, she acknowledged glumly as she pressed the elevator button. Clear the air. Even though he had already drawn the line last night on their little tête-à-tête going any further, his being a client was more than enough incentive for her to keep her distance. She would never risk her career for a fling. She would reassure him of that, reiterate her commitment to the job. Hopefully, that would be enough.

The elevator doors slid open. She stepped inside and pushed the button for the third floor. The doors started to close when a hand shot out. A small alarm beeped and they slid open to reveal a stone-faced Prince Nicholai Adamović.

"Going up alone?"

She frowned at his frigid tone.

"Unless there's a ghost lurking in here with me, yes."

"I didn't know if you were waiting for Chris."

Frustration pumped through her as she narrowed her eyes. "You're my client. That entitles you to know my professional background, skills and what I'm doing with your project. It does not give you the right to know who I choose to spend time with."

The elevator door started to beep more incessantly. Nicholai stepped inside. The doors closed, leaving them alone.

She knew it was impossible for spatial relationships to change. But her brain insisted that the elevator shrank because suddenly it seemed like no matter where she moved, she would be inches away from touching the Prince.

"How did you arrange it?"

Her brows drew together.

"What?"

"Last night. What was your plan? Draw me out, have a photographer waiting to capture us?" He leaned down, the gold flecks in his eyes a vivid flash against dark green. "Were you trying to trick me into a compromising position, or perhaps have some gossip to sell to a magazine?"

"'A compromising position,'" she echoed. "Did you steal my copy of *Pride and Prejudice*? This isn't the Regency era. A man and a woman are allowed to have a private conversation without being engaged or married."

He looked away and ran a hand through his hair, muttering something in a deep, guttural language that stirred the air and, despite her irritation, made her heart beat a little faster.

"It's not the same for someone like me."

"Okay," she said slowly. "Look, I know neither of us expected to see each other again. But I want to reassure you that I—"

"Are you sure you never intended to see me again?" The venom in his voice put her on high alert as he pinned her in place with his gaze. "Or did you know who I was all along? Did you decide to sneak up onto that roof with the hope of capturing my attention?"

Irritation burst into righteous anger. She tried, and failed, to swallow the words that rose up.

"One, you will never speak to me in that tone again. Understand?"

Nicholai blinked. "Excuse me?"

"You're a prince. Congratulations. That doesn't give you the right to talk to me like I'm trash. Second, do you really think last night was a setup?" She cocked her head to the side. "I mean, it makes perfect sense to me. I went up on the roof of the hotel my boss booked for me a week ago, to a spot that was out of the line of sight of your room, on the tiny whim that you might go to the window and look off to the side? Oh, and that you," she said with a stab of her finger in his general direction, "would develop a superhero complex and jump off of a balcony to rescue me?"

His brows drew together.

"Surely even you have to see how—"

"Even me? A lowly commoner? No, apparently, I'm too simple to see how any rational human being could picture last night being a setup."

The elevator dinged. The doors slid open and she brushed past him.

"Madeline."

The sound of her name, uttered in that husky accent, slid over her. Heat pricked her eyes as she remembered how he'd said her name last night, of how special she'd felt under the magic of a Parisian sky.

She whipped around. He stood in the door of the elevator, one arm braced against the frame, a thunderous expression on his face.

"Don't worry. I'm going to pretend like last night never happened. As far as you and I are concerned, we met for the first time this morning. I won't say anything to anyone, including my team, reporters or anyone else you're concerned might find out. If you can treat me with slightly more respect and politeness, then we'll get along just fine."

He sighed and scrubbed a hand over his jaw.

"Madeline—"

"Have a good day." She punched the button to close the door, grateful when he stepped back.

And couldn't resist one last parting shot. She grasped her skirt in her hands and dropped into a deep curtsy as the doors started to slide shut. "Your Highness."

CHAPTER FOUR

"LUNCH IS SERVED."

Nicholai looked up as Marina, the head flight attendant, set a plate on the table in front of him. The familiar savory scent of cuttlefish and risotto relaxed the tension that had gripped him since yesterday morning.

The team had arrived a half hour before their departure time. J.T., Julie, Andrew and Chris had been excited at riding on the private jet chartered by the palace. The plane had been divided into three sections, with the first dedicated mostly to crew space and a guest bathroom. The primary section, the main cabin, boasted a mix of luxurious ivory leather chairs, a sofa at the front and one at the back and a long table the same gleaming black wood as the floors. The back of the plane included a private suite with a bed, shower and walk-in closet. Even if it was more ostentatious than Nicholai preferred, he appreciated the intimate setting.

The luxury hadn't seemed to faze Madeline one bit as she'd given him a brief nod, glanced around the plane, and then moved as far away from him as she could get.

His eyes strayed toward the back of the plane. Madeline sat in one of the plush chairs with her legs curled under her. With her blond hair pulled into a messy bun on top of her head and a pair of round glasses, she looked more like a college student than an architect as she sketched.

Watching her hand fly over the paper made him remember the drawing tucked safely in his briefcase. A drawing he'd pulled out at least twice since she'd given it to him. Once, when he'd awoken the morning after to an ache in his chest that had plagued him until the moment he'd walked into the courtyard and seen Madeline's beautiful face frozen in surprise. An ache replaced by a thrilling jolt, then squelched by anger as he'd fought to make it through the meeting without demanding answers.

The second time had been after she'd left him speechless in the elevator. He'd smoothed the crinkles left in the paper from when he'd crushed the drawing against her back as he'd kissed her. The light of day had shown him the details he'd missed in the night: the rivets climbing up the side of the tower, the intricate latticework, even the detailing on the bridge where the couple stood, spoke to her talent, both as an artist and as an architect.

A breath escaped him. Franjo's betrayal had made him distrustful. Madeline had paid the price for his irrational suspicions. For someone who usually held himself to the pillars of honor and duty, he'd screwed up. Royally.

Chris crouched down next to her chair and murmured something. Madeline looked up and blinked owlishly. She glanced over at the table, watched Marina set more plates down, then shook her head with a small smile. Nicholai's fingers tightened around his pen as whatever Chris said next teased a laugh from her. When he patted her on the knee as he stood, Nicholai nearly snapped his pen in half.

He'd seen the way the architect had looked at Madeline at the hotel, had overheard his invitation to explore around the museum. He couldn't remember the last time he had ever wished someone would trip over their own feet or walk into a window.

But he had entertained numerous thoughts of that nature in the past twenty-four hours about Chris.

The younger man looked up and caught Nicholai's gaze.

His expression faltered. Inwardly cursing, Nicholai forced a slight smile and nodded before turning his attention to the dish in front of him.

"This looks great." Andrew grinned, his teeth white against his dark brown skin as he took the seat next to Nicholai's. "Seafood?"

"Cuttlefish. Known as *crni rižot* in Croatia."

"It smells amazing." Julie, the project architect, took her seat next to Andrew. "I've never had black risotto before."

"The color comes from squid ink."

Julie blanched. "Oh."

Nicholai smiled at her. "I promise it's worth a taste. But the crew can prepare something else."

Julie sighed and picked up her fork. "I'm always getting on to my kids about trying new food. Can't do that if I don't practice what I preach." She scooped up a forkful and paused, scrunching her eyes before she took a bite. Her eyes flew open. "Oh, wow. Wow, this is really good. Maddie!"

Madeline's head jerked up. Her eyes flickered to Nicholai, then to Julie.

"Maddie, you are missing out!"

"I'll have some later." Madeline nodded toward the pad in her lap. "I'm on a roll here."

"Madeline is very good at design work," Julie confided as she dug into her dish. "So is Chris."

Chris smiled and shrugged. "I'm decent. Madeline's the true talent on the team."

Nicholai gave him a thin-lipped smile in return. Even the man's humbleness grated on his nerves.

"I'm not familiar with the different roles you all play."

"So I'm the project architect—"

"Big boss," Andrew clarified as he slathered butter on a thick slice of *pogača* bread.

"Big boss," Julie agreed with a grin. "Andrew is our site architect. He's the one who makes our lovely pictures come to life. J.T., of course," she said with a nod toward the back where J.T. dozed, "handles all the administrative things, although he used to be a legendary designer himself. And then Chris and Madeline are the design architects."

As Julie rattled off the details of all the roles she had just mentioned, Nicholai tried to listen. Tried to focus on what would be not only an important project, but one that carried a lot of pride for the people of Kelna. After centuries of being forgotten, they were finally being recognized for the incredible country they'd created and sustained over generations.

Yet his eyes kept straying back to Madeline. How she chewed on the tip of her pen or tapped it against the paper in her lap when she was puzzled. How at one point she glanced at everyone seated at the round table and, thinking no one was watching, pushed off the wall with her foot and spun in a circle.

His lips curved up.

"So what do you think?"

Nicholai froze.

"I'm not sure." He shook his head and smiled at Julie. "I apologize. I tuned out for the last part of our conversation. Could you repeat the question?"

Julie waved her hand. "Just me jumping ahead to business. I'm sorry. I'm just so excited to get to work."

This time, the smile Nicholai gave Julie was reassuring. "No need to apologize. I'm honored to work with a team as excited about this project as I am. It's why my father wanted to work with J.T.'s firm."

"Thank you, Your Highness."

"Nicholai," he gently prodded her. "Now, you mentioned children. How many do you have?"

Julie's cheeks turned pink with pleasure. "Three. Two boys and a girl…"

As Julie spoke, awareness sparked across Nicholai's skin. He looked up, saw Madeline watching him, a furrow between her brows. Pink swept over her cheeks when their eyes connected. She hurriedly glanced back down at the papers in her lap.

Unreasonably pleased at her reaction, he refocused on Julie and her stories about her children. Andrew and Chris chipped in with tales like when Julie's daughter had let the family's new puppy loose in J.T.'s office during an important client meeting. The rest of the flight passed in casual conversation, with the team sharing everything from how they got started in architecture to their favorite places in Kansas City.

Nicholai leaned back in his chair. His father had chosen well. He liked J.T.'s team, even if he didn't want to like Chris. They were talented and worked well together. The personal touch they brought, the camaraderie, all of it spoke well for the work they were about to do.

"Ladies and gentlemen, *dames i gospodo*, we are beginning our initial descent into Kelna."

The pilot, Nada, spoke smoothly over the speaker.

"Oh!"

The simple breathless syllable made Nicholai look up. Madeline had moved to a window and now had her hands pressed to the glass like an excited child. He got up from the table and made his way back to her.

"What do you think?"

"It's like looking down on a...a..."

"Fairy-tale kingdom?"

She glanced up at him, her eyes slightly narrowed. When she saw the small smile hovering about his lips, she grinned in return, an uninhibited gesture that made his chest tighten.

"Exactly."

She turned back to the window and he followed her stare. The deep blue waters of the Adriatic Sea lightened into shades of aquamarine as they neared the coast. A beach covered with golden sand hugged a promenade that stretched the length of the town behind it. Lepa Plavi stood in its proud, historic splendor beyond the beach. Buildings of pale stone were made vivid by their red-tiled roofs. As the plane drew closer, the narrow, winding streets became visible, along with the bustle of people visiting the markets, shops and restaurants.

And to the left, on a hilltop overlooking the sea, stood the Palace of Kelna. The limestone walls gleamed like a jewel in the afternoon sun, with over a thousand years of history residing in its ivory-colored walls.

"How do you ever leave here?"

"It's hard." He nodded toward the mountains in the distance, the green hills sloping up to thick pine forests that covered all but the snowcapped tops of Kelna's majestic peaks. "My country has something for everyone. The entrepreneur, the family, the explorer." His eyes roved over the familiar sights beneath him before straying to a site just beyond the wingtip of the plane. A site that had changed drastically in such a short amount of time. "Now for the industrialist, too."

"You're not certain about that."

Surprised, he looked down at her.

"What makes you say that?"

One shoulder rose and fell. "You hesitated."

Slowly, he released a deep breath. "This port will bring great prosperity to our country. But also, great change."

"Change can be good."

"Yes."

His eyes returned to the site of the new port. Massive cranes stood against the backdrop of the sky, mechanical and out of place next to Lepa Plavi's mix of Roman and European architecture.

"But how does one know when there is too much change?"

Madeline tried to keep her ears tuned to the guide escorting them through the winding hallways.

And failed miserably.

Marble dominated the palace, from the gleaming floors to

soaring pillars. Over two hundred rooms made up the complex. The palace library boasted two floors of books, complete with dark walnut bookcases and actual sliding ladders. From the vaulted ceilings painted with elaborate designs in the grand hall where official guests were welcomed to the more solemn yet still elegant columns that marched down the art gallery, it was magnificent.

The ballroom was another story, and just as over-the-top as it had appeared in the photos. Whereas rooms like the Hall of Mirrors at Versailles exuded historical charm, this looked like it had been done purely to show how much money the old King had had to waste. Andrew scribbled note after note on his tablet.

The project was massive.

She couldn't wait to get started.

They passed by the large bay windows of a room that overlooked one of the numerous gardens. Her eyes roamed over the stone paths that meandered through lush lotus plants, colorful orchids and acacia trees.

Had Nicholai played here as a child? Explored the paths and pretended he was a pirate or a wizard? Or had he been studious, focused, even as a youngster?

Irritated with herself, she quickened her pace to catch up to the group. She'd managed to hold on to her indignation from his ridiculous accusations all the way onto the plane. Even when she'd caught him looking at her, she'd ignored him.

Until he'd been kind and talked to Julie, shown genuine interest in her colleagues. Until he'd looked down at the shores of his homeland and spoken with both pride and the gravity of someone who understood the depth of his responsibility and duty.

She blew a stray hair out of her face. She didn't want to like him. Didn't want to think about his good qualities, which would inevitably lead her back to that night in Paris.

Focus on your work! Not a prince who is completely off-limits.

A prince who had thankfully seen them off in two small limos at the airport before departing in his own. He'd met them on the front steps of the palace, where an aide had escorted them to a charming conference room overlooking well-tended gardens. The meeting was quick and effective. Members of the survey team, along with people from departments like finance and public affairs, had met to review the detailed reports. It had been one of the most prepared client sessions Madeline had ever attended. She'd even managed to keep her mind on their work.

Mostly.

Except for when Nicholai had laughed at something Andrew had said. The deep sound, a moment of relaxed amusement, had slid over her and made her breath catch. Or when she'd caught him nodding appreciatively to some of the questions she asked. When he had excused himself before the tour had started, she'd been equally relieved and disappointed.

The guide turned into a room that looked like a formal living room. The elegant furnishings stood out against the pale blue walls that added a touch of calm to the affluent setting.

"We've arranged for you to have some refreshments before you're shown to your rooms." Goran, a slender man with a silver mane of hair and a calming smile, gestured to a sideboard table laden with water pitchers, glasses of champagne and an array of fruits and cheeses. "Please, enjoy yourselves, take all the time you want and notify me when you're ready."

"I'm ready!" Julie said with a laugh. "I haven't walked this much in a long time."

J.T. echoed her sentiment. Goran led them out one of the doors, leaving Madeline alone with Andrew and Chris.

Andrew sank down into a chair and continued to scribble furiously. Chris picked up two glasses of champagne and handed one to Madeline.

"This is incredible."

"It is." Madeline's eyes roamed over the rectangular room,

drank in the sight of rounded bay windows offset by elaborate columns, the marble fireplace at the far end. "I wish we could stay longer. Twenty-four hours isn't nearly enough."

"We'll be back in four weeks." Chris nodded in Andrew's direction. "Andrew's already got all the blueprints and a crew coming through later this week to take photos. We'll have everything we need."

"True." She wrinkled her nose. "Not a fan of the accelerated timeline."

"At least it'll be a challenge," Chris said as he clinked his glass to hers.

"True." She sipped the champagne, enjoyed the dance of bubbles on her tongue.

"Never one to back down." Chris smiled at her. "I like that about you."

Some of Madeline's joy disappeared. She inwardly groaned. She didn't want to hurt him. But her more passive approach had done nothing to discourage him. She liked Chris, appreciated him as a work partner and as a friend. She didn't want to lose that, especially with the largest project of their careers on the line.

"Chris—"

"Miss Delvine."

Nicholai's voice swept over her. Chris frowned, his gaze shifting from her face to the Prince behind her.

Swallowing hard, she turned and dipped her head. "Your Highness."

"May I have a word?"

Her heart kicked up its pace.

"Of course, sir." She glanced over her shoulder at Chris, shrugged to show him she didn't know what Nicholai wanted and followed Nicholai out into the hall. He led the way to a small alcove set amongst a pair of columns.

"Yes?"

Nicholai glanced around before pinning her with his intense gaze.

"I wanted to apologize."

She loathed that her heart gave a traitorous leap. "Apologize?"

"For my discourtesy yesterday. My accusations were thoughtless and insensitive."

She threaded her fingers together and rocked back on her heels as nerves fluttered in her belly.

"Thanks. It's okay."

"But it's not. I was rude."

"You were. But," she added with a sigh, "I wasn't exactly polite myself."

Nicholai's lips twitched. "You had just cause."

"Still, it's not the way my mom raised me to behave. Especially to a prince." She stuck out her hand. "Truce?"

"Truce."

His hand enveloped hers. Energy sparked between them, curled up her arm and flooded her with sensation. Her breath caught in her chest. Her eyes swept up, met his equally stunned gaze.

"Sir—"

"Please call me Nicholai." He blinked, as if shocked by his own request.

"Nicholai."

She repeated his name softly, saying it in its entirety for the first time. His fingers tightened around hers.

"Madeline—"

"Maddie?"

She gasped and yanked her hand away as Andrew called down the hallway. Suddenly frantic at the possibility of being caught in a secluded alcove with the man who would be signing off on her company's paychecks, she moved into the hallway.

"Yes?"

Andrew cocked his head to one side as she walked toward him.

"What were you doing?"

"Exploring," she replied with a bright smile, her stomach twisting at the lie. She barely resisted looking over her shoulder to see if Nicholai had followed. "What's up?"

"Goran is taking Chris and I up to our rooms. We didn't want to leave you behind."

"Great. I'll join you."

She followed Andrew back to the reception room. It had been a good thing, she told herself, that Andrew had interrupted whatever had been about to happen.

But it didn't stop her from pausing in the doorway and risking a discreet glance down the hall.

The hall was empty.

CHAPTER FIVE

BUTTERFLIES FLUTTERED IN Madeline's stomach as she slid a cover over the final illustration.

You've got this. You've got this.

She'd been repeating the same mantra since yesterday when she'd boarded a plane from Kansas City to Paris with Chris and Julie, followed by another private jet to Kelna. J.T. and Andrew had gone out a week early to meet with a team of civil engineers to discuss the technical details of the new ballroom.

She stepped back and surveyed the easels set up at the far end of what Goran had described as the "Ivory Room." An elegant conference room painted a creamy white that made the azure-colored waves of the Adriatic, viewed from arched windows that took up most of one wall, even more striking. A long cherrywood table dominated the middle of the room. She'd laid out enough copies of the presentation folder for the royal family and the Forge team. Everything was in order, which meant the worst part had arrived.

Waiting.

In less than thirty minutes, she and her team would present their initial plan to King Ivan, Prince Nicholai and Nicholai's sister, Princess Eviana. Designs that normally took months, but had been produced in just one.

The past four weeks had been chaotic. Ever since they'd landed back in Kansas City, they'd put in twelve-to-fifteen-hour days to meet Nicholai's demanding deadline. If the royals approved, the proposal would be submitted to a committee of citizens who would cast the final vote.

No pressure. No pressure at all.

The punishing pace had had one upside. It had kept her focus on her work and off those last, fraught seconds with Nicholai in the alcove.

Except for at night, when a glimpse of the stars from her bedroom window or a taste of wine at dinner stirred the memories she'd fought to push away.

She didn't want a relationship right now. She needed a break, time to be alone, before she dated again. Even if she was ready to date, Nicholai was the Prince of a rapidly growing European nation. She was an architect from the Midwest. Interested or not, a relationship was out of the question.

In a moment of weakness, she'd looked him up on the flight home. The sheer number of reports speculating on his love life had been overwhelming. For all the gossip and rumors, one theme had emerged: Nicholai would most likely wed in the next year as his father's health deteriorated. His future bride would be an integral part of Kelna's growth.

Madeline felt sorry for the poor woman already. To have that kind of weight resting on one's shoulders before even saying "I do"? To have a marriage rooted in strategy and policy instead of love?

No, thanks.

The tabloid speculation had also planted a seed of discomfort in her chest. Nicholai had told her there was no woman in the picture. Technically that was true. But the fact that he might be married within a year was something he'd forgotten to mention.

She sighed. The tabloids could easily be writing fiction to sell stories. And why was she pondering any of this when none of it mattered? No, he hadn't told her. But he didn't owe her an explanation. One kiss didn't entitle her to all his secrets, or him to hers.

She needed to stop ruminating and refocus her attention on her work. On the biggest presentation of her career so far, which would take place in just a few minutes.

Relax. Take a breath. Be calm. Professional.

She drifted over to the large bay windows that overlooked the sea. She leaned her forehead against the glass, much as she had the month before as the plane had descended into Kelna.

Something about the country called to her. Yes, there was the initial excitement of being in a new place. But she'd felt something deep in her bones the first time she had laid eyes on the beaches, the pine forest, the sea. A feeling reinforced by the evening she'd spent in Lepa Plavi. J.T. had treated the entire team to dinner at a local restaurant, then set them loose for a couple hours. She'd wandered the cobblestone streets and narrow passageways, navigating buildings cloaked in history. The architect in her appreciated the strength, the sheer will that had kept the town standing for over a thousand years. The romantic in her had fallen in love with the country that had stood the test of time.

Her eyes drifted back to the easels. Chris had followed her lead the past four weeks, giving her free rein over the designs, even when she had caught a raised brow or a slight frown. The royal family's direction, to design a new ballroom that would bring it in line with the palace while updating it for the twenty-first century, had been vague at best. She'd made several sketches of the large lawn where the new ballroom would go, taken numerous pictures the morning they'd flown back home. Reviewed more photos of the existing palace and some of her favorite rooms from her tour.

And come up with the design that would be unveiled in just a few minutes. Whether it achieved what the King, Prince and Princess wanted remained to be seen.

Awareness prickled over her skin. A sharp inhale brought a scent of cedar mixed with a masculinity that painted a vivid image of a handsome smile and green eyes crinkled at the corners.

"Hello."

Squaring her shoulders, Madeline turned and laced her fingers together as she faced Prince Nicholai.

"Your Highness."

He looked incredible. Dressed in a charcoal suit with a dark green tie, his hair combed back from his face, he looked every inch the austere royal. His face was smoothed into an expressionless mask that made his sharp features look more like a statue than those of a living person.

Something inside her chest twisted. She missed the carefree smile he'd given her on the rooftops of Paris, the naked emotion in his eyes when they'd met in the alcove. On those occasions, she'd seen the man behind the crown.

Now, though...now he looked distant. Unreachable. Untouchable.

For the best. No touching the handsome prince.

"How was your flight, Miss Delvine?"

"Fine, thank you."

Silence descended. The longer it grew, the more tense it became. If Madeline thought she had imagined the attraction between them, the tension spoke otherwise.

Frustrated, she abandoned her pretense of appearing calm as she ran a hand through her hair.

"Look, I know there's—"

"Hello."

A woman appeared just behind Nicholai. Madeline instantly recognized the long black hair that hung down to her waist, the pixie-like features, and the green eyes, the only feature that Princess Eviana shared with her brother.

Madeline dipped into what she hoped was a passable curtsy.

"Your Highness."

Eviana's lips tilted up into a small *Mona Lisa* smile that radiated regality. She crossed the room and held out her hand.

"You must be Madeline."

"I am."

Madeline took the offered hand, trying to mask her surprise at the faint roughness of the Princess's palms.

"My brother's told me a lot about you."

Madeline's eyes flickered to Nicholai, then back to Eviana. The Princess's smile deepened to something genuine, edged with a touch of smug satisfaction that told Madeline she had just given something away.

Alarm flared. Surely Nicholai hadn't told his sister what had happened between them in Paris. But then again, even though he was a royal, he could still share things with his siblings like the rest of the world.

"I've enjoyed getting to know him and learn more about your country."

She hoped her answer sounded professional even as her heart raced so fast it was a wonder she didn't pass out.

"Diplomatically spoken." Eviana glanced back at her brother. "We're looking forward to seeing your work today, aren't we, *braco*?"

Thankfully, the rest of the team walked in just then. More introductions were made. Nicholai and Eviana took their seats at the far end of the table. Whatever Madeline had sensed between her and Nicholai disappeared as he resumed the mantle of prince.

Which is good, she told herself as she and Chris moved to the front of the room. *Business. This is business.*

Another man entered the room. Despite his hunched shoulders and paper-thin skin, he still exuded a calming regality that spoke of power entwined with a personality she wouldn't have expected from a king. Illness had not dimmed the intelligence in King Ivan Adamović's eyes, nor robbed him of his presence as he moved forward with the assistance of a simple black cane.

Nicholai and Eviana both stood, as did Andrew, J.T. and Julie.

J.T. bowed. "Your Majesty."

Chris and Andrew followed suit, as Julie dropped into a curtsy. Madeline hastily copied Julie's gesture.

"Please." King Ivan waved a wrinkled hand as he approached J.T. "Friends do not bow to one another or address each other so formally."

The men hugged. Madeline smiled at the obvious affection between the two. But her smile faltered as she took in more details of the King's appearance, from the sunken cheeks to the deep blue network of veins beneath his skin. Saw the bittersweet regret on Eviana's face as the Princess watched her father. Realization hit.

The King wasn't just sick. He was dying.

Nicholai tried to keep his eyes on the easels, the folder in front of him, anything but her.

It proved almost impossible.

She'd opted for a cream-colored dress with, if he wasn't mistaken, an actual petticoat beneath that made the wide skirt flare out. The dress, he realized with a small smile, was covered in a pattern of vintage airplane blueprints. Her navy blazer and matching belt added the right touch of professionalism to an outfit that was purely Juliette. Creative, whimsical and unique.

Frustrated, he looked down at the brochure, but not before seeing Eviana's pondering gaze and hint of a teasing smile. He inwardly cursed. He hadn't gone into detail about what had happened between him and Madeline in Paris, other than to admit that he found Madeline intriguing. But a sister as perceptive and nosy as Eviana hadn't needed much to piece together that something significant had happened.

"We are ready."

Nausea settled in the pit of his stomach. Once his father's

voice had boomed out to the thousands of people in Kelna, addressing crowds at festivals, holiday celebrations and other royal events. Now those tasks had fallen to Nicholai, along with numerous others, as his father's illness took its toll on his lungs, his energy, everything that had made Ivan great.

A leader does not let personal matters take them away from their duty to the people.

His father's oft-spoken words centered him. He raised his head and found Madeline watching him. Sadness tinged her gaze as her eyes flickered to Ivan, then down at her clasped hands. Her throat moved as she swallowed hard.

She knows.

Instead of stirring concern or even anger, the realization provided comfort. When she raised her head again, she didn't look at him with pity or concern or doubt. Her gaze radiated compassion and an understanding rooted in the shared sense of losing someone one loved.

Ivan slowly eased down into a chair. Nicholai and Eviana followed suit. J.T., Andrew and Julie all took chairs closer to the front of the table. Madeline and Chris stood in the center in front of the covered easels. Chris leaned down and said something to Madeline that brought a smile to her face.

Nicholai's chest tightened. Four weeks. Four weeks Madeline and Chris had been working together. Chris seemed far more interested in Madeline than she did him. A fact that brought little relief when he remembered that when this project was over, Madeline would return to Kansas City and live out the rest of her life thousands of miles away.

While he would stay here and serve as king.

"Please," Ivan said with a smile. "Begin."

Madeline nodded, tucking a stray lock of hair behind her ear. She breathed in deeply, glanced down and then looked back up. Calm softened her expression as she made eye contact with each person in the room.

Bravo, Madeline.

Proud of her, of seeing her in her element, Nicholai sat back and gave her his undivided attention.

Madeline dived into a summary of what she and her team had considered as they put together the designs for the initial proposal. She talked not just with her voice but with her hands, her facial expressions; the passion she'd felt for Kelna when she'd first glimpsed it from the air evident in her animated gestures, her excited tone.

She glossed over the history of the country, rightly assuming the people present knew far more than she did. Although, Nicholai acknowledged, the facts she did cite rolled off her tongue like she'd been studying Kelna for years instead of weeks. She rattled off the architectural styles used throughout the palace.

"Which led us to your request." She turned and placed one hand on the first easel. "To bring the Grand Ballroom into the twenty-first century."

The room fell silent as Madeline lifted the cover off the first easel. The schematic drawing mirrored the first page in their folder. Circular in nature, the drawings noted walls made almost entirely of glass.

"The third and fourth pages in your folder are artistic renderings of what we imagined for the ballroom. Our design blends with the rest of the palace while bringing it into the twenty-first century," Madeline continued as she moved to the second easel. "It honors the past and everything that brought your country to this moment of change."

She lifted the cover. This drawing turned the flat two-dimensional design into a jaw-dropping reality. Marble steps swept up to the main entrance of the ballroom. Recessed lighting on the stairs made the limestone glow. At the top, two double doors set into a vaulted archway welcomed visitors. The walls were fashioned of glass and curved into a rounded shape, with marble pillars every dozen feet to hold up an elegant domed roof built of material in the same shade of red as the roofs of Lepa Plavi.

Conflicting emotions tightened Nicholai's chest. He liked the traditional elements, the use of the pillars and arches.

So much glass... Madeline's drawings were stunning, no doubt about it. Part of him understood the appeal. The current ballroom would be gutted, the new ballroom expanded out onto a green space with stunning views. The glass would give nearly a three-hundred-and-sixty-degree perspective on some of Kelna's most incredible scenery.

But it would also be a huge change. The most modern exterior update the palace had ever received.

Nicholai liked to think of himself as a forward-thinking man. One who had accepted the country's need to modernize.

It was also coming fast. Too fast.

The last cover came off, revealing the imagined interior. A grand chandelier hung from the top of the dome. More recessed lighting built into the simple but elegant white molding above the glass made the interior of the dome glow. The walls were finished in the palest of golds, a color that shone under both the light from above and the sunlight streaming in through the large windows.

"It's stunning."

Nicholai glanced at his sister. She was gazing at the designs with a rapturous expression. Resentment crept over him, surprising and unwelcome but present nonetheless. Eviana fulfilled her role in multiple ways, including serving as the patron of numerous charities and sitting on committees for education, the new hospital and tourism.

But ever since they were children, their roles had been clear. Nicholai would one day inherit the throne and rule with a queen by his side. Eviana would support, but never lead. Kelna had had ruling queens before. The line of succession, however, had always favored the firstborn, with the primary responsibilities falling to the heir and their spouse.

It hadn't been something Nicholai had ever questioned. But as Kelna grew, Ivan stepped back from more of his royal duties, simply because he couldn't physically handle them anymore. Nicholai couldn't stop the occasional feeling of being stranded out in the middle of the ocean on a ship bravely charging through the waves, even as they rose higher and higher, lapping at the deck and threatening to pull it under at a moment's notice.

He blinked and looked away. It wasn't Eviana's fault. She was doing what she had been raised to do, as was he. She loved their father just as much and was taking his failing health hard. She had little memory of their mother, who had passed when Eviana was only two years old from an infection that had moved quickly and savagely.

Losing Ivan would be the first major loss she would remember. Begrudging her for the order of her birth and the easier load of duties she carried was selfish at best.

"Thank you," Madeline said with a deferential bow of her head in Eviana's direction. She motioned to the navy folders on the table in front of them, marked by Forge's logo. "Inside, you'll find everything you see here, which includes the layouts of the ballroom and how it will align with the existing palace."

"Normally the artistic designs are not included in the first presentation," J.T. added. "But we're fortunate to have someone with Madeline's twin talents of precision and creativity."

Madeline smiled slightly at her mentor. Something heavy settled in Nicholai's chest. Madeline wasn't just great at her job. She loved it. He'd asked himself more than once in their time apart if there was some way around their circumstances. A possibility for them to get to know each other.

But there was no point. He belonged in Kelna. Asking her to give up her career, her life back in America, would be like asking him to give up the crown.

"Thank you, Miss Delvine." Ivan nodded to the folder open

before him. "A moment for my children and me to review, please."

"Of course."

Silence fell, permeated only by the whisper of paper as the royals flipped through the carefully prepared materials. The team at Forge had been thorough. Nicholai knew he had pushed them on the deadline. But the palace was paying for the expedited process. If it meant Ivan would see the finished ballroom, hopefully for celebrating a royal wedding, then it was worth every penny.

But unless his father, who favored the tradition and history of the palace, agreed with Eviana, they would be asking for Forge to revise their proposal and opt for something more in line with the rest of the palace's aesthetic.

Ivan sat back and steepled his fingers in front of him as he regarded Madeline with a thoughtful gaze.

"I agree with my daughter."

Nicholai's head snapped around.

"Thank you, Your Highness... Majesty."

Pink tinged Madeline's cheeks at her faux pas. Ivan waved it away with a quick flick of his hand.

"Do not trouble yourself over titles here, Miss Delvine. The designs are wonderful."

All heads turned to Nicholai.

"It is very well done."

Madeline's expression tightened for a brief moment before she forced a slight smile to her face.

"But you have concerns?"

He hesitated. He didn't want to hurt her. But, he reminded himself, she was a professional. She deserved the truth.

"The modernity. It wasn't what I pictured."

"What would you change?"

He drummed his fingers on the tabletop, not wanting to share the tangled web of emotions behind his reticence.

"I don't know." He shot her a smile. "If my father and sister approve, any minor concerns of mine don't mean anything."

Madeline frowned. "But they do. This is your home. If something needs to be changed—"

"Nothing needs to be changed." Suddenly frustrated with himself for his irrational feelings about a damned building, and about Madeline's pressing for his opinion, he responded to her tight smile with one of his own. "It has my seal of approval. *Otac?*"

Ivan nodded, his eyes cautious as he glanced between Nicholai and Madeline.

"Good. Eviana?"

Self-contempt dug deep into his skin, little barbs that pricked his pride and his sense of honor, as the excited light in his sister's eyes dimmed, replaced by concern.

"I do like it. But I agree with Madeline. If you—"

"Then it's settled." Nicholai nodded to Madeline, Chris and the rest of the team. "If you could put everything into a report for the Citizens' Committee, we'll forward it to them for review."

He was about to make his exit when Ivan stopped him with a raised hand.

"The ball."

His jaw tightened. "Of course. Would you like to extend the formal invitation, Eviana? It was your idea."

"Yes." Eviana recovered enough to smile at the team. "We're hosting a ball this Saturday. It's a national holiday and we've invited a number of public service employees, palace staff and some international guests. The Citizens' Committee meets the Friday before and will have an answer before the ball. If they're approved, we'd love to unveil the designs and have you there as our guests."

"And even if they aren't approved, we would still be honored to have you," Ivan added with a comforting smile.

Nicholai looked away. His father had always excelled at

building relationships, at making people feel seen and heard. From what little he could remember of his mother, she had been the same. He enjoyed talking with people, yes, and knew he was an adequate speaker. Some had even compared him to his father, words he had taken as a compliment for years but now sounded ghoulish in the light of his father's illness. Unfortunately, engaging with the public often fell by the wayside as he focused his time and attention onto his ever-growing to-do list.

"I've never been to a royal ball." J.T. grinned. "Ivan, I hope you have a suit I can borrow."

"Eviana is familiar with several shops in Lepa Plavi that would be happy to supply you with evening wear." Nicholai glanced at his sister, who nodded. "And of course, you're welcome to stay at the palace."

The others quickly agreed. Madeline was the last to respond, and then only with a tiny smile and a soft "thank you." Their eyes met for one heart-pounding second. And then she looked away as she began to collect the designs.

He contemplated staying, waiting for a moment to talk to her and explain why he had hesitated. To reassure her that it was nothing to do with her work and everything to do with the inner turmoil he fought as he faced inheriting his father's throne.

He stood, hesitated. Then, with a nod and quick quirk of his lips that passed for a smile, walked out the door. Sharing with her would mean acknowledging the pull he felt toward her, the desire to be in her company. Feelings he had no business pursuing when his future was tied to his country and his crown.

CHAPTER SIX

MADELINE SMOOTHED THE skirts of her dress as she hesitated next to a potted plant. The murmur of hundreds of voices rose and fell in the ballroom, backlit by the strains of a professional orchestra. People moved about, talking and sipping champagne, completely at ease in the gaudy surroundings. Even the garish colors and over-the-top paintings had been softened by the glow of candlelight.

The ball had kicked off half an hour ago. Madeline had spent far too much time debating whether the off-the-shoulder scarlet gown she'd picked out from the nearly half dozen dresses Eviana had sent to her room was suitable. She'd barely made it down in time to hear King Ivan welcome his guests. The whispers that had circled around the ballroom like wildfire had been hard to ignore.

"He's so thin."

"Oh, no. I knew he was ill, but it's worse than I thought."

"Nicholai will be King before the year is out. I'm sure of it."

Her heart had broken for Nicholai, who had taken the stage shortly after his father. She'd seen men in tuxedos before. Alex had worn one to a black-tie gala at the National World War I Museum in Kansas City. But where Alex had tugged at his bow tie all evening and grumbled under his breath, Nicholai wore his with confidence. Coupled with his engaging smile and warm tone, it wasn't hard to picture him taking over the reins from his father and leading the country.

When he had officially announced the beginning of the ball, the room had erupted into applause.

Madeline's smile had disappeared as more than one elegantly clad woman had approached Nicholai. Some had murmured a quick word and shaken his hand or dipped into a curtsy. But several lingered, one being bold enough to lay her hand on his arm in a gesture of intimacy that made Madeline feel sick to her stomach.

"Are you hiding?"

Madeline started as Julie appeared beside her.

"More observing. I've never been to something like this."

"Me either." Julie grinned. "I'm starting with the food. My house is almost strictly pizza, macaroni and cheese, and grilled cheese sandwiches."

Madeline followed her to the buffet at the back, the tables draped in snow-white tablecloths and laden with food. Delicacies like marinated scampi, truffles and *fritule*, battered doughnut balls dusted with lemon zest and infused with rum, were artfully arranged on silver platters next to a glass tower, each layer covered in chocolates and bites of cheesecake drizzled in raspberry sauce. By the time Julie and Madeline had made it back to their table, their plates were loaded with nearly one of everything. Chris and Andrew had joined them. The camaraderie distracted Madeline enough for her to enjoy her food.

Nicholai walked onto the dance floor to formally open the ball with Eviana at his side. Whispered speculations flying around the room about the King not dancing with Eviana died as the two siblings laughed and smiled through the waltz.

Madeline smiled. She liked how close the royals were. The King exuded a quiet sense of power and a touch of reserve that was almost imperceptible. But she had yet to see him without kindness in his eyes or friendliness in his smile.

Eviana carried the same reserve as her father. Glimpses of a bubblier, sweet woman had come through. But those moments were fleeting, like she wasn't quite sure who to fully trust with seeing the true depth of her character.

And then there was Nicholai. A man who had yet to falter in public, but who struggled in private with the massive changes taking place in the Kingdom. A man who loved his father and, she suspected, worked hard to keep his grief private as he prepared to lead.

She'd been disappointed at his response to the designs. Yet she'd sensed something else lurking beneath the surface, a suspicion confirmed by his strong reaction to her prompting him.

It had hurt to see him walk away. But she'd reminded herself, in the long run it didn't matter. The designs had been approved, both by the royal family and by the Citizens' Committee. Part of the King's welcome had included the announcement of the new ballroom and directing guests to view the mock-ups on prominent display by the main door.

A night of triumph. She needed to buck up and enjoy the moment instead of ruminating over someone else's opinion.

The music wound down. Nicholai and Eviana separated. Nicholai bowed as his sister dropped into a graceful curtsy. Thunderous applause broke out as the crowd stood. Nicholai accepted a microphone from a palace aide.

"Let the celebrations begin!"

People moved onto the dance floor. An older man with a thick gray beard and a stunning blonde approached Nicholai. Clad in a black gown that followed her tall, slender figure, the woman curtsied as if she'd been doing so her whole life. The bearded man said something and Nicholai smiled down at the woman.

Madeline's heart twisted. Frustrated with herself, she pushed back her chair.

"Maddie?" Chris shot her a smile. "Want to dance?"

She wavered. As she'd watched Nicholai and Eviana move through the dance with graceful movements, she'd imagined what it would be like to dance like that. Not just dance, but dance at an actual royal ball wearing an incredible gown gifted to her by a real-life princess.

"Go on." Andrew nudged her. "I'll dance with Julie if you dance with Chris."

"Now you have to!" Julie said as she hopped up. "Don't leave me hanging."

Madeline laughed. "Peer pressure wins again."

Chris took her hand and led her to the dance floor, Julie and Andrew trailing behind them. Out of the corner of her eye, Madeline saw Nicholai take the blonde in his arms and begin to dance. Her stomach knotted. She turned away and focused on the man in front of her. The one who hadn't told her there could never be anything between him. The one she wished she could feel something for besides friendship.

Chris settled a hand at her waist and smiled down at her. "Ready?"

"To trip over my own feet? Yes."

He tugged her a fraction closer. She didn't resist. He surprised her by confidently guiding her into a turn before pulling her back to his chest. She let out a surprised laugh.

"Where did you learn to dance?"

"I took a ballroom dancing class in college."

"Ballroom dancing? In college?"

"Also took scuba diving, an introduction to painting and beginner's French."

"An eclectic mix."

"And a great way to meet women."

She laughed again. The easy conversation, coupled with dancing with someone who knew what they were doing, the light glowing from the chandeliers above, all of it swept away her earlier agitation. Determined to enjoy herself, she agreed to another dance with Chris, followed by a dance with Andrew and even one with J.T.

When she glanced at the towering grandfather clock behind the buffet, she realized over an hour had passed.

"I need champagne," Julie said with a laugh as she joined Madeline back at their table.

"I need water."

"Yes." Julie glanced over her shoulder. "I saw you and Chris dancing together."

"He's a good dancer."

"Any potential there?"

Madeline shrugged. "Chris is a good friend. But I'm not looking to date anyone right now."

Julie's face sobered. "Sorry. I shouldn't have pried."

"It's okay. I think Chris would like for there to be more, but after Alex, I just need time by myself."

"Wise." Julie plucked two champagne glasses off a passing tray. "I'm someone who didn't find her Prince Charming until the second wedding because I rushed into my first marriage after a bad breakup. Having some time to yourself is very smart."

"Thank you."

Madeline clinked her glass against Julie's and took a small sip.

"I think I could use some fresh air."

"Another smart idea." Julie glanced back at the ballroom. "I'm going to take advantage of not having to wake up with my kids in the morning and dance a little more."

"Go on. I'll join you in a bit."

Madeline drifted along the edges of the ballroom, her eyes roaming over the glamorously dressed people, the synchronized movements of the orchestra as she listened to the rise and fall of conversation in over a dozen languages. It was as close to perfect as a moment could get. Her nerves tangled with excitement and satisfaction. She was in a brand-new country with coworkers who felt more like family, and the biggest project she had worked on to date had been accepted by a literal king, prince and princess.

Life was good.

As she neared the glass doors leading out into the garden, she glanced over her shoulder and nearly stumbled over the hem of her dress. Nicholai was back on the dance floor, this time with one arm wrapped intimately around the waist of a voluptuous brunette he appeared to know very well. He was smiling down at her as she spoke, his attention focused solely on the woman in his arms. One hand came up and rested on his lapel as she leaned up and whispered something in his ear that made him throw back his head and laugh.

The sudden, crushing disappointment floored her. Yes, she was attracted to Nicholai, had thoroughly enjoyed their kiss in Paris. Getting to know him a little bit on a personal level, to learn more about the man behind the crown, had made her like him even more.

But she had written off her interest as something that would pass with time. Never had she entertained the possibility that seeing him with someone else would matter. Let alone two someones. He hadn't struck her as a playboy.

Yeah, because you're so good at judging men.

For the first time in her life, she felt a crack in her heart, one that hinted her feelings went far deeper. She'd never experienced anything like this with Alex. The strength of her emotions, coupled with how rapidly they'd developed, frightened her.

Nicholai and his partner spun. His head came up. His gaze locked on Madeline's. She inhaled sharply, then picked up her skirt and hurried out the door. There were a few people milling about the terrace and a young couple walking up the short flight of stairs from the garden. Lanterns flickered along the stone balustrade. A full moon glowed bright over the palace and dusted the waves of the Adriatic with a sheen of silver.

"Champagne?"

Madeline nodded to the waiter and accepted a flute off the tray. Having something to hold in her hands steadied her. She moved down the stairs, taking a sip as she crossed the grass toward the rose garden. Music drifted out from the open doors of the ballroom, but the farther she walked, the more it served as a background, the lyrical strains adding a touch of magic to her surroundings.

She walked beneath an arch of white roses that glowed in the moonlight, breathing in the deep, heady scent of rose petals and a faintly sweet smell coming from plants dripping with lavender blooms shaped like little bells. The garden, she realized with a small degree of delight, was comprised of a series of circles. The circles themselves were cobblestone paths. In between the circles were carefully tended beds of roses. The entire garden was contained by a series of stone arches that matched the stonework she had seen in Lepa Plavi. At the center of the garden stood a magnificent, tiered fountain.

She moved from circle to circle, stopping here and there to inhale the various fragrances. When she finally made her way to the center, she stopped, staring at the play of water as it fell.

A flash of white beyond the fountain caught her eye. Curious, she circled the water feature and found another path, one fashioned of pale stone that wound and twisted through a thick grove of evergreen trees.

Then she emerged from the trees into the closest thing to Heaven she'd ever seen.

A white terrace had been built on a cliff overlooking the sea, the intricate stonework surrounded by a balustrade with thick columns that reminded her of ancient Rome. The moon made the terrace shine as if it were lit from within.

She moved to the edge, let one hand rest on the cool stone as she watched the waves rise and fall a hundred feet below. A sigh escaped her lips as her thoughts turned back to the Prince dancing in the ballroom with a woman who looked very at ease in his arms. She would have to deal with whatever emotions Nicholai had stirred in her, and soon, so that it didn't affect her work. She'd been fortunate that it hadn't been a problem so far.

She also needed to do it for her own sake. As much as she loved her stories of romance, there was no such thing as love at first sight. And even if there were, she had no interest in falling for a man who lived half a world away.

The footsteps behind her had her whirling about. Champagne sloshed over the rim of her glass and spilled onto her hand.

Nicholai stood just a few feet behind her, his hands held up in a gesture of surrender.

"You have got to stop sneaking up on me," she gasped.

"Well, if you would stop sneaking out to odd places, maybe I wouldn't have to follow you."

She narrowed her eyes at him. "Seriously?"

He grimaced. "Bad joke."

"Very."

They stared at each other for a long moment. A sudden urge to laugh crept up Madeline's throat. She tried to hold it back, but ended up letting out a very unladylike snort before she gave in and laughed.

Nicholai arched a brow even as one corner of his mouth twitched.

"What?"

"I almost bashed you over the head with a champagne glass. First a wine bottle, and then a champagne flute."

"If I didn't know any better, I would think you a very poor assassin. Or at least an attempted one."

Madeline contemplated the remaining bit of champagne in her glass. "If it makes you feel any better, I'd rather not waste it on your head."

"Comforting," he replied dryly.

She held up the glass in a toast to him. Suddenly shy, she took another sip to give herself something else to focus on.

"What is this place?"

Nicholai glanced around. "I'd actually forgotten about it. I think my great-great-grandmother had this commissioned in the late nineteenth century."

"It's beautiful."

"It is."

She leaned against the banister. "Do you come out here often?"

"Do you mean why did I follow you out here?" At her nod, he approached to stand next to her at the banister. "I saw you come out. You looked upset when you left the ballroom."

Embarrassed, she looked back over the sea. "Just a little overwhelmed, I think. There's a lot going on."

She felt him move closer. Her breathing grew heavy as she felt his presence at her back.

"Did Chris upset you?"

Startled, she looked at him. "No. Why would you ask that?"

The thunderous expression on his face took her by surprise.

"I saw how much the two of you were dancing together. Didn't know if you had had a lovers' spat."

"Chris and I are not, and never will be, lovers."

"Does he know that?"

Guilt surfaced and dug its claws deep into her skin. "I haven't explicitly said no. I need to."

"Yes, you do. Because I see the way he looks at you."

"Oh, really? Is it the same way the curvy brunette you were just dancing with looks at you?"

Nicholai's brows drew together. "Amara?"

"Sure. The gorgeous woman you were dancing with, who could be a brunette version of Marilyn Monroe."

"You noticed."

"How could one not notice? She's beautiful and sexy and—"

"Would you like me to introduce you?"

Madeline contemplated if sticking out her tongue would be too childish.

"Amara is a friend."

"Nicholai," she said softly, "you don't have to explain anything to me. I know we didn't get a chance to have a full discussion about what happened between us in Paris, but it was one hour. One kiss. After this project is over, I go back to Kansas City, and you stay here to be an actual king." She smiled at him in what she hoped was a reassuring manner that didn't reveal the ache growing inside her at the thought of never seeing him again. "You don't owe me anything."

"Well spoken, Miss Delvine."

Put out by his casual acceptance, she inclined her head to him.

"Thank you. Now, I think I'll rejoin—"

"Except there's one problem." Nicholai stepped in front of her. "I haven't been able to stop thinking of you since Paris."

Madeline nearly dropped her glass. "What?"

"I know that nothing can happen between us, nothing permanent. I have my life here—you have your life back in America." His hand came up, hesitated in the air between them, then settled on her face with such tenderness it made her eyes grow hot. "I think about that hour I spent with you on the rooftop in Paris. It was the first time in a very long time that I was able to be…" His voice trailed off.

"Just Nick," she prompted softly.

"Just Nick," he echoed. "To forget about the responsibilities, the committees, the economic forums, all the change happening in my life. And when I saw you dancing with Chris, I wanted to cross the ballroom and rip him away from you. I'm not a violent man, Madeline. But seeing him touch you…" His voice trailed off as he stared deep into her eyes. "I could barely stand it."

Madeline's breath froze in her chest. One wrong step and she would fall, fall further than she ever had with Alex.

And yet, whispered a tempting little voice, *what if you fly*?

Slowly, she set down her champagne glass, then held out her hand.

"May I have this dance?"

Nicholai's mouth curved into a reluctant smile. "I'm supposed to ask you."

"So ask."

He captured her hand in his, brought it up to his lips and grazed a kiss over her knuckles. She swallowed hard.

"Miss Delvine, would you do me the honor of sharing a dance with me?"

"I'd love to." The faintest notes of music drifted across the lawn, over the roses and through the trees to the cliff. Chris had been a fun dance partner, but Nicholai was a master, sweeping her into elegant turns as he kept one hand firmly at her waist and the other wrapped around her fingers, leading her in a dance she had only seen in movies. Had she thought earlier in the ballroom that life had been perfect? Because it paled in comparison to this moment.

Nicholai held her close, the intimacy of his hand at her waist thrilling her senses and making her feel like the most beautiful woman in the world.

Too soon, the music wound down. They drifted to a stop next to the banister, the distant roar of the waves crashing on the beach below eclipsing the dwindling music. She wanted to keep going, to pretend that real life was not waiting on the other side of the evergreens.

And knew that to pretend anything different would only be delaying the inevitable.

She stepped back, dipped into a curtsy.

"Thank you. Your Highness."

Nicholai's face tightened.

"You know as well as I do," she said quietly even as her heart twisted in her chest, "this can't go anywhere."

Nicholai hesitated, his lips parting as if to say something in protest, before they thinned back into a line.

Her heart felt like it was breaking, but if she could spare him some of the pain she was experiencing, she wanted to. She'd seen the hurt in his eyes when he looked at his father, the uncertainty as he gazed out over an evolving Kingdom from the window of a plane. His life was here. Hers was not.

She started to walk around him, to rejoin the ball. Nicholai's hand shot out, wrapped around her arm, and before she could say a word, he pulled her against him and claimed her lips with his own.

She kissed him back, throwing her arms around his neck and pouring every emotion she had been fighting for the past month into their kiss.

He pulled her close, his mouth moving over hers with passion and a hint of desperation, as if he knew this would be the final time.

He pulled back. She didn't stop him, letting her arms fall to her sides. Slowly, she raised her eyes to his.

"It's a shame, isn't it?" she finally said.

When he didn't respond, she turned and walked away, the crack in her heart deepening with every step.

CHAPTER SEVEN

NICHOLAI AWOKE TO a frantic pounding on his door. Groaning, he rolled over and glanced at the clock. It wasn't even 7:00 a.m. He pulled a pillow over his face, hoping whoever had dared to intrude this early after a ball that had kept him up past midnight would just go away.

The knocking intensified.

Exhausted and irritated, Nicholai flung back the covers and got out of bed. He pulled on his robe with swift movements before he stalked to the door.

"What—?"

"Oh, no." Eviana barreled into his room and slammed the door shut behind her. "I'm the only one who gets to ask questions this morning." She held up a newspaper. "The first of which is, what were you thinking?"

Frowning, he grabbed the newspaper. Dread crept over him and squeezed his chest with an iron grip as he realized what he was looking at.

The pictures splashed across the front page of the Kelnian national newspaper were almost as bad as the headline: "Is Kelna's Future King a Playboy?"

One picture featured him and the tall, blonde British Duchess Dario had introduced him to for the second dance. Another had caught him and Amara in the middle of a waltz. The photographer had managed to capture the perfect angle that showed off the sweetheart neckline of Amara's bodice and her rounded curves. The third...

Nicholai's fingers tightened on the paper. The third picture was of him and Madeline kissing on the cliffside terrace. Despite the graininess of the picture, it was clearly him.

The article featured detailed biographies of the duchess, Amara and Madeline. The duchess's biography included a summary of her wealth and lauded family background. Then it jumped into speculations on his and Amara's decade of friendship and rumors from supposed sources that there had always been "something more" between them.

But the one that made his blood boil were the gleeful sentences dedicated to Madeline's first trip to Kelna the month before. The reporter had gone so far as to rehash her childhood in Kansas City and include a mention about an ex-fiancé named Alex, a prominent lawyer back in Missouri.

The last paragraph about her broken engagement made his stomach twist. She'd said nothing about being engaged before.

But then again, when had they had time to discuss much of anything? Really, what did he know about her?

His eyes strayed back to the photo of him and Madeline locked in a passionate embrace. She stirred feelings he'd never experienced before. Not just attraction and warmth, but jealousy. The burning in his chest when he'd seen her dancing with Chris, the bitterness that had swept through him when she'd laughed up at the other man had bothered him. Was this infatuation? Obsession?

And now…now he was faced with the consequences of not being able to keep himself under control. Of letting his emotions over his father's illness, the numerous changes taking place in Kelna and his own doubts about taking the throne sway him from duty.

The desire to crumple the paper into a ball and hurl it in the trash nearly overcame his resolve. He set the paper down on his bed and moved to the window.

"Well?"

"Well, what?"

Eviana appeared next to him. "What are you going to do?"

"Talk with Father first. Then public affairs. Find out the best way to handle this."

"What about Madeline? Don't you think you should talk to her, too?"

"Eventually yes. But this is a palace affair."

Even as he said it, discomfort moved through his chest. If she wasn't already, Madeline would become the focus of intense scrutiny in the coming days. She had made her desire to steer clear of any royal entanglements clear. She had a life, a career, family back home. Any woman he dated now would automatically be seen as a potential contender for the title of queen. The reminder soured his mood, fanned the flames of a growing anger. He had dated in his twenties, yes. A couple of casual relationships, and one lengthier relationship with an Italian countess that he thought might lead to the altar. But they had all ended, most due to the capriciousness of youth, a couple when one or both of them had realized that they were simply not right for each other.

But now he felt the pressure to be seen as dependable, stable. That meant a prince with a princess by his side, one who would help lead the country. At one point he had thought he'd had all the time in the world to find a woman, fall in love and propose because it was something they both wanted. Yet as the media scrutiny grew, the women he was introduced to seemed more focused on his crown than on him.

Although, he thought as a dull throbbing started to pulse in his temples, he was no better. Letting Dario put together a list of suitable candidates and reviewing their backgrounds as if he were interviewing someone for a job instead of spending the rest of their life with him.

Which made his situation with Madeline all the more painful. That night in Paris, when she had not known who he was, had been one of the best nights of his life in recent memory. Her being a dynamic, intelligent woman with a happy personality that invited one to enjoy life as much as she did made his future look all the more bleak by comparison.

"It will affect her, too."

Nicholai narrowed his eyes at his sister.

"Did I miss you and Madeline becoming best friends? You just met her."

"I like her." She planted her hands on her hips in a gesture that reminded him of when she had been four and thrown a royal tantrum in the reception room after their father had announced that he would be gone for two weeks at a summit in Spain. "Even if I didn't, it's the right thing to do. Especially with how you feel about each other."

"You don't know what you're talking about."

Instead of backing down from the icy censure in his voice, Eviana drew herself up to her full height. Even being nearly a foot shorter than he was, she still made an impressive figure as she poked him square in the chest.

"I know what I saw, Nicholai. However you two decide to handle it is up to you. If you both want to pretend like there's nothing going on, even though anyone with eyes can see that you two obviously care about each other, then that's your affair." She picked up the newspaper, dangled it from her fingers with a smirk. "Or rather anyone with a subscription to the *Kelna National News*."

Nicholai picked up a pillow from the nearby sofa and launched it at his sister's head. She ducked and scampered for the door.

"Talk to Madeline first."

"You don't know what you're talking about, Eviana. You don't have to worry about things like this."

"Only because you won't let me help."

Confused, he stared at her. "What are you talking about?"

"Nothing." She shook her head. "Wrong time, wrong place. Please, consider talking to her first."

"I can't, Eviana. The situation has to be contained."

"Does 'contained' mean she won't be able to work on the ballroom?"

He scrubbed a hand over his face. *Probably.* It wouldn't be appropriate to have the woman he'd been caught kissing working on the ballroom while he searched for a wife.

"Most likely not. It wouldn't be in the best interests of the palace or the country."

"Spoken like a politician." The disappointed expression on his sister's face cut him deep. "Looks like you're ready to be king after all."

With that parting shot, she moved out of the room. The door shut behind her with a click, the sound echoing in Nicholai's head as he turned back to stare out over the sea.

The need for his father's guidance tugged at him, urged him to seek out the King and talk with him.

But the man who had been thrust to the edge of inheriting the Kingdom, who would have to make decisions on his own far sooner than he had expected, resisted. He was a grown man. A man who would lead over half a million people and have to make split-second decisions that affected their lives and the lives of future generations. A notion his own father had impressed upon him from the time he'd been a teenager.

"We won't always make the right decisions, son. But we have to make the best ones we know in the moment, not just for this generation, but for future generations to come."

Nicholai scrubbed a hand over his face, then wrapped his fingers around his jaw. One of his first major crises, and it all came down to not being able to keep his hands off a feisty American architect.

A knock sounded on his door.

"Go away, Eviana."

The door creaked open. Nicholai spun around.

"I said…"

His voice trailed off. Madeline stood in the door, wearing a white robe over a T-shirt and pajama shorts. Her hair hung in blond, tussled waves about her face. The lack of makeup enhanced her youth, drove his sense of guilt even deeper.

"Madeline."

She closed the door behind her.

"We need to talk."

Madeline's heart sank as Nicholai stared at her with an unreadable expression on his face. He watched her for a moment before he turned away and began to pace.

She'd woken up to a barrage of text messages and missed phone calls. Screenshots of her kiss with Nicholai were now flashed across the worldwide media. Embarrassment had ruled as she'd flipped through everything from congratulations to a mortifying message from her mother asking what she had gotten into.

But as her initial panic had subsided, her mind had turned to Nicholai. The drama she faced right now wouldn't impact her future much. Yes, she didn't relish her name popping up in articles years from now if she ever decided to work for another firm.

But despite the mention of her broken engagement, the writer had painted her in a neutral light, focusing primarily on her career and how she had come to be at the ball in Kelna. It was Nicholai who had been vilified with a list of women he'd been spotted with in the past year as well as a rather flowery description of his dance with Amara. He'd been painted the aggressor, a playboy indulging in his position.

"I don't have the time to discuss this right now, Madeline."

Frustration surged through her. "Then when is the right time to discuss this?"

"Later."

"No." She moved closer. "This affects both of us."

"I'm aware."

She reached out, grabbed onto the back of a chair with both hands and squeezed tight. "What can I do?"

Nicholai pinched the bridge of his nose, and let out a harsh breath. "The best thing you could possibly do right now is go back to your room and stay there until I've talked with the public relations department."

"Hide?"

He whirled then, tension vibrating from his frame. "Yes, hide. This is my world, not yours. You don't know what could happen in the next hour, two hours, twenty-four hours. My leadership has already been called into question by that blasted article. The people who have invested in Kelna's advancement will, at the very least, have questions. The kind of questions that carry underlying threats, such as if the stability of Kelna is not guaranteed, neither is their money."

The full weight of how a simple kiss could affect hundreds of thousands of people hit Madeline with the force of a freight train.

"Nicholai... I'm sorry."

"Don't apologize. It only makes it worse. I saw you go out. I followed you. I put you in this position. I put the country in this position." He stopped pacing and turned, his face thunderous. "Go back to your room, Madeline. Someone from Public Affairs will be by soon." He sighed. "I'll have to speak to your team at some point today, too."

Alarm skittered through her. "My team? Why?"

"I don't like contemplating this, but..." His voice trailed off as he closed his eyes. When he opened them, he looked at her with a regret that turned her alarm into full-on panic. "I don't think Forge Architecture continuing to work on the ballroom will be a good fit. Not with this press."

Shock rendered her speechless as shame kept her feet glued to the floor. The biggest job J.T. had ever landed. She'd put that all at risk. Yes, Nicholai had followed her, initiated their kiss. But she'd asked him to dance. She'd kissed him back. She'd been a more than willing participant to it all.

Her mind scrambled, trying to grasp onto something, anything she could do.

"There has to be something that can make this better."

"If you can somehow convince the world I'm not a playboy who toys with women's emotions, then yes, by all means, do something."

"What would reassure the investors? Anyone who might doubt your ability to lead?"

"Nothing." Nicholai closed his eyes, breathed in and then out before opening them again, his brown eyes dark with pain. "Nothing except being engaged or married. A clear sign that I am not, in fact, a playboy."

The mad idea entered her head. She batted it away. No. It was too ridiculous.

But it was a stubborn idea, one that slipped in and coaxed her, inch by inch, to say it out loud.

"What if I pretended to be your fiancée?"

CHAPTER EIGHT

WHAT?

Nicholai stared at Madeline. Surely, he had heard her wrong.

"Excuse me?"

She looked as though she'd swallowed something sour, her lips pinching together as pink bloomed in her cheeks. But then she squared her shoulders and raised her chin.

"What if we pretended to be engaged?"

"This isn't a romance novel, Madeline. This is real life with real people's livelihoods and an entire country at stake."

Her eyes narrowed. He stifled a groan. He'd hurt her.

"You said your leadership had been called into question. That the people funding all the development going on might pull out. My problem is on a smaller scale, but my employer and coworkers could lose the largest project they've ever worked on. Wouldn't revealing a secret engagement be less—" her blush deepened as she cleared her throat "—scandalous? Reassure your investors and the rest of the country. And Forge could stay on the project."

The more she talked, the less crazy it sounded. Logical, even.

He would still have to deal with the press coverage surrounding Amara. She was a beautiful woman, but he had never entertained romantic thoughts of her, had barely even seen her over the past two years as she'd pursued her career in England. A quick conversation and statements from both the palace and her representatives would smooth that over. And the Duchess had been mere conjecture. Emphasizing that the prime minister had introduced the two of them would squelch any rumors.

But Madeline... The picture was damning, to say the least. The photographer had caught them at just the right moment, wrapped in each other's arms, her hand on his face.

Yes, that one would be much more difficult to explain away. Never mind, he thought crossly, that he was a man and should have a moment or two out of the spotlight. A moment to kiss a woman he found interesting and engaging and kind, but had no future with.

It seemed life would prefer he not even have those precious seconds of normality.

He looked back at Madeline. She looked so young, so innocent, standing there with rumpled hair and a worried wrinkle between her brows. She had made it clear that her home was in Kansas City, that her career was important to her.

There was no future for them. And he couldn't bring himself to enter into an engagement, even a fake one, knowing that it would end.

"I appreciate your offer, Madeline. It's very generous. But there has to be a better way."

A blankness swept across her face, erasing all hint of emotion.

"Of course." She dipped her head. "I'll be in my room if you need me."

And then she was gone.

With a groan, he sank down onto the edge of his bed.

"...there has to be a better way."

He certainly could have phrased that differently.

Another knock sounded on his door.

"Come in," he called wearily.

The door swung open and King Ivan walked in. Nicholai rushed forward.

"Otac, what are you doing up?"

"I'm sick, *sin*, not dead."

Ivan's fingers clutched the knobby head of his cane as he moved into the room and chose a chair close to the door. He sank into it, his breathing labored.

Nicholai's hands tightened into fists at his sides. He wanted to turn away, knew without a doubt that his actions last night and the resulting media frenzy this morning had heaped stress on his father's already overburdened shoulders.

But he stood his ground, prepared to face whatever punishment his father thought best.

"How are you this morning?" Ivan asked in a raspy voice as he settled in amongst the cushions.

One eyebrow shot up. "If I said 'well,' would you believe me?"

Ivan chuckled. "Not in the slightest." His face sobered, his pale eyes far kinder than they should have been, given the circumstances. "*Sin*, you made a mistake."

"I did." Nicholai sat down in a chair across from his father and threaded his fingers together. "I have no excuse. I let my emotions and attraction to Madeline get the better of me."

"Nicholai. You are allowed to a kiss a beautiful woman. I was referring more to kissing her in a public place."

He stalked around the room. "But I shouldn't have kissed her at all. Not when I'm supposed to be married...soon."

Ivan's face tightened. Despite the illness that ravaged his body, he still maintained the regality that had set the tone of his reign. A man who loved his people and his country, but also knew when to invoke a stricter, at times harsher, leadership. He did not suffer fools or those who preyed on them.

"Our public relations department tells me the photo was taken with a long-range lens. It was outside the palace grounds and a clear violation of our privacy. Had it not been you, it could have very well been one of our other guests."

"Except it wasn't another guest. It was me. And now my ability to lead has been called into question."

Anger flared, made his muscles tremble with the sudden fierceness of it. His latest struggles with taking over the throne, of replacing his father, suddenly seemed foolish when confronted with the possibility of having to step aside, to forgo the crown that had been in his family for generations. While he didn't think it would require a drastic act like abdicating, he would do it if it meant keeping the patronage of the wealthy organizations pouring money and resources into Kelna.

Ivan sighed. "Things were much simpler when I took the crown. There were photographers, yes, but not like this. You will replace the Forge team?"

Nicholai stood and began to pace. "Most likely, yes. I'll never be able to get rid of the speculation with her nearby."

Ivan nodded, even though his expression was sad. Guilt dug deeper into Nicholai's skin, sharp little barbs he wasn't sure he'd ever be able to rid himself of. The results of his actions grew worse by the minute.

"And Madeline is not a consideration?"

"No. She would not give up her life in America."

"Work can be done from almost anywhere these days."

"True. But Parliament still has to approve my choice of bride. They prefer nobility and prestige over personal preference."

Based on his last conversation with Dario, he was certain of it. Besides, what was the point in pressing the issue anyway? Of creating more stress and change when it wouldn't change Madeline's mind.

"But you don't know if you don't ask—"

"She's made it clear her heart is in Missouri."

Ivan blinked at Nicholai's curt tone. Inwardly cursing, Nicholai held his father's gaze even though he wanted nothing more than to look away.

"This is best for everyone. I promise you," he added at the doubtful expression on his father's face, "I'm doing the right thing."

Ivan sighed, the sound hoarse and raspy. "I trust you, *moj sin*. I simply wish you would extend others the same trust. Not try to conquer everything on your own."

Nicholai frowned. His father's words echoed Eviana's sentiments before she'd walked out. It bothered him that his family thought he didn't trust them.

Before he could reply, Ivan spoke again.

"Your and Madeline's pictures have already reached the United States. They're jumping on the story. Public Affairs has arranged for a press conference at eleven this morning so you can address the nation."

Nicholai nodded. "Done."

"Normally I would advise against a conference and let Public Affairs release a statement. But I've already had calls from Verde Construction and two of the shipping firms in Greece." Ivan's voice firmed, his irritation evident. "They're asking for reassurances that last night was simply bad press and not a pattern."

The knife twisted deeper. *"Otac—"*

"No. I disagree with how they're handling this media attention. You, and our country, have shown them how capable we are over the last year. But we are beholden to them for many things that will impact Kelna. I don't require an explanation, *moj sin*. Just a promise to fix this, to show them you can handle things."

Handle things.

A euphemism for what so many seemed to know, yet no one would talk about. Unless a miracle happened, his father would be dead within a year. He had wanted to lead, yes, to follow his father's and grandfather's legacy. But not like this. Not with his assuming the role because he took the crown from his father's grave.

Ivan started to rise.

"Let me—"

"Please." Ivan held up a wrinkled hand. "Let me do the

small things. Better to struggle than not be able to do them at all."

He finally got to his feet and walked toward the door, the thud of his cane on the floor echoing throughout the room. He turned and gave his son a small smile. "You will be king one day soon, *sin*. I trust you to make the right decision for our people. While we serve them first, I hope you will also consider yourself in this equation, too."

The click of the door closing sounded like a gate slamming shut on a prison cell.

Nicholai turned and moved to his windows with slow, deliberate movements. Inside him, anger and fear raged. Anger at himself, at the blasted photographer, at the heavens for cursing a good man and a good leader with such a terrible illness.

And fear. Fear that he would make the wrong choice. He'd already made one last night—he'd told himself repeatedly as he'd followed Madeline into the gardens that he should let her go.

But he hadn't. Seeing her laugh and dance without him had made him crave her presence as he never had another woman's.

His thoughts turned back to her offer. No matter how he turned the situation over in his mind, he couldn't think of another solution that would immediately quiet the swirling rumors. Even if he refuted the playboy angle most outlets were running with, the news vultures would descend in bigger numbers on any sighting of him with a prospective wife. Whether the women on the prime minister's list would even want to be seen with him right now was another question. Yet the issue of how people perceived him paled in comparison to the very real threat of companies pulling out of Kelna because they doubted his ability to lead.

An issue that could be solved, at least temporarily, by one simple proposal. A proposal he would have to run by the prime minister and reassure him the engagement would be for appearances only until the press coverage died out. Then he and

Madeline could part ways, her with her reputation intact and her firm still on the job, he with the confidence of his country and the investors helping it flourish.

But will you be able to let her go?

He'd given into weakness not once, but twice now where Madeline was concerned. If he agreed to her offer, what was to say he wouldn't make the same mistake a third time? What if he fell for her, truly fell, but still had to let her go?

The sun rose from behind the mountains, glimpses of the orange orb glowing behind sharp peaks still capped with snow. A wind whispered across the pine forests below and made the treetops sway. Beyond the forest lay another town, Drago Selo. He could see the red roofs, imagine the people already up and bustling about the small farming community.

So many people who depended on his family. Who, in a short time, would come to depend on him. Whether he could keep his heart safe meant nothing compared to their well-being and future.

He turned from the window and dialed Dario's number. He had decided.

Madeline plucked at a piece of toast on the tray that had been brought to her room. Eviana had stopped by just after she'd gotten back. Instead of being angry, she'd been incredibly kind, offering to order Madeline breakfast and keep her company. She'd also threatened a variety of creative punishments on the photographer who had taken the lurid photo and managed to tease a reluctant smile from Madeline. The reserve Madeline had observed before had completely disappeared, revealing a sweet young woman beneath who, in another life, Madeline could have been very good friends with.

When the food arrived, Eviana had sensed that Madeline needed time alone. She'd given her a tight hug and a recommendation to not go into a meeting with anyone in the public affairs office unless Eviana was present.

"They mean well," Eviana had said with a wrinkle of her nose, "but they can be overbearing."

The reminder of the damage Madeline had managed to inflict with her thoughtless actions had sent her back into a state of numbness. It was the only way she was managing to make it through the morning without breaking down and crying. The one time she'd tried to settle into the comfort of a plush chair and draw, she'd ended up running the pencil in a circle over and over again until she'd worn the pencil down to a nub.

Her phone had been blowing up with calls and texts from family and friends. Her brothers' and sisters' messages had ranged from curious and excited to one threatening damage to Nicholai's person for daring to drag Madeline into the international spotlight. That last one, from her youngest brother, Cliff, had made her smile despite the gravity of the situation.

Her mother had left a voicemail, the soft voice bringing both comfort and shame.

"Darling, call when you can. I'm worried about you." A lengthy pause. *"Don't let someone take advantage of you. You don't need a man to be happy. You're enough."*

She could only imagine what this was doing to her mother. Madeline's biological father had met her mother at the diner where she had worked in college, convinced her to give up her schooling and marry him. Madeline remembered him being handsome with a charming smile and a quick joke.

Qualities, her mother had told her in later years, which had blinded her to his flighty nature, his inability to hold down a job or provide for the family he said he had wanted. They'd moved five times before Madeline had started school, usually because her father had helped himself to the rent money for some get-rich scheme or to travel somewhere under the guise of picking up work.

But her mother had fought her way out of it, had gotten a divorce and made her own way with Madeline and her sister Greta. She'd told Madeline more than once that she had thought Father was the answer to what had been missing in her life at the time.

"A dangerous way to think, Maddie. Never let someone else be the answer to your happiness."

She blinked back hot tears. At first, when she'd started dating Alex, she'd enjoyed his company. Then, as their relationship had deepened, she'd thought herself in love.

Yet, as the warning signs had started to show, from Alex's intolerance of her work schedule to his irritability over trivial things, she had brushed them aside. She'd wanted the wedding, the marriage, the kids and the house with the yard. She'd wanted a dream so badly she'd nearly let the rest of her life become a nightmare to achieve it.

Slowly, she uncurled her fingers and let the mangled bread fall onto the plate. She didn't know the first thing about being in a relationship, let alone with a prince. Not that Nicholai had asked her to be in a relationship. While they hadn't discussed the explicit details of what his future queen would do, he had agreed with her brief assessment when they'd talked in the alcove on her first visit to Kelna. The future queen would be needed here.

The rehashing did little to assuage her damaged pride. Nicholai's emphatic rejection of her idea had hurt. She hadn't made the offer lightly. But she had felt responsible for her role in the debacle. She'd been the one to invite Nicholai to dance, had most definitely kissed him back. Forge losing the contract of a lifetime because of one moment of indiscretion made her sick. Add in the possibility of Kelna's meteoric rise falling apart because she'd kissed the Kingdom's heir and she felt so heavy she could barely sit upright.

She glanced at her phone again. Thankfully, no one from Forge had reached out yet. Given that the sun had barely been up for an hour, they probably wouldn't learn of her mistake for some time yet.

And getting fired because of me.

Miserable, she moved over to the bed and flopped down, curling around her pillow and hugging it tight. The underlying thought that had been circulating since Nicholai had rejected her now rose to the surface. She couldn't do anything to help Nicholai. But there was one thing she could do to help her team. The people who had supported her through thick and thin.

Resign from Forge.

Her throat tightened as she sucked in a shuddering breath. It would kill her. She'd worked so hard for this. Her job had become her life, especially in the last year. She'd chosen it over Alex.

The right choice. And now I'm going to lose it all.

She would eventually find work. But the scandal would follow her for some time. Kissing a client was not exactly a résumé enhancer. She could strike out on her own. Except how many clients would want to work with her? Even if they did, she was still relatively new. Yes, she was confident in her skills. But she still had a lot to learn.

Doesn't matter.

It wasn't fair for everyone else to lose their chance at an assignment that could catapult their careers into stardom. Resigning was the right thing to do.

Why, she thought as she closed her eyes against a hot sting of tears, *is the right thing so damn hard sometimes?*

A knock sounded on her door.

"Not now," she called.

The door swung open. Startled, she sat up in bed as Nicholai stepped inside. She barely stopped her mouth from dropping open as he shut the door.

"I would like to take you up on your offer."

This time she wasn't able to stop her lips from parting in shock.

"But...you said—"

"I changed my mind."

"Just like that? In twenty minutes?"

"Does your proposal still stand?"

My proposal.

Heat flamed in her cheeks. Although the situation was entirely different, she had, in fact, proposed to a prince this morning. Cautious hope swirled inside her even as she kept an iron grip on her pillow.

"It does."

Nicholai exhaled a harsh breath that sounded more like accepting something disdainful versus a sigh of relief.

"All right. A representative from our public affairs office will be down in twenty minutes to brief you on the official story."

"Official story?"

"Yes. How we met, our whirlwind romance, et cetera."

Her brief moment of relief flickered and died. An underlying sense of nausea crept in.

"Why not just keep it simple? That we met in Paris—"

"We will. But we need to make sure our stories match." He ran a hand through his thick hair. "I'll drop by after the people from wardrobe come by and we'll discuss terms—"

"Wardrobe? What are you talking about?"

"We will hold a press conference at eleven to announce our engagement."

The floor dropped out from under her. "What?"

"It's best to get ahead of the story as soon as possible. The quicker we address it and perform for the cameras, the sooner we can get back to normal."

The nausea grew. How had she gone to bed with the bittersweet memory of their dance and woken up to this horrid hell that had taken the second-best kiss of her life and turned it into tabloid journalism for the world to consume?

Somehow, she forced a smile to her lips. "Of course."

Nicholai gazed at her for a long moment, as if he was waiting for her to say something else. Humiliated and suddenly exhausted, she remained silent.

He stood and moved to the door, pausing just before he went out.

"Thank you, Madeline. I owe you."

The nausea pitched into her throat. She nodded once, kept her face devoid of expression until the door closed behind him.

And then she broke down, letting her tears fall silently down her cheeks.

CHAPTER NINE

MADELINE TRIED NOT to wrinkle her nose as she looked down at her dress. The public affairs representative had picked out a black dress with sleeves down to her elbows and matching black heels. The rep had called it dignified, posh.

Madeline thought she looked like she was going to a funeral. *Might as well be.*

The meeting had been hideous. The rep had obvious loyalties to the crown, loyalties that came out in clipped responses and hardly any eye contact. If this was what the rest of the world was going to think, that some upstart American had managed to snag herself a prince and drag him through the mud, then her time as the supposed fiancée of Prince Nicholai Adamović was going to be unpleasant.

She glanced down at her bare ring finger. The one detail that no one had mentioned. For the most part, the rep had emphasized keeping her mouth shut during the press conference and only speaking if Nicholai prompted her. Otherwise, "His Highness" would field all inquiries. When Madeline had asked why, the rep had responded that he had experience, whereas Madeline didn't.

The public affairs version of "sit down and shut up."

Her hair had been styled into an elegant French braid. Tiny drops of pearl adorned her ears. She looked very proper and put together.

Very much not herself.

Her phone had continued to blow up with messages, especially after the palace had announced a press conference with Prince Nicholai and Miss Madeline Delvine with some "exciting news." Shortly after eight, her team started texting her, too. Julie had been cautiously congratulatory. Andrew's simple statement of his being available if she ever needed to talk had signaled he knew more was going on. J.T. had actually stopped by to check on her and tried to pepper her with questions until the public affairs rep had stopped by and politely but forcefully escorted him out. The worst had been Chris, congratulating her and apologizing if he ever came on too strong.

How had this spiraled out of control so quickly?

The dress seemed to tighten about her ribs. Madeline stared at her reflection.

Sighing, she turned away from the mirror. She knew what the Public Affairs Department was going for. No hint of scandal. A united front that emphasized decorum and all the values that had been called into question by hers and Nicholai's midnight make out session.

It was, she kept reminding herself, all for show. In a month, maybe two or three, they'd probably make some quiet announcement about how they'd realized they were no longer suited and would part ways. Given that she was playing out the biggest lie of her life, it shouldn't have mattered that she was lying yet again in the way she presented herself.

Except it did matter. She felt like she'd slipped back into her past, into mistakes that had nearly swallowed her whole. She had started to acquiesce to some of Alex's requests in the months leading up to their breakup. Little things, like wearing a slightly longer dress, or toning down the red lipstick she preferred to wear when she went out. The more she stood up to him on things regarding her career, the more he had pushed her on things she thought of at the time as mundane. Small requests that he had phrased as perfectly reasonable and, in her attempt to mitigate some of her guilt about how much time her career demanded, she had said yes to.

She'd sworn never to do it again. To give up her independence for a man. To be someone she wasn't.

Yet here she was, once again playing a role.

Suddenly frustrated with herself, she unzipped the dress and let it pool at her feet in a black, shapeless mess. Most of the gowns the representative had brought to her this morning were from a high-end boutique in Lepo Plavi, a shop that catered to the wealthy vacationers taking advantage of the Dalmatian Coast's sunshine and seascape.

Even if they weren't her style, the exquisite detail and attention to design were evident. Most were black or various shades of blue.

But buried beneath the mound of clothing, was a deep emerald dress. Sleeves came down to her elbows, although the scooped back probably dipped a little lower than the Public Affairs office would have liked. The bell skirt came to just above her knees, a respectable length. She swapped out the pearls for glittering citrine orbs from her own luggage. The earrings had been a gift from her mother and stepfather when she graduated college. A matching bracelet and nude heels made her feel more like herself. Classy, sure, but with a dash of much-needed color. Accents that reminded her of her family thousands of miles away.

A knock sounded on her door.

"Come in."

Nicholai walked in. His eyes swept up and down her form. "Hello."

"What are you wearing?"

Her back went up.

"A dress."

"They told me that you were wearing black."

"I changed my mind."

"You can't just change your mind."

She narrowed her eyes at him. "What's wrong with this dress?"

"It's too bright. Not the image we're wanting to put out today."

She cocked her head to one side. "Do you really think all the newspeople that are combing through my social media right now and looking at photos of what I normally wear are going to for one second believe that I—" she pointed to the mound of fabric on the floor "—would actually wear a black dress like that?"

Nicholai blinked, as if the thought had not occurred to him.

"If I was wearing a thigh-high dress and go-go boots, I could understand the concern. But this is a perfectly acceptable dress that covers more than enough and still feels like me."

"Except you're not you anymore." He didn't say it meanly, which almost made it worse, as though he were talking to a child who didn't understand. "You're the fiancée of a prince and the future queen of Kelna."

Madeline gritted her teeth. "I'm not changing. If that means the deal's off, then I guess the deal is off. But I will not be told what to wear again by you or by anyone."

Nicholai's face darkened. "Again?"

Madeline inwardly groaned. "It's nothing. Forget it."

"It's not nothing."

Nicholai advanced into the room, his eyes narrowing in anger.

"Alex?"

Her chest tightened. She hadn't told him about Alex. But then again, she remembered with a sigh, she hadn't needed to. That stupid article had drudged up her entire life. It was a wonder they didn't include that she'd failed Mrs. Farmer's English exam in tenth grade.

"You know what's worse than making a mistake? Having literally the whole world know that you made a mistake."

"Did he try to control what you wore?"

Her anger twisted, morphed into humiliation. She had made such a hideous mistake with Alex, making excuses for him until one day he'd pushed her just far enough to finally yank the wool from her eyes. That it had taken months of his controlling behavior to get her to leave was a thorn she had yet to pull out of her side. That, coupled with her mother's warning about not letting a man take over her life, made her current predicament embarrassing.

"He had very strong opinions."

A muscle ticked and Nicholai's jaw.

"Did he hurt you?"

"Not physically." She let out a small, strained laugh as she turned away, unable to face Nicholai. "But emotionally, mentally, yes. He hurt me. He knew how much being an architect meant to me. He only cared more about himself, about what I could do for him, instead of being partners. And when I pushed back, he found other ways to troll, to make himself feel better by at least having a say in something." She sucked in a deep breath, then faced him, her arms crossed over her chest. "I want to help, Nicholai. I know what's on the table. But please don't ask me to lie more than I have to. I know you can't completely trust me after what's happened in the past few days. But I promise I will represent Kelna as best I can—"

"Stop right there." Nicholai stalked toward her, his eyes dark and thunderous. "I take responsibility for what happened. I followed you out into the gardens to the terrace. I kissed you."

"I kissed you back."

The atmosphere in the room changed, shifted into one of awareness.

"Yes, you did." Nicholai let out a harsh exhale. Longing flashed in his eyes, a look that pierced her heart. Then it disappeared as he regained control. It was unsettling, to see a man shift from vulnerable to a commanding leader in the span of a heartbeat.

"We both know where this is headed."

Instead of feeling strong for sticking to her priorities or relief that they were on the same page, she just felt miserable.

"Yes."

"Then we won't discuss how this started any further. It's in the past." He scrubbed a hand over his face. "There will be times during this charade that I will have to ask you to do things you don't want to do. However, knowing your history, I will endeavor to make sure that what you wear is not one of them."

"Thank you." She scrunched up her nose. "Sometimes I can be independent almost to a fault."

"Shocking."

"I will try to temper some of my usual responses."

"This life is not for everyone, Madeline. Yes, it's depicted in books and movies as being hard. But the true depth of what's required of us as royals can only be understood by people in a similar position. Not," he added, "that we don't reap benefits from it. It's one of the things I have to remind myself of when I start to feel trapped."

"Trapped?" His words from the rooftop in Paris suddenly came back. "You mentioned feeling caught between two worlds."

"Yes. The Kingdom my father ruled is very different than the one of today. In the past two years it has grown rapidly, as has the scrutiny we live under from the media and the public. The number of duties has increased tenfold. So have the expectations. I receive a life of luxury, one which I strive to be grateful for. There are times when I look at the sheer amount that needs to be done and I falter. But no matter what my wishes are, or are not, I am pledged to lead in the best interests of my people."

Floored by the level of his commitment, and stunned by the depth of her own emotional response, Madeline took a physical step back. Never had she been so moved by a man's commitment to a purpose, or really anything in his life. Alex had been dedicated to his career, yes, but so much of that had been wrapped up in the money, the prestige.

Stop. She couldn't let herself feel anything more than she already did for Nicholai. Leaving was going to be hard enough as it was.

"We'll make it through this, Nicholai."

"We will." He cleared his throat. "On that note, we need to discuss the terms of our engagement."

She nodded, suddenly exhausted. "Okay."

"I spoke with the prime minister. Aside from us, he is the only one who knows this engagement is a fake."

"Not even your dad?"

"No." Nicholai paused, then rubbed at his jaw. "He has enough to be concerned about. And my sister, as much as I love her, can't be trusted to not let something slip to the wrong person."

"If this is so hush-hush, then why did you need to tell the prime minister?"

"Because he oversees Parliament. I need the ministers' approval of my fiancée."

Madeline's jaw dropped. "What?"

"It's part of the law of our country."

"That's archaic!"

Nicholai stared at her for a long moment. Something flashed in his eyes. Disappointment? Frustration? Then it was gone.

"Perhaps. But here, it's part of the law. And he agreed to help us."

Madeline held up a hand in surrender. "Okay. I'm sorry. I didn't mean to insult your country. It's just...very different."

Nicholai nodded. "Thank you. Would two months be agreeable to you?"

Her eyes widened. "Two months?"

"Long enough for the furor to die down before we announce that we have decided to step back from the engagement."

"What would happen during these two months?"

"The first month you would stay here."

"Here? As in—" she gestured to her room "—here?"

"Yes. In Kelna." He'd settled back into his lecture mode, regarding her with a neutral gaze as if he wasn't turning her world on its head. "We need to be seen together, and regularly, to sell the engagement."

"But my work...my life back home—"

"J.T. said this was your primary project at the moment. You can work on it here. Your life in Kansas City will be waiting for you when this is over."

"So that means Forge will stay on the project?"

At his nod, she sagged in relief. Forge wouldn't lose the contract. She could keep her job, as long as J.T. didn't kick her out for bringing all this press attention to the firm. While she didn't relish being away from her home for a month or more, there was a concrete end date to this arrangement.

Suddenly lightheaded, Madeline sat down hard on a settee. Her eyes drifted to her reflection in the mirror. Beneath the expertly applied makeup, she looked pale.

"I imagine this isn't what you had in mind when you made your suggestion."

A giggle rose up in her throat, a sound that would probably come out as hysterical. She managed to swallow it by pressing her lips together and shaking her head.

"Madeline..." He knelt before her. His handsome face was the definition of serious. "If this is too much—"

"No." *Get a grip, Maddie.* "It's overwhelming, yes. But I'll make this work."

"If you're sure?"

"I am."

"All right." He stood. "We can discuss upcoming appearances and such later. Someone will be by from Public Affairs to bring you down."

"We aren't going down together?"

The thought of another stranger, someone who would probably be judging her with every step they took, made her feel sick.

"I have to meet with several people before the conference."

"Oh." Smoothing things over, no doubt. "Okay."

He turned to leave. As he opened the door, he glanced back at her.

"You do look beautiful."

The words shot straight to her heart. For one moment, as he stood framed in the doorway, she saw the man who'd drunk wine with her in Paris. Who had waltzed her about a seafront terrace. Who had kissed her like she was the only reason he wanted to keep on living.

And this time, when the wall came down and he slid back into his role as Prince, she saw him differently. Not as someone austere and unreachable. No, she saw a man who bore the burden of an entire country on his shoulders and did so with a dignity and commitment she greatly admired.

Once the door closed behind him, Madeline pressed the heels of her hands to her eyes.

I cannot fall in love with a prince. I cannot fall in love with a prince.

No matter how many times she repeated the phrase, she feared it was too late.

CHAPTER TEN

NICHOLAI ALLOWED HIMSELF to relax a fraction. Lights flashed as cameras snapped numerous pictures of him and his bride-to-be. His opening statement, carefully composed by the Public Affairs Department, had struck the right note of contrition for last night's misstep and excitement for his upcoming engagement. That his and Madeline's romance had supposedly been a whirlwind courtship begun in Paris, and the future princess was an American from an average background, had delighted the reporters thronging in front of the podium.

So far, thankfully, no one had bothered to dive too deeply into Kelna's laws. He had almost shared them with Madeline this morning. But based on her reaction to his needing the prime minister's approval for his choice of bride, he'd decided not to. It wasn't a law he liked himself, and since Madeline would be gone in two months' time, what was the point in further upsetting her? She'd put herself out on a limb to help him and Kelna recover. If he could spare her any more unpleasantness, he would.

Although she'd held up extremely well during the conference. She'd maintained a calm expression throughout, answering briefly when questions were directed to her. When one reporter had asked where her ring was, she'd looked up at him, a momentary flare of panic in her eyes. He'd slid his fingers through hers and squeezed. A soft murmur had swept through the crowd. Belatedly, he had remembered the encouragement of Public Affairs to maintain a low level of public display.

But Madeline had drawn strength from the contact and turned to face the reporter with a sweet smile.

"I'm excited to see what Prince Nicholai surprises me with. I didn't need one to say yes to his proposal." She looked back up at him then, her gaze warm and affectionate. "It's an honor to stand by his side today."

It's just an act.

But even as he felt relief that their charade was being accepted so readily, his earlier trepidation that he would fall too hard for Madeline solidified in his veins.

"Miss Delvine?"

Madeline nodded to a silver-haired reporter with a strong blade of a nose and a pen clasped in her hand like a weapon.

"Yes?"

"Sarah Tomlin, American press. How do you feel about having your engagement unveiled to the world the day after not only having *your* picture published but that of *two* other women dancing with your affianced?"

The room fell into a stunned silence as all eyes swiveled to Madeline.

Anger surged forth. He'd known this was a possibility, been lured into a false sense of security by the first round of mundane questions. He stepped forward, opened his mouth to speak.

"I would have certainly preferred to not have that photo in the papers." Madeline's slight smile, coupled with embarrassed amusement in her voice, solicited a few chuckles from the audience. Nicholai paused. Madeline had proven herself an adept speaker during her presentation to his family. While Public Affairs wanted him to do the talking, he didn't want to silence her if he didn't have to. She was already sacrificing enough.

The reporter's lips thinned. "What about Amara Atis?" she pressed. "Surely there are questions about your sudden engagement so soon after the Prince being pictured with not one but three ladies in a single evening."

Done. Madeline was well-spoken. But they were wading into dangerous territory, where the slightest mistake could be cruelly twisted and used over and over again as a weapon. They had built up a significant amount of goodwill during the first part of the conference. One wrong word could decimate it all.

He leaned towards the microphone, ready to take over.

"My fiancé talking to another woman is not a crime."

Madeline's voice had cooled considerably. Out of the corner of his eye, Nicholai saw a Public Affairs rep trying to signal him. Indecision kept him silent. If he intervened and cut her off, what impression would people form about their relationship? While Madeline was speaking more frankly than he would, she wasn't saying anything inappropriate.

"As to Miss Atis, I understand she is a longtime friend of Nicholai. I don't understand the concern."

"When your fiancé is dancing with a woman dressed like that, it's only natural—"

"Like what?"

Nicholai could feel the tension radiating down Madeline's arm and coming through her tight grasp on his hand. His own body stiffened. *Kravgu.*

He squeezed her fingers, tried to give her a silent cue to stop while she was still ahead.

She ignored it.

"If the question is simply because of what dress Miss Amara chose to wear," Madeline said in a quiet but icy tone, "then I'm disappointed."

Another ripple flew through the room. Reporters shared shocked glances. Never before had the royal family spoken so plainly. That the new fiancée of Prince Nicholai was doing so, and at her first official press conference, would be talked about for months to come.

"Disappointed?" Sarah repeated, her teeth bared like a

shark. "Don't the Kelnian people have a right to know if their prince can be trusted?"

"But he can." Madeline's voice rang out, strong and sure. "I've never known anyone like the Prince. The passion he feels for this country, the support that he pours into it. I knew when my team first met with him that the addition of a new ballroom was not a vanity project. It was something that meant a great deal to him, to his family." Her voice trailed off before she rallied again. "To answer your first question, no. I have no concerns about the Prince, nor where his loyalties lie. As for Miss Atis, I hope she knows that she is always welcome here and," Madeline added with a devilish curve of her lips, "that any further gossip about her dress focuses on how well she wore it last night."

The room erupted, more questions being shouted out as conversations took place, cameras clicked away and recorded. Nicholai stood frozen in place, barely remembering to keep a faint smile on his lips.

What had she just done? What had he just let her do? Never mind how her passionate defense of him had rocked him in a way that had made him feel like a god even as it had shaken his foundation to be so responsive to someone else's opinion. His personal reaction had no place here.

Heart thumping, Nicholai leaned into the microphone.

"That concludes the press conference for today. Thank you."

He strode offstage, Madeline's hand still clamped firmly in his. He didn't stop until they were down the hall and safely ensconced in a private reception room with the door closed behind them.

He released her hand and stepped over to a silver cart on the far side, pouring himself a cup of black coffee as he sought to get his racing thoughts under control.

"Well," Madeline said from behind him, her voice cautious, "that was interesting."

"Yes. You made it even more so."

Silence reigned behind him. He took a deep drink of his coffee, inwardly cursed as the liquid scalded his tongue.

"You're upset with me."

"A little." He turned to face her. "You had explicit instructions on how to handle the questions."

Her nose wrinkled. "The question was directed to me."

"Yes. But did you not feel me squeeze your hand?"

"I did. I thought you were encouraging me."

"No, I was trying to stop you. You can't say things like that."

Bewilderment crossed her face.

"Like what? Defending you? Standing up for Amara? Refuting the nasty insinuations from that reporter?"

"When you respond like that, all you do is give them fuel for more gossip. You took what should have been a staid, polite press conference and catapulted it into what will surely become international news once again."

He knew even as he spoke that he was going too far, letting his anger at himself for letting personal whims prevent him from stopping her meld with his disappointment at how their first event had gone. She had promised him that she would represent Kelna in the best light. And then she went rogue on a reporter.

She's never been in a press conference before, his conscience whispered inside his head. *How is she supposed to know how to respond to such a question?*

"Is the motto of the royal family to roll over and take it?"

Any voices encouraging moderation or compassion disappeared. His jaw tightened as heated anger swept through him.

"Do not dare to question my family's honor."

She drew back, her lips parted in shock at the ferocity of his words.

"So you'll defend Kelna to the death, but not your fellow man? Or in this case woman?"

"What they said was unpleasant, yes. But if I would have

said anything positive, they would have brought it back to the rumors of us dating. Amara and I have been friends since university. That's it. We have never, and will never date. She's used to the media scrutiny."

"But she shouldn't be." Madeline leaned forward, her hands curled into fists as she glared at him with a disapproval that nearly penetrated his own shield of ire. "She shouldn't have her choice of dress ripped apart."

"I'm surprised you even stood up for her, given how upset you seemed last night."

Madeline stared at him like he'd grown an extra head. "I was jealous of her. But I don't know anything about her. I don't know if she's kind or friendly or funny. I know nothing other than she looked amazing in a dress that made her look beautiful and she got to dance with you. For that reporter to suggest anything about her character based on a dress that— oh, my God—showed a little bit of her back, was hideous."

Reluctant admiration filled him. As he scrambled for the right words, her shoulders slumped as her face fell.

"How could you not stand up for someone you told me is a friend?"

They stood at opposite ends of the room; their earlier camaraderie erased by the gaping distance between their roles in life.

Finally, Madeline looked away.

"It's a good thing this engagement is all for show. Because I don't understand this life at all."

Her words stabbed him in the heart. This morning, after their conversation in her room, he'd known a moment of optimism. Even if the charade ran its course and Madeline returned to America, their arrangement had given them something he hadn't thought possible: time. Time to get to know one another, to enjoy each other's company.

But with this chasm gaping between them, knowing the depth of her disgust, there would be no time spent together other than the carefully arranged appearances by Public Affairs. What would be the point? They were from two different worlds.

Hope withered, died.

"Fortunately, you don't have to."

She flinched as if she'd been struck. Disgusted with himself and his heartless response, he reached out to her, but she turned away.

"J.T. is having some of my equipment sent back when the team returns to Kansas City tomorrow. Unless I'm needed for some other show-and-tell, I'll be in my room."

The skirt of her green dress swayed like a bell as she disappeared out the door. He wanted to go after her, to tell her that even though her response to the reporter had flown in the face of every public relations lesson he had ever received during his lifetime, her defense of him, even his friend, had meant something to him. He wanted to brush the hurt from her face, soothe her anger with a walk in the rose garden in the light of day instead of skulking around at night like they had something to hide.

He turned his back on the door and moved to the window. Those were things that a man would do for his actual fiancée. Not things a prince would do for the woman playing a role to save him from public damnation.

CHAPTER ELEVEN

MADELINE SMILED AND nodded for what had to be the hundredth time in the past forty-five minutes, as a hospital administrator walked them through a door out into the bright morning sun. She blinked just as a camera clicked and silently cursed.

Get a grip. It's the third day.

Somehow, she stretched her smile just a little wider and nodded toward the photographer before redirecting her attention to the courtyard. Pastel-colored flowers and thick bushes with velvety leaves lined the meandering walkways. Benches set into the blooms offered pockets of privacy. A small fountain babbled at the far end. Despite the two dozen people in the space, the sound of the water calmed some of Madeline's tension.

She'd been left blessedly alone the rest of the afternoon and evening following the press conference. Her solitude had been ruined early the next morning by the insistent knock of a young woman who'd introduced herself as Jelena, the new aide to the future princess.

She hadn't had time to think, much less work, since. Wardrobe fittings, endless meetings, a few minutes here and there to eat while someone rattled off an endless round of trivia. If her five-year-old self could see her now, she would seriously rethink asking for that princess dress-up set for her birthday. Being a royal, even a fake one, was exhausting.

Her eyes flickered to Nicholai as the entourage moved around the courtyard. His attention was solely focused on the hospital administrator, a slight smile playing about his lips as he nodded. More than one of the doctors and nurses they'd met had given him an appreciative glance. He really was handsome. And, based on how attentive he'd stayed throughout the tour, he was good at what he did.

She inhaled deeply, exhaled softly. Nicholai was a good leader. If nothing else came of this charade, Forge would keep the palace contract, and Nicholai would be well received as king when he took the throne. From what little she'd seen, he would do the role justice.

The subject of her thoughts glanced her way. Her breath caught in her chest as their gazes met. His eyes held a question, almost as if he were checking on her. The simple moment softened her smile.

The sharp click of a camera shutter made her smile disappear. A veil dropped over Nicholai's eyes as he looked at the photographer, then turned back to the hospital administrator. Had she imagined it all? Projected what she'd wanted to see versus reality?

Probably making sure you don't run amok again.

She had been proud of herself after the press conference announcing their engagement, had thought she had handled things well, only to be faced with that blank stare Nicholai adopted so well when he was in official mode. She had thought back over what she had said, had even forced herself to watch a couple news clips that had circulated online and still could not understand Nicholai's stance that she should have just kept her mouth shut.

But she hadn't handled their post conference conversation well, either. More of an argument, really. Her last words had been spoken out of anger and hurt. Never a good combination, and, judging by the pain she'd seen flash across Nicholai's face before he'd agreed with her, she had hurt him back.

One of the few positives to come out of the situation was that her sparring with the iron-willed Sarah Tomlin had actually been well received. People lauded the future "Cinderella princess," who hadn't been afraid to speak her mind and stand up for a fellow woman. While some traditional outlets had criticized her for speaking too plainly, others had praised her for being a fresh face amongst royalty and politicians.

At least it was good for Kelna. But judging by the way Nicholai had barely spoken to her in the days since, the good press didn't matter one way or another. In his eyes, she had screwed up. While she felt sorry for the way she'd handled his reaction, she didn't, and wouldn't, regret one thing she'd said.

In the end, it didn't matter anyway. Even if Nicholai had entertained any thoughts about pursuing a romantic relationship with her, any kind of commitment to him would mean surrendering everything she held dear. She'd almost lost herself once. She would not do so again.

She glanced around the courtyard and, seeing no clock in sight, cast a glance down at her wrist. Fifteen more minutes. Then, if she remembered correctly, they would head back to the palace, where she would have just over an hour to take a shower, change and meet Nicholai, his father and his sister for a "family tea," their first get-together since this whole debacle had begun.

A headache started to build in her temples. Her hand drifted up, then fell back down to her side as she saw another camera aimed her way.

Almost over.

She'd actually enjoyed the tour. Hearing the capabilities of the new hospital compared to the old one had been interesting. The staff had been incredibly nice, a few even shyly asking for autographs. They'd also met a couple of patients and their families, who had all been lovely. It had been fascinating, too, to see the similarities and differences between American and Kelnian hospitals.

But the cameras…everywhere she turned, there was a camera, watching her every move, documenting every blink, every wrinkle of her nose.

Nicholai had texted her last night with details about the hospital tour and a request for her to join him. She'd typed out, then deleted numerous replies before finally settling on "Sure." Not the most eloquent of responses. But every other variation, from irritated refusal to grudging apology, hadn't felt right. Simplicity had won out.

Sooner or later, though, she would have to put her foot down. Part of the agreement of her staying at the palace had included time for her to work. She hadn't touched the detail designs in days. If she went more than a day without sketching, even if it was just the view outside her window, she felt the loss like a part of her had been carved away.

At last, the tour concluded with photos with the hospital staff. As they walked out, a young couple approached, asking for an autograph. Nicholai waved off his security guards as he signed a hospital brochure. A small crowd grew, drawn by the Prince and future princess of Kelna. Napkins, scraps of paper and even a book were shoved in her face, all with requests for her signature. Even though the attention overwhelmed her, she drew strength from Nicholai at her side. He took the attention in his stride, smiling as if he were enjoying it. He crouched down to talk to some young children and returned the enthusiastic hug of an elderly woman.

At last, the crowd thinned, helped along by the quiet yet firm guidance of two security guards who cleared the way to the waiting limo.

"You're really good at this," Madeline observed as they walked down the stairs.

Nicholai smiled slightly. "Thank you. I don't get to do much of it."

"Why not?"

"Too many other official duties."

"But you like talking to people?"

"Usually. Sometimes I need solitude. I don't get much of either."

Madeline hesitated, unsure of how to phrase the thought that came to mind. She waited until the doors were shut and they were ensconced in the privacy of the limo before finally saying, "I imagine doing your work while trying to take on more is hard."

"It is. I was not prepared to take on my responsibilities as well as my father's during such a critical time for our country."

"Why not ask Eviana for help?"

Nicholai frowned. "Eviana has her own duties. I've been raised for this."

The firmness in his voice signaled the subject was closed for discussion. As the limo pulled away from the hospital, she waited until they passed the archway over the gate before leaning her head back and closing her eyes.

"Are you all right?"

She kept her eyes closed as she nodded. "I'm used to client meetings and delivering presentations. I'm just not used to having a camera on me all the time."

Something rustled across from her.

"I've never gotten used to it."

Slowly, she opened her eyes. Nicholai was glancing through a sheaf of papers inside a leather portfolio balanced on his lap. His tone was conversational, certainly friendlier than it had been since their confrontation.

"How do you manage it?"

He glanced up, his eyes focusing on some distant thought before shifting to her.

"I know it's what best for the country. For me to be seen outside the palace. So, I do it."

"You make it sound so simple."

"It's far from simple, Madeline." He exhaled slowly. "Something I forgot when I chastised you after the conference."

That made her sit up in her seat. "Oh?"

"You had all of a few hours to prepare for something others would have had months, perhaps even years, to plan for. I was overly harsh."

"Thank you." She debated for a moment on her next words. "But you still think I made a mistake."

He closed the portfolio and set it down on the seat next to him. "I don't know what to think about your statement. The reporter was overly aggressive. Her line of questioning was inappropriate. I've been trained not to respond to such things. To date, ignoring the drama seekers has served me well. However," he added as she opened her mouth to argue, "this situation is unique. Whether or not you followed palace procedure, your response has been well received. I can't argue against the results."

She sighed. "I don't know whether to be offended or appeased."

His smile flashed, quick and unexpected, a straight shot to her heart.

"You gave a human face to our country. You did what so many times I have not done. Instead of accepting things as the way they'd always been done, even wanting them to stay the same, you did something new." He reached out then and grabbed her hand. Her breath caught. A simple act, but one that made her feel accepted. Cared for. "Not only did you stand up for me, but you stood up for Amara. It meant a great deal to her."

"I'm glad." She inwardly cursed at the hint of weakness in her tone. Nicholai had told her twice now that Amara was just a friend. Even if Amara had meant more to him at some point, she had no right to be jealous.

"Amara is a friend. She's never been anything more, and never will be anything else."

Madeline ducked her head. "It's none of my business."

Nicholai tugged on her hand, waited until her eyes met his.

"This may not be a traditional engagement. But as long as we are in this together, there's only you, Madeline."

She released a shuddering breath. "Thank you. Same. There is no one. Hasn't been in over a year."

Something flared in his gaze, something that made her feel warm inside.

"I'm glad," he said softly.

He squeezed her hand before releasing it. The loss of his touch speared through her as her fingers automatically lingered, sought him before she snatched her hand back and placed it firmly in her lap.

Oh, Nicholai.

In just one conversation, he'd swept away the tension and awkwardness and replaced it with something far worse.

Wanting. She wanted Nicholai, wanted more time with him, the possibility of something more. Wanted to get to know the man behind the crown and what inspired him to return over and over again to the role that demanded so much.

"Thank you."

Unsettled by his words and the glimpse of the personal side she'd first experienced in Paris, she looked away. Vulnerability was not something she wore well. The tumultuous early years of her life had forged her into a fiercely independent child who preferred constancy. Qualities she had maintained into adulthood, minus her brief lapse with Alex.

She liked being strong. Liked the routine of her life. Yes, what she had thought of as her Paris adventure had been exciting. But she'd flown to Europe knowing she would have her apartment to go home to. Her family and friends. Familiarity. Stability.

Nicholai, on the other hand, offered the opposite of what she was usually drawn to. His life was chaotic, a constant evolution as he pivoted from one thing to the next. She'd spent mere hours in his actual presence.

Yet he drew her in like no one else had. As the limo passed

by a plaza, the limestone square surrounded by elegant pillars and archways and tourists and locals moving among a sea of umbrella-covered shops and pots of the lavender flowers she'd glimpsed in the royal gardens, she felt that tug again. A sense of belonging she hadn't experienced anywhere except home.

The limo stopped at a light. Madeline looked ahead, then did a double take as she spied the large green space up ahead, partially eclipsed by rows of pine trees on either side. Stairs built into the hillside marked the beginning of a cobblestone path that wound its way across the grass. What looked like stone statues stood at random intervals on the lawn.

"What is that?"

"The Markovic. Kelna's own *muzej*, housing historic art and several exhibitions from England, Japan and America." Pride deepened Nicholai's smile. "It opened two years ago."

Madeline eyes widened as the limo passed by. "Oh, wow."

At the far end of the lawn stood a magnificent building, at least three stories tall, with pointed arches and numerous windows stretched across the front. The vivid white of the pillars and matching trim around the arched windows offset the pale redbrick walls. Terraced stairs swept up from the lawn to the main doors, wooden behemoths at least ten feet tall.

"It reminds me of the Nelson back home."

"The museum your stepfather took you to?"

Surprised and touched that he remembered, she glanced at him. "Yes."

Nicholai glanced down at his watch. "Would you like to go?"

"To the museum?"

"Yes."

Yes! "When?"

"Tonight. I'll arrange for a private tour after the museum closes to the public."

She couldn't stop her excited smile. "Really?"

"Really. We could both use a break."

"Thank you." With her spirits lifted, she pulled out her phone and typed in the Nelson's website. "This is where I spend a lot of my time when I'm not in my office."

She held up a picture of the museum's south lawn. Green grass dominated half the image, dotted with couples strolling and posing for photos, families picnicking, and a father flying a kite with his son. The trademark shuttlecock sculptures stood out in vivid white and bright orange. On the far right, the newer addition of the Bloch Building rambled over the landscape, the frosted glass walls a modern contrast to the towering stone pillars that marked the museum's regal southern entrance.

"Are those...birdies?" Nicholai's brows drew together as his lips quirked. "Like you hit in badminton?"

She chuckled. "Yes. A husband-and-wife team designed them. They imagined the museum as a net on a badminton court. There are three sculptures on the south lawn and one on the north side."

"Interesting."

She wrinkled her nose at his dry tone. "A lot of people didn't like them when they were first installed. Thought it ruined the museum's aesthetic. And now they're a symbol of Kansas City. Something fun that people enjoy."

He tilted his head to one side as he looked back down at her phone. "Do you think that's the most important thing for a museum housing prominent art?"

"The most important? No. Very important for a free museum that serves it community? Yes."

His lips twitched. "Touché, Miss Delvine." He pointed to the glass structure on the far right side of the picture. "Different style of architecture."

"The Bloch Building. Another bit of a scandal when it was being built."

"Oh?"

"A lot of people thought it was too modern. Didn't fit in with the rest of the architecture."

"I can see the argument."

"I can, too. Although in an odd way, I'm glad people got upset. It means it meant something to them. Architecture is art. And that's the beauty of art—everyone's allowed to have an opinion. A lot of people thought it looked like a shed or storage container."

Nicholai's lips twitched. "I see the resemblance."

"But," Madeline said as she took her phone back, "for me, I see glass. Natural light. Feeling like you're a part of the landscape. Not obscuring the original architecture, but supporting it."

"Finding a way for the old and the new to coexist."

Wincing, she remembered his reaction to the initial designs. "I wasn't trying to—"

Nicholai waved his hand. "I didn't think you were purposely saying anything, Madeline. Just an observation. You're passionate about what you do. I like that about you."

Her lips parted as warmth flooded her body.

I like that about you.

She'd imagined hearing someone say sweet things to her one day. Someone who paid attention not just to the big things, but the little things, too.

Like what museum her stepfather had taken her to on their first outing.

For the first time in what felt like forever, the thought of going home to Kansas City didn't initiate an instant feeling of contentment. Instead, it filled her with an ache at the thought of never seeing Nicholai again.

How, she thought morosely, *am I supposed to walk away from this with my heart intact?*

CHAPTER TWELVE

MADELINE'S PENCIL FLEW across the paper, leaving curves and lines of graphite. She stopped, leaned her head back and frowned. With a deft movement, she flipped the pencil about and applied the eraser with intentional ferocity.

Nicholai's lips tilted up as he watched her work. In a few minutes, they would pose for their official engagement photos. When his knock had gone unanswered, he'd suspected the reason and quietly let himself in.

It wasn't just the tumble of blond locks, carefully styled in preparation for their upcoming engagement photos, that entranced him. Although the sight did make him think, for just a moment, what it would be like to brush the hair from her neck and place a soft kiss on her skin. Nor was it just the way she nibbled on her lower lip when she concentrated on something, even if it did remind him of the last time they'd touched like lovers on the cliffside terrace.

Part of Madeline's allure was her passion. She poured herself into her art and work. He'd witnessed it here and there since meeting her in Paris. The evening after their visit to the hospital, though, had finally given him the chance to see Madeline's talent on full display.

It had been incredible.

They'd met his father and sister for tea in his father's royal quarters. Madeline's excitement at the prospect of visiting the museum had been visibly subdued when she'd first entered his father's sitting room. But Ivan and Eviana had quickly put her at ease. By the time they'd adjourned for dinner, Madeline had been sharing stories of her upbringing in Kansas City, much to his father's amusement and Eviana's delight.

That night, they'd met one of the curators for a private tour. Madeline had made the man's day by asking intricate questions and giving him her undivided attention. When she'd asked for an hour to wander, the curator had practically stumbled over his feet to offer her as long as she'd needed.

Nicholai had made himself scarce, ambling through the European exhibit that featured paintings reminiscent of the ones hanging in many of the rooms in the palace. When he'd realized it had been over an hour, he'd gone in search of Madeline. He'd found her sitting cross-legged on a bench in front of an oil painting of the palace from the early nineteen-hundreds, chewing on her lower lip as she'd drawn. Every now and then she would look up, her dark blue eyes flitting over the painting, before returning to her drawing.

He didn't know how long he'd watched her before he'd finally approached. It hadn't been until he'd sat down on the bench next to her that she'd even noticed his presence.

"It's not finished yet," she'd told him shyly before handing over her sketch pad.

She'd drawn an elegant, pointed archway of the new ballroom she'd envisioned, with glass doors flung open. Inside, vague sketches of men and women danced. Above the arch, embedded in stone, had been a cluster of blooms he'd recognized as bellflowers.

"I'm thinking keystones above each arch. Adds a touch of that tradition you like."

His fingers had settled on the flowers. "Why bellflowers?"

"The national flower of Kelna. I saw them everywhere and asked Eviana about them."

Did any of the women on Dario's list know Kelna's national flower? Would a seemingly small detail even matter to them?

It mattered to Madeline. That it did meant something to Nicholai.

He hadn't yet had time to examine the implications of that feeling. The rest of the week had passed by in a blur. Press coverage had been positive, including one picture of Madeline looking at him in the hospital courtyard with a sweet smile on her face that had social media users swooning around the world. Every day since the tour had been filled with meetings, public appearances and preparing for the royal engagement photos. Nicholai had finally selected a ring, a silver band set with tiny diamonds and topped with a halo diamond, in preparation for the photos. Dario had paid Nicholai a personal visit when he'd learned of the photos and asked just how far Nicholai intended to take the charade. Nicholai's response— "As far as I have to for the sake of the country"—had pacified the older man.

For now.

Even if it didn't begin to address the labyrinth of tangled emotions coursing through him where Madeline Delvine was concerned.

He glanced down at his watch. He hated to interrupt her work, especially with how much time she had given him. But it had to be done.

"Madeline?"

She sat up and looked over her shoulder. "Oh." She frowned. "Am I late?"

"Not yet."

"Good." His chest warmed as she smiled at him. "I had an online meeting with the Forge team yesterday morning. The design development phase is my favorite part of a project."

She held up her sketch pad. As he drew closer, the sweet scent of jasmine teased him.

"All the details come together. The windows, fixtures, everything."

There were familiar elements, like the pointed arches and

domed ceiling that he'd seen around Lepa Plavi and other Kelnian towns. Features that had always been there, that he'd taken for granted.

Unlike the first revelation, when all he had been able to see was change, he now saw the blend of old and new. Saw the way the glass walls let in the light and, as he flipped through the sketches, provided stunning views of Kelna.

"Do you like it?"

"I do."

"You can tell me if you don't like it. I've had clients use all sorts of adjectives to describe their feelings about my work."

"Then believe me when I say it's nothing like what I imagined. It's better."

Her smile grew. "Really?"

"Really." He sat down in the chair next to her. "I will never fully be a fan of the modern. But the context you gave on things like the sculptures and the modern addition to your museum, learning the reason and intentions behind it, helped me look at the designs a different way. And seeing this," he said as he looked back down at the drawing, "the ways you've incorporated Kelna into this design, makes it seem both familiar and new."

"Thank you, Nicholai. That means a lot."

"You're welcome."

She stood and smoothed out the full skirts of her dress. Ice-blue with a lacy bodice and soft folds of fabric that fell into a sweeping skirt, the dress and the woman who wore it reminded him of a classic movie star.

"Do I look royal enough?"

"You look beautiful."

Pink suffused her cheeks. "Thank you. I don't think Public Affairs was a big fan of the dress that I picked."

"They don't have to be." Nicholai held out his hand. "Something you've taught me over the last few days is that while tradition has its place, so too does change."

Madeline's lips curved up. She accepted his hand. His fingers wrapped around hers. He heard her slight inhale, saw her eyes widen a moment before she looked up at him.

Time froze. His heart thudded in his chest. It had been over a week since they'd last kissed. A kiss he never thought would be repeated, even after the announcement of their engagement. Royals did not kiss in public.

But as his gaze drifted down to her mouth, he suddenly wished there was such an occasion.

A knock on the door made them startle and draw apart.

"Your Highness?"

"Come in," Nicholai ordered.

The door swung open. Ana, one of the Public Affairs representatives, walked in and bowed her head.

"They're ready for you."

Nicholai turned to Madeline and offered his arm.

"Shall we?"

Madeline swallowed hard, but accepted his arm, tucking her hand into the crook of his elbow. Tension remained thick between them as Ana led them to a balcony that overlooked one of the private coves along the sea. The photographer made quick work of arranging them in various regal poses, from standing side by side to a close-up of Madeline's hand resting on his arm, the ring on full display.

"Now smile," the photographer ordered.

Madeline made a noise that sounded suspiciously like a snicker.

"What?" Nicholai murmured out of the corner of his mouth.

"I've just never been ordered to smile in such an aggressive manner."

He couldn't have stopped the laugh even if he'd wanted to. She glanced up at him with a cheeky glimmer in her eyes.

"Perfect!"

Nicholai looked toward the photographer, who was grinning at his camera screen.

"That was excellent, Your Highness. I'll have proofs to Public Affairs within forty-eight hours."

Madeline ran a finger over the soft fabric of her skirt as the photographer packed up his equipment.

"That only lasted twenty minutes."

"The palace is known for its efficiency."

"Still," she said as she moved back and forth, making the skirt flare out about her knees, "maybe I'll just wear this in my room the rest of the day."

Inspiration struck.

"What would you say to a tour of Kelna?"

She wrinkled her nose. "I was actually looking forward to having an afternoon where I didn't have to do anything official."

"Nothing official. What would you say to a drive around Kelna? See our country beyond the conferences and corporate meetings?"

"And I still get to wear the dress?"

"Yes."

She grinned. "I'm in."

Madeline's eyes devoured the terraced hillsides of Kelna's wine country. The road they were on wound its way through clusters of evergreens, past groves of olive trees and then up a hillside covered in rambling grape vines. It had been, she thought with a lazy smile as she leaned her head back against the plush leather headrest, one of the nicest afternoons she'd spent since arriving in the country.

When they'd first left the palace, with Nicholai at the wheel of an old roadster, she'd been acutely aware of the black car trailing behind them. But as he'd driven through the streets of Lepo Plavi, taking her past courtyards, shopping districts and historic sites like a grand cathedral with a mix of Roman and Baroque architecture that had made her swoon, the car had faded from her mind. Hearing him talk about it away from the spotlight, hearing the genuine warmth and appreciation in his voice, had taken her initial passion for the country and fanned it into something more. As the city gave way to homes, and the homes to fields, Nicholai had pointed out the rolling hills, the soaring peaks of distant mountains and the hint of another city in the valley beyond.

The more she saw, the more she fell in love. They passed by a stone villa with dark brown shutters. She counted at least three terraces as they drove by.

She'd loved Paris: the sight of the Eiffel Tower, the mix of languages, the scent of freshly baked bread from a *boulange-rie*. Never had she imagined living there.

But here...she could imagine waking up here. Going to work at a desk with a bank of windows that offered stunning views of the sea.

It was a strange thought, given that she had never imagined anywhere but Kansas City as home. But the beauty of this country, the incredible architecture, seeing it through Nicholai's eyes, had made her fall even more in love with Kelna.

She glanced at her fake fiancé. The setting sun highlighted his handsome profile. She'd wondered that day after the hospital tour if she'd be able to stop herself from falling for him. Each passing day had made it harder to keep her heart safe. Seeing the work he did, how he committed himself to everything he did, and how his actions contributed to a stable country that was growing and providing for its people, added to her respect and admiration.

All while pulling her closer and closer to an edge she wasn't sure she could stop herself from falling over.

She stifled a sigh and looked away. When her relationship with Alex had been falling apart, she'd had friends to talk to. Family. Her mother especially. But now, she had no one. Her family wouldn't sell her story to the press. But one innocent slip to the wrong person could erase all the work she and Nicholai had put into their arrangement.

It had been easy over the past week to maintain the secrecy surrounding their engagement. The few times she talked with her team, the conversations had been focused on work. Texting and emailing allowed her to keep distance with her friends.

The phone calls with Stacey Delvine were a different story. She knew her mother suspected something wasn't right. It didn't sit well with her that she was lying to the woman who had taught her to be independent, who had stood by her and her decision to walk away from Alex.

A few more weeks, she told herself. *A few more weeks and you can tell her everything.*

The thought didn't bolster her spirits. Rather, it sent them plummeting. The thought of leaving Kelna, of leaving Nicholai, was becoming harder and harder with each passing day. And there was the question of what would face her on the other side when they officially announced the end of their engagement. Some people would be sympathetic, sure. But she had a nasty feeling that, given the press they had received in the last few days, she would be a subject of interest for quite a while. When she was ready to move on, would anyone want to date a woman who had been affianced to an actual prince, who had not one but two supposed broken engagements?

A warm, comforting weight settled on top of her hand. Her eyes drifted down and she watched as Nicholai's strong fingers wrapped around hers. His touch instantly soothed some of the tension tightening inside her chest.

"Are you all right?"

She started to offer a glib answer. But when she looked at him, saw the genuine concern in his eyes, she opted for truth.

"Thinking about the future."

"Do you mean with your job?"

"My job. What my life will look like after this."

He squeezed her hand. "You know that we'll do everything in our power to smooth the transition for you."

"I know." She smiled a little. "I'm going to miss this place."

His arm tensed on top of hers.

"I miss it every time I leave."

"I won't miss all the media attention. I don't understand all the protocol or the need for some things to be done the way they are. But you have a beautiful country." She thought back to the people she'd met outside the hospital, the ones who had been so excited to see their prince. There had been respect in their eyes, too, not just fawning over a celebrity. "You and your family make a difference here."

"That means something to you?"

"Of course it does. It's one of the things I love about art and architecture. I love the creative side," she said with a smile, "but I also love seeing the work we do make a difference. Like the ballroom. There's a lot of pride in Kelna. Knowing that your family is going to make an effort to include the people in events held at the palace makes the project so much more meaningful."

"I'm glad."

His voice came out rough, but when she looked at him, he was facing forward, his eyes fixed on the road.

"What are your future goals for your career?"

"One day I'd love to open my own architecture firm."

"How long will that take?"

"At least another ten years. I still have a lot to learn, and it's not exactly cheap to start up a business."

"What would you focus on?"

Warmth curled around her even as the setting sun ushered in a coolness that seeped in through the open window. Alex had never asked her about her future goals. He'd only cared about his own vision for their future, which had included a lavish house and expensive vacations. That Nicholai cared enough to ask brought about a contentment that made her relax and share more than she had planned.

"I don't want to limit myself. I've worked on libraries, houses, even a university building. I love the variety, getting to challenge myself, incorporating different styles of art with people's preferences and dreams."

"Will you always work in Kansas City?"

Her heart fluttered in her chest. A week ago, she would have said yes without hesitation. But now, as the car turned left and climbed higher still, providing the most incredible view of the valley to the west, she wasn't sure. Not only was Kelna an incredible country, but it had pushed her out of her comfort zone. Made her think about possibilities beyond the path she had always envisioned for herself.

"We'll see."

Lights appeared up ahead. As they drew closer, Madeline saw a redbrick building materialize against the backdrop of pine trees. Curved windows marched along the front, lit up from within with a golden light. Outside, a patio offered wrought iron chairs and pots overflowing with colorful blooms.

"Where are we?"

"A winery. My mother's family has owned it for over one hundred years."

Surprised, she turned to him as he pulled the roadster into a parking lot. The security car, which she had completely forgotten about, pulled in alongside them.

"That's amazing!"

"Wine is one of our top exports." He said it matter-of-factly but not without a great deal of pride. "My grandfather served as the minister of agriculture for years. Owning a vineyard was his idea of relaxing."

A hostess greeted them at the door and led them through the tasting room and out a back door, where a private terrace surrounded by grapevines awaited. String lights created a golden glow over the smooth stones of the patio. To the east, the mountains soared up, the setting sun painting the slopes with hues of orange, pink and violet. To the west, the terraced hillside was brushed with the darkness of encroaching night. A sommelier joined them on the patio and offered several wines for tasting. After Madeline requested a rosé and Nicholai settled on a port, the sommelier poured and left them alone on the patio.

He leaned back in his chair. "Tell me about your life."

"My life?"

They were interrupted by a waiter who came to take their food orders. Once he left, Nicholai pressed her.

"Back home. What's it like in Kansas City?"

"I already told you some in Paris."

"You did. Tell me more."

So she did. She told him about the jazz club that catapulted one back to the Roaring Twenties, the distillery where she'd bottled gin in college, the various districts with their unique shops and venues. The botanical gardens to the east of the city that blended prairie with forest. The soaring tower of the museum honoring those who served in the Great War.

"Paul got my sister Greta and me hooked on BBQ. You'll have to try it if you ever travel there."

"I will." He cocked his head to one side. "You mention Paul a lot. May I ask what happened to your birth father?"

She glanced down at her wineglass.

"I apologize. That was rude—"

"No. No, it's just… I rarely talk about him. Sometimes I forget he was ever a part of my life." She blew out a harsh breath. "My father flitted from job to job, sometimes disappearing for days and weeks at a time. We moved five times before I started kindergarten, usually because a check bounced or we were evicted for nonpayment. When he was gone, Mom was working herself to the point of exhaustion, but we were always happier." She ran a finger up and down the stem of her wineglass, her eyes distant as she revisited the past. "Those years shaped me. I love my work and where I live. But I also like the familiar. The knowing that I always belong somewhere."

"Where is he now?"

"I don't know. I have a vague memory of him coming back,

sitting at the breakfast table, and saying something about need-ing more money." Her lips curved up. "What I do remember, vividly, is my mother packing up our belongings and stuffing them into a rusted tank of a car. We moved to Kansas City. Mom found work fairly easily, first as a waitress, then a bar-tender, and then a restaurant manager. She met Paul there."

"And they lived happily ever after in a home along the river where you watched the fog roll in."

Her eyes crinkled at the corners as she smiled. "Yes. The rest of my childhood was a happy one. They set the bar high."

She leaned back in her chair, her eyes drifting up to the sky for a moment before her gaze returned to his. Her expression reminded him of Paris, made his heart leap as she looked at him with such warmth it made him long for endless nights like this.

"Thank you for this, Nicholai. Tonight, and the museum trip... I needed these breaks."

"You're welcome, Madeline." He held up his glass.

"What are we toasting to?"

He paused for a moment. "How about the future?"

She smiled and held up her own. Their glasses clinked. "To the future."

CHAPTER THIRTEEN

NICHOLAI SHOOK HANDS with Arthur Brandon, head of Brandon Consulting and one of the primary benefactors of Kelna's recent economic fortunes.

"We are very pleased with what we've seen, Your Highness."

Arthur smiled. The gesture was cold, edged with a steely strength that had catapulted the finance consultant to the head of a global firm that could make or break fortunes in a matter of hours. Arthur's reputation for rigid control also made him very selective about who he worked with. Any sign of risk and he had no problem severing ties and moving on to his next project. With a significant percentage in one of the shipping companies that would be utilizing Kelna's port, he wanted to ensure its success.

"Thank you, sir."

Arthur turned his attention to Madeline. His face softened just a fraction.

"And you, Madeline. It's nice to finally meet the future princess who's caused such a stir."

"For the right reasons this time, hopefully," Madeline replied with a slight smile.

Arthur's lips formed into something reminiscent of an actual grin. Nicholai blinked. He wouldn't have believed it if he hadn't seen it with his own eyes.

"Everyone is entitled to a mistake here and there," Arthur said.

But his eyes flickered to Nicholai, a hint of warning in the sharp depths. Nicholai kept his expression neutral, not deigning to play the man's game of control. Yes, losing Brandon Consulting's investment would be a huge setback. But it would not be the end. Kelna was too strong to be at the mercy of one man.

Nicholai glanced down to see Madeline's lips part, as if she were about to utter a retort. But then she pressed them together into a thin line.

"Thank you."

"Until our next meeting then." Arthur bowed his head to Nicholai. "Your Highness. Ma'am."

Madeline waited until the door closed behind Arthur before spinning around, her eyes snapping fire.

"That man is awful."

Nicholai chuckled. "Thank you for not saying that in front of him."

Madeline wrinkled her nose. "I wanted to say that and more. But I'm working on my diplomacy. I could see that self-righteous jerk pulling all of his financial support."

"He's been known to do that over far less."

Madeline's hands moved over the cups and saucers, pouring tea in one and coffee in the other. It had been two days since their winery adventure. Business had kept him from spending any more time with her. So when Arthur's team had requested a meeting with both the Prince and his fiancée, Nicholai hadn't even regretted that he would have to meet with the pompous financier. Not if it meant more time with Madeline.

He watched as she added a dash of milk and a small spoon of sugar into the coffee, stirring it before she brought it to him. The moment, simple yet domestic, struck him. The few women he had dated hadn't brought him coffee, much less taken the time to notice how he preferred his.

"I'm assuming Kelna does not have the financial resources to tackle all this development alone."

"No. But we will become financially independent. Until then, we play the game."

Her hands cradled her cup, as if she were drawing strength from the heat seeping through the porcelain.

"It seems like a dangerous, ugly world to me. But then I think back to some of the contracts, some of the people we've done business with." She blew on the surface of her tea, ripples chasing each other across the surface. "It's not as different as I thought. Putting on one face to convince someone to pick our firm. Putting on another to get money from an investor."

Shoulder to shoulder, they gazed out over Lepa Plavi. The bell tower stood tall and proud over the city. The bell had been used for centuries to warn of everything from an invading army to an approaching storm. History, culture, so much uniqueness that made his country home.

Beyond the city, the crane he had seen from the window of the plane when he'd flown into Kelna with Madeline and her team nearly two months ago broke the peacefulness of the landscape.

As if sensing how much the site of the construction bothered him, Madeline leaned her head against his shoulder.

"Why does it bother you so much?"

"It's the first decision my father truly put in my hands. There's responsibility. I always thought of myself, too, as modern. Forward-thinking." He nodded to where bulldozers moved back and forth shoving heavy mountains of rock to the side to make way for the new. "The buildings that were there were old, abandoned storefronts and an old hospital that we had once thought about turning into apartments. Nothing significant."

"Still, a part of your country's history. Change can be bittersweet."

"It can. Being beholden to so many and their goodwill makes the change heavier."

"And adds more responsibility you hadn't anticipated."

He gave in to desire then, slid an arm around her waist and pulled her close, taking strength from the simple contact. The beautiful peacefulness of being able to touch the woman who seemed to understand him like no one else, who had shown up when he'd needed her most, calmed him even as it warmed his heart. A woman who continued to stand strong and rise to the challenge of meetings and public events and unwanted media attention with increasing grace and confidence.

He breathed in, savored the light floral scent that clung to her hair.

"It is a bit jarring," she finally said as she continued to watch the frenzy of construction.

"The finished port will be similar to your design of the ballroom. Same coloring and stone style as Lepa Plavi. Blending of old and new."

She was quiet for a long moment. "And you truly like the ballroom design?"

He smiled against her hair. "It's grown on me."

She laughed. "Seriously, though."

"I do like it, Madeline. Not what I expected. But the more I've seen it, the more I know it will be an excellent addition to the palace. It will be the kind of space we can host guests and visitors with pride. The views will be unbeatable."

The morning after their trip to the winery, he'd walked out to stand in the spot where the new ballroom expansion would reach. Picturing the views from the glass walls had made him further appreciate the work Madeline had done, the vision she had created.

The door behind them burst open.

"Your Highness!"

An aide rushed into the room, tears streaming down her face. Fear exploded in his chest.

"The King?"

"No, sir. A bridge collapse. A school bus was on it—"

Nicholai was running for the door before she'd finished her sentence. He felt Madeline just behind him.

"There's nothing you can do," he said over his shoulder.

"Don't give me that." Madeline followed him through the

maze of hallways to the grand hall, quickening her pace to keep up with his determined jog. "I'm not just going to stay here at the palace. There must be something I can do."

He glanced down at her, at the determination on her face. "All right."

For the second time in two weeks, the limo made the journey to the hospital, this time at a more rapid pace. *The hospital's new trauma center*, Nicholai thought grimly as the car pulled up to a private entrance, *is about to be tested.*

They were rushed inside by palace security. A hospital security guard guided them to an administrative wing just down the hall from the emergency room. A grim-faced woman met them in the hall.

"Your Highness. Miss Delvine. I'm Marta Horvat, one of the hospital administrators."

"An aide briefed me on the way in. The bridge just crumbled?"

"Yes, sir. Fortunately, the drop was only ten feet or so. Other bridges in the area are over thirty to forty feet. It could have been much worse."

Nicholai steeled himself. "How many casualties?"

"Twenty with minor injuries. Three will require surgery, and two are in critical condition."

"But no deaths?" Madeline asked quietly.

"Not so far, ma'am."

Madeline sagged in relief as the pressure eased in his own chest.

"Thank you. Miss Delvine and I will be staying on for a while."

"I'll have the hospital security team—"

"No." Nicholai softened his order with a hand on Marta's shoulder. "Your team needs to focus on your patients and your staff. Don't worry about us. Pretend like we're not even here."

Marta sucked in a shuddering breath. "Thank you, Your Highness."

Nicholai waited until the woman was out of earshot before he turned to Madeline.

"This isn't going to be easy. There's the potential..." His voice trailed off, not even wanting to contemplate the possibility of what awaited them in the emergency room.

"I know." She reached up, cupped his face in her hands. "I know that this engagement is only for show, and temporary at that, but while it lasts, I'm not just going to show up for the nice and pretty events. I'm here to help you." Her hands tightened. "Let me help you."

He gave in, dipping his head to kiss her. It wasn't the sweet romance of their kiss in Paris, nor was it the frustrated passion that had brought them together on the seafront terrace. This was desperate, a need to connect before they walked into the unimaginable. His arms came around her, hugged her close, as she kissed him back.

A woman's voice cut into the moment through a loudspeaker in the ceiling, speaking first in Croatian, then English.

"Ambulance arriving, ambulance arriving. Status critical."

Nicholai and Madeline broke apart. Her eyes glinted bright in the light of the hallway, but her jaw was determined, her shoulders thrown back as if readying for battle.

"What first?"

"I need to find out what happened. If there're any risks to other bridges in the area." The sound of a distant sob came from the doors leading to the emergency room. "I need to meet with the families, too."

"What if I see the families while you talk with someone who knows what happened? Then come back here and meet with the families."

Some of the tension eased from his shoulders. He was used to doing things alone, especially after Ivan's illness, to dictating and trying to get through his priorities as quickly and efficiently as possible. The novelty of having someone to share the burden with, someone he trusted, was an unexpected gift.

"Let's go."

Five hours later, Nicholai could barely stand. So far, every patient was stable, even the driver who had borne the brunt of the damage when the bus had driven off the edge. After traveling out to the site and meeting with emergency crews and the Transportation Division, he'd returned to the hospital. Eviana had joined Madeline while he'd been at the scene of the accident. Together, they had already met with most of the families. The emotions of the people he'd met with ranged from shock and disbelief to bone-deep anger. Feelings he certainly did not begrudge them as initial facts started trickling in.

The bridge, it seemed, had been in desperate need of repair for months. The inspector responsible, however, had decided to write the bridge off as passing inspection instead of doing his job. Nicholai had already consulted with the police to ensure his arrest would be swift. Public Affairs was putting a conference together for later that afternoon, one that would be presided over by the King, Nicholai, the head of transportation and a representative from the hospital.

Nicholai rubbed the bridge of his nose. Orders had already been placed for new inspections on every bridge the inspector had been responsible for in his three years on the job. It amounted to nearly a third of Kelna's bridges. Nicholai had agreed with the transportation director's decision to order emergency closures, which would create traffic nightmares for a good portion of the Kingdom.

Better to have a traffic jam than any more accidents or, God forbid, deaths.

Nicholai glanced up and down the hall. The palace had stationed security guards at every entrance. Several others walked through the halls, ensuring that the only people allowed in or out were medical personnel or families of the victims. Not just for Nicholai, Eviana and Madeline, but to provide the families with much-needed privacy as hordes of news vans and reporters gathered outside the hospital.

He frowned as his eyes swept the chairs and couches in the waiting room. Madeline had been by his side for the past two hours, hugging crying mothers and fathers, consoling siblings and listening to the shouts of one particularly furious parent that had nearly resulted in security intervening.

She had stood up to it all. Perhaps she had just needed a break.

"Are you looking for the Princess?"

An older woman dressed in blue scrubs with fatigue etched into her dark brown skin, stopped next to him. He started to correct her use of the title, then stopped. A trivial detail, especially given what Madeleine had done today.

"Yes. I assumed she was taking a break."

A small smile crossed the nurse's face.

"No, sir. I'll take you to her."

She stopped outside a door marked with a patient number. After a gentle knock, she opened the door and poked her head inside. She glanced back at Nicholai and put a finger to her lips.

"They're still sleeping."

Nicholai walked in. Then stopped, floored by the sight in front of him.

Madeline sat in a chair in the corner. A little girl was curled up under a blanket on her lap. Her head rested against Madeline's shoulder, tousled curls covering most of a white bandage across her forehead. Their chests rose and fell with their deep, even breathing.

The little girl whimpered in her sleep. Madeline started, her eyelashes fluttering as her arms tightened around the child. The girl settled and both slipped back into sleep.

Tenderness flooded him. He had thought occasionally of having children, but it had never been something he'd paid particular attention to. It was inevitable, of course, for ensuring the line of succession.

But as he watched Madeline and the little girl sleep, he saw a future in stunning clarity. One with Madeline as the mother to his children, showering them with unconditional love as she brought a much-needed dose of normalcy to the chaos of living in a royal household.

Nicholai barely covered his start of surprise as he realized the nurse still stood behind him. He racked his brain.

"This is the girl whose parents are out of the country?"

The nurse nodded. "The family friend who was watching her had to leave to go pick up her own children. Your fiancée offered to stay, Your Highness."

Nicholai nodded, trying to fight past the tightness in his throat. "Thank you."

"I hope it's not too forward of me to say, but you chose well, sir."

Her words stole some of his contentment as she exited the room. He hadn't chosen at all. It had been Madeline who had put forth the idea, Madeline who had risen not once, not twice, but now three times, giving her all to their fake engagement, and who, with her fierce independence and kind heart, was winning over not only his country but the world.

He slipped out, but not before stopping to glance back. Dark shadows covered the pale skin beneath Madeline's eyes. The bun at the nape of her neck had come loose, wisps of hair sticking out at odd angles.

She had never looked more beautiful to him than she did in that moment.

He knew, as he closed the door behind him, that he would not be the only one who would mourn when their engagement came to an end.

CHAPTER FOURTEEN

MADELINE WOKE TO hushed whispers in the hospital room. The weight of Mina on her chest registered a moment before she would have stood.

Slowly, she opened her eyes. A couple stood on the other side of the room. The woman, with the same ringlets as Mina, except in a darker shade of blond, had her arms crossed tightly over her chest. A tall, heavier man stood next to her; a protective arm wrapped around her shoulders. Nicholai and the nurse who had brought Madeline in stood talking with them in hushed tones.

As if sensing her awaking, Nicholai's eyes shifted to hers. The emotion burning in his gaze hit her hard. Challenging as it had been, the afternoon had brought them closer together. Her respect for Nicholai, as well as her appreciation for the role he served, had deepened even more. Now she better understood the pressure Nicholai put on himself, how seriously he took his role.

"Oh." Mina's mother hurried over, her eyes focused on her daughter's sleeping form. "Thank you, Your Highness. For caring for our little girl."

"Oh, I'm not—"

"Mommy?"

"Mina!"

Mina launched herself from Madeline's lap into her mother's and father's arms. Madeline barely managed to blink back her own tears as she got to her feet and set the blanket aside.

"How can we ever repay you for being here when we weren't?" Mina's mother asked as she clutched Mina to her chest and rocked her daughter back and forth, tears slipping down her cheeks.

"By continuing to be the kind of parents that obviously love their daughter very much."

Her words made Mina's mother cry harder as Mina's father shook her hand and then pulled her gruffly into a hug. Nicholai kept a watchful eye on the man until he released Madeline. The man echoed his wife's words of thanks and then joined his family on the sofa.

She and Nicholai exited the room, leaving the united family in peace.

"How long was I asleep?"

"At least an hour, possibly more."

"I'm sorry. I left you to deal with all of it alone—"

"No."

Nicholai took her hands in his and stepped close. She knew the display of affection was discouraged by protocol, making his touch even more meaningful.

"You comforted a little girl in her hour of need. You were doing exactly what you should have been." His expression darkened. "If I had known our agreement would lead to this, I never would have agreed to it."

"I would have." She looked around the bustling corridor, at the slightly calmer expressions of the families now comforted in the knowledge that their children were at the very least safe. "This has really opened my eyes to what you and your family do."

"Speaking of," he said, as he released her hands and began to walk down the hallway with her at his side, "we have another press conference this afternoon. Eviana is still visiting with some of the other families, but she will join us at the podium to present a united front. My father's doctor advised against him coming to the hospital, but he will lead the press conference." He looked down at her. "Will you come with us?"

"Are you sure you trust me to keep my mouth shut?" she asked with a sassy grin, trying to lighten the somber mood.

He stared at her with complete seriousness. "Completely."

Touched, she swallowed hard and nodded.

"Good. They've arrested the inspector who falsified documentation saying that he had performed a complete inspection last year."

"What?" Outrage filled her as a nurse wheeled a child by in a wheelchair, his leg wrapped from ankle to knee in a thick bandage.

"He will be punished to the fullest extent of our laws. We've also demanded emergency inspections on all the bridges he was responsible for during his time with the transportation department. This will not happen again."

She believed him, knew that he wouldn't stop until he had ensured his country was safe.

A thought hit her.

"Nicholai..."

"What is it?" he prodded gently when she fell silent.

"The ballroom. It's not right moving forward with it right now."

"The money covering those projects comes from two different funds. But I see your point." He thought for a moment, then nodded. "I'll have to verify with my father and Eviana, but I think you're right. It would be in poor taste to continue right now."

"Perhaps when the new bridge is up and the others have been inspected?"

Nicholai gave her a small smile. "I know the thought of a royal life holds no appeal for you. But you would make an excellent princess."

He turned and left her staring after him, at a loss for words. Was Nicholai suggesting that he wanted to turn their performance into something more? Something that would result in her actually accepting his ring as the future queen of Kelna?

Two weeks ago, her answer would have been an immediate no. But as she watched Nicholai bend down and speak with the grandparents of one of the victims, she no longer knew the answer to that question.

The next week passed swiftly. The press conference was well received, as was Madeline's idea of postponing the ballroom project. Ivan had proven that his illness, while devastating, could not stop him from rising to the occasions that required his leadership, with he and the other leaders of the various agencies that had responded receiving accolades for their quick action.

In the wake of the immediate arrest of the inspector, coupled with Nicholai and the Transportation Department's quick action regarding the remaining bridges and Ivan's immediate pledge to cover any and all medical and other associated costs of the victims and their families, the reception had been surprisingly positive. So, too, had been the immediately proposed policy that would add a second inspection to all future inspections.

It hadn't hurt that the kindly nurse who had shown Nicholai to Mina's room had snapped a photo of Madeline and Nina fast asleep, one that she had shared privately with Mina's mother. The mother had then shared it on her social media with a heartfelt thanks to the Prince and Princess for stepping up in her absence. The photo had spread like wildfire, catapulting Madeline back into the spotlight.

Nicholai pushed back from his office desk and moved to the window. Madeline had made several more visits to the hospital and had sat in on meetings with Nicholai. Doing everything an actual fiancée would.

Making him wish more and more that this could be an actual engagement.

Then had come a true test for their fake engagement. J.T. had requested Madeline's presence back in Kansas City for a couple of days to meet with the team and the structural engineer. Saying yes had been one of the hardest things he'd done in a long time. When Madeline had left, she'd hugged him, but they hadn't repeated their kiss from the hospital. A fact that now pricked the skin between his shoulder blades and created a restlessness he couldn't ignore.

He was falling in love with Madeline. He'd known it was a possibility, had told himself he would be able to hold up if it happened and carry on.

But more and more, he didn't want to. Unfortunately, his own wants paled in comparison to the fact that Madeline was uncomfortable with royal life. That, and her career, were steep obstacles. Nor the issue of the requirements of the Marriage Law. Numerous problems he didn't have any solutions for.

His cell phone rang.

"Yes?"

"Your Highness." Charles, the chief public affairs officer, sounded grim.

"What is it?"

"Miss Delvine's ex has given an interview. It was published in a local Kansas City paper this morning."

A fury unlike any Nicholai had ever known pounded through him.

"What did it say?"

"It could be far worse. But he makes certain intimations about his and Miss Delvine's relationship."

Nicholai moved back to his desk and typed in Madeline's name. The most immediate results still focused on her and Mina in the hospital, as well as her involvement in the aftermath of the bridge collapse. But a couple links down, he saw the article in question.

Exclusive Interview with Future Princess Madeline Delvine's Ex-Fiancé

"Has anyone spoken to her yet?"

"No, sir."

He hung up. Why, of all weeks, did her weasel of an ex have to pick this one to crawl out of his hole and drag her name through the tabloids? He wanted to go to her, to hold her and reassure her that it would all be okay. But she was thousands of miles away.

He dialed her number.

"Hey." The waver in her voice told him she'd already seen the article.

"Are you all right?"

"I've been better."

Guilt punched him in the gut. Madeline had hinted that her ex had been manipulative. To him, it had sounded like abuse.

"I'm sorry, Madeline."

"It's not your fault my ex is a jerk."

"No. But what were the chances that he would have come back into your life if not for this?"

"I don't know."

The weariness in her voice alarmed him more than anything else could have in that moment. She had stayed strong through so much.

"What are you doing this week?"

"Hiding in my apartment. People were showing up outside the office. Reporters were calling. J.T. finally suggested I take some time off and go home."

Her misery cut him deep. To have her work cut short and her visit home tainted made him furious.

A chill crept up his spine. He was in love with Madeline, yes. But would asking her to be his lead only to misery?

Even as he felt like someone had ripped his heart out of his chest, inspiration struck. A small way that he could give Madeline a break from the chaos. Buy him more time while he figured this out. It was a selfish idea, he freely admitted.

"Meet me in Los Angeles."

A beat of silence followed, then, "What?"

"It's, what, 10:00 a.m. there?"

"Yes, but—"

"I'll charter a plane to fly you from Kansas City to Los Angeles. It'll be ready within an hour. Can you take a few days off?"

When she spoke, the smile in her voice bolstered his spirits. "J.T.'s already put me on leave. So yes."

"I'll be there as soon as I can."

Nicholai called his secretary next. Minutes later, he was walking down the hall to his father's office. He knocked before announcing himself.

"Enter."

The weakness in his father's voice made him hesitate. What was he doing? Flying off on some exotic vacation while the King struggled?

"Nicholai?"

Nicholai pushed open the door. Ivan sat behind his desk, glasses perched on the tip of his nose. Stacks of papers were arranged in neat piles on the surface.

"How are you, *otac*?"

"Alive," Ivan replied dryly. "I've had better days. But today is not the worst." He gestured to the laptop in front of him. "I assume you are here because of the story?"

"Yes."

Ivan stared down at the screen for a long moment. "Fortunately for both Madeline's sake and the country, the recent positive press only makes this young man look more like a *dupe*."

Nicholai couldn't hold back his smirk. "I can't remember the last time you cursed."

"I like Madeline. She makes you happy. And one day soon, she will be my daughter-in-law."

Nicholai's chest tightened. What had he expected when he started this charade? His first and primary goal had been to save Kelna from the fallout of his impetuous actions. He hadn't envisioned Madeline becoming so important to him, nor to his family.

But now, as the lie continued to grow, he felt ensnared by the web he'd spun.

"How is she?"

Nicholai blinked and refocused on his father. "All right. I hate that she wasn't here when the story was published."

"Why not go to her?"

"That's actually why I came." He cleared his throat. "I want to take her away. To truly give her a break from the press."

"For how long?"

"A few days."

"Do you trust your sister and me enough to leave us alone for so long?"

Even though his father's eyes twinkled as he said it, Nicholai frowned. "I don't know why you and Eviana think I don't trust you."

Ivan's gaze darkened with sadness. "You think I don't see the burden that has been placed on you? The knowledge of what will come to be? The position that will leave you in?"

Cold fingers reached into Nicholai's chest, wrapped around his heart, and squeezed.

"It's my duty."

"It doesn't mean it's not a heavy burden to bear. I benefited greatly from my father's tutelage. I had over a decade of assuming more and more responsibility. Not a year."

"No."

Nicholai paused, allowed himself a moment of grief so deep it clawed at him, threatened to tear him apart.

And then pulled himself back together.

"I won't fail."

"I have no doubt you won't fail the Kingdom. But," Ivan added gently, "I worry you will fail yourself. It is not a weakness to ask for help, to open one's self to another. To trust them to love you at your best and your worst."

Like Madeline.

She had seen him at his worst after the first press conference. Had stood by his side through scandal, the mundaneness of everyday life and heartbreak as Kelna had faced down one of its worst accidents in years.

For better or for worse.

Vows he intended to utter within the year. Before Paris, he would have said them for the sake of his country and preserving his family's line.

But now...now he wanted to say them for all of that and more. For a woman who brought out the best in him as a leader, whom he suspected was coming to love Kelna like it was her own country.

Could he offer her enough? Would the life of a working royal sustain her the way her career did? Would he be asking too much of her?

"She is a good person, *moj sin.*"

Nicholai quelled his errant thoughts as he nodded. "She is."

"And now you must go to her." Ivan smiled at him. "Enjoy this reprieve. You both have earned it."

Guilt flickered through him as he left. He had deceived his father in the beginning because he'd thought to handle the situation of his scandalous kiss with Madeline on his own. Now he was paying the price of the lie that lay between them, of not being able to talk with his father about his evolving feelings.

Frustrated, and anxious to get to Madeline, he headed to his chamber to pack. Whatever happened during this sojourn to paradise, he was going to enjoy every last minute he could with the woman he could no longer picture his life without.

CHAPTER FIFTEEN

MADELINE PULLED BACK the gauzy curtain and stepped out onto the patio. Just below the patio, crystal clear water lapped at the stairs leading down into the lagoon. Beyond the breakers, the deep blue waters of the South Pacific stretched to the horizon.

When Nicholai had told her to meet him in Los Angeles, she'd expected a weekend getaway, perhaps a trip to California's wine country or somewhere else where they could be away from the prying eyes of the paparazzi. A car had been waiting for her in Los Angeles and whisked her away to a prominent hotel in Malibu. The penthouse had afforded stunning views of the Pacific. She'd dived into the sea of faces surrounding her and gone out for dinner at a wonderful Italian bistro, followed by a large glass of wine at a sidewalk bar.

The brief return to normalcy had been a much-needed balm for her wounded pride after Alex's article had come to light. Once again, she'd been hit with a barrage of text messages, phone calls and, worst of all, another conversation with her mother, who was growing increasingly worried about Madeline's cryptic responses to her supposed engagement.

Things were about to come to a head. She was sure of it. Even though she had sensed her and Nicholai growing closer, he had said nothing about making any changes to their arrangement. Still confused herself as to how she would reply if he asked, she had said nothing.

Coward.

She brushed that aside as she leaned against the rail and breathed in the heady mix of sea and tropics. The following morning, the front desk of the hotel had called to let her know a car would be by at 10:00 a.m. The car had taken her back to the airport, where Nicholai had been waiting next to another private jet.

When she'd seen him, she hadn't been able to stop herself from running to him and throwing her arms around his neck. Instead of stepping away or chastising her, he'd crushed her to him in a tight embrace that instantly washed away the strain of the past couple of days.

They boarded the plane, with Nicholai responding to her repeated questions as to where they were headed with an enigmatic smile. It hadn't been until the plane turned and continued out over the ocean that Nicholai had finally told her they were heading to Bora Bora.

And now she was here. On a private island resort for the world's elite who needed privacy and vacation in equal measure. Sharing a two-bedroom over-the-water bungalow with her fake fiancé.

Her bed sat on a see-through floor. With the flick of a switch, the glass would go from opaque to a window into the lagoon beneath her. Last night, she'd pressed the button that had turned on lights beneath the floor, giving her an incredible view of the sea world at night.

They'd eaten on the plane, so Nicholai had only ordered champagne and chocolate-covered strawberries as their welcome meal last night. They had sat at the mosaic-inlaid table for two, saying almost nothing and simply enjoying the novelty of anonymity in a luxurious surrounding that, two months ago, Madeline could never have pictured herself enjoying.

She glanced over at the other bedroom suite. When Nicholai had told her that the bungalow had two bedrooms, she felt like he had been waiting for her to say something. Part of her had wanted to tell him then the conflict she was feeling over her growing feelings for him versus her uncertainty about being a part of the royal family.

Except the attention she had received following Alex's interview had been yet another reminder of the intense scrutiny the people in Nicholai's world faced. Even if she could adjust to that, accept it as a part of a new life, how could she possibly give up her career? Something that meant so much to her on both personal and professional levels? Something that brought her joy? Would she come to regret what she had given up, possibly even become resentful of Nicholai and the crown?

"Good morning."

Madeline turned to see Nicholai smiling at her. In a black V-neck shirt and tan linen pants, he looked the most relaxed she'd ever seen him.

"You were thinking deep thoughts."

"I was."

"Care to share?" he asked as he joined her at the rail.

"Not at the moment." She reached over and laid her hand on top of his. "I think right now the moment calls for relaxing and indulging." She smiled up at him. "Thank you, Nicholai. This is exactly what I needed."

"I know." Regret colored his tone. "When Public Affairs told me about that article…"

Madeline tightened her fingers over his. "I'm a big girl. I didn't fully understand what I was doing when I offered to be your fake fiancée, but I still proposed it and I continued with it, even after I realized what it meant." Before Nicholai could continue down his path of self-flagellation, she nodded out at the lagoon. "We have four whole days at our disposal. What should we do?"

Nicholai's brows drew together. "I hadn't thought beyond getting here and escaping the paparazzi."

"My mother taught me that on a vacation, you should do one thing a day. Anything more and you risk getting burned out. And always build in days for resting."

"Sounds like a wise plan."

"I have friends who go in with a full itinerary. Scheduled stops, tour guides, the works. They enjoy it. But I don't."

"Sounds like an average day to me."

She lightly nudged him with her shoulder. "So, let's change that up. Get you to relax a little."

"I'd like that, Madeline."

The sound of her name on his lips, said with caressing warmth, filled her. She resolved in that moment that, no matter what happened at the end of their vacation, she would enjoy herself and her time with Nicholai.

She walked toward the stairs leading down into the water. "Let's start with a swim."

She slid into the warm water. Nicholai joined her after changing into a pair of black swim trunks that made her take a second look at his impressive physique. She paddled languidly through the water as Nicholai moved with sure, strong strokes. Several times he disappeared beneath the surface, popping back up with a shell or a bit of sea glass to show her.

At one point, they both drifted lazily on their backs, staring up at the impossibly blue sky.

"I can't remember the last time I just relaxed," she murmured.

"I know when I did. Paris."

The answer surprised her enough that she lost her buoyancy and righted herself in the water.

"Really?"

"Yes." He treaded water next to her, his eyes boring into hers. "That was the first night in a long time where I could just be myself. Part of it was you not knowing who I was. But a large part of that was you, Madeline."

"Nicholai…"

He reached out, his fingertips trailing over her cheek. "For the next four days, I want to be those two people we were on the roof that night."

"Just Nick?"

"Just Nick," he repeated with a small smile, "and Madeline. No titles, no crown, no paparazzi—"

"Or pompous investors?"

"Or pompous investors," Nicholai agreed with a chuckle. "I care about you a great deal, Madeline. Would you join me in that? Just being us for a few days?"

She swam closer until their legs brushed against each other. She reached up, cupped his face.

"I'd like that very much."

He leaned down and sealed his lips over hers. She surrendered herself to the moment, the novel sensation of kissing a man she cared deeply about while balancing in the waves of a far-flung tropical getaway.

Yet even as he deepened the kiss, hugged her closer against him, she couldn't ignore the whisper of warning across the back of her neck at the finality she had heard in his words. The resignation that, after their time in Bora Bora, their time together would be over.

It was one of those incredible days that seemed to extend forever and yet slipped by in the blink of an eye. They kayaked out to the breakers, dozed on the hammock stretched out over the water and indulged in a long soak in the hot tub on the patio. Dusk seeped into the sky with a rainbow of colors, from rosy pink and deep violet to fiery orange and the deep blue hint of night spreading up from the east.

Madeline had just finished showering and stepped out onto the patio as a butler finished laying the table. On the white tablecloth, a low candle flickered next to a vase holding a single red rose. The butler poured them each a glass of wine, bowed and departed as silently as he had arrived. They savored *poisson cru*, succulent fish marinated in lime and coconut milk and served on a bed of onions, cucumber and tomatoes, grilled mahi-mahi and *po'e*, a baked pudding, for dessert.

"I don't think I can move."

Nicholai laughed. "Perhaps I should ask the palace chef to replicate some of the recipes."

Madeline made a soft humming noise in response. Allowed herself the indulgence of imagining a future where she would dine at the palace with Nicholai as his true bride.

Stars winked into existence overhead, peppering the night sky with their glittering brilliance. Madeline breathed in, exhaled as she savored pure contentment.

"You know, when we were in Paris, the one thing that disappointed me about that night was that I could only see a few stars."

"I'm glad to know that was the only thing that disappointed you."

Madeline shot him a saucy smile. "How could I not be impressed by your Superman routine?"

He rubbed the back of his neck in a self-conscious gesture. "I was worried about you."

"And you didn't even know who I was." Whether it was the wine or the ambience or the man sitting next to her, the magnitude of what she had just said hit her. "You really are a good man."

Nicholai started, a frown crossing his face.

"What?"

"You literally jumped from a balcony to help someone you thought was in need. When our picture showed up in the papers, you were worried about the effect it would have on Kelna instead of yourself." She smiled at him. "I don't think there are many men like you left in the world."

He stared out over the darkening scene. Tendons tightened in his neck.

"Nicholai?"

"You say I'm honorable. Except what I'm thinking right now is far from honorable."

"Tell me," she urged softly.

He pulled his phone from his pocket, his fingers tapping across the screen. A moment later, the lilting strains of an orchestra filled the air. He stood, placing his phone on the table and extending a hand to her.

"Dance with me."

She took his outstretched hand, let him tug her to her feet and pull her close as they swayed on the patio against the darkening sky blending into the ocean. She rested her cheek on his chest, felt the beat of his heart against her skin. She pressed a little closer, wanting to savor his woodsy scent, the strength of his embrace, all the details she feared would one day fade from memory.

"Madeline…"

She looked up into eyes that echoed both her own wants and fears.

"Stay with me tonight."

She rose up on her toes and let her kiss serve as her answer.

Nicholai watched the sun rise over the waters of the lagoon. He'd fallen asleep last night with Madeline in his arms, the most content he could ever remember being. He'd awoken at dawn with her body curved against his, her breathing soft against his chest.

Since that first night, they'd spent every night together. Their days had been filled with exploring the resort, hiking the nature reserve, swimming in the waters of the lagoon, their adventures interrupted only by exquisite meals and long stretches of doing absolutely nothing other than lounging on the patio or relaxing in the hot tub.

One of his most vivid memories had been lying in the hammock with Madeline's head on his shoulder as she had read one of her classic novels and he'd thumbed through a mystery he had been meaning to read for well over a year. The water lapping beneath them, and the sky stretching above them, had brought him a peace he hadn't even known he'd been searching for.

A peace that had evaporated with the coming dawn.

Inside, a war raged on. A selfish part of his character, one he hadn't even fully known existed, demanded that he ask Madeline to stay. To become his fiancée for real and the future queen of Kelna.

But the rational part, the man his father had raised him to be, argued against temptation. Madeline deserved a normal life. She deserved to have the career she had worked so hard for.

He scrubbed a hand over his face as her words from their drive came back to him.

I'm going to miss this place...

Would she miss it enough to consider giving them a chance? To stay and see if their relationship could turn into something more? Something permanent?

The buzzing of his phone interrupted his thoughts. Frowning when he saw the prime minister's name on the screen, he answered.

"Yes?"

"Your Highness." Dario's tone was grim. "The duchess is engaged."

"Excuse me?"

"The Duchess. You met and were photographed with her at the ball."

"Oh." He vaguely remembered the blonde woman Dario had introduced him to shortly after the start of the ball. She'd been pleasant to talk to. But there had been no spark, nothing beyond two professionals meeting and considering a mutually beneficial arrangement.

"Forgive my impudence, Your Highness, but how much longer are you going to continue this charade?"

Nicholai's fingers tightened on the phone. "I told you. As long as it takes."

"For the country or yourself?"

"Watch yourself, Prime Minister." Nicholai's voice turned to ice. "I don't take kindly to being questioned in such a manner."

"And I don't enjoy doing it. But it's been almost a month."

"I said a month, possibly two."

"The longer you wait, the harder it will be to move on."

"You mean select a wife from your list of potential candidates?"

"A list you agreed to, Your Highness," Dario replied, his voice a step away from defiance. "Are you considering turning this pretense into a real engagement? With a woman you told me yourself has no interest in residing in Kelna?"

"What I am considering or not is not your concern."

"Given that you must receive Parliament's approval on your choice of a wife while meeting the requirements of the Marriage Law, it is very much my concern."

"Approval you have already voiced publicly." Dario's silence gave Nicholai a small sense of satisfaction. "I understand the law, Prime Minister. I will wed within the year of assuming the throne. But who I choose—"

A creak sounded behind him. Dread filled his chest with a heavy weight.

"I'll call you back."

Steeling himself, he stood and turned. Madeline stood framed in the doorway. Dressed in white cotton shorts and a blue tank top, with her hair in a tousled blond halo around her face, she looked beautiful.

And heartbroken, he realized as the weight grew and dragged his heart down with it.

"What did you hear?"

"Enough."

"Madeline—"

He reached for her. She flinched and stepped back.

"There's a *law* that requires you to marry?"

His hands fell to his sides. "Yes."

"Why didn't you tell me?"

"It's an old law. One that hasn't been enforced for nearly two-hundred years. The Kings before me were much older and already married before they ascended the throne."

"So what?"

"When the prime minister told me about it after my father's diagnosis, we agreed it was best not to draw public attention to it. We wanted the future queen to be…"

"Someone from your list of potential candidates?"

The bitterness in her tone alarmed him. She wrapped her arms about her waist as if to shield herself from him.

"You only heard part of the conversation."

"I heard enough. When you kissed me in Paris and told me you weren't free to pursue anything, it's because you were looking for a wife like you were shopping for groceries."

Irritated by her casual dismissal of the conundrum he faced, he shoved his hands in his pockets. "It wasn't my first choice. But, Madeline, I'd just learned that my father was dying and I had to not only take over the throne but marry, too. When the prime minister offered to compile a list of candidates, it seemed like the right choice."

"What changed?" Her lips parted as the color disappeared from her face. "The ball. The blonde woman he introduced you to, the duchess. She was on the list, wasn't she?"

His jaw hardened. "Yes."

"But I wasn't."

"No." The word was torn from someplace deep inside him. He wanted to lie, to soothe away the pain on her face. "But I've come to care about you, Madeline. Deeply. I want to try and make this into something permanent."

"Do you? Or do you just want me because I'm convenient? Because I can get you something you want?"

Hurt made his chest ache. "Do you truly believe I would do that?"

"I don't know what to believe. I've believed before, and I've gotten hurt."

His gut clenched at being compared to Alex. Realizing her mistake, Madeline hastened to rephrase her words.

"I only meant—"

"You don't need to explain."

He shook his head. Of all the ways he'd pictured the morning going, this had not been one of them. He had envisioned telling Madeline how much he cared, that he wanted a chance for them to see where this relationship could take them.

Nowhere.

He had hurt her too much, and she him.

"I'll arrange for you to fly home."

"Home," she echoed.

"Yes. Kansas City." He inclined his head to her even as his heart fell to his knees. "Thank you, Miss Delvine, for all of your help."

And then he turned and walked away from the woman he loved.

CHAPTER SIXTEEN

MADELINE TAPPED HER pen against her desk. The steady rhythm echoed in the empty office. It had been over a week since she had returned from Bora Bora. The media had gone blissfully silent, distracted by a scandal involving an international pop star. Aside from a news blip about one other bridge in Kelna being found unsafe and in need of repair, the world had temporarily moved on from their obsession with the tiny Adriatic country.

Everyone, that is, except her.

Whenever she thought back to those last moments on the patio with the rising sun illuminating Nicholai's handsome, solemn expression, grief hit her just as it had when he'd walked away.

She had thought Nicholai was going to join her on the flight home. But when the car had pulled up, he had come out only to say goodbye, telling her that he was catching a different flight that would take him west and back to Kelna faster than going east would. She had accepted his excuse, contemplated kissing him one last time, and then decided it would be too painful for both of them. She'd gotten in the car and let herself be driven away without a backward glance.

A move she had almost instantly regretted, but hadn't been able to bring herself to fix.

The tapping of her pen intensified. She'd let her own hurt and past fears get the better of her. Had judged him harshly in the moment instead of placing herself in his shoes. She knew Nicholai. Knew the kind of man he was. The pain on his face when she'd insinuated he was anything like Alex haunted her every night.

That and running away instead of fighting.

Why had she not told him the true depth of her feelings? Because she was scared? Scared that he wouldn't feel the same way? Frightened that loving him and even contemplating the possibility of somehow making a relationship work would mean repeating past mistakes and forfeiting independence?

Her fear, rooted in her past, had overridden what she'd known both in her heart and her mind. Nicholai was not Alex. Not her father. Would things have been different if she had shared that, somewhere along the way, she'd fallen in love with him? That his commitment to his people, the honor he brought to his role, the way he had treated her like a partner even in the midst of their charade, had pulled her deeper into the emotions he had awakened that first night in Paris?

She sighed and leaned back into her chair, letting her head fall against the headrest. She regretted it now, and yet still couldn't bring herself to call him. To take that final step.

"There you are."

Madeline let out a little shriek and whirled around. Her mother stood behind her, hands on her hips, with that motherly look that conveyed Madeline was in trouble etched onto her porcelain skin.

"Hey, Mom."

"Don't 'Hey, Mom' me." Stacey Delvine marched up to her daughter's desk and sat down in the chair across from her. "It's time you told me what's going on."

Madeline nodded. "Yeah."

Stacey blinked. "I was expecting more of a fight."

Madeline let out a watery laugh. "I don't think I have any fight left in me."

Stacey's eyes narrowed.

"Has he hurt you?"

"What?"

"That boy. Has he hurt you?"

"The boy you're referring to is a prince."

"I don't care if he's the King of England. Did he hurt you?"

Madeline sucked in a shuddering breath. "Yes. But not in the way you think."

She told her mother everything, starting from the night in Paris with Nicholai's superhuman jump onto the rooftop, how the illicit kiss on the terrace had happened, the fake engagement, all the way up to that horrid morning in Bora Bora when they had parted ways.

Stacey sat back in her chair. "Well."

"Yeah."

"Quite a mess."

"Mild way of putting it."

"What are you going to do?"

Madeline massaged her temples as a headache began to form. "I don't know, Mom. This feels different than what I went through with Alex."

"It is different." Stacey leaned forward. "Alex wanted to control you. From what you've told me, Nicholai is the opposite. He knows you. He cares for you."

"I thought he did. But the law...the *list*..."

"I'm not saying he handled things well." Stacey cocked her head. "But do you think he really concealed all of that to hurt you? That he was searching for a wife all this time?"

"No."

"Then, time for the most difficult question of all." Stacey gathered Madeline's hands in hers. "Do you truly believe he agreed to the engagement simply because you were a convenience? Or because, even in the beginning, he wanted you in his life?"

She stared down at her mother's hands wrapped around her own. The touch grounded her, allowed her to breathe and push away the mess of insecurities and heartache. She looked out the window at the familiar sights of the city that had been her home for so long. The tower of the World War I museum, smoke spilling over the stone rim from the eternal flame. The circular fountain outside the impressive stone facade of Union Station. The tracks of the streetcar that whisked Kansas Citians and tourists alike up to the River Market. Her eyes strayed to a brick office building, one of the first projects she had worked on as an intern.

If she looked past her own hurt and really thought about giving a relationship with Nicholai a shot, she knew it would mean letting go of some things she cared deeply about. It made her sad, but in a bittersweet way. Saying goodbye to one stage as she stood on the precipice of a change she knew could bring her and Nicholai great happiness.

"You love him."

Madeline looked at her mother with heartbroken eyes. "I do. I was so insistent on being alone for a while, on not dating, on not forming any romantic attachments. I thought that's what I needed. But looking back on it, it was more to protect myself. I fell for Alex and ignored the warning signs because he was familiar. Easy. I wanted to be married. I wanted my own family. Wanted the same kind of stability Paul brought to our family, the dream of being a wife and mother. And I lost myself in that." She ran her hands through her hair. "Yet I'm now in love with a man whose future wife must do exactly that. Surrender herself to a rule, to an entire country."

When Stacey spoke, her voice was thick with tears. "I can't think of a single good thing in my life that has not required some sort of sacrifice. Even being a mother meant I had to give some things up."

"I know. I don't want to end up in the same position you were forced into by...him."

Even now, all these years later, she couldn't bring herself to call the man who had treated them so horribly by the title of *father*. "You told me you gave up everything, and all he did was take more and more."

"You truly think Nicholai would do that to you?"

"No. But being a queen... The day that I went to the hospital was one of the most humbling experiences of my life. And I know moments like that are not the norm. But they could happen at any time. Where I might have to leave my work, my own children, to serve the people." Her heart ached. "I'm coming to understand, just a little bit, the pressure that Nicholai feels to lead. To be the best representative he can be. Even if he would agree to try again, I don't know if I'm strong enough to do that."

Stacey reached over and squeezed her daughter's hand. "During a faked engagement, you stood up to the international press and spent hours with a frightened girl in a hospital. You didn't buckle under the pressure of an ex giving a tell-all interview."

"Yeah. But that was a few weeks. I don't know if I can keep that up for years on end."

"Darling, tomorrow J.T. might lose the business. The economy might collapse. War could break out. Yes," Stacey said as she reached up and smoothed a curl back from Madeline's face, "know your strengths. Know your weaknesses. Know what your limits are. But what I see is a young woman more than capable of seizing that life with both hands and making the most of it next to the man she loves. And she's letting herself be held back by fear."

The truth of her mother's words hit her hard.

"Well. When you say it like that, suddenly it all makes sense."

"Which is why you should have come to me sooner."

Madeline laughed. "I should have. But I didn't want to betray his confidence."

"I understand that." Stacey blinked back tears. "Believe me, I am not a fan of my daughter moving halfway around the world. And maybe you'll go and talk to Nicholai, and you won't be on the same page."

The possibility nearly tore Madeline in two. "I hurt him, Mom."

"And he hurt you. If you stay together, it will happen again. But," Stacey added softly, "if you love each other, if you work through those hurts together, it can lead to an even greater love."

"I love him," Madeline whispered softly. Then, as a smile stole over her face, she said it louder.

"I'm in love with a prince."

Nicholai stared at the rapidly forming skeleton of the new bridge. He saw the stone foundation, the massive pillars, the long threads of iron that would be laid into the cement. He saw it all, but hardly any of it registered.

"Your Highness?"

Nicholai turned to the newly appointed bridge inspector at his side.

"I apologize. My mind was elsewhere. You were telling me of the tentative construction schedule."

The inspector nodded enthusiastically.

"Yes, we expect for it to be ready in six months."

"And done to code?"

"Yes." The inspector's expression turned grave. "I will not make the same mistakes as my predecessor."

Nicholai offered his hand to the young woman. "I know the transportation director chose well."

He moved on to tour the rest of the site, conscious of the photographers huddling. There had been an audible murmur of disappointment when he'd emerged from the royal car alone.

Even though their vacation had been uninterrupted, it hadn't stopped photos of their private plane leaving Kansas City and then Los Angeles from making the rounds on social media.

Public Affairs had begun to forward him the various articles and trending posts in a daily report. Yesterday's report had included a picture of Madeline with her mother walking down an avenue of trees at the Nelson. Their arms had been entwined, smiles wreathing their faces. Stacey Delvine was still a beautiful woman, and the relationship between the two was clear in the pointed chin, the slight tilt to their nose, their dark brows a pleasant contrast to their blond hair.

Another regret. Not meeting the family that had raised such an incredible woman. A woman he'd let get away because, as he'd made his own plans, he hadn't opened up, hadn't confided in Madeline and told her everything until it was too late.

The tour of the site completed, Nicholai returned to the palace. The next few hours flew by as he dealt with one matter after another.

A knock on his door made him blink.

"Enter."

Eviana walked in with a tray in her hands. "It's almost seven."

He glanced at the bay of windows. "It's still light outside."

"When was the last time you ate?"

He glanced at his watch, frowned. "I think breakfast."

Eviana sighed and set the tray down in front of him. The delicious aroma of roasted chicken and rice wafted up from the covered dish.

"Thank you."

Eviana prowled about the room, stopping to examine a book or one of the folders he had left out.

"Was there something else?"

"What happened between you and Madeline on your vacation?"

Nicholai looked at her with narrowed eyes.

"What do you mean?"

"Don't give me that. Ever since you came back, you've been moping around like a lovesick teenager."

"I'm a prince. I don't mope."

Eviana's face softened. "Nicholai, you look like you've lost your best friend. What's wrong?"

No longer hungry, and resigned that his sister wouldn't rest until she'd discovered the true story one way or another, Nicholai set the fork down.

"In a week or so, Madeline and I will announce the end of our engagement."

Eviana's eyes bugged out of her head. "What?"

"Don't play coy, Eviana. You had to have suspected that Madeline and I had an arrangement, not a true engagement."

"I had a pretty good idea of why you were suddenly engaged to someone I had barely met, but you two are good together. Good for Kelna." She slammed her hands down on the desk and leaned forward. "You're in love with her."

Nicholai's heart twisted in his chest. "Yes."

"And she loves you."

"She cares for me."

"She loves you," Eviana repeated.

"Whether or not she does is irrelevant."

"Did you tell her how you feel? Did you ask her to consider being your actual fiancée?"

He thought back to their last conversation on the patio of the bungalow. Relived those final, gut-wrenching moments.

"I alluded to it, yes."

"But you didn't ask."

"She learned about the Marriage Law and the list of candidates the prime minister composed. She said she didn't know if she could trust that I wasn't asking for our relationship to become real because I cared about her or because it was convenient." He pushed the memory out of his head. "Besides, she loves her career. I doubt she would give that up."

"Why can't she do something related to architecture here?"

Nicholai gestured to the bustling construction site on the horizon. "Kelna is growing, Eviana. faster than any of us anticipated. I can barely keep up with things as it is. And when

Father…" He breathed in deep. "When Father passes, my responsibilities will increase even more."

"Why haven't you asked me?"

Nicholai looked at the sister. "What?"

"Why haven't you asked me for more help?" She almost sounded hurt.

Nicholai frowned. "You have your own life. The charities you work with, the public appearances—"

"Which does take up a lot of my time, yes. But it's not nearly the amount of work compared to the load you carry."

Nicholai rubbed the back of his neck. "I never thought to ask."

Eviana looked down at the desk, traced her finger across the pattern on the wood.

"I sometimes wondered if it's because you didn't trust me."

"Nothing could be further from the truth." His eyes moved back to the construction site. "It was just always the expectation that I would take over one day. When Father got sick about the same time that Kelna began expanding, I became so focused on what I had to do that I couldn't see anything else."

"You always were independent."

His lips worked at the corners. "So is Madeline. Eviana, I can't ask her to give up her life."

"What if it's not giving up her life but adapting, changing it? Think about it, Nicholai. If I were to take on some of the duties that you currently handle, and then Madeline takes over some as the future queen, that will be three instead of one."

"Even if we were to share duties, that doesn't solve the problem of her career."

"There are at least two architecture firms right here in Lepa Plavi. Have Madeline take on the occasional project that she wants, or maybe even serve as a consultant for her firm, make time for her to be able to do what she loves."

He almost didn't want to entertain the possibility, allow himself to hope. "I don't know if she can forgive me for not confiding in her sooner. If she can believe that I care about her for her and not because of some archaic law."

"And she may say no. But don't you owe it to her to give her that chance, to hear all the possible options and decide for herself?"

"And what about you, Eviana? This would be taking on a massive responsibility. It'll change your life as well."

She nodded. "It would. And no, it's not what I envisioned for my life." She shrugged. "I would be lying if I said it was my first choice, but I would rather have some of what I wanted and help lead than see you shoulder the burden alone. Especially if it means letting someone like Madeline get away."

"She really is something."

"When I heard her defend Amara at the press conference, I knew I liked her as a woman. And then, when she held that little girl at the hospital, I liked her as a leader for our people." She moved to Nicholai and flung her arms around his neck just like she had when she'd been a little girl. "You carry so much weight for our family. It's time to share the burden and finally go after something you want."

He returned her hug, fought past the tightness in his throat as he spoke.

"Thank you."

Suddenly filled with an iron resolve, he moved to his desk.

"I have two meetings tomorrow—"

"I'll cover them."

"I'll miss the economic forum."

Eviana wrinkled her nose. "Not my favorite, but I'll manage."

"Thank you." He pulled open his drawer. "Could I get your opinion?"

"Sure, on what?"

Her eyes widened as he pulled out a blue jewelry box. "I thought she already had a ring."

"One picked out by Public Affairs."

"How long have you been holding on to this?"

"A little over a week."

He flipped open the lid, satisfaction curling through him at Eviana's delighted gasp.

"Nicholai...it's perfect."

"Let's hope Madeline thinks so, too." He shot her a sudden, confident smile. "Hopefully the next time I see you, I'll have a princess by my side."

CHAPTER SEVENTEEN

"MESSAGE CAME THROUGH for you."

Frowning, she took the slip of paper J.T. held out to her. "From who?"

"Potential client. They really liked your design of the ballroom and are wanting to talk to you about a similar project."

Madeline looked at the paper. "They want to meet at the Nelson?"

J.T. gave her an encouraging smile. "I told them it was an inspirational site for you and your work. I can vouch for them. Nothing sinister."

Madeline laughed even as she rolled her eyes. "The fact that you have to clarify it's nothing sinister makes me wonder what you're up to."

J.T. sobered. "I know the last month has been rough on you, kid."

Madeline struggled to keep her smile in place even as her heart twisted inside her chest.

"Nothing I can't handle."

She nearly squirmed under J.T.'s somber gaze. The man usually had the jovialness of Santa Claus, but when he chose to, he could be frighteningly perceptive.

"I know there's more to this engagement than you're telling me."

She lifted her shoulders and tried to give him an enigmatic smile.

"I'm worried you're going to get hurt again."

His kind words chipped away at her stubbornness. "I think it's too late for that. But I made choices. And this time... Nicholai isn't like Alex."

Just saying his name hurt. But no matter what happened, she would not regret her time with him.

Her answer seemed to satisfy an unspoken question. "Okay." He nodded toward the slip of paper. "Got time to meet with them in an hour?"

She glanced at her computer. With the ballroom construction project on hold, and the other projects the team had been working on nearly completed, she had experienced an unusual and yet very necessary decline in demands on her time.

"Sure."

"Great." J.T.'s eyes twinkled. "Let me know what you think."

She hesitated. "Would you ever let someone be a consultant?"

J.T. brows shot up.

"Consultant?"

"Yeah." The idea took hold, a bridge between a life she had never envisioned and the work she loved. The look he gave her made her think that he knew exactly what she was alluding to.

"For you? Absolutely." He smiled down at her with fatherly pride. "You are one of the most creative, talented architects I've ever had the pleasure of working with."

She swallowed past the lump in her throat. "Thank you."

"But something I've learned in my sixty-two years on this earth is that sometimes the life we thought we were going to have isn't what's meant to be. That doesn't mean we can't still make it into something we love."

"You're wise in your old age."

He squeezed her shoulder even as he narrowed his eyes at her. "Off with you, young lady. Go meet that client."

She waited until J.T. walked away before she went online

and typed in Nicholai's name. A new story posted early yesterday afternoon included pictures of Nicholai touring the bridge construction site, speaking with the new inspector, and shaking hands with some of the construction crew. He looked tired, his lips drawn tight, lines edged deep into the skin around his eyes.

Was he ill? Or had he been having trouble sleeping, just as she had, since they'd parted? After her conversation with her mother, she had decided to reach out to Nicholai and apologize. Then, whether he forgave her or not, she would tell him she loved him. If he rejected her, then she could at least walk away knowing she'd done everything she could.

Now, she thought grimly, she just needed to find the courage to make the call.

She arrived at the Nelson and parked along the side street. She could glimpse the south entrance between the trees. Glancing at her watch, she realized she still had ten minutes or so before she met the client at the base of the stairs.

It was after five, and the museum had closed for the day. Dark clouds heavy with rain hung in the sky, chasing people from the lawn. She reached into the back of her car for an umbrella. Perhaps after meeting the client, she could convince him or her to join her for a drink at a restaurant on the Plaza to discuss whatever project they had pitched to J.T.

She followed the winding path of one of the sidewalks that ran between a low stone wall and majestic trees that stretched up to the stormy sky. The distant sounds of traffic and city life faded as she mentally composed what she would say when she called Nicholai.

Nicholai, I think I'm in love with you.

No, too abrupt.

Remember how I said I couldn't picture giving up my career? What if I found a way to make it work while being in Kelna?

So lost in her thoughts was she that she didn't see the man standing in front of her until she ran smack into him.

"Oh! I apologize, I..."

Her voice faded as she stared up into Nicholai's handsome face.

"Hello, Madeline."

"Nicholai?"

She launched herself at him, flinging her arms around his neck, burying her face against his shoulder. His scent enveloped her, woodsy with that hint of spice, a fragrance that had become so familiar in such a short time. He crushed her against him, brushed his cheek against hers, caressed her hair.

"I missed you."

"I missed you, too."

He drew back, cradled her chin in one hand and kissed her. Her eyes fluttered shut, tears clinging to her lashes as the last bands of tension wrapped around her heart loosened and fell away.

Thunder grumbled overhead. Rain started to fall, the leafy branches overhead providing some shelter.

They broke apart. Madeline tilted her head back and laughed.

"I've always wanted to be kissed in the rain."

He ran his thumb over her lower lip. "I'm glad I could do that for you."

"Seriously, though, Nicholai, what are you doing here? Where's your security team?"

He gestured to the trees bordering the road that ran alongside the museum. "Close by. It took some convincing for them to not accompany me up here."

She glanced at her watch and sucked in a breath. "Oh. I have to meet a client—"

"Interested in a new venture with Forge?"

Her lips curved up. "J.T. knew this whole time, didn't he?"

"I called him yesterday and asked him for a favor."

Her fingers reached up, traced the sharp line of his jaw, the coarse stubble on his chin, then down his neck before laying her hand over his heart. The steady beat beneath her palm summoned the memories of their time in Bora Bora, the intimacy of lying side by side and the simplicity of enjoying each other's company.

"You could have just called or texted me."

"This seemed more romantic." He nodded to the stone steps and giant birdies standing proudly on the lawn. "I couldn't pass up the chance to see the larger-than-life shuttlecocks in person."

She laughed as he grabbed her hand and tugged her down the lane. The cool mist turned into big raindrops. Belatedly, she remembered the umbrella and popped it open, holding it above both their heads as the rain drummed steadily on the fabric.

"When we last spoke, I told you I cared about you."

Her pulse accelerated.

"You did. And I—"

"Wait."

He stopped, tugged her around to face him.

"The first time I saw you, I thought I was going to have to save your life." He silenced her laugh with a sweet kiss. "But I was wrong. You're the one who ended up saving me, Madeline."

Confused, she leaned back. "How?"

"I wasn't dealing well with the change in my life. My father's illness, Kelna's expansion, the new port. I was so focused on my responsibilities, on the ways things used to be, that I couldn't see the possibilities in the future." He smoothed a lock of hair back from her face. "I also didn't realize how much my own need to control something in my life was preventing me from asking for help."

"I'm not exactly one to judge on that front."

"No," he agreed with a slight smile. "But you've made me

a better leader, Madeline. You showed me the value in slowing down, in enjoying my life instead of just moving through it without stopping to look at what was around me."

One tear escaped and traced a hot trail down her cheek.

"Nicholai…" She swallowed hard. "Thank you. Although you helped me grow, too, you know."

"Oh?"

"I was so focused on my need for familiarity that I closed myself off to so many possibilities. And then you introduced me to your beautiful country and I…" Her voice trailed off as she blinked back tears. "It pushed me out of my comfort zone. I started looking around and seeing things beyond my own interpretations. All of the meetings and commitments I saw at first as confining, but then I saw what a difference they made. What a difference you make. I love my work and what I do." A tear slid down her cheek. "But I loved being a part of something bigger, too."

He brushed his finger over her cheek. "Don't cry, *moja ljubav.*"

"They're not sad tears, I promise." She swallowed. "I have a question to ask."

"Which you can. After me."

With that pronouncement, he dropped to one knee. The rapid beat of her heart catapulted into a gallop, one that thundered so loudly in her ears she barely heard the words that came out of his mouth. He released her hand and pulled a jewelry box out of his pocket. He flipped the lid. Her hand flew up to her mouth.

Could she have imagined a more perfect ring? Delicate silver, fashioned into three strands that wove over each other in an elegant braid, made up the band, with a square blue topaz sitting on top and surrounded by the tiniest drops of diamonds.

"This belonged to my mother. She was much loved as a queen." Nicholai glanced down at the ring, then back to her, his heart in his eyes. "I knew I would one day marry. I wondered if I would have the luxury of a marriage based on af-fection. When I told you in Bora Bora that I cared about you, I lied. I love you, Madeline. I never pictured that I would fall so deeply in love with the woman I want to be my wife, my queen and the mother of our children. Will you marry me?"

Barely had the words left his mouth before she leaned down and kissed him. The umbrella tumbled to the ground, forgot-ten as the rain drenched them.

"Yes," she breathed against his lips. "Yes, Nicholai. I love you. I love you so much."

"I almost lost you." He gripped her tight, kissed her cheeks, her neck, before holding her tight in his arms. "At first, I told myself I was doing the right thing letting you go. Not making you choose between a life here and a life with me."

"But this is different." She ran a hand through his hair, smoothing the wet locks back from his forehead. "That was the lesson I had to learn. When you love someone and you want to be with them, there's sacrifice. Compromise. And I want to be with you, Nicholai."

He slipped the ring on her finger.

"Your mother will be relieved."

"My mother?" Madeline echoed.

"I called her. I asked her blessing for your hand. She said she's going to miss you and she'd toss me in the river if I hurt you."

Madeline choked out a laugh. "Sounds like her."

"Promising her her own mother-in-law's quarters, available for her exclusive use whenever she wanted to visit, seemed to help."

"Another expansion to the palace?"

"More a renovation of existing rooms. Which reminds me…" He brought her hand up to his mouth, kissed the tips of her fingers. "I'd like to add an office."

"An office?"

"For you. If you're interested, there are two architecture firms in Lepa Plavi, as well as an opening with the country's development authority."

The hope that had taken root in her chest during her earlier conversation with J.T. now bloomed, filling her with an elation so bright it made her lightheaded.

"But what about serving as queen?"

"My sister and I talked. Kelna is growing, and so are the needs of its people. She has agreed to step up and assume more of the royal duties. Instead of being just one or two, we'll be three, perhaps four if she decides to marry."

"And you're okay with that?"

"I know I'm asking you to give up a lot, Madeline. I can't solve the problems of the media, public scrutiny, having to have a security guard when you travel. But I can offer you a way to do what you love and continue to make a difference." His thumb brushed away a drop on her cheek. "Are these more tears or raindrops?"

"Probably both," she said as she smiled. "I asked J.T. before I came here if I could be a consultant. I was going to call you this weekend and tell you I love you, that I wanted to see if we could make this work."

He stared down at her. "You were going to give up your career? For me?"

"Not give up. Just…change things. I want to be with you, Nicholai. I need to draw, to design. But I also want to do more giving back. I fell in love with you, but I also fell in love with your country. I want to serve it as best I can."

"I have no doubt you will." Nicholai looked up as the rain started to fall harder. "And now, Princess Madeline, it's time to get inside."

She let out a shriek of laughter as he scooped her up into his arms and carried her down the lane. She leaned up and kissed his cheek.

"Do you remember in Paris when I said it didn't get more fairy-tale than that moment?"

"I do."

"I was wrong," she said on a sigh of happiness.

"As was I." He pressed a kiss to her forehead. "Here's to happily-ever-after, Your Highness."

EPILOGUE

Eighteen months later

THE SUN ROSE above the palace, casting a rosy glow over the walls as it slid high above the mountains to the east.

Madeline sighed and reclined in her chair. She'd woken up before dawn, too excited to sleep. In just a few hours, she would say "I do" and officially be crowned as Queen Madeline Adamović.

Nicholai's wife.

After he'd officially proposed, he'd spent the night at her apartment. The next morning, Stacey had joined them to meet her future son-in-law. There had been lots of tears, hugs and questions about Kelna. Seeing her mother at ease with Nicholai in a way she'd never been with Alex had made Madeline even happier, a feat she hadn't thought possible.

They'd flown back to Kelna shortly after to confess their charade to Ivan. The King had simply smiled and embraced them both.

"I knew you would find your way eventually."

Nicholai had invited her to meet with the prime minister with him, a sign to show that he would work on no longer doing everything alone. They'd sat before the stern-faced man, hands laced together, as they'd told him of their commitment to each other.

"The women on your list were meant to lead Kelna." Nicholai had looked at Madeline, love shining from his eyes, and squeezed her hand. "Madeline put her life on hold and her reputation on the line to help our country in a time of need. She served our children during a dark hour. She loves Kelna as if she were born here." He'd looked back to Dario. "What more could I or the people want in a queen?"

Nicholai still maintained that Madeline had imagined the flicker of emotion in Dario's eyes. Regardless, he had agreed to support their engagement and their marriage.

The next few months had sped by. Madeline had continued to work on the ballroom with the team from Forge, mostly through remote work, but with occasional trips back to Kansas City. Ivan had lived long enough to see construction begin before he had finally succumbed to his illness.

Madeline's hands tightened on her mug. Losing his father had hit Nicholai hard. But they'd leaned on each other and Eviana, forming their own tight-knit family as the nation had mourned with them.

The decision to postpone the wedding had been an easy one. They'd set it for one day after the anniversary of when Nicholai had been crowned king, a nod to the Marriage Law that had been quietly repealed by Parliament a month after Nicholai and Madeline had reunited.

I'm getting married today.

She smiled and let her head fall back as she soaked up the warmth of the rising sun.

A shadow fell across her.

"Good morning."

"Nicholai!" Laughing, she set her mug down and stood. "It's bad luck to see the bride before the wedding."

"I thought that was seeing you in your dress." He leaned down and kissed her. "I couldn't start my day without you."

Sighing happily, she leaned into his embrace. "Just a few hours."

"And then a week of nothing but sun, sand and waves."

"I'm excited to go back."

She felt his smile against her hair. "It will definitely have a happier ending than the last time we were in Bora Bora."

Nicholai suddenly tensed.

"What is it?"

He held a finger to his lips and leaned over the railing. Madeline turned to see Eviana by the evergreen trees. And she wasn't alone. A man stood with his back to them, hands gesturing wildly as Eviana glared at him. She leaned in and said something too low for them to hear. Judging by her angry expression, though, it wasn't anything pleasant.

"I should go down there," Nicholai growled as Eviana stalked off, leaving the man staring after her.

"She's a big girl. And she respects you. She'll come to you if she needs help."

Although she would be sure to check in with her maid of honor before the ceremony started. Ever since Eviana had returned from a sabbatical three months ago, she'd been quieter, more subdued. Perhaps the young man who was now marching off in the opposite direction had something to do with her morose mood. "Maybe." Nicholai sighed and turned back to her. "Given how I feel about my baby sister talking to a man, I can only imagine how I'm going to feel if we have a daughter."

"Maybe we can find out next year," she teased as she looped her arms around his neck.

"Maybe." He smiled down at her. "Wedding first. I'm very much looking forward to sliding that wedding band on your finger and letting the world know you're mine."

"So we can live happily ever after?" Madeline laughed as Nicholai responded to her teasing by sweeping her into his arms.

He leaned down, his lips brushing hers.

"Ever after and always."

* * * * *

MILLS & BOON MODERN IS
HAVING A MAKEOVER!

The same great stories you love,
a stylish new look!

Look out for our brand new look
COMING JUNE 2024

MILLS & BOON

COMING SOON!

We really hope you enjoyed reading this book.
If you're looking for more romance
be sure to head to the shops when
new books are available on

Thursday 4th July

To see which titles are coming soon, please visit
millsandboon.co.uk/nextmonth

MILLS & BOON

MILLS & BOON ®

Coming next month

UNEXPECTED FAMILY FOR THE
REBEL TYCOON
Rachael Stewart

'Where's Fin?'

'He's in the front room, doing his summer project for school.'

'He's doing *what*?'

Matteo flicked Porsha a look to find her staring at him, and grinned. 'I know, wonders never cease, right?'

She shook her head and fisted her hips, her blouse pulling taut across her front, not that he was noticing or reacting in any way, shape, or form—*Neighbour. Friend. Fin's parental figure!*

The mental mantra was getting tired. Stepping in as Fin's manny for the summer had been an easy offering, one that Porsha had eventually accepted and one that was going swimmingly in all ways but one…*this.*

The incessant pull he felt towards her, the attraction, the chemistry…

Experience told him it should have eased by now.

Instead it was doing the opposite.

Maybe that was denial for you…evil.

But seeking out a fling right on one's doorstep was